PRA

THE SILENCE IN THE SOUND

"An exquisite debut from a thrilling new voice. *The Silence in the Sound* is a poetic story, powerfully told. Emotional yet exhilarating, Dianne C. Braley's novel is alluring through every page."

—Anna David, *New York Times* best-selling author of *Party Girl*, founder of Legacy Launch Pad

"An engaging story of love, grief, and remoteness on Martha's Vineyard."

—Kirkus Reviews

"*The Silence in the Sound* is an unflinching look at the legacy of addiction and the soul-destroying effect it has on family and friends. Love does not conquer all for George, and her long journey from anger to forgiveness is grueling. In George, author Braley has given us a believable, flawed character whose story compels the reader to root for her."

—Susan Wilson, *New York Times* best-selling author of *One Good Dog*

"In *The Silence in the Sound*, Dianne C. Braley weaves a gorgeous, heart-wrenching, and very real tale of love, secrets, and resilience. The engaging plot peels back the façade of wealthy, seemingly idyllic Martha's Vineyard to expose the lives and struggles of the island's year-round working-class locals—the nurses and carpenters who labor, mostly unappreciated, behind the scenes. Laced with love and gritty with addiction, *The Silence in the Sound* is a compelling, memorable read."

—T. Elizabeth Bell, author of *Counting Chickens* and *Goats in the Time of Love*

"In *The Silence in the Sound*, Dianne Braley fashions a moving tale in which complicated love—for an alcoholic father, a testy patient, an unnervingly enigmatic lover, and Martha's Vineyard—interweaves to create a compelling narrative. Georgette returns as an adult to the island, lured by the memory of a significant weekend there as a teenager with her father. She becomes the private nurse to the famous author Mr. S., for whom, despite his difficult nature, she develops a deep fondness. But Georgette can't outrun the damage from growing up with an addict in a dysfunctional home as she becomes entangled in a complicated relationship with Dock—a local contractor with a mysterious past. Brimming with rich characters and a provocative storyline, Braley movingly explores if our history indelibly determines our future."

—Abby Remer, published author and writer for the
Martha's Vineyard Times

"Braley has a distinctive and energetic voice and a lyrical style. She writes with confidence and easygoing fluidity that belies the fact that *The Silence in the Sound* is her debut novel. Engrossing, psychologically intricate, and poignant, the book is multilayered, fresh, and immersive. Not only is it compulsively readable, but the characters stayed with me days after I'd finished it. *The Silence in the Sound* is beautifully written, emotionally charged, and highly recommended."

—Penny Haw, author of *The Wilderness Between Us* and
The Invincible Miss Cust

"Georgette, a young nurse, is on a crash course to follow her family's historical trajectory of love, loss, and alcoholism. But nature's healing beauty on Martha's Vineyard and a deep connection with a terminally ill celebrity author for whom she is first a caretaker and then a friend intervenes to change her life.

"*The Silence of the Sound* takes the reader on a ride as a young woman reckons with generational loss and grief from the ravages of addiction and codependency. With empathy, Braley writes a story with hard, honest consequences in a young woman's fear-based solutions to problems. In the end, Georgette forgives herself and those she has loved in order to move beyond the blame game and carve a life of hope and health going forward."

"Dianne Braley's beautifully written, lyrical and insightful debut weaves the disparate threads of the journey to wisdom and maturity into a wondrous fabric. *The Silence in the Sound* plumbs the depths of relationships—with a famous author, with a lost father, and ultimately with oneself—to measure the sometimes dark pathways that bring us to where we are. A brilliant read, and a first novel that promises great things to come."

"Searing and truthful, this story plumbs the inner depths of desire, regret, self-understanding, and ultimately the power of love and connection that make it all worthwhile. The setting of Martha's Vineyard provides a sense of rootedness and identity that is itself a healing force amid the turbulent lives that seek a toehold on the shifting sands of life. Read it and feel deeply."

"A beautifully-written and riveting tale of love, resilience, friendship, devotion, and the heartbreaking impacts of addiction. Braley does a masterful job weaving George's quest for love and peace with fascinating intersecting story lines, past and present. For those who love Martha's Vineyard, it's also a special treat to see the island lovingly rendered as a character in its own right."

The Silence in the Sound

by Dianne C. Braley

Published by

 köehlerbooks™

3705 Shore Drive
Virginia Beach, VA 23455
800-435-4811
www.koehlerbooks.com

The
SILENCE
in the
SOUND

Dianne C. Braley

VIRGINIA BEACH
CAPE CHARLES

To my mother.
And for William Styron, who inspired me
not to be afraid of the dark.

"Somehow, I still could not believe that this life we all have together would ever be changed."

—William Styron

CHAPTER 1

July 6, 2007
I'm exhausted from goodbyes.

• • •

A kiss is just a kiss until it's more, and then everything changes. Growing up, my mother hummed the song "As Time Goes By" by Dooley Wilson, not occasionally but incessantly. It appeared a compulsion of sorts, or possibly a coping mechanism from having to deal with us kids and my alcoholic father. Nearly every morning, you would find her in the kitchen, doing the previous night's dishes and making coffee or lunches for the day, and you'd hear her. Initially, it would be a slow hum; she seemed unaware of the beginning of the song's lyrics. Next, she would break full-on into the song, and then she'd return to the hum of the chorus.

• • •

The song replayed over and over in my head as I entered Falmouth, and I heard myself humming. I'd done it for years, a nervous tick passed from my mother that was now ingrained in me. I slowed with the traffic, seeing it backed up at the Palmer Ave lot. The cars began to move, and I stared at the picture of a ferry boat on a sign for Martha's Vineyard. I felt my heart thump in my chest and looked at the time.

I'd be lucky if I made my ferry reservation, and I prayed that I would. I usually did; although it had been a few years since I'd had to catch the ferry, I figured not much had changed. Hurrying back now felt familiar, but this time was different. I didn't want to be going back. I had left and put it all behind me. At least, that's what I tried to convince myself. Running from things—I was good at that; I ran here, but it seems the things you run from always catch up to you.

My palms slipped along the steering wheel, and dampness grew across the small of my back. I put the air conditioner on, wondering why I hadn't done so an hour ago after my minor panic while leaving the coffee shop in Bourne.

The Jeep glided down the winding road to Woods Hole. I'd driven it so many times before. Heading back to it all now, I couldn't imagine how I'd face any of it. But I always knew one day I would have to.

I just have to get there.

I'd assumed over the years no one day would be better to return than any other, but I was wrong.

The clock stared at me as I passed the golf course. I had fifteen minutes, and it seemed I'd make it. The tension in my neck subsided, and I relaxed slightly, easing my foot off the gas. The Jeep slowed as I took in my surroundings. I knew every bump and bend in this road and enjoyed the familiarity of it all, forgetting everything for a moment as I looked ahead. It was becoming cloudy; I'd noticed after turning near the bed-and-breakfast on the corner.

Raindrops pelted the windshield, startling me. Sleep had eluded me for days, and I was both tired and wired, living off coffee after getting the news. It's funny how, though you know something terrible is coming, you expect it and are ready for it, you think, but then it happens, and it blindsides you. You are never as prepared as you think you are, if at all. I'd been here before, and I wasn't remotely ready. This time was no different.

More drops fell, and my eyes welled as if the rain had somehow triggered me to join it. The sun was bright in the sky ahead of me, past the clouds near the Oceanographic Institute. I slowed the Jeep, pulling onto some open grass on the side of the road. Tears spilled down my face, and I rested my head on the steering wheel, the moisture hitting my legs below my skirt. The rain tapped on the windshield in a loud rhythm, aligning with my heartbeat, which I was intensely aware of in my anxious, caffeine-fueled state. Inhaling deeply, I held my breath, then blew out slowly against the steering wheel.

"I can't do this," I whispered, turning my face toward the vent for the cold air to dry my tears. An overwhelming feeling of panic and dread came over me, and I reached for my throat, feeling as if I were choking, and tried to clear it.

"I fucking hate you." I breathed out, hanging my head and sobbing, clutching the steering wheel as hard as I could. Hobo touched me with his paw. I ignored him, watching a string of saliva fall from my mouth onto my legs, joining the wetness from the tears.

I wiped my mouth, smearing lipstick across my hand, and stared at my legs, feeling numb. A few moments went by; then the Jeep vibrated from the rumble of a truck passing, and I lifted my head. I looked through blurry eyes, seeing the clouds now gone and the sky bright and blue where the trees cleared a few yards up. Suddenly, I remembered where I was.

The tiny Coast Guard lighthouse sat on the little patch of land, the whitecaps breaking against it. The dark-blue ocean stretched for miles, and seagulls called to one another as they hovered over the two ferries docked below. The blue of the sea was slightly darker than the blue-gray sky that met it. The contrast of the colors in front of the golden and rust-colored sands of the island's cliffs several miles from shore was calming and comforting, and I closed my eyes. This was the point where the happy and calm came. I put the Jeep in drive, inching along the grass a hundred yards past the clearing, and rolled my window down. Leaning on the opening, I rested my chin on my forearm and looked to the left. My lips turned up in a small half smile, and I inhaled the clean, salty air.

There it was across the water—the island, my island, or it used to be. It was a place I'd never wanted to leave. I resented that I'd had to. I resented Dock. The anger built inside me again. I resented the anger, too, and didn't want to feel that today. The island was mine before all of it. It was mine the day I landed on it that weekend with my father all those years ago. Coming back now, I wanted it to be mine again, but so much had happened.

Ferries pulled in and out, down the small hill at Woods Hole terminal, taking islanders, workers, and vacationers with their cars and bikes back and forth to the island. I drove down the embankment, thinking of my father's truck bumping toward the boats that weekend we came. Looking ahead, I could almost see him, leaning against the truck, tilting his face toward the sun. So much about him annoyed me then that now makes me smile.

The black from my mascara had mixed with the lipstick I foolishly put on this morning, smearing and making a mess as I wiped my eyes with the back of my hand. I was going back today, and for a reason I never wanted. It all seemed like a lifetime ago. I stared ahead at the *Islander*, her name written in big black letters on the giant hull's side. People walked down the ramp, leaving her, as I waited to get in line to board. I pulled over, giving my name to the man at the kiosk, catching a look at myself in the rearview mirror. Black half-moons of mascara stared back at me from beneath my eyes. I hurriedly put on my sunglasses to cover them.

I still love him.

The man in the kiosk was young and smiled kindly. He didn't seem to notice anything wrong and only checked my reservation. I turned away from him, observing a young couple walk past with their black Lab, who seemed to smile. Hobo barked, seeing them, wagging his tail. The woman was laughing and touching the man's hand as her golden highlights caught the sun. He felt her hair and slid his hand to her back as the dog pulled him along.

"You're all set, miss. Miss?" the man in the kiosk said.

Still staring at the couple, I ignored him.

Finally, a hand waved across my windshield, breaking my trance.

"You okay, miss?"

"I'm sorry." I laughed nervously.

"Lane twelve; have a nice trip." He pointed out where I should go, waving the car behind me up.

Everyone is so lovely who works here, I remembered as I pulled behind a black Lexus with a New York plate. The island was full of New Yorkers in the summer. Rude, entitled New Yorkers. Lots of islanders would say that. Others argued against that premise and appreciated the revenue they brought.

Most held an opinion somewhere in the middle. To have your opinion matter anyway, you had to be an islander, which meant that you had to be born there, which I wasn't. So no one cared what I thought, although I'd lived there long enough to know both "rude" and "entitled" were slightly appropriate words, at least sometimes. Being from the city, I occasionally enjoyed the rushing, impatient energy that city people brought, as it was familiar. It excited the slower island pace I became accustomed to while living there.

The city folks probably didn't realize their behavior. I didn't when I first moved to the island. It was a survival mode they developed, serving them well in the city's concrete chaos. I didn't judge it. I had it too, or at least I once did. Most who came to the island appeared to magically drift away from such behavior by day three of their visit, give or take a few days. This, I was sure, was why they continued to come.

My mind raced, and I tapped my arm, still gripping the steering wheel. I hummed, trying to distract myself. Families got out of their cars, stretching and chatting with each other as they waited to board. I was lucky to get a reservation at all at the height of summer. Part of me wished I had not come back, but I'd never have forgiven myself. I had to see him and say goodbye.

The ferry loomed through the windshield of the car ahead of me, and the fear and sadness subsided some. I looked in the rearview mirror, seeing a wreck of the woman I was a few days ago. My eyes and nose reddened. The older, tired face in front of me looked broken and irreparable. I touched my finger to my cheek to see if I felt real. My black dress had fallen from the hook in the back and lay crumpled on the floor in its dry-cleaning bag. I turned to pick it up but then left it and watched as Hobo circled on top of it before plopping down his dirty white little body. Something about it all made me feel good. I looked again at the mirror, seeing Dock's sleepy eyes staring back at me, enormous and green. They mesmerized me. They always had.

I tried hard to collect myself, mustering a smile before turning around. I picked up the white teddy bear on the seat and moved him in front of my face, peeking my head out, then back again, hearing the little giggles. Everything felt better, if only for a moment.

Suddenly, I felt someone watching from outside. A little girl holding an ice cream sandwich stared in through the passenger side window, probably curious what the crazy lady was doing. I smiled, watching as her ice cream slid out of the sandwich bottom onto her pink dress, then slowly made its way down the fabric. She didn't seem to realize or care. In the mirror, I noticed my sunglasses crooked on my face. I left them and looked over at her, smiling. She made a face at me and rolled her eyes, then stuck her tongue out and walked away.

New York assholes.

People climbed into their cars as they loaded the *Islander*. The *Nantucket*, a freight boat, had pulled in next to her, and giant trucks pulled off, along with a few cars and people.

God, I hope I'm not on the damn freight boat.

The *Nantucket*, along with the other freighters, was open to the air. There was just a tiny enclosure for people if it was cold or rainy. This meant there was no bar, and that would be a problem right now. It shamed me that this was my first thought, but soon I realized it wasn't the alcohol I cared about. I hadn't had a drink in quite a while and honestly didn't miss it much. Everything was so different now than it was, and although I would love to feel numb, my desire for a cold beer came from the opposite impulse. Suddenly, I wanted to feel again. I wanted the familiar, the happy. I wanted to feel like before, before it was all gone. I wanted back the girl who ordered an Offshore Ale while sitting on the top deck, looking ahead, excited to return home.

They waved me onto the *Islander*, and I was thankful to be the second to the last car in. I pulled up behind another SUV, with two big yellow dog heads hanging out the windows. Two little boys hopped out on the other side and ran past my car, laughing. The giant metal door closed, entombing the vehicles in the boat's belly.

A symphony of familiar sounds played around me. I had always loved the noise of the ferryboats: metal cranking and men shouting to each other as they cast her off or pulled her in, dogs barking and kids laughing. I pushed my sunglasses high on my face to hide my eyes as I climbed out of the Jeep, Hobo dropping to the ground beside me. Shutting the door, I looked again at the black dress I had brought, still feeling it belonged there on the Jeep floor. I resented the dress; I wanted to rip it from the plastic bag, stomp on it, and then tear it into a million pieces.

We followed the two little boys and the yellow dogs, heading up the stairs to the top deck and the small cafeteria, and found a good-looking kid with perfect teeth at the counter.

"I'll have an Offshore Ale, please," I asked, rummaging through my purse for cash, remembering they didn't take cards.

"We don't sell that anymore, ma'am," the bartender said, smiling widely. He had the whitest teeth I'd ever seen.

Ma'am? Now I'm a ma'am? Great.

He encouraged me to try a Nantucket Ale, saying it was similar. Nothing made sense anymore. The Vineyard and Nantucket were rivals of sorts, and I didn't feel right drinking something from there.

"Are there any other Vineyard-brewed beers?"

"No."

"They shouldn't be selling Nantucket beer on this boat. They never used to," I said to him in a catty tone disguised with a smile to not come across as so bitchy.

He shrugged and handed me the beer. Now seeing the credit card machine, I took the drink, gave him my card, and then crumpled the cash, putting it in the tip cup that said *College Fund* on it.

Everything's changed.

I walked through the doors and stepped onto the deck. Leaning against the railing, I stared at the water, taking a sip. After a few minutes, the steam whistle blew, and the boat jolted ahead as we made our way toward the island. Seagulls hovered over the boat, appearing suspended in the air as we moved. They patiently waited for some kid to lose a french fry or someone to toss popcorn as they usually did. I sipped my beer; I wasn't pleased with it, although I enjoyed the warmth it brought for a moment, along with a slight tingle in my head. It could have been precisely the same as the Offshore, but because it wasn't Offshore and had Nantucket's name, I hated it. I hated it all.

The couple and the dog from earlier at the kiosk stood across from us. She looked so familiar. Her golden hair blew gently against her right cheek as she held the railing, scanning the watery landscape. She was twenty-five, I'd guess. Her skin was fair like mine, with a few scattered freckles. She was getting a little pink at the top of her forehead under her hairline, like I always did. She reached into the shirt pocket of the man next to her, pressing against his chest, then took out his sunglasses and put them on. Smiling at the dog, she patted him on the head as the man held the leash at his side. She took the leash from him and shot him a flirty smile as the wind whipped her hair into her face.

The man brushed her hair from her forehead. Her smile was wide and bright. He said something to her as he grabbed her hand. It was subtle, but I noticed. Her face changed, and her lips turned. She looked stunned. Like someone had taken the wind from her sail. I twisted back to face the water—a pit formed in my stomach.

Suddenly, I knew why she seemed familiar. I knew her face; I recognized the change in it. She was smiling and carefree a moment before, and in an instant overtaken by disappointment or sadness—I was unsure which.

She reminded me of myself, if only for a moment. She looked like me, except younger and without despair. I wondered what he'd said. All the disappointing whispers canceled out the other ones. The promises that never came to be. I glanced toward her again. She seemed not entirely sad but more let down, I thought, as she pulled her hand away from his and walked away. The happiness, the letdowns, the constant sadness, the highs and the lows, the insanity. My mother and all her subtle looks of disappointment at my father. I felt connected to my mother now, which no longer enraged me. I understood, but I should have known better. I was better, or I could have been, but Dock knew different, or love did.

Continuing to watch them, I took another sip of my beer, oblivious of whether they noticed me. I looked past them at the open water as we headed into Vineyard Sound. Was she losing herself? Like my mother did, like me and so many others? I wanted the woman to hold on to her smile, to keep walking.

The tears returned, and I tried to blink them back, pushing my sunglasses tight against my face. We made the turn passing in front of West Chop, and I looked ahead toward Mr. S.'s house, past the Yacht Club, trying hard to spot it through the trees and the tears. It seemed like yesterday I was sitting with him on the porch, watching the ferries pass by. Guilt pulled at my insides. I'd wanted to be with him to the end and wasn't sure I'd ever forgive myself that I wasn't. My patient, my friend—I left him. He graciously let me go. I still wondered how he knew.

I reached down, feeling my bag, checking it was there along with my journal—his book, I carried with me always, like a security blanket reminding me to be strong. I traced the hard-square edges, remembering the woman and her choice, wondering if I'd made the right choice in leaving then. I knew I had, but I still wondered. Turning, I looked toward the rear of the boat, biting my bottom lip, trying to steady it, relieved no one was looking. People never looked toward the back. Everyone looked forward and toward where they were headed, not backward to what they were leaving.

I am not that girl anymore. The smiling one. The naïve one. The city girl starting a new life. I envisioned myself riding my bike by East Chop Light with the wind blowing my wavy brown hair in the blue bandanna I always wore.

I took a sip of the beer so I could wipe my cheek unnoticed as I brought the cup to my face. Sick to my stomach unexpectedly, I gripped the railing, squeezing it as hard as I could with my free hand. I tried to push it all from my mind but couldn't.

Dock and the cottage. His face in front of me, his upturned smile, was there every day. I still felt him, and right now, it was more than I could bear, except I never wanted it to end, the feeling.

I'd been kissed by a few men by then, maybe more than a few. But none had ever kissed me as Dock did that night. I've never been one to believe in being swept off my feet in love, but after that night in the cottage, I did.

The funny thing is, he had kissed me before, just not like that. With that kiss, everything changed, and going back now was more than I could stand.

The boats in the harbor came into view as the ferry turned toward the pier. Nothing was here anymore except ghosts—their ghosts, my ghosts, and the beautiful sadness of it all. I stared at my sandals and crossed one foot over the other, tapping the ground, humming softly. At some point, I'd fully accept that I wasn't so different from her, my mother.

As it always did, the humming calmed me, until I became aware I was doing it. "*. . . just a kiss.*"

CHAPTER 2

December 31, 2002
The waters, still and surrounding, protect me,
but then there are the memories.

T he sky was clear, and you could see every star in it. Vineyard nights were beautiful, no matter the season. I wasn't sure moving to the island was the best idea, especially in the winter, but I was excited about a new start. I still had the same feeling as when I came that weekend with my father when I was seventeen, so I hoped it would all work out. I'd been here a while now, and so far, it had. I'd moved to the island this time last winter, nearly ten years after visiting. I loved the island; I fell in love that weekend, and it hadn't changed, but winter could always be a little lonely.

It was cold but not as cold as it usually was on New Year's Eve in the Northeast. New Year's always seemed to be one of the coldest nights of the year. But Vineyard weather was different and unpredictable. Being on an island, and one in New England, you never quite knew what the weather would be. I sat in the chair outside the guest cottage I had moved into a few days earlier. It was nice to have my own space and be out of the hospital housing. I had long overstayed my welcome and was supposed to find living arrangements of my own, but the rent here was a fortune, and it was slim pickings.

Nursing hadn't exactly been a passion of mine, but growing up blue collar, it was a route many girls took. I didn't care much for people at all, which made it an odd career choice for me, and to most, that might seem like it would make me a bad nurse. In many areas of the field, it might, but I knew my strengths and was self-aware to an extent. After graduating, I took a position on a surgical floor at a hospital close by. Surgical nursing required being slightly tougher and more encouraging than nurturing, which suited me well. My mother always said I should become a nurse first and pursue my passions later, which was the one thing I ended up listening to her on.

"It's job security and good pay," she would say, followed by, "and at least you'll be able to pay your bills."

"You're wicked smart," Aunt Rita agreed in her thick Boston accent while my mother nodded.

"Sounds so exciting," I'd mumble sarcastically, disappointed, realizing how sadly working class we were.

All I could think about was escaping the city after our lives changed. I thought about travel nursing or moving far away. I had my own apartment by then but was still too close. Another winter in our broken family was more than I could bear. There had been far too many, and it depressed me, thinking of how long and cold it would be.

I stayed late at work one evening, which I did most evenings; you could never finish your work on time.

"You're still here, George?" Janice, the charge nurse, said, startling me. I'd had my head planted in my patient's chart.

I put down my pen to look at her. She was blurry, and my eyes hurt. It took a minute to refocus. "Room 304 kept me busy all day." I picked up the pen and tapped, wishing she would go away. "I'm almost done."

She's just worried about signing the overtime.

"All right, I'll go grab your timecard and initial it. Hurry and get out of here so you have some of your evening left," she said, smiling her phony smile, rubbing her pregnant belly.

I looked out the large windows as I walked through the hospital lobby to the garage; seeing it was already dark outside depressed me more. I waited for the elevator and noticed a new picture hanging in the lobby—or I'd just never noticed it before. It showed a small sailboat alone in the water with a faded red sail, and there was something about it I liked. I stared at it a moment, then out at the darkness again, dreading the coming winter.

Turning my wrist to look at my watch, I hurried, seeing the time. My evening was empty, but I still had to get home to Hobo, the little white Lhasa Apso I'd adopted from the shelter up the street a few weeks before.

"What kind of name is that?" I'd asked the girl helping me at the shelter.

She looked stoned, staring at me, confused.

I looked at him again with his weird underbite and dirty white fur. *He kind of looks like a Hobo. Maybe it fits.*

My name was odd, too; at least, I thought so. *Georgette—weird.*

I was too lazy to change it—Hobo, I mean, especially if he already responded to it, which I couldn't tell if he did. I called out, "Hobo," and he tilted his head.

Initially, I went in looking for a Shih Tzu, knowing they're usually friendly dogs. In Revere, just north of Boston, where I grew up, everyone had one. I was never sure why, but Italian people seemed to like them. Shih Tzus, gold, and leopard—can't forget about leopard. Usually printed on slippers or a shirt, but all the Revere ladies wore a little leopard when they weren't in all black.

They had no Shih Tzus that day, but I saw Hobo as I walked by one of the last cages. He kind of looked like a Shih Tzu except a little bigger. *How different can little white dogs be?*

It turned out little white dogs can be quite different, and Hobo was stubborn, an escape artist, and every chance he got, he ate my shoes. His name suited him perfectly.

We can both have weird names.

Georgette is my name, but most called me George for short. My father named me, often telling the story of a girl he knew growing up named Georgette. She was beautiful and had become a famous dancer, he said once while drinking a giant Schlitz beer, both of us sitting on the porch and watching a thunderstorm over the ocean.

I immediately wanted to sign up for dance classes and begged my mother. That fall, I joined the Arthur Murray dance group that many kids in my class were in. At the end-of-the-year recital, we danced to the Eurythmics, "Here Comes the Rain Again." I was miserable, stuffed into a black-and-white striped leotard, clodhopping around the stage, trying hard to keep up. It seemed that I was not the gracious-gazelle dancer type like this fantastic, famous dancer Georgette my father so admired he named me after. Or like Keri Ann Thomas and Lynn Melody in my class, who laughed at me, saying my legs were too short and fat for dancing. I ripped off my silver-sequined headpiece on the drive home and threw it in the back seat and cried. Ray, my brother, patted me on the shoulder from the back seat and told me I was good as he flung the headpiece back at me.

"You were great, George," my mom said. "Why are you so upset?"

I pouted for a while, then sobbed again, looking at myself in the side mirror.

"I hate my stupid name," I said, sniffling.

I turned toward my mother, watching her face change. Her mouth curled downward, and her eyes narrowed as she kept them on the road. I tried to stop crying, nervous she was mad at me.

After a few moments, she spoke.

"Listen, George," she said. "This Georgette thing your father told you, well, it's, it's . . ." She paused, seemingly nervous, taking a deep breath. "It's a load of crap, okay?" She exhaled.

"What?" I was surprised, wiping the tears and snot from my face with one of the white satin gloves from my costume.

"You can't always listen to him," she went on.

I had already known that about my father but never thought the story of my name and the beautiful, talented dancer could be untrue.

It had to be true. I nervously waited for her to go on.

She touched my cheek, continuing to drive, and wiped the moisture away, letting out a heavy sigh.

"Truth is, George, is that he saw a comedian one night on TV named George Carlin and liked him. He's famous, you know?" She paused, slowing to a stop at a red light and watching my reaction. "I was pregnant with you, and we thought you were a boy for a while. My favorite uncle's name was George, and he liked George Carlin, so it stuck." She looked at the light, waiting for it to turn.

I stopped crying, listening attentively, unsure I wanted her to continue.

"When we found you were a girl, he was stuck on the name George and thought of how to make it into a girl's name."

She kept pausing and glancing over to see if she should go on. Eventually, she did. It was too late to turn back now. The light turned green, and she drove. She turned onto the beach and said nothing again, only letting out another sigh.

"Mickey from next door came by, and they came up with adding 'gette' to the end of George," she finally finished, looking frustrated again. "Okay, doll?" She brushed my hair back and wiped at my face.

I pushed her hand away.

"It's a beautiful name," she exclaimed as if trying to convince herself.

I wasn't sure how I felt. I was relieved I didn't have to be a famous dancer anymore, but my namesake was a man who told jokes. *After a guy that made him laugh one night on television? That's how you named me? Your daughter?*

Emptiness filled my stomach as I tried to make sense of it, and I nervously picked at my cuticles. That my name was as significant as a quick laugh one night with the weirdo-drunk next-door neighbor made me sick. Suddenly, I wished there were a dancer.

The car was quiet for a few moments, then Ray giggled.

"Stop it, Ray," my mother snipped.

He giggled again, trying to control it, but couldn't help himself.

My face became hot, and I curled my fist, knowing Ray wouldn't let this go.

"They named you after a guy!" he yelled, belly-laughing in the back seat.

My mother yelled at him again to stop it, reaching back and smacking at his legs as she pulled into a parking space near Kelly's Ice Cream and our house. She put the car in park and turned to me, ignoring Ray, who kept laughing.

"Let's get some ice cream. How about it, George?" She slapped at Ray's legs again, missing them.

I stared out the window in silence.

He didn't come to my stupid recital anyway, so what did it matter? *I hate him.*

• • •

That night, as I returned late from the hospital for the umpteenth time, I walked in the door and threw my keys on the table. I was grabbing Hobo's leash when I remembered the picture of the sailboat again, and it came to me.

The Vineyard! The painting in the window on Main Street.

Suddenly, it all came back. The painting in the lobby looked just like the one I'd admired on the island; it all felt like a lifetime ago. I grabbed at my necklace, fiddling with the small island charm, remembering my father and that weekend. The following day, I called Martha's Vineyard Hospital and asked if they were hiring, then made my escape.

CHAPTER 3

July 10, 1992
As always, I am unrelenting,
just like his twisted desire for poison.

"Wanna go to Martha's Vineyard, Georgie?" my father said with excitement in his voice as he tossed his keys on the table. He rarely sounded so chipper. The boots he wore made a familiar clackity-clack sound as they climbed the stairs. I'd heard that sound nearly my entire life. He stood before me in the kitchen, but I never looked up. I felt him mustering something to say while I took my time painting my nails at the kitchen table. I enjoyed rare moments like this, watching him be uncomfortable. Moments where he needed something from me or had something difficult to say, with me knowing it and not making it any easier, I found humorous. I tried my best to make them last.

"Why Martha's Vineyard?" I asked, painting my last nail, using a casual, unimpressed tone after enough time had ticked by, leaving him to linger in the doorway.

I lifted my head slowly and replaced the cap on the nail polish, careful not to smudge anything. I finally looked up, and he smiled. He still wore his sunglasses, which annoyed me. He always looked the same:

aviator sunglasses, jeans, and a sleeveless T-shirt with a pocket to keep his cigarettes. He wore his Teamsters Local 25 union jacket, despite the warm day, and his old brown boots that clicked. He rarely strayed from this look, and if he did, it was only for a wedding or funeral. That was a whole other look, and it annoyed me too.

He leaned against the doorframe, his smile fading. I glanced at his boots, seeing some mud fall to the floor when he moved. He followed my eyes and kicked them one by one against the threshold.

"Don't act so excited," he grumbled. He walked into the kitchen and pulled out a chair to sit across from me.

I waved my hands to dry my nails and pretended to yawn, disinterested. He crossed his legs, leaning back in the chair.

"I'm delivering some things there for Marty, bringing a truck over. Thought you might want to go. I don't know?" He shrugged, looking out the window, tapping his fingers on the table.

Blowing on my nails, I stared at his hand, watching him tap, again taking my time to respond. Of course it had something to do with Marty. Good cover. Marty had been a friend of his for years, but he was a sketchy character. He was also supposedly in recovery from booze. I didn't trust him either.

I chose my words carefully, trying to catch him off guard while he gazed out the window.

"An interesting time for this, with Mom and Ray away," I snarked, scrutinizing his behavior, frustrated that I couldn't see his eyes hidden by his stupid glasses.

He stopped tapping. And then silence. It was our usual father-daughter standoff that had become our way of communicating. The dance we did to get closer and have some sort of normal relationship after the drinking years' wreckage. He was fortunate enough to probably not remember as much as I did; I figured it was more of a giant blackout for him.

Like some alcoholic profiler, I was still looking for signs of deception in his body language. I didn't exactly know what I was looking for; I never did, but I figured I'd know it when I saw it. In our relationship, I sometimes felt like the parent, and he was the sneaky teenager. Or we were both sneaky teenagers. But he wasn't supposed to be. So, if I could help it, I'd make sure he wasn't, and if he was, I'd know about it and tell or hold it over him.

This trip seemed odd, especially now, with my mom and Ray visiting her friend in Maine for the weekend. I was supposed to go too, but my grades were terrible, and my attitude was worse, so my mother said to stay home, which I was okay with anyway. I didn't care much in those days. Of course, at seventeen, I wasn't supposed to care, but I extra didn't and made it known.

I glanced at him suspiciously, waiting for the rug to be pulled from under me, like always. I never wanted to get too comfortable in his sobriety. That would mean I trusted him, the alcoholic, the ones you shouldn't trust. Although things had changed, I hadn't. I wouldn't let my guard down. That's how you get the real hurt—the hurt that you feel foolish for feeling because it was stupid to hope; because you got comfortable and lost your edge. If you expect it, the hurt doesn't hurt as bad, and you don't feel like a fool. You also get to say, "I told you so," which I enjoyed, although it gained me nothing.

He looked relaxed and didn't move except for the foot hanging over his knee, slowly rotating around and around. I stared, watching him roll his ankle clockwise, then counterclockwise. Suddenly, I had a lump in my throat. This was familiar. Here was my aha moment. The tell!

He usually only did this if he drank, and I never remembered it until he did it, or at least that was when I noticed, but it had been a while. He had so many tells that I would forget until I didn't, and by then, what did it matter? It changed nothing, but at least I could let him know he wasn't getting one over on me, although it never mattered except to me.

Resting my chin on my knuckles, I inched my face closer to him, trying to sniff at him while he twirled his ankle. I smelled nothing more than the usual odor of aftershave mixed with menthol-cigarette abrasiveness. The whiskey and beer I had been familiar with for most of my life were absent. I couldn't remember that stink anymore. Sometimes I tried, if I suspected something, but it's hard to remember smells until you smell them. I hoped that I would never smell it again but was prepared for the day I might.

"Why do you still have your glasses on?" I said in the tone I crafted specifically for him. I was interrogating now. Marty never took his glasses off either. That's partly why I didn't trust him. I could never see his eyes.

Why don't these people take their glasses off? Shady fucks.

I became incensed.

"What is this with the third degree?" he snapped, irritated. He leaned forward and started to say something, stumbling on his words, clearing his throat. "Look, George, do you want to go or not?"

He stopped circling his foot now, moving it quickly like a windshield wiper back and forth. I shifted my chin and rested it on one hand, smirking, saying nothing.

Give them enough rope, and they'll hang themselves.

I recalled hearing the expression but forgot where.

What is he up to?

He took his glasses off and tossed them on the table.

"If you want to stay at home, you can. I don't care; you're old enough." He tapped his fingers again. "But don't tell your mother."

He seemed disappointed in my lack of enthusiasm. He uncrossed his legs and stood, looking defeated. This gave me a small amount of pleasure until I listened to him click down the hall, and his bedroom door shut a little harder than usual. A pang of guilt came.

Maybe he wants to spend some time with me?

I had to accept that this was in the realm of possibilities, but I quickly put it out of my head, sure there was an agenda.

In a moment, I forgot him in my excitement at being home alone all weekend and immediately started planning. I'd invite Maria and Lisa, and we would smoke cigarettes.

I rose to grab the phone, lifting it off the receiver, and stopped, my stomach sinking. My weekend of freedom wasn't to be. Lisa's parents were punishing her for sneaking out last weekend to meet some stupid guy on the beach. Maria and I had told her it was a bad idea. And Maria was away at a dumb singing camp her mother paid a lot of money to send her to.

"Goddamn it," I mumbled, pushing the tangled phone cord away, knocking the receiver to the floor in the process. I picked it up, slammed it back hard, and noticed two smudged nails. "Fuck!"

I peered down the hall to see if he'd heard me. The bedroom door stayed shut. I trudged across the hall to my bedroom, sitting on my bed, pouting in frustration and then lying back, letting my legs dangle to the floor. The small desk fan in the corner blew up my shorts, and it felt good in the heat.

I could call Sammy at the Chowder Pot and ask if they need help at the counter. God knows I need the money. I'd like a car and to get out of here someday.

Tapping the bed frame with my heels, I swung my legs back and forth, continuing to think. It was hot today and would be hot all weekend, or so the weatherman said this morning. Running back and forth from the counter to the kitchen, sweating and smelling of fried clams, made me anxious, and I put that idea out of my head. I glared at my smudged nails, becoming angrier and angrier about the weekend that could have been. I wished my stupid father had said nothing; ten minutes ago, I was okay with sitting around.

I couldn't stand him.

I sat up on the edge of the bed again, the air blowing on my neck and face. I turned into it and closed my eyes.

Martha's Vineyard. *I guess it could be okay.* I tried hard to convince myself. I had always wanted to see it, and with my options limited, I eased up on my suspicions.

If he was drinking, I'd find out. I always did. *Why would he want me around to put a damper on it if he is, anyway?* I rationalized to myself. That made no sense.

This change of heart suited my current needs, and I decidedly hung up my detective hat. At least for now. It was a lot of work with no reward.

Nothing good ever came from it. Either you found absolutely nothing and wasted a lot of time, or you found out everything, which was never good news.

I learned about this and other things in the meetings we went to near my grandmother's in Boston for kids of drunks and addicts when we were younger. Every Thursday, we had dinner at her house—something resembling a Howard Johnson's dish, the place where she waitressed for twenty-five years. Chicken patties with overcooked spaghetti and tomato soup as a sauce were my favorite. Ray liked her famous tuna melt on Wonder Bread, which she'd cut diagonally, adding chips and a pickle sliced in half on each side of the plate.

At the meetings, my mom went to a group upstairs from us, for adults affected by the addicted people. After going for a while, and as much as I thought they were stupid, I couldn't deny things became a little better. The yelling lessened at home; my mom was "working her program," she'd say.

I didn't know what that meant, except it had something to do with our Thursday groups, and it was helping. One of the first things we learned was that you were not supposed to call them drunks or talk about them like they were less than other people. They had a disease, and you were to be empathetic to it.

I struggled with thinking of it as a disease. His "disease" had caused me many problems, and I had a hard time relating it to something like cancer. That was what one of the group leaders said—to think of it like cancer. Even as a kid, I knew cancer didn't make someone swim to the middle of a lake on your family vacation and pretend to drown to make your kids cry for fun. I'd never heard of cancer causing someone to ruin breakfast, passing out on their plate. Or drive someone to put ketchup all over themselves, then stand on the roadside, pretending to be injured in front of Denny's so their wife would stop to get them. I'd never seen cancer cause someone to leave anyone at Denny's, then circle the rotary with kids crying in the back, driving past ketchup-bleeding Dad, mumbling, "Fucking cancer" repeatedly under her breath. I couldn't see how cancer was comparable.

Being older now, I was supposed to try Alateen, for teenagers of the diseased people. I firmly said no, resentful that people who had done nothing wrong had to go to these places and do all this extra work because they were affected by someone else's cancer. How was that fair? My mother agreed but said it was what it was; we were involved whether we liked it or not. Well, I didn't like it, and it made me want to punch my father and his disease in the head. I was sick of needing help. It seemed we were more infected than affected. Like we had some plague that the other kids didn't have.

Poking my head out of my room, I glanced down the hall again, making sure his door was still closed. I walked to the kitchen and leaned against the wall, twirling the phone cord in my hands. I couldn't act happy about it. I didn't want him to think I wanted to go—more that I was settling to go.

Continuing to twirl the cord, I studied my reflection in the mirror across from the kitchen table. My brown hair was a mess from the fan, so I smoothed it back, hating how it looked not done. I picked at one of my freckles, which I've done for years, trying to scratch them off as a kid. I hated them then, but they didn't bother me much now.

Tired of waiting, I let the cord fall and headed down the hall. Just before I reached his door, it opened, and he came out, nearly running into me. He held a small bag that hit my legs, causing me to stumble back, and I huffed loudly, throwing my hands up.

"Watch where you're going." I smiled. Not a full smile but big enough to let him know I was approachable.

He grunted an "uh-huh" or something I couldn't make out. I could tell he was still irritated as he made his way by me.

"I think I'll go. Okay?" I said, turning toward him as he passed down the hall, disappointed that this was all the cleverness I could come up with.

He stopped, looking back at me.

"Yeah?"

I couldn't tell if he was happy or didn't give a shit.

"Yeah," I said, shrugging.

"All right then." He adjusted his glasses. "I'll get the truck and bring it back here. Pack your stuff, and we'll leave at seven o'clock to make a late-morning boat." He stared at me, waiting for a response.

"Seven in the morning?" I returned to my irritable tone. "So, what are we gonna do there?" I asked, as if he had forced me to go, while looking at my nails.

He turned away, switching his bag from one hand to another.

"I don't know. George, I don't know," he mumbled, holding his free arm up. He continued down the hall, returning his arm to his side, then walked out the door. "Maybe see a beautiful island," he shouted.

His dark hair blew in the breeze as he disappeared from view. I walked to the door and watched his Cadillac drive off down the boulevard.

"I hate that car," I groaned, then went to my room and packed.

CHAPTER 4

December 31, 2002
On the coldest night of the year, somehow I felt warm.

Everything was quiet except the waves lapping against the shore. I lit a cigarette from the pack I'd found the day before in a coat pocket and inhaled, cringing at the stale taste. Occasionally, it still surprised me that I lived here, and sometimes I felt worlds away from anything else. Mostly, I liked that, but tonight I struggled with being alone. I inhaled again, watching the smoke escape into the cold island air. I shivered, hugging my knees, pulling them up on the chair. My phone rang, startling me. I'd forgotten it was on my lap.

"Hello." I barely got the word out before Bobbie interrupted me.

"So, are you going out?" She laughed in her familiar sounds-funnier-than-it-is way. I had left her a message earlier asking her advice about going out alone on New Year's Eve.

"I'm in crisis," I said, taking another puff off the cigarette, clutching my legs close to my chest.

"Just go, George," she said. "I went out alone all the time when no one was around there."

I could tell she had already started celebrating.

"Well, you're cooler than me, I guess." I laughed. "And you've never lived here in the winter, so spare me."

I stubbed out the cigarette and headed into the cottage. Hobo stared up at me, tail wagging, head tilted.

"Go to Seasons and hug an Edgartown boy." Bobbie giggled, knowing the bar would have all the island people in it tonight and not just the usual Oak Bluffs crowd.

We didn't like Edgartown boys, Bobbie and I had decided; they were stuffy and snobby. It was Oak Bluffs guys for us, we said, toasting our beers after venturing to the Wharf, a bar in Edgartown. We'd wanted to try something new, needing a change of scenery, but we didn't get the attention we felt we deserved. It wasn't like Oak Bluffs, where everyone knew us.

"I don't know," I said, looking around the cottage at my half-unpacked boxes. I had a lot done, but I still had so much more to do before starting full-time with Mr. S. in a few days. "Maybe I'll stay in and finish in here. Happy freaking New Year." I sighed loudly.

"Who cares about that?" Bobbie went on. "You have all winter."

"Wish you were here and not in the awful city." I walked into the bathroom, looking in the mirror to check if I was presentable enough to venture outdoors.

"Me too, but unlike you, I still like the city, although I'd rather be on the island even though it's a ghost town now. Now go find a little Vineyard summer fun tonight." She laughed and sang along to a song in the background.

When I moved here, I was sure I'd made a mistake not long afterward. Then I met Bobbie, a traveling nurse who worked at the hospital in the summers. She also worked a few weekends in the winter, coming up from Boston, and we hit it off right away. One night, sitting at the nurse's station, I told her I was thinking of leaving.

"No, you're not." She glared at me.

She begged me to hang tight for the warmer weather, which I did reluctantly. Then summer came, and I got more than I ever bargained for.

"You're right," I said, swiping on some dark lipstick, thinking it was too dark but not caring enough to take it off.

"You'll be thankful next week when you're stuck in with the man every night," she said.

"I know, I know."

"The man": I called him Mr. S., after picking it up from Delia, their live-in house woman. I didn't want to call him by his first name as it was unprofessional as his nurse, but saying his full last name seemed too formal, as I'd be with him nearly every day. He didn't mind what you called him, and I thought it was a good fit.

"Go have fun. Gotta run, bye." She laughed again and hung up.

I filled Hobo's water bowl and grabbed my coat, figuring I'd head to Seasons Bar and see where the night brought me.

• • •

Seasons looked packed, from what I could tell by the many cars lining the street. The island was small, and I felt I knew almost all the year-rounders, at least in Oak Bluffs. I liked it most of the time, until I didn't. Everyone knew your business, and you knew everyone else's. The plus side was that it made it hard to judge, and if you did, you'd better have nothing to hide because if your stuff came out, you were in trouble. I was used to that, anyway, living with my father. We never had the luxury of judging, so I was in my element.

The previous summer was the best I'd ever had in my life, and I wasn't sure much could top it. I had made a home here and loved everything, except a cold and lonely New Year's.

The island was a quiet, sleepy place in the winter. Everyone sort of hibernated and ventured out only around the holidays with all the fun things to do. After that, it became a ghost town. Year-rounders didn't seem to mind; summer was plenty busy and filled with things to do. Most looked forward to the last of the vacationers leaving on the ferries at the end of the season, when the island became theirs again. Then it started all over. Springtime came, and all the summer houses slowly opened one by one. Workers were out, planting and painting, getting ready for the season ahead. The sounds of hammering and saws buzzing stimulated excitement for it all to begin—the madness and fun the warm weather brought. The island soon filled with new faces. Late nights and fun-filled days. It was a life you became accustomed to, and I never wanted to leave.

I took my stethoscope out of the glove compartment and hung it on the rearview mirror. It was a reminder nurses at the hospital gave the police to not write a ticket or to leave you alone if you'd had a few beers and drove home. It might not have been right, but it benefited us.

"Hey, Vince," I said, giving him a giant hug as I walked in and wished him a happy New Year. "How's your grandmother?"

"Great," Vince said, eyeballing a few guys who were getting a little rowdy across the room.

Vince was the doorman at Seasons. His grandmother was a sweet woman and a frequent flyer at the hospital, so we nurses knew her well. It was a genuine question but also a way of reminding him to forget our cover charge. He usually did anyway but occasionally would forget if he was in a mood.

"Karaoke is starting again in fifteen minutes, girl," he said, smiling. His teeth looked fluorescent in the darkness. Not only was Vince the doorman, but he also ran karaoke most nights, which seemed odd, but it worked.

"I'll see what I can do." I laughed.

People filled the bar from wall to wall, and I recognized no one, which irritated me. In the winter months, most places in the other towns were closed, so people who would generally be out in Edgartown, the next town over, headed here. With this, along with many of the island's college kids being home for Christmas break, no one looked familiar.

I shouldn't have listened to Bobbie. New Year's brings out the weirdos.

I headed to the bar and gently pushed my way in. It was already late, and people looked noticeably drunk, which was never fun when you were sober.

I held up a twenty, trying to get Betsy's attention, but she walked right by, not noticing me. She hurried around, trying to keep up with the demanding crowd; then suddenly her eyes caught mine, and she smiled.

"One minute," she mouthed.

Suddenly, I felt a push and a sharp pain. I looked at my arm, now wedged between the guy next to me and the bar.

"Whoa," I said, trying to move it with everything I had.

The man's full weight was leaning against it, and it was killing me. He looked irritated, watching as I struggled to free myself, not changing his position to make it easier. I realized that in his intoxicated state, he didn't see the connection. I wouldn't waste my breath explaining it to him. He looked at me angrily now, his eyes glassy and red. I pulled as hard as I could, stumbling backward while he stood swaying as if he were in a strong wind, not saying a word. He smiled as I corrected myself, but it didn't appear to be a friendly one. I knew this look well and wanted no part of him.

"Nice jacket," he said, looking me up and down.

I glanced at my sleeve and remembered I was wearing my dad's leather coat from Sears. It was harsh, like something from an old gangster movie, but I liked it and had it tailored to fit me. I sometimes forgot people here didn't dress like this so much. The island vibe was a more casual, laid-back look, either beachy with sandals or jeans and a sweater. You didn't see high heels or much leather. Most of the year-round men wore work jackets and boots like this guy did. I knew a lot of the island guys now, but he didn't look familiar.

"Thanks," I said, pretending he was sincere.

"It's kind of stupid," he said, touching my lapel. He laughed, falling into me, steadying himself with my shoulders.

"All right, buddy, relax." I looked at him earnestly, gently pushing him away and turning to face the bar to get Betsy's attention again.

I felt a push on my arm and stepped back, nearly falling into two girls. The music was loud, and I apologized, yelling as they stared at me. I smiled, saying sorry again, righting myself as Betsy put a beer in front of me and stood there. Her eyes darted around, and she seemed to notice something was wrong. I put my hand up, letting her know it was okay.

"Stop it, Brian," she said, walking away to tend to the people across the bar.

I didn't know Brian, but it appeared Betsy did. I was slightly concerned. He turned to talk to someone; with relief, I thought he would probably forget me and hopefully fall on someone else. I scanned the room again, searching for familiar faces. I thought I saw Meg from the lab in the corner, but I couldn't tell with her back facing me.

I took a sip of my beer and looked ahead, then felt a warm breath on my neck.

"Nice fucking jacket," the voice drawled. I spun and was face-to-face with Brian, the drunk asshole, again.

"Back the fuck off," I said as sweet as I could say it, turning and taking a large sip of my beer.

Casually, I lowered the beer bottle by my side and emptied half on the floor, unnoticed. I was nervous now and turned my hand, gripping the bottleneck tightly. I didn't want to but prepared myself to hit him if he touched me again. In Revere, these types of situations weren't entirely uncommon. I had been away from that for a while but knew no one here tonight and started feeling paranoid.

I should just leave. But fuck this guy.

Sometimes, the city girl in me didn't make the best decisions, and I thought I was a lot tougher than I was. I held the bottle tightly, then turned to face him again, realizing having my back to this person was not the best idea.

He stared at me as if trying to say something but couldn't get the words out. His eyes were mean and redder than only a moment before. He was drunk, very drunk. I didn't know Brian—maybe he could be a great guy; but right now, I could see in his eyes he wasn't in there, whoever he was.

I loosened the grip on the bottle as better judgment came over me, and I moved a few steps toward the door to leave. Although I shouldn't have, I was unable to resist smiling at him while I passed, knowing this would piss him off. Foolishly, I turned my back to him again, but I was rusty, also misjudging how fast my exit would be through the crowd. I still had the bottle when I felt something on my right shoulder pull me backward, swinging me around. I stumbled, the bottle slipping from my grasp to crash on the floor. I fell to one knee, and saw it was him. He had balled his hand into a fist as if he was about to hit me. I had no time and nowhere to go, so I turned my face and closed my eyes, bracing for the blow.

I felt a breeze as something moved across me, and when nothing happened, I opened my eyes. A man stood between us. I rose and stepped back, watching. He towered over me like a giant and had Brian by the throat.

"You fucking stupid drunk," he yelled over the music.

Brian's eyes were wide and scared. Two guys behind him yelled.

"C'mon, Dock, let him go, let him go," they screamed.

The man, Dock, didn't let him go. He stood holding Brian, who now looked unable to breathe, with ease. I looked down and saw Brian was on his tiptoes, kicking his feet, struggling.

"You want to fucking hit a girl, you piece of shit?" Dock went on.

Trying to see this Dock's face, I stepped outward, away from the bar. He clenched his teeth, rage in his eyes. His arm shook as he held Brian's throat.

Vince came running in alarm, asking if I was okay. He didn't wait for me to answer before turning his attention to Dock and Brian.

"Let him go, Dock," he said calmly, resting his hand on top of Dock's shaking arm. "Let him go," he said again, moving his hand to his shoulder.

Dock appeared to snap from his trance, acknowledging Vince but still holding Brian. He looked at me; our eyes met, and he smiled. I felt odd about smiling back during this potential murder, so I dropped my head and turned toward Vince.

"You've always been a piece of shit," Dock said, then let him go.

Brian stumbled backward into his group of friends. He looked sober suddenly and grabbed at his throat, coughing.

Dock turned away and headed for Vince and me. Betsy came around the bar, sweeping up the glass from the broken bottle. The people all around us resumed talking and celebrating as if nothing had happened.

"New Bedford boys," Betsy mumbled, rolling her eyes.

Then the voice again.

"Fuck you, Dock," Brian yelled, moving toward us.

Dock spun around and moved quickly while Vince darted in front of me.

I made my way through the crowd and out to the street, not looking back.

The cold air felt good on my face. I took a deep breath, wishing I had a cigarette, remembering I'd left the pack at home. I saw no smokers around to bum one from, but the craving went as quickly as it came. I was hurrying to my car, figuring that was enough drama for one night, when someone called out behind me.

"Hey, Leather." The voice echoed through the quiet night air.

Terrified, I moved faster, digging in my pocket for my keys. Whoever it was, they were coming fast. I turned quickly, holding my keys tight and putting one between my fingers in case I could stick him in the eye.

"Just leave me the fuck alone, okay?" I yelled, trying to finish with the word *asshole*, but I stopped, seeing it was Dock. "Oh, it's you." I smiled, embarrassed. "Sorry. I thought you were—"

"One of those assholes?" He laughed, taking a few steps closer.

I relaxed a little but kept up my guard. I looked past his shoulder to see if anyone else was coming. He kept a safe distance, possibly sensing I was rattled.

He seemed familiar, but I knew that I'd never seen him before. He wore a Carhartt coat and jeans with work boots like the rest of the year-rounders, so I figured he was one.

It was dark, but the holiday lights glowed around him. He had olive skin and dark, thick hair that angled toward his face. He looked Italian, but I figured he was Portuguese as the island had a large population. I stared at him for a moment, saying nothing, and watched as he reached in his pocket. He pulled out a cigarette pack and leaned over, offering me one. I noticed the white-and-green label.

I loathed menthols and hardly knew anyone who smoked them except my father and Black people in movies.

"Who smokes menthols?" I asked, sounding judgy but still taking one from the pack. I didn't smoke much but liked one with a drink or when others were smoking. I wanted one now, and beggars couldn't be choosey.

He lit it for me, still staying back a reasonable distance.

He either knows how intimidating he looks or thinks I'm still scared.

"Thanks." I smiled, trying to let him know I felt safe.

"I do," he said, leaning against the car in front of me, watching me.

I looked at him, confused for a moment, then realized he was answering my question, although I didn't mean it to be a question—more of an insult.

He smiled, raising his eyebrow at me.

Oh, he knows.

I watched him take a long drag and blow out into the night air. His hand looked giant holding the cigarette, and I noticed one of his knuckles appeared swollen as though he'd fractured it at some point.

"So, did you leave people dead in there?"

He smiled but didn't answer, taking another drag, and I noticed his hand again. He had a tattoo next to the busted knuckle. I couldn't see well in the dark, but it looked like dots, how they appeared on dice.

I inhaled, coughing as the harshness of the menthol burned my throat.

"So, does that jacket always get you in trouble?"

"Jesus Christ. Like, what, have none of you islanders seen a leather jacket before?"

Rolling my eyes, I crouched down, stubbing the cigarette on the ground.

"I'm not an islander." He looked at me strangely. "So, yes. I've seen, and I own, a leather jacket," he finished, then walked over to the curb. He sat, stretching his long legs in front of him, crossing one boot over the other.

I studied his face under the streetlight, his dark skin and large green eyes. He was handsome. He had a larger nose, and his lips seemed to turn at the corners even though he wasn't smiling. He leaned back and looked to the sky. His breath puffed in the cold night air, and suddenly I was freezing.

"Nice night," he said, dropping his gaze to me now. "So, what's your name?" His voice was deep and raspy. He was older, I could tell, but I wasn't sure how much.

"Georgette," I said hesitantly. "But people call me George usually." I smirked, waiting to annihilate him if he said something dumb.

He flicked his cigarette across the sidewalk. I watched it fly and hit the tree in the middle of the square, becoming irritated.

"George," he said, as if seeing how he felt about it.

I was ready to pounce, but something about him intrigued me, and I didn't want to be too much of a bitch.

"George, I'm Dock." He got up and brushed his hands on his pants, extending his arm toward me.

I shook his hand and smiled at the silliness.

"So, Dock, is that a nickname? Like you're a doctor or something?" I said sarcastically, as it was apparent that he wasn't.

"That's a no." He laughed. "Dock like a boat dock. My parents had a thing for boats—I don't know." He shrugged.

"With that name, are you sure you're not an islander?" His hand felt warm, and I hated to let it go, but I did. "Well, Dock, I'm freezing, so I'm gonna head home."

His eyes met mine and held me there until I turned my head, uncomfortable. I opened the door to my car and leaned in to start it, looking at him as I sat.

"And thanks again for your help tonight." I started to shiver. "I guess I owe you one."

Why did I say that? Stupid.

He put his hand on top of my door, looking mischievous.

"I'd like to see you again, Leather." He looked at my stethoscope hanging on the mirror. "Do you work at the hospital?"

I paused, wanting to be careful with my words.

"Not anymore." I turned up the heat.

"Leaving?" He looked in my eyes again, holding me there like a prisoner.

"Just changing jobs. Going private."

"Ahh." He moved away from the door. "A nurse for one of the rich kids, I'm guessing."

I rolled my eyes but smiled.

"Well, I'm glad you're staying," he said, lighting another cigarette.

"I'm never leaving, except I'm leaving now." I laughed. I was unsure if my attempt to be cute worked, but it was so cold I didn't care.

He grabbed the door handle, holding the cigarette between his teeth.

"So, again, I'd like to see you again." He was aggressive in a subtle way, and I liked it.

The island was small, and he could find out everything about me if he wanted to; I figured I'd see if he made the effort. I touched his hand on the door handle.

"So, see you then."

He coolly took another drag from the cigarette and blew the smoke into the night.

"I plan to," he said with confidence and gently shut the door.

I backed out onto the avenue, looking at him as he watched, then headed home.

CHAPTER 5

July 11, 1992
Driving was long, longer than time,
because of the infection that slowly ate us.

The alarm clock rang and vibrated on my nightstand, and I slammed my hand on top of it. At seventeen, having to be ready by seven in the morning was nearly impossible, and someone would pay dearly. That someone was my father, who had to deal with my complaining until we hit the Bourne Bridge before crossing into the Cape.

"This truck is horrible!" Irritated, I shifted on the tattered vinyl seat, reaching under my legs, wiping the sweat away. "Gross." He ignored me. "This is a long drive," I continued, staring right at him, making sure he could see I was bothered.

"Not really," he mumbled, then opened his mouth and made the retching sound, drumming up a giant loogie. He turned his head and launched it out the window. Unrelenting, I pretended my eyes were laser beams vaporizing him.

"That's beyond disgusting." I lifted up from the seat to wipe my legs again. "So gross."

"All right, all right!" he finally responded.

A giant sign made from carved bushes in the rotary read, *Welcome to Cape Cod*, and I was relieved to be almost there. We followed the green-and-white sign pointing to Woods Hole, Falmouth. I had only ever been to the Cape once, which was weird as I'd lived in Massachusetts my whole life. Aunt Rita, my father's sister, rented a house in Cohasset for a week after she got settlement money from a car accident.

I remembered all the adults sitting around and hearing "settlement" over and over and my father saying, "Ya did good, kid" while patting her on the head.

Most folks on the North Shore didn't go to Cape Cod or the Islands. We usually headed further north to New Hampshire or Maine, while the people who lived south of Boston opted for the Cape or the Islands since they were closer. Living in the ocean-side city of Revere, most of our vacations consisted of us going across the street to the beach, which was okay with us; it was America's first public beach, to be exact, as noted on the signs exclaiming this.

Revere was a tough, blue-collar city with a few Irish and Jewish people scattered about. But really, everyone and everything in the city was Italian, except for us. At least, that's what it felt like. The bakeries, restaurants, and all my friends were Italian, and I wished I were too.

My friends and I hung at the beach and lay in the sun most summers, them with their long dark hair, olive skin, big brown eyes, and me with my fair, freckled skin and reddish-brown hair. I liked my blue eyes, and my hair was long, but I looked like a ghost next to their tanned, glistening bodies. I'd watch them slather themselves in baby oil and become darker. Then I'd do the same and burn red like a lobster. My mother yelled at me to stop pretending I was Italian and to be proud of my Irishness, as they were the most beautiful people in the world. Looking at my reflection and my pasty skin, frizzy hair, and freckles, I disagreed, but in silence.

There were tons of guys around Revere with nicknames like Johnny Rockets or Broadway Joe. Everyone had a nickname. Fat Ricky cashed everyone's checks and had an illegal cab company with a few old 1970s limos. We had about ten Blackys, and two of them lived near us on the beach. My father was "Richie from the Beach." Even at a young age, I thought I could have come up with something a little cleverer. None of these people seemed to have jobs—or regular jobs, anyway. "Blacky from the Beach" ran numbers, my father said, although I didn't know what that meant. My dad was a truck driver, but it seemed he didn't work much either.

• • •

For a little while, I believed my father might be a gangster like the ones from the movies he watched on TV. He and his friends looked and talked like those guys, and many of them drove the same types of cars.

One night, I watched *The Godfather* while he slept on the couch. I stretched out on the green shag rug, listening to him snoring next to me, unaware I was there. Michael, the main character, had the same enormous eyes as my father that were also slightly turned at the corners. I couldn't believe Michael, who seemed like a smart guy on a good path, would get involved with and then lead the Italian Mob and hurt people. I guess he had to, but it wasn't what his father wanted for him. I watched until the end and then lay in bed, wondering if my father could be one of those guys. He drove the car and was in the union, which they talked about a lot. He dressed like them—or tried to, anyway. We weren't Italian, so he couldn't be a made guy, but a lot of Irish guys and others worked with them.

Maybe I was onto something.

I woke up the next morning and went to the kitchen. He was sitting at the kitchen table, hurriedly rolling one of his "cigarettes," as he called them. He never seemed to roll these if my mom was home. I couldn't understand why he was afraid of her seeing the cigarettes he rolled himself. She didn't care about the Kools, and she smoked too. She had been trying to quit recently, though, so maybe that was it, but I wasn't sure. It seemed he was up to something.

I grabbed a Bubba Cola from the fridge—like a Pepsi, but for poor people; my mom bought them at the weird grocery store down the street. None of the products there had names like the ones in regular stores or on TV. They also didn't have bags for your stuff, and you had to put it all in boxes yourself after paying. Ray hated that store and refused to drink Bubba Cola.

"Why can't we be normal? Can't we have Coke and Doritos like everyone else?" he'd cried the other day while chewing on the end of his clip-on tie. He stood, showing my mom the Bubba Cola can, then walked over and pulled the bag of Nacho Cheese Chips with a giant *Great Value* sticker on the front from the cabinet, pointing to it.

Ray had worn a clip-on tie since he could dress himself. He told us all that he was an executive and didn't care what anyone said because that was how executives dressed. He also told us an executive wouldn't drink Bubba Cola. My mother ignored him and changed the subject.

"What's up, Georgie?" my father said as he rolled his cigarettes, looking past me nervously, watching for my mom. I sipped my cola as he stuffed the cigarette in his pack of Kools, then brushed off the table.

"Are you a gangster?" I asked, taking another sip.

His hurried movements suddenly slowed, and he stared ahead, then turned and smiled strangely. I was relieved after worrying the question would make him angry. In the movies, they didn't say that word in the family. It seemed only the police referred to them as gangsters, so I didn't want to get in trouble for going against the rules. I smiled, pleased, and swung my legs underneath me. I stared at him for a moment, my smile fading.

He shouldn't be smiling. He should be serious, like Michael in the movie.

He suddenly didn't remind me of Michael anymore. He seemed more like Michael's brother Fredo instead. I studied him. His eyes bloodshot, he looked weird. Fredo was a guy who was around because they had to let him be. Maybe he was like that. I felt sorry for Fredo and thought he was stupid.

He stopped smiling and came over, leaning in close. I pulled away in surprise. The familiar beer-cigarette-aftershave mixture made me choke, and I turned my head to cough.

"If I were, you'd never know it," he whispered, quickly kissing me on the cheek.

He stepped away and smiled down at me proudly, patting me on the head, and then made his way to the stairs out the back door.

I put my can in the sink and then went to my room and plopped onto my bed. I pulled my diary from under the mattress, taking the pen from the holder, writing my last entry for the day: *My dad is not a gangster.*

• • •

I stared out the window as we drove the narrow stretch of road into Falmouth.

"Almost there," he said, sounding excited.

I felt a little excited too. I was eager to see this place, even if it was with him. I glanced at him, thinking maybe he wasn't that bad.

I had grown up by the North Shore, so the Cape seemed familiar, only prettier and cleaner. Also, the people seemed fancier, and I liked that. We pulled down into what looked like the town center and stopped for gas across Main Street, next to a few small shops and restaurants. I remembered little of our trip here with my aunt except for my father ending up drunk and leaving on a bus after my mother decked him. I never forgot that. Ray and I were sitting on the dock, eating freeze pops Aunt Rita had given us, when we heard yelling from the house. Ray ignored it, as he usually did, and playfully pushed me over.

"You're a jerk," I yelled, starting to push him back, then hearing a door slam and more screaming.

We looked at each other, raising our eyebrows. I tried my best to put it out of my mind and stay right where we were, pretending things were fine. That's what Ray would want. But I never could and convinced him to come with me and see.

"Let's go see what's going on." I stood, making my way toward the stairs. I turned back. Ray wasn't moving. "C'mon." I gestured for him to get up.

"I don't want to know, George," he sighed. His blue lips from the pop made him look dead.

We slowly walked to the house. I listened hard, trying to figure it out, but there was no sound. I tiptoed up the stairs and quietly opened the screen door to the porch. Ray stood close behind, looking in every direction except in front of him.

"You're leaving!" my mother yelled.

We could see through the doorway to the living room. My father clutched the fireplace, appearing to steady himself. He was drunk. Even in the dimly lit room, I could tell. He looked like he needed a bath, and just hours before, he'd looked clean.

Something came flying toward my father. It looked like clothes, but it was hard to tell. I stood at the entrance of the porch, clutching the plastic pop wrapper. I turned to Ray, who was chewing on his, twirling it in his mouth and staring at the ceiling.

"I'm not going anywhere," Dad said, slurring, attempting to make his way toward where I assumed my mother was standing.

He took a few steps; then suddenly she came into view. He took another step toward her and suddenly was thrown back over the rocking chair. It all happened in slow motion. He looked like liquid spilling from the chair onto the floor. My mom walked over and glared down at him. He didn't move. I turned to Ray, whose eyes were wide, still twirling the ice pop wrapper in his mouth. Noticing us there, my mother turned in horror. She ran to us, kneeling, assuring us he was okay.

"Sorry, guys, I'm so sorry," she said.

I could tell she was trying to hold back from crying.

"It's not your fault, Mom," I said, rubbing her head.

"Did you hit him, Ma?" Ray's voice came from behind, and I stared at him with fire.

A tear fell from her cheek. She looked away from us, wiping it with the back of her arm. My eyes filled, and I tried holding them back. I hated crying, but seeing her cry bothered me.

"How about a ride in the rowboat?" She hopped up, glancing again at my father.

"Is he alive?" Ray asked, looking past her.

"Oh my gosh, Ray." She grabbed his shoulder. "Yes! Yes, of course he is, Ray. He's just sleeping," she said, hugging him tightly.

Ray didn't move.

"Drunk sleeping," I whispered, watching him. "Let's go to the dock again, Ray. Come on." My eyes met my mother's. "We can make fishing rods and try to catch something."

"Great idea!" my mother chimed in, pretending to sound excited so we would be. "I'll grab some line and some bread for the fish."

She walked to the kitchen, past my father, who still wasn't moving.

It stunned me that she had hit him. She'd never done anything like that. He deserved it, or I guessed he did. He was breathing, and after watching him for a moment, I saw his hand move. I was glad he wasn't dead.

CHAPTER 6

January 20, 2003
He is challenging, melancholy, irritated,
and at times impossible. We are a fine pair.

"George!" Mr. S. yelled from across the hall. I had ignored him once already, so I couldn't again. I made my way to his room. Our usual morning song and dance had become my every morning since coming on full-time with him. I had worked for him here and there throughout the summer after Bobbie asked if I was interested in the job. One night at the hospital, she called him by his full name as if I'd know who he was. It sounded familiar, although I couldn't place it.

"You know him," she said, her blue eyes glaring at me. Her strawberry-blond hair appeared redder than usual under the nurse's station's fluorescent lights.

Finally, someone more Irish looking than me. More freckles.

"Sounds familiar," I answered, turning away to grab a patient's chart.

"The Pulitzer Prize winner?"

I thumbed through the chart, not paying attention.

"The movie? The book?" She kicked my chair.

"What?" I turned to look at her.

"*The Choice!*" She stared at me, raising her shoulders.

"Oh," I said, realizing who he was. "Great movie. Maybe I'll read the book." I laughed at her annoyance, then yawned uncontrollably, noticing the clock. It was three in the morning, the witching hour where patients rang for you or something crazy always happened.

"Are they high maintenance?" I asked, referring to Mr. S. and his wife. I watched closely for her response to make sure she was truthful.

"Maybe a little," she answered after a long pause.

I lingered a moment, then shrugged.

"Whatever, I'm in." I yawned again. "I could use the money."

The call light blinked for room 107, and a voice yelled loudly down the hall.

"Here we go," she said, and we looked at each other, then broke out laughing.

Bobbie worked a few shifts a week for Mr. S. after meeting Jan, his full-time nurse, one night over the summer. Bobbie knew everyone on the island, and everyone seemed to know her. It was the thing I liked best about her—how easily she talked with people and made everything look effortless.

I worked mostly evenings for Mr. S. with a weekend day here and there. It was a straightforward routine, except that he wasn't a trusting sort, and it took a long time for him to get comfortable with me. He intimidated me at first, saying little, and when he said something at all, it was often cynical and questioning my competence.

"What are you doing with that? Where are we going? Why are you doing it like this?"

Others might have left. Jan eventually did, and I'd heard there were previous exits before. Jan left abruptly, abandoning everything the day before Thanksgiving. They were about to return to Greenwich, Connecticut, and their main house for the winter as they did every year, and Jan was to go with them. I came that evening to work, and his wife, Lilly, appearing desperate, asked me if I had an interest in a full-time job. I called my mother, and we talked a little. It was nice to have something new to discuss, avoiding everything we should talk about, which was our usual.

"It'd be a unique experience," she said.

My initial thought was no, and I had no intention of leaving the island, but I thought again, adding the figures in my head. I gave my notice at the hospital when Lilly assured me that they would stay on the island this year to entice me, and I finally agreed.

Working for him—or them, as that's what it really was—I found challenging, and it involved a lot more than being a nurse. Lilly, his wife, and Delia, the house woman, had strong personalities, and it was a juggling act between all three of them; sometimes they all could be difficult. But the difficulty didn't bother me much, and I was reasonably good at handling it.

I tried extra hard at first to gain his trust, exhausting myself. When it didn't happen as fast as I'd have liked, I figured I'd just let it happen organically if it happened at all. He probably felt abandoned by the nurses who'd left, and I was sure he was unaware he was part of the problem.

"Mr. S., do you want something to eat?"

"No."

"It's probably time to get out of bed. Let's get going."

"Not now."

"It's time for your medications."

"Later."

This was our routine. Thankfully, I was numb to it. It was often crazy, but crazy I was comfortable with.

His declining health and aging body left him vulnerable, and he didn't like it. Lots of aging patients suffered from this, I'd experienced, and I felt he was struggling with the same. He needed help, which angered him, but I could tell he wanted to feel safe with someone he could trust. I called out sick one Tuesday; I wasn't ill. Bobbie and I and a few other nurses ended up on a yacht after meeting some guys at Nancy's Bar in Oak Bluffs—until getting kicked off.

"Put some clothes on, ladies," a voice had rung out as a giant spotlight nearly blinded me.

It was the harbor police on a smaller boat below us. We were jumping naked off the bow into the water.

"Shit," Bobbie said, turning to me.

I grabbed my sweatshirt, then watched, stunned, as she ran and jumped one last time, getting us banned from the harbor for the summer.

I called early on when I knew the night would turn wild and got Barbara, a nurse who worked a few shifts over the summer, to cover for me. Mr. S. wasn't happy about it.

"Where were you?" he snapped when I came into the living room the next day. He was waiting silently on the couch for me.

"I was sick, Mr. S."

I hate lying.

"Oh." He leaned over, grabbing his glasses, picking up the book next to him.

"You were in good hands with Barbara," I said, knowing he was upset with me.

"She's old and heavy."

I struggled not to laugh, feeling bad he was irritated. I tried justifying it in my head. Then Bobbie's ass jumping from the boat popped in my head, and I looked away from him in guilt.

He said nothing else, but he must have been worried that I wasn't coming back. He tried hard to push me away every day, testing me to see if I'd leave. I knew he didn't want me to, but he couldn't trust me unless he knew I wouldn't. I was familiar with this, learning it somewhere.

Maybe in the meetings as a kid? I wasn't sure, but I had trust issues too, so I got it.

After seeing me nearly every Tuesday and Thursday throughout the summer and my only calling out once, he seemed more at ease, but he still challenged me. The routine was the same, except there was a repetitive morning sequence now and all kinds of other nonsensical habits to contend with. This, along with Lilly throwing an unexpected visitor in or a forgotten appointment or trip into the mix.

Mornings, I'd get there early. In a matter of minutes, after I headed up the stairs, he would call out, checking if I was close. He always wanted me close, mostly if Lilly was away. I'd typically yell back, but sometimes, like today, I'd let him call twice.

"George!" he called again, letting out a cough that echoed in the hall.

"I'm right here!" I yelled, to which there was no reply. "Do you want to get up now? It's ten o'clock." I stood in the doorway, watching him stare ahead.

He said nothing, which was his way of saying yes. I came in and gathered his clothes onto the bed, then headed to the bathroom to grab his toothbrush and washbasin, filling it with soapy water.

"Did you want a shower?" I asked, already knowing the answer, while setting the basin down.

"I'll fall."

"You didn't fall yesterday. Why today?"

"You're a small woman," he reasoned.

I assured him he'd be fine, but nothing I said eased him.

"I can't win," I went on. "If I were fat and large, you wouldn't like it, or if I was too young or too old. Now I'm too small."

"Is Lilly back?" he grumbled and coughed. I held a cup to his mouth to spit.

The best doctors in the country treated him. I figured it was because of who he was, the genius Pulitzer Prize winner—seeing how no doctors, at least that I knew, would fly to see just any patient. They had good plans, some of them, but you had to have a willing participant with the drive and determination to try. I wasn't sure why they couldn't see that Mr. S. didn't. But the doctors seemed to spend more time talking about him than with him, so maybe they didn't know.

"No, she's not back yet," I said, wiping his mouth with the washcloth. He reached up, taking it from my hand.

"I'm not a baby," he growled, coughing again.

"I think she flies in later," I said and pulled his shirt over his head. "She's still in London at the board meeting, remember?"

He nodded, tossing the washcloth on the floor.

"Then we head to New York to see your therapist," I said, knowing this would rattle him.

I was half glad because it rattled me. I hated flying in the small private plane to his appointments. We had already been there three times in three weeks, and I was over it. I carried the briefcase with all his medical records and spoke to whomever he saw, talking all the medical jargon that seemed to impress Lilly.

"What's the weather?" he asked, reaching his arm through his sleeve, getting stuck. He pushed hard and accidentally hit me in the side. "Sorry," he grumbled, seeming unscathed by New York, which was unusual.

He was nervous about the weather on the island in the winter. He asked every day, so I made sure to listen to the news before I came to the house.

"Cold and clear, it said on the news this morning, Mr. S." I fixed his collar as he nudged my arm away. "But it's New England; you can't go by them."

"Drooling like a baby." He nodded, reaching for another tissue while I fixed his collar again.

As he couldn't hold his head upright for long from the weakness that occurred, it hung forward, causing an increase in the "drooling," as he called it. It embarrassed him, and I knew this was why he was often irritated. I'd try to be patient when he angrily grabbed at tissues or nudged my hand when I wanted to help him. I often said nothing.

"My body is deteriorating, George."

He said this nearly every morning, usually while looking at his arms or hands as if he didn't recognize them.

"All of ours is," I whispered.

"Did they say snow?" He lifted his head a little and looked at me, his eyes gray and watery.

"Not that I heard."

We finished up for the morning and headed downstairs to the living room. He was more unsteady than usual today, and I held on to him tightly. He used a cane but never correctly, and I was sick of arguing with him about it. I glanced at some pictures of Lilly and him on the wall as we passed by. He looked so intense as a younger man and much more intimidating. It was odd seeing the picture next to the thinner, frailer man in front of me. I often wondered what he was like then, in his prime. He had a presence about him. I felt it when I first met him that day at the beginning of summer.

I had heard all the stories from the house woman, Delia, and other staff. Some of them were so outlandish I wasn't sure I believed them, but Delia had been with the family for over thirty years, so I figured there must be a little truth there.

A few weeks ago, in the kitchen, she told me of the epic fights he and Lilly had in their house in Connecticut, after he'd be up all night drinking and writing.

"Oh my gosh, he would come down and throw the pots and pans, yelling at everyone! He'd demand that woman type his work; then he'd get in his car and drive to New York and disappear," she said loudly in her thick Jamaican accent, nearly hysterical.

Delia always called Lilly "that woman" when she spoke of her to people who worked in the house. They had a tumultuous relationship that I couldn't quite understand. They would yell at each other, and Delia would bang things around. I wasn't sure why Lilly put up with it; Delia was the hired help, after all. After so many years, I guessed she was part of the family, and maybe Lilly had loyalty to her for being there when she wasn't. Lilly was always off on some trip, doing her human rights work. If nothing else, it seemed they both were loyal.

I sat Mr. S. on the sofa's right side after moving a stack of Lilly's papers. She always put them there, on the right side, where he sat every day, which I found strange as there were five chairs and countless other tables to put them. I wondered if she bore resentment toward him, doing it unconsciously. It sounded like it would be understandable, but what did I know? I recalled my mother behaving similarly toward my father before starting the meetings, making me think of her.

I wish things were better between us.

I handed him the *New York Times*, and he opened it, staring at the page. I'd watched him reading the paper a few times now and wondered if he could see well enough to read. He had glasses, but he often looked like he was just staring at the page. His eyes didn't move, and he once had it upside down. It made me sad, but I said nothing. I empathized, figuring it must be hard for someone whose life has been all about the written word not to be able to see words anymore, if that was the case. I wasn't sure if it was his depression, which he struggled with considerably for years, or part of his neurological decline affecting this. I made a mental note to let the doctor know in private sometime during his appointment tomorrow, although there probably wasn't much he could do.

I went to the kitchen, and Delia motioned for me to sit. A plate of buttered toast and a cup of hot tea sat on the table. I was starving and thanked her, taking a bite. I didn't want the tea, but I sipped it graciously to not set her off. She could be difficult too.

"Someone special is coming for a visit," Delia blurted, staring at me intensely. She slapped her dishrag on the counter, smiling, holding back from laughing. She appeared eager for my reaction, and I only looked at her, confused.

"Special?" I took a sip of the tea, black and cloudy, feeling it burn my lip.

"Yes, yes!" she squealed in a fit of laughter. Her teeth beamed white against her dark skin, and she threw her head back, slapping the dish rag again. I'd never seen her so animated.

"His special friend, she is coming." She laughed again, tucking a loose hair back into the turban I'd never seen her without.

"I, I don't know what to say." I smiled, lifting my shoulders. I touched my lip with my fingers. "Why is she special?" I asked.

Her smile became more abundant, and her eyes widened.

"I'm making them brunch!" she squealed again.

Feeling strange about it all, I thought of asking for more details, wondering who this friend was. I'd heard chirpings around the house about things, but I left it alone. Mr. S. called from the living room just as a knock came from the kitchen door. I went to see what he needed, irritated; I wanted to see who it was.

I poked my head around the corner. "I'm here. Do you need anything?"

"No."

I sat in the chair across from him and listened, straining to hear voices in the kitchen.

"Any New Year resolutions?" I asked, making small talk, which he hated.

"No." He cleared his throat, shaking the paper out.

"Me neither," I said. "It's stupid."

"Yes," he agreed, half smiling. "Stupid," he repeated.

He liked it when I was negative or disagreed with things against social norms. Something had come on the television one night about the hidden germs at restaurant buffets, and I commented how disgusting I thought buffets were. He perked up on the sofa and gave me a half smile, which I'd never seen before.

"Atrocious and gluttonous," he said.

I had never heard him so peppy.

"Like pigs at a trough," he went on.

I laughed, enjoying our interaction. "Agreed."

Now we sat quietly for a few moments. I heard a noise and watched cringingly from the corner of my eye. The newspaper slid out of his hand, making its way down his lap. I nodded, watching it fall onto Lady, his skittish brown dog lying by his feet. I knew what was coming next and braced myself.

He brought his hand to his face, looking at it as he always did, as if it were some brand-new appendage. His lips turned down into a scowl and his face turned pink.

"This hand!" he yelled, turning it back and forth in front of him.

Lady leaped to her feet and scurried from the room. He visibly became more upset, as if he were about to cry watching her.

He only ever gets emotional about the damn dog.

It was his dominant hand, his writing hand—and one of the first things to become affected by his disease. The contracted hand left him unable to grasp things. Pens, papers, anything would slide out. He referred to it as a claw and told me once he felt this was a punishment of some sort. His psychiatrist thought his other disease, his depression, was contributing to his hand-function loss. I wasn't entirely sure.

"Punishment for what?" I asked then, afraid of his response.

"Isn't it obvious?" he had groaned, holding it in the air. "Fitting," he went on, staring at it.

I knew it had something to do with writing but didn't say a word.

Lilly had every therapist imaginable come to work on his hand. I would massage it, doing the prescribed exercises when he let me. He'd tell me nothing worked, and I'd nod in agreement, continuing to do them anyway.

Delia hurried in from the kitchen; she must have heard him yell.

"You want something, Mr. S.?" she said breathlessly.

"No!" he snapped, still staring at his hand.

"Okay, okay, jeesh," she said, which I barely understood. Sometimes her accent was thicker, especially if something upset her. She looked at me and rolled her eyes.

He and Delia had an odd relationship. The whole family's relationship wasn't conventional, and I kind of liked it, mostly. Delia had spent a lot of time with the kids when they were growing up because he and Lilly were away a lot. Rosalie, the cleaning lady, told me all of this when I helped her fold laundry the previous week. They were literary folks and didn't get all bogged down with guilt and nonsense, putting the art first, I figured. Or they lived in the "let's pretend" world, like my family did. I wasn't sure which.

Artsy types, more accepting, I had told myself, wishing I had an excuse for my clan.

I'd thought they bore no guilt until a few days before when I told him that his youngest daughter, Annie, was coming for a visit, which I'd heard as I was doing his hand therapy one morning.

"I was an awful father," he had exclaimed out of nowhere.

I wanted to hear more and was careful in how I proceeded. He was not a man who enjoyed many spoken words, so you had to carefully pick what you said if you wanted something in return.

"Really, why was that?" I said, waiting for him to ignore me or get angry and shut down.

I'd once overheard Lilly saying he wasn't the best father and was a less than stellar husband as she talked to a woman outside on the porch one afternoon. She laughed, going on about him being such a gifted writer and how he couldn't possibly be both. From what I could tell, she seemed fine with it, and I liked her honesty, although I wondered if she was as fine as she appeared.

"I wrote and drank," he answered, wiping his mouth with his sleeve. "I yelled too," he went on matter-of-factly.

He never elaborated much, and it was clear he lived in his head, which I knew could be dangerous.

"Does this make you feel bad now?" I asked, careful not to move or distract him.

I knew he was a drinker from what Delia said. One evening, I also heard him talk about alcohol and how he used it to write while speaking to a woman who was writing a book on alcoholism and wanted a quote from him about it.

"I wasn't good when I stopped drinking either," he grumbled to me.

He appeared deep in thought. He had a puzzled expression I'd not seen before, as if all of it confused him.

"Maybe you were a dry drunk," I said, knowing I was pushing my luck. I stood next to him, holding his medicine cup of pills and trying not to break his concentration. He said nothing. "Have you heard of that term?" I asked, hoping this wouldn't offend him, and then immediately regretted it.

"No."

I paused, wondering if I should go on, but he seemed interested, so I continued.

"A lot of people, when they get sober, are sort of miserable and angry. They think they'll be happy without the substance, but it's all they've known for usually a long time. When you don't have your 'crutch' anymore, it's a real struggle, and often people forget whatever made them happy before it."

I didn't think I articulated this great, but I tried my best.

He looked at me with interest. His mouth hung agape, and I reached with a tissue, watching him grab it fiercely with his contracted hand, wiping and then tossing it on the bed next to him.

"Maybe that's what I was."

"Only you would know." I put the tissue in the barrel.

"How do you know this?" he asked, attempting to make eye contact with me.

"About what?" I asked. "Dry drunks?" *My favorite subject.*

"Yes, that."

"My father had a drinking problem, and I saw it. I also used to go to meetings about it all when I was a kid."

Maybe I'm getting too personal.

"Really?" he mumbled, pointing toward the floor at a clump of tissue.

I picked it up and threw it in the basket.

He stared at his hand again, and I felt a knot starting in my stomach. He looked at it like a dog looked at his tail before chasing it.

• • •

After my New Year's comment and his Lady-scaring outburst, there was no further talk, and I rose to leave the room. I smelled Delia cooking something and hoped my toast was still warm. I heard voices, now remembering the mysterious visitor, and I tried to envision who it might be.

"Where are you going?" he asked, gazing out the window as the ferry glided by the dock.

"I'm going to talk to Delia. There are a few things we need for you at the store."

I lied. I wanted my toast and to eyeball his guest.

He reached for the newspaper, then quickly gave up and made a fist, pushing off the couch to get up, nearly falling sideways. I hurried to help, grabbing his cane, which was pointless but a habit.

He's impossible! "I wish you'd give me some notice when you want to do that, okay?"

"Delia can't read or write," he scoffed.

"Stand up tall," I reminded him, putting my hand on the small of his back. "Delia's okay," I said, putting my arm through his and heaving him straighter.

"She's not educated, George. She hardly ever went to school," he said. *Why is he telling me this?* Hunching over, he stumbled toward the dining room.

"We'll figure it out."

"Who's here?" he asked, alarmed at hearing the voices.

"I, I guess someone is coming for brunch," I responded, feeling awkward.

"Oh, right, Karla." He brought his sleeve to his mouth and coughed into it. "Take me there." He pointed to the chair at the head of the table.

He didn't complain or have a negative thing to say about someone coming, which he always did. I had learned from my short time with him that he seemed to dislike everyone no matter who it was. No one impressed him enough to want to see them, at least no one that I'd seen, and there was always someone coming. Lilly brought someone she thought important for a meal or a chat almost every day when she was home through the summer. He complained every time she announced there would be a visitor. Sometimes, he would yell and refuse to come down, and other times, he'd sit quietly until he felt comfortable, although never appearing so. He occasionally seemed to enjoy the people, but rarely, and complained incessantly about their arrival beforehand. He showed little interest in anyone she brought, and their celebrity status meant nothing.

I figured this was why she didn't tell him until the last minute anymore, and she kept it from me now too. Last week, a man walked up the dock path with two men in suits, having just come off a boat. I noticed what looked like wires from an earpiece in one man's ears through the picture window as they came closer. I continued massaging Mr. S.'s hand, trying to make out who it was. Mr. S. noticed me staring, then turned to look as they walked up the lawn. He pulled his hand from me, glaring out the window.

"Who is that, George?" he asked, annoyed, trying to see.

I moved closer to the window.

"It looks like—"

"Damn Kennedys!" he had erupted, seeing it was the senator of Massachusetts.

Now Lilly walked in with a woman, Karla. She was tall and thin and had auburn hair. She appeared younger than the old couple, but not by much.

"Let's all sit," Lilly said, hurrying around the table. "Delia will bring some food soon. Hey, George." She smiled, gritting her teeth weirdly. "George, this is Karla."

We greeted each other, smiling. I looked again at Lilly, who looked stiff, and I wondered if something was wrong. She spoke in a more pretentious tone than usual, and she had a giant smile plastered on her face. Lilly could saunter with the likes of anyone, and I'd never seen her flustered, at least not in social situations—that was her element.

I think I'll make my exit.

"George, could you tell Delia we would like water?" Lily smiled.

She was already sitting, which was also unusual; she never sat, at least not long.

"Sure," I said.

"Sit, Karla," Mr. S. barked from his chair.

Karla pulled her chair out. She seemed comfortable, and it made me second-guess things.

I went out to the kitchen, relaying to Delia the water request. She raised her eyebrows and smirked.

"They're all crazy, Georgie." She leaned over, pinching my cheek, then headed out with a tray.

Mumbling under her breath, Lilly marched through the kitchen, nearly knocking me over. She grabbed her coat from the chair. Delia came back in and ignored her to wash dishes at the sink. She quickly turned to me and winked.

"Where you headed, Mrs. S.?" Delia asked while Lilly fumbled with her notebooks on the table.

Lilly always had notebooks and papers of all kinds around the house, with scratching and numbers all over them. They were all of vital importance, she'd say. One of us would search for some piece of paper at least once a day while she jumped about in a panic, calling for us all to look.

"I'm heading to visit with Sunny and Ann," she responded, looking underneath the table and picking up a bunch of papers that had fallen to the floor. "When is Kelly coming, for God's sake?"

I'd never seen her so irritated, watching as she piled all the papers, hugging them to her chest.

"Next week she is here, I believe, Mrs. S. I talked to her this morning." Delia turned, hurrying over, picking up another fallen paper.

Lilly's assistant lived in Connecticut and worked for her when they were there. Lilly didn't like change, and those who worked for her, she kept—or tried to. She always made any arrangements needed for it to work. It would probably have been easier to get another assistant on the island, but instead Lilly had Kelly come for weeks at a time to help her, probably costing her much more. Lilly was also tricky; people didn't always work out, I had heard.

"Thank God," Lilly said, exhausted. "I have two poetry workshop groups coming to stay in the guesthouse, and then I'm flying to London again, and then there's Paris." She seemed to be thinking out loud.

Lilly was also a writer, a published poet, with a few books. Everything was always of great importance to Lilly—every phone call and every interaction, if you were someone worth the exchange. She was from wealth and lived a privileged life growing up. Although she was kind and generous to "the common folks" and made you feel as though you were friends, you knew your place if someone more important came by, which, again, happened frequently.

"George." Lilly glanced at me. Her silver hair curled perfectly, and a piece fell in her face, which she brushed back with her coat sleeve, sending another paper flying toward me. "Could you put these in my office?"

"Sure thing." I chomped my last bite of toast as she handed me the papers and headed toward the door.

Delia laughed loudly, nodding as she did after nearly every interaction with Lilly. Lilly usually ignored her, except this time. She whipped her head angrily, stopping at the door, and glared at Delia.

"Is something funny, Delia?"

Delia stopped laughing, immediately knowing her place.

"Nothing. Nothing funny at all, Mrs. S."

"Good," Lilly said firmly, turning again, and headed out. I glanced at Delia, who kept her head down.

I could only imagine what that was about. After thirty years, their relationship probably had its ghosts and goblins. They argued and fought and sometimes screamed at each other, but I had never seen Lilly make Delia know her place.

Delia disappeared upstairs, and I sat at the kitchen table, looking out at the trees. They swayed in the wind, and I sipped the cold tea, soft voices drifting in from the dining room. I couldn't make out any words but moved to the chair across from me, feeling intrusive, trying not to hear—although I wanted to. I enjoyed the quiet, knowing it wouldn't last.

The sky darkened over the sound; it looked like a weather front was moving in soon. I recalled someone talking of snow at Mocha Mott's this morning. I smiled, watching the whitecaps blow across the ocean, excited to see what would happen next.

Sheila and I had made small talk at Mocha Mott's as we usually did, and I thanked her as she handed me my cup. She'd seen me in line and had it ready for me. I tapped Bandit, the old black Lab, on the head as he lay by the door in the same spot as always. His tail wagged.

I panicked when I noticed the time on the wall clock. Hurrying to my car, I dug in my pocket for my keys, figuring Mr. S. was probably already yelling for me. Of course, I spilled my coffee. Jumping back as the hot liquid hit the ground, I pulled the stuck keys from my coat and wiped coffee from the outside of the cup with a sigh.

As I went to get in my car, something caught my eye, and I looked closer, puzzled. Then it came into focus. A single cigarette stood upright against the driver's window. Seeing it was menthol, I quickly spun my head around but saw no one. I'd nearly forgotten the New Year's events at Seasons after keeping my eye out around the island for him for a while, thinking I saw him once or twice.

"How romantic," I scoffed, trying hard not to smile.

I picked up the cigarette and headed back up Main Street.

CHAPTER 7

July 11, 1992
Maybe I want to be a Winterfresh kid.
Perhaps I was supposed to be; then,
there was some cosmic misfire.

"Are we almost there?" I asked loudly, changing the radio station to something I'd listen to other than Van Morrison. Hot and cranky, I was regretting my decision to come. I glared at my father in annoyance, but he didn't notice.

"Yeah," he said disinterestedly, eyes on the road ahead.

"It smells like old weed in here."

"We aren't far now," he mumbled, clearly irritated.

It's like I couldn't stop myself from being a jerk, but I also wanted to be one—sometimes, not all the time, but sometimes. I guess I had a lot of anger.

We slowed at a red light. Ahead was a sign with a small ship that read, *To Woods Hole and Martha's Vineyard* with an arrow. I watched him drive, lost in my thoughts.

"Do you like driving so much?" I finally asked, trying to make conversation and change the air I'd created with my complaining.

"I don't mind. I guess it's what I know," he said.

I pictured the truck-driving awards hanging on the wall of our living room—his father's, my grandfather, who was a union guy and drove for a living too. Dad didn't talk about his father much. He died when I was two. My mother said from drinking.

I guess they give awards for anything.

We arrived at the ferry terminal and pulled to the left with the other trucks waiting to get on the freight boat tucked alongside the larger ferry against the dock. The air, crisp and salty, blew through the window, and I pulled down the sun visor mirror, making sure my hair was in place. Seagulls mewed above us, and the men tying off the ship directed the people on and off, yelling back and forth to each other while making small talk with the people coming and going. My dad got our tickets and stayed outside, smoking a cigarette. I got out to stretch my legs. I jumped from the truck, catching my shorts on a tear in the seat where something metal stuck out, causing a small rip in my cutoffs.

"Shitbox," I said, twisting, trying to see if there was a hole.

The salt air smelled strong. A cool breeze came off the water, and I was thankful as it hit the sweaty moisture behind my knees. I took in the scenery of the busy terminal. I had always wanted to visit the island, but I figured you had to be fancy and rich to go. I saw I might not be far off, immediately noticing nearly everyone dressed nicer than us. It suddenly dawned on me that we just delivered the goods to the fancies. It wasn't like I didn't know it, but now it was clear. *We're the help.*

I looked at my father and then twisted again, trying to make sure there wasn't a hole on my butt. A glare from the ground caught my eye, and I followed it to my scuffed-up boots. The right one had a tiny tear on the top where the sun reflected off the steel toe's exposed metal from under the leather. I angrily side-stepped to a shaded area beside the truck. I stood there, annoyed, watching my father take a long drag off his cigarette, staring up toward the sky.

Watching him, I rolled my eyes.

A group of girls a little older than me stood in line by the ramp leading to the ferry. They looked like an advertisement for Winterfresh

Gum, crisp and clean looking. Smoke from my father's cigarette blew past my face, and I coughed loud so he could hear me. The elite's lifestyles intrigued me, and I tried my best to be a little bit fancy in my inner-city, "Great Value" world. I also expected more of life than I was willing to give, which made me resentful of those who got ahead on their own accord. But what enraged me more were the ones who had it all and did nothing except come from the right womb. I guessed I wasn't so different from Ray wanting to be an executive.

Maybe we both want an out. Something better.

Watching the cars pull onto the boat next to ours, I studied the people. I glanced over at the Winterfresh kids again, noticing how they dressed. One of them wore a colorful navy-and-pink floral dress with silver sandals. She had a yellow dog next to her, and his coat matched her golden hair, almost as if they'd planned it. The dog's leash was green with blue whales on it, and I watched the girl next to her laugh, tossing her hair back in her light-red shorts and powder-blue loafers. Her tanned shoulders were bare, and the ruffle from her white top billowed in the breeze. Her highlighted hair hung down her back in loose waves, and she playfully pushed a boy who walked by them wearing sunglasses and a polo shirt. His belt looked like the dog's leash, except instead of whales, it had anchors.

They all dressed for summer in a casual, put-together way, but casual fancy. The girl in the navy dress looked over, saw me staring, and smiled. I was leaning against the front of the truck with my legs crossed carefully so my boot didn't catch the sun again, and I turned my head, embarrassed. A bead of sweat rolled from my hairline, and I pulled at the ends of my long black hair. I stared at the lifeless, dry pieces. Maria's older sister was in hairdressing school and had dyed it black accidentally after I let her practice on me for a free haircut and color. It was supposed to be brown with highlights like the girl with the ruffled shirt, but it wasn't.

I moved away from the truck, not wanting to be seen with it or my father, and glanced over again, watching them smiling and laughing.

They looked like something from the expensive clothing catalogs Aunt Rita had on her coffee table. I could never figure out why she had them, as she only ever wore a housecoat. But I liked to look through them and picture myself in the different places they showed, wearing the clothes.

I continued observing, trying my hardest to hate them. I called them privileged assholes in my head, envisioning moving my boot into the sun again and directing the laser beam of light onto their group, incinerating them.

Navy-dress girl smiled at me again, and I half smiled back this time. Smiling at someone staring made little sense to me. She was supposed to say, "What the fuck are you staring at?" I didn't trust her.

"Privileged assholes," I mumbled under my breath, picturing them burning up with one move of my foot. *Ghetto superpowers.*

I laughed out loud at my thoughts.

The attendants waved toward us as they began loading the freight boat. I jumped in the cab, careful not to catch my shorts again.

"Hurry up," I said out the window, watching him finish the last of his cigarette, still leaning against the truck. The sun reflected off the gold rim of his sunglasses. He didn't move. "You're so cool," I said sarcastically. He ignored me and got in after the attendant yelled at him, causing me to smirk. "Told you."

We pulled on with ease as another guy waved us to the side and told my father to cut the engine. The whistle blew, and we lurched forward.

"That's the island straight ahead of us." He pointed. "It's seven miles out."

Following his finger, I looked. The truck pulled against the side of the open-aired boat, and I heard the waves lapping against the hull. He lowered his arm to the seat. I cringed at seeing Kate's name on his forearm. It still caught me off guard, though I'd seen it a million times by now.

I remembered the day Ray and I built a sheet fort in the living room and told my mom we would camp out for the night. We played GI Joe and Barbies, and she let us stay up late. I was making Barbie kiss GI Joe, and Ray yelled that was gross. Suddenly, an arm reached in between the sheets, and in a loud monster voice, my father—although unknown to us as yet—yelled, scaring the crap out of us. Ray jumped so high the sheet fort fell on our heads, scaring us more. I saw the tattoo on the arm when it came in and realized it was him, but it didn't register in enough time not to be terrified.

"Gotcha, scaredy cats!" he said, peering under the sheet, laughing, then helped us put our fort back.

After we got settled in again, I kept wondering about the tattoo. We never talked or asked about it. I'd seen it many times, but that night I felt the need to address it, at least with Ray.

"Who the heck is Kate?" I said in a loud whisper, staring at the sheet ceiling. I turned to him, watching him move GI Joe's legs into a split, then push them straight again.

"Who?" he said, bending Joe's knees.

"Kate. You know, the tattoo on Dad's arm? Who is that?"

He shrugged. "I don't know," he said and put the figure down, rolling on his side. "Goodnight."

"Ray!" I yelled, gently shoving him.

"What?" he groaned, not moving, as if he had fallen asleep already, which was entirely possible.

"I want to know who this Kate is; don't you?"

He rolled on his back to stare at the ceiling.

"I guess . . . I don't know," he said, now looking concerned.

"Well, Mom's name is Jane, so who the heck is Kate?" I stared at his face. His right eyebrow was up, and his mouth was open. It was his "I'm thinking" look I knew well. "What if, like, Mom isn't our mom, and this Kate is or something?" I said, wondering if we looked like our mother, staring at Ray's features.

"What?" he said, alarmed. "No, no." He shook his head as if convincing himself, then picked up the action figure again, turning its arms.

"Well, it's weird, Ray. It's weird, and I am getting to the bottom of it."

The next morning at breakfast, things seemed different. We sat extra quiet as we ate our cereal, prompting my mother to ask us if we got a good night's sleep. I looked her up and down, then looked at Ray. Ray stared back at me, continuing to eat his Captain Munch, the generic cereal from the weird store. He didn't get mad at the cereal even though the box was right in front of him. Usually, my mother poured it and kept the box from his view so he wouldn't get upset.

Was he thinking like me now: about Kate and the tattoo?

It never dawned on either of us to ask who Kate was. No one seemed to do that in our house. We lived in this strange Irish world of "Don't ask, don't tell" and pretended that everything was fine. I only knew it to be an Irish quality from what Maria's mom told me. I commented once how I liked that the Italians talked a lot and hugged and cried after her father, Maria's grandfather, died. The whole house was packed, and people laughed and ate while others collapsed on each other, hugging and crying. There was so much emotion, and no one seemed to hold anything back. After everyone left, I said something to Maria as her mom poured us some milk and gave us one of her homemade whoopie pies I loved so much.

"You're Irish, George," she said, cutting my whoopie pie in half. "They say nothing about anything." She laughed and patted me on the head.

Ray and I said nothing, keeping with our heritage, and I forgot after a while. Then coincidentally, a few months later, we found out. Ray and I were outside, fixing the tire on my bike, when my father walked up after pulling into the driveway one day. He stared at both of us for a moment, pulling a cigarette from his pocket, lighting it, taking a long inhale. We stopped fooling with the tire and sat on the ground, waiting for him to speak, which seemed to take forever.

"Listen, guys," he said, sounding exhausted. He paused and blew the smoke in our direction. Some came out of his nose.

"Gross," I mumbled so only Ray could hear, and he giggled.

Dad stared at us, then turned his head, looking at the fence in apparent concern.

"Your sister is coming to stay with us for a week," he exclaimed, turning back to us.

He took another drag off the cigarette before stubbing it out, and then wordlessly walked toward the house. I looked at Ray, stunned. Ray said nothing, instead picking up the tire rim, pretending to inspect it, and trying not to look at me. Everything seemed to happen in slow motion. I wanted to throw something at Dad, but he was almost at the door, and nothing was near me I could grab fast enough.

"Sister?" I yelled at the top of my lungs. "What sister?"

We found out my father had been married before. No one spoke of it. Kate was his ex-wife, and Mary was six years older than me and eight years older than Ray. She came a few days later, walking right by Ray and me as we watched TV in the living room. My mother came in not long after with Mary behind her and introduced us all. Mary seemed annoyed but forced a smile, and I forced one back, sizing her up.

Ray extended his hand to her. "Nice to meet you," he said, to which she smiled.

She was pretty with medium-length, feathered brown hair and braces. I wanted braces so badly but still had a few teeth to lose. She had boobs and long, dark eyelashes. She asked what we were watching, and I thought I heard an accent. It seemed Southern.

Did my dad live in the South before?

We all were silent, trying hard not to make eye contact until my father came in, ushering her from the house somewhere, and we didn't see her the rest of that day.

The following day, while brushing my teeth, I heard my mother whispering about Mary. I lowered the water pressure and put my head to the door to listen.

"Mary got friendly with Bernie," she said, followed by something about how she was happy that it was someone close to Mary's age. My father grunted.

My cheeks felt on fire, and I boiled with anger. I went to the sink and spat, nearly choking on the bit of toothpaste left in my mouth.

Bernie, with his dark tan and sandy-blond hair, lived downstairs, and I had been in love with him since I was seven. Now, being nine, that was a long time. He was sixteen, and I was sure he loved me too but didn't know it yet, but I would pretend that he did. I figured one day our age difference wouldn't matter, and then he would realize it.

I looked at myself in the mirror, staring at my mousy brown hair sitting in a clump on the side of my head. I ran my hand over my freckles and picked at one, seeing if I could scratch it off my cheek. Tears running down my face, I rubbed my giant, yellow front teeth. I wiped the tears away, continuing to look at the chubby, round-faced girl in the mirror, hating her.

I didn't speak to Mary the next few days, which wasn't hard as my dad kept us all separate the entire time she was there. His two worlds colliding seemed like more than he could handle, and I was thankful for that. He acted differently with Mary than he did with us, and I wasn't sure why. Did he love her more?

The last day she was there, I saw them in his car as I headed out to meet Lisa, my best friend, at the park down the road. It looked like he was crying, which bothered me.

I heard him saying, "I'm sorry," over and over.

Mary said something I couldn't understand and yelled, "Liar!" She got out, shutting the door hard, and stormed up the steps to the house, and just like that, she was gone.

Things got worse after that, and my father drank more. I never knew why Mary left or why she yelled. It was weird seeing my father cry, and I wondered if he had ever cried over me. I figured he promised her something and didn't keep it. He did that when he drank. He did it a lot to Ray, but not so much to me anymore. I had stopped believing him.

This went on for a while until, one day, he got into a big fight with my mom. He fell and broke his nose, passing out in the hallway in front of us after she told him to leave. Seeing all the blood, Ray cried and yelled to call the doctor. He turned, terrified, asking me if he was dead. I was sick of wondering if he was dead, and it was the first time I didn't think I cared if he was, which scared me.

"He's not dead, Ray," I said, pointing to his back, instructing Ray to watch it go up and down with his breathing.

My mother made a call, and a little while later Joey G. and Big Ray, my dad's friends from the union, came over. They put him in a car, and he was gone too. My mother told us he was going into a program to help him stop drinking. I went into my room and pulled my diary from under my mattress, opening to any page, not caring it wasn't in order. I scrawled the words in giant letters, *I FUCKING HATE MARY*, and *I HATE MY FUCKING FATHER*, tracing each letter so many times it tore through the pages.

CHAPTER 8

March 30, 2003
Like the island, I slowly come alive.
God, how passionless I'd been.

The sun crept in through the blinds, and I jumped in alarm, worried I was late. The winter had been long, and my personal life had become nonexistent. The cigarette on my window seemed like a distant memory, and I ached for some excitement. I sat at the edge of the bed a moment, enjoying the light coming in from outside. It excited me that spring was near, and I sat listening to the birds chirp outside, ignoring Hobo at the door. I had been working nearly every day all winter. I heard Mr. S. calling for me in my dreams now, and it was haunting. Working with him was different, and some days I felt like we were morphing into one person. Not only was he dependent on me, but I had become weirdly attached to him. It became suffocating at times.

Unlike the hospital, I was with my patient every day, nearly all day, and now overnight sometimes when Lilly was away, which was new. It was more comfortable to sleep in the guestroom instead of having Delia walk through the bushes over to the guest cottage, scaring the life from me. She did this the past week to tell me Mr. S. needed me at three in the morning; I didn't sign up for that and immediately planned on setting boundaries but instead slept there. I hated being spineless about it, so I put my foot down, requesting Lilly to hire another nurse so I could have at least one day off. Lilly agreed, but Mr. S. didn't like it, and I knew it would be a difficult task.

"Give me a minute, for the love of God," I said to Hobo, watching him wag his tail and spin in a circle.

Today Lilly was home, and I was thankful for some alone time in the cottage. It was quiet and cozy, surrounded by bushes and plantings and tucked away down the small path alongside the Yacht Club. The ferry whistle sounded, and Hobo barked, still not used to how loud it was here, so close to the sound. I popped the coffee that I hadn't finished yesterday in the microwave and decided I'd sit outside for the five minutes I had. Hobo watched me wrestle with my coat. I opened the door expecting warmth, but it was colder than usual. I was still grateful for the sun, which was brightly shining as I stepped outside.

Hobo took his time, finally deciding on the hydrangea bush that showed a few signs of life. Two tiny leaf buds were pushing their way from the stem at the bottom. It surprised me to see them so early.

I sat on the larger of the mismatched Adirondack chairs, noticing the hole in my sweatpants. I felt a draft through the nearly disintegrated concert T-shirt I wore most every night and pulled my jacket around me. The shirt had had its day, but I couldn't part with it. It was comfortable. I pulled at my necklace as I always did and took a sip of my coffee. I noticed dirt, brushed my old leopard slippers, and then tucked myself in the chair. Leopard print always reminded me of the Revere ladies, and sometimes I missed it.

The sun was mid-sky over the water, and I turned my head toward it, feeling it on the side of my cheek, closing my eyes, listening to the sounds of the island. Birds chirped, and the wind echoed from under the dock at the club. I heard the waves gently breaking under it, making the hollow sound that had become familiar.

A sudden buzzing noise rang out and then stopped. I peered around nervously, unsure who would be here this early, and tried figuring out where the sound came from. A hammer knocked, and the buzzing came again, sounding nearly on top of me. I looked by the Yacht Club, noticing a large truck and some men working just past the bushes that separated us, surprised I hadn't seen it before. I resented being bothered in my moment of quiet, but saws buzzing and hammers banging meant the island was coming to life again. Summer was on the horizon, and I smiled.

I took my last swig of coffee and ran in to feed Hobo, then hurriedly got dressed. I swept my hair in a bun and pulled on the pants from two days ago slung over the chair, along with the black cardigan sweater under them. I swiped on mascara and lip gloss, grabbed my medical bag and coat, and headed toward the door.

"I'll be back," I said to Hobo, rushing out the door. I typically cut through the narrow arch between the house and cottage instead of going around, saving me time. "Oh my God! I'm sorry," I yelled as I crashed into the back of a man on the other side of the bushes. The man twisted, nearly falling, then steadied himself.

"Jesus, lady," he said, clutching his hammer to his chest, staring at me in confusion.

I started to speak but instead said nothing, staring at his face.

I recognize this face.

I studied it for a moment, trying to place it, when it came to me.

Dock! He looked exactly like Dock, except he was shorter with different eyes from what I remembered from that night. His hair was lighter too, but everything else seemed eerily similar.

"I could've hurt you." He laughed uncomfortably, looking at his hammer.

"Oh, I'm sorry. I . . ." I stammered, following his eyes to the hammer and then back up at him. "I'm just cutting through to work." I rubbed my throat, feeling as if I'd cough, trying not to.

I glanced at the truck pulled alongside the club, trying to make out the name on the side. It looked like it said *New Bedford*, which was odd. During summer, you'd see all kinds of workers from different places, but not now. I recalled Dock being from New Bedford, or so Betsy said that night.

Weird coincidence.

"Well, have a good day." I smiled, brushing past his shoulder.

"You too."

I felt him shift to watch me as I passed.

A loud bang and a voice in the distance yelled. I turned to see.

"Hey, Will, come help me with . . . this."

The raspy voice.

Our eyes met. He dropped a large wood plank he was holding into the truck bed, and it slapped against another one, causing another loud echo.

It was him; it was Dock. I hadn't seen or heard anything from him since the cigarette on my car that day a few months ago, and I figured I'd never see him again. He looked surprised at first, then quickly changed his demeanor, leaning with ease against the side of the red truck, smiling at me coyly.

"I know you." He laughed and crossed his arms for a moment, but made his way toward me when I didn't move. I changed my deer-caught-in-the-headlights expression and quickly tried coming up with a creative response.

"Long time no see," I said, putting my hands in my pockets, wishing I'd thought of something better.

Will, the other man, stood between us.

"You two know each other?" He smirked, appearing puzzled. "Who don't you know, Dock?" He nodded, mumbling something about women coming out of bushes, and walked past Dock, slapping him on the arm. "Work, Dock, work."

Dock came close, gently touching my shoulder.

"Hey, how are you?" he said softly.

He had large teeth, and his lips were pink and moist. He looked the same as I remembered, but better.

"I'm good," I whispered back, not meaning to.

"How's the jacket?" He chuckled. "Did you retire it?" He stared as if looking through me and held eye contact slightly longer than was comfortable.

"Never, it's vintage."

Oh my God, if he's working at the club, I'll see him every day!

"So, is that your brother?" I asked, knowing there had to be a relation.

"Yup, that's Will, my little brother."

"Eleven months apart, so not so little," Will chimed out, hearing us. He loaded wood on his shoulder and headed toward the water.

"And much more mature," he yelled, disappearing down the sand.

"This is true," Dock said. The sun glinted off the yellow in his green eyes as he turned toward the cottage. "You live right here?" he asked, patting his jacket pocket.

I smiled, knowing he was looking for his cigarette pack. "Maybe you should quit smoking."

"You are one hundred percent right," he said, looking at the green-and-white pack and putting it back in his pocket. "Maybe if I had a nurse to teach me all the dangers about it . . ."

He pulled the pack out again and put a cigarette in his teeth, lighting it.

He had aggressive energy. I'd noticed it the night I met him. There was nothing nervous about him at all. It was different and attractive. I could see him better than that night. He had darker skin, and his face had stubble on it and seemed fuller. I stared at his hands, watching him inhale the cigarette, noticing the dots of the tattoo again.

Impulsively, I grabbed the cigarette gently from his lips, putting it to mine. I took a long, slow inhale, being careful, knowing the menthol would be strong. I blew out toward the water, then looked up, meeting his eyes.

"Maybe a nurse should," I said, cocking my head, handing it back to him. "Gotta go." I smiled and headed toward the house, aware of his gaze. I turned, walking backward a few steps. His lips quirked. "Hey, how long are you on this job?" I tried to sound casual, not knowing what answer I wanted.

He looked at the club, then back at me.

"A few weeks at least," he called. "So I'll be seeing you."

I turned again, walking away. He was watching, and I hoped I didn't stumble.

Delia sounded hoity-toity as I walked in the door. "Mr. S. has been calling for you."

"Sorry, I had a run-in with someone," I shouted, heading up the back staircase.

"What? Who?" she called back.

Delia always wanted to know the details.

"George?" Delia called up the steps again.

I pretended not to hear.

"George!" Mr. S. bellowed through the hall as I made my way toward him.

"Coming; I'm here!" I took off my coat, throwing it in the closet.

He was upright in bed as I had left him, staring ahead with his mouth open. I looked at his half-unbuttoned pajama shirt, pulled high to his neck, and walked to the window to open the blinds.

"Good lord, not yet," he barked, lifting his hand, attempting to shield his face.

"It's late," I said, only half opening the blinds.

I noticed the dusty books on the wall shelf and figured I'd tidy his room today. It wasn't my job, but I didn't think Delia or the housekeepers cleaned very well.

"Where were you?" he asked, sounding more concerned than angry, which was a pleasant surprise.

"I got a little tied up walking over here," I started, trying to think of an excuse he would find acceptable or amusing.

"Tied up?" He turned his head toward me. The pajama shirt tightened at his shoulders, and I went over, fixing it as best I could.

"You desperately need a shave."

"What's the point," he groaned. "Tied up how?"

Jesus.

"Some off-island workers are at the Yacht Club. They were asking me all kinds of questions." I threw the tissues all over the bed in the barrel.

"You know, they don't know the island, so they were bugging me where to get different things." I couldn't come up with anything else, and the truth wouldn't interest him.

"People are fairly stupid." He reached for a tissue, knocking the box over.

"Yes, they are," I agreed. I handed him the box.

"Let me lie here for a while." He closed his eyes, refusing to see the look of disapproval on my face.

"Fine," I mumbled, putting the tissues next to him.

I closed the door halfway and quietly headed down the hall. Peering out the small window near the closet, which gave me a nearly unobstructed view of the club over the bushes, my heart sped up, and my stomach felt tingly. It'd been so long I'd almost forgotten how liking someone felt.

I went into the bathroom to get the shaving cream and basin ready, prepared for when he yelled again, then noticed myself in the mirror. I dropped everything in the sink, disappointed at my lackluster look, then annoyed at myself. *Do I like this guy? I don't even know him.*

I walked to the window again. *Where is he?* I wondered, then spotted him leaning against the truck. Just then, he turned his face toward the house. I leaped back, mortified, but figured he couldn't possibly see me from where he was.

"I guess I'm interested." I laughed out loud.

• • •

"George!"

The morning was the same routine as usual, except he had a doctor's appointment.

"That doctor is a quack" was all he said as I held open the door for him when we left after the visit, careful not to let go of his arm.

"He's okay, I guess. Why do you say that?"

"None of them do anything." He wiped at his mouth, then threw the tissue on the floor, stepping on it. It stuck to his shoe.

As a nurse, I wanted to argue and defend medicine and the people in it as there were so many excellent doctors, nurses, and specialists treating and curing diseases, saving lives. But I couldn't argue his point. No one was doing anything for him except giving a lot of double talk and false promises, as far as I could tell. Not everything was curable or even treatable. I wasn't sure they were honest about his disease and its progression because of who he and Lilly were, but I felt slightly fraudulent in it all. I didn't say much, but I threw in some honesty here and there, which he seemed to appreciate.

"I'm not sure there's much they can do," I said nervously.

Maybe I shouldn't have said that.

"But try," I added after pausing awkwardly. It gave a little hope but not much.

I'm no better.

We headed into the house. He called loudly for Lilly and hurried to the living room, taking the cane from my hand, holding it but not touching it to the floor. I hurried alongside him, making sure he didn't fall and directing him to the couch, quickly moving Lilly's bags and notebooks. He called again and peered at her through the window in her office on the side of the porch. She waved at us, phone to her ear.

"She's on the phone," I said, helping him out of his coat.

"Yes." He looked disappointed. Lady came in from outside, and he touched her head.

I went to the kitchen for a drink and found Delia stirring a pot on the stove.

"Anyone coming over?" I asked with a grin.

"Always," she cackled. "That senator is coming by again; he loves my fried chicken." She dropped a chicken breast in the pot, and it made a loud crackling sound. "They're all crazy, George." She smiled, wiping her hands on her apron.

I left him and Lilly alone in the living room before she could tell him someone was coming. I told Delia I'd be back and headed across the lawn, passing the senator and his security on the way. I stopped to say hello, and he greeted me with his charismatic smile. I had the urge to call my mother and tell her, thinking this would be a good conversation. We had a picture of the three brothers hanging in the dining room growing up. She loved the Kennedys, but I was too tired to be phony.

I peeked through the bushes to see if the truck was still there, but the flowers were starting to bloom with the warmer weather, and I couldn't see through them. Then, suddenly, the hiss of a saw sounded out. My heart bubbled as I passed through the archway, pushing my hair off my face. I looked toward where the truck was earlier but saw it now tucked near the kayaks on the sand in a different spot. I tried hard to discover where the sawing was coming from without stopping and making it obvious. I finally noticed Will when the sound stopped. He was leaning near the side of a foundation I hadn't seen before that looked freshly poured. He wiped his face with a bandanna. His back was toward me, but he turned and noticed me looking.

"Hey there." He put the saw down and waved.

"Hi again," I said, feeling awkward.

Does he think I was staring?

"Home for the day?" he asked, shuffling to face me on his knees.

"For a while," I called back. "It's a never-ending gig." I smiled.

There was an uncomfortable silence for a moment, and I tried hard to think of something to say.

"Would you like water or something?"

Do I have any bottled waters?

Hearing my voice, Hobo barked from inside. I had to hurry before he peed.

"Sure, that would be great." He stood, arching his back and stretching, then brushed off his knee pads and made his way toward me.

I hurried into the house and pushed past Hobo, opening the fridge, seeing nothing, but I noticed three bottles on the counter.

And where is Dock?

My mind raced. I put Hobo on his leash and grabbed a plastic bag, letting the screen door slam behind me. He was standing by the Adirondack chair now, and I handed him the water.

"I'm sorry it's not cold." I smiled, watching Hobo sniff his legs and bark. "Shut up, Hobo," I snapped, glaring at him, pulling his leash. I noticed Will's hands. They looked like Dock's, large and weathered.

"Dog's cute." He opened the water bottle and tipped his head back, bringing it to his lips, nearly drinking the entire bottle.

I laughed. "He sucks." He nearly spit out the water.

He was more soft spoken than Dock. He kept his distance, seeming shy and a little nervous, unlike his brother. On the truck I now saw *New Bedford Builders* on the side in gold lettering.

"New Bedford, huh?"

He turned and looked. "Yup, born and raised." He smiled, taking another sip from the bottle.

"Tough town."

"It is, but it's what I know. Are you from the island?" He paused. "You don't seem it."

"What does that mean?" I widened my eyes.

"Nothing, you just . . . don't seem, I don't know . . ." He kept smiling.

"Spit it out."

"I don't know. You don't seem as chilled and hippie, if that makes sense?"

He seemed nervous, now tapping the water bottle on the chair.

"I know what you mean, and I'm not. I'm from Revere, the New Bedford of the North Shore, kind of." I shrugged. "What brings you boys here? No work in New Bedford?"

"Plenty of work, but I'm trying to extend things here. I handle most of the New Bedford jobs, and Dock is gonna get the island going because he's here full-time."

"Oh, that's good; you guys will be busy." I kneeled and pulled Hobo over, wiping the brown gunk on his face with my finger.

"Hope so; that's the plan. I'm hoping to move or be here a lot eventually. At least, I'm thinking about it. We'll see how business goes, and my brother." He shook his head, scratching the bottle against his face.

It seemed they hadn't been in business long together. I wanted to know more but didn't want to sound like I was interrogating, so I left it alone.

He looked toward the sky, rubbing his head through the black knit hat he now had on. His skin was rough and coarse-looking, and he had grayish eyes that looked kind. I'd noticed that immediately earlier. His accent was thick but didn't sound so Boston, like mine. I try to curb mine a lot, thinking it sounds harsh and mannish, but it comes out when I'm with people with the accent too, or ones like it, like now. Will's sounded almost New York, Brooklyn maybe. Dock had it also, but not as much. I figured it was a New Bedford thing.

My stomach rumbled. I was starving and had to eat before heading back to the house. I was sure Lilly would go out for the evening after dinner, so I'd be there for most of it. I hated having to rush and wanted to chat more, needing a social distraction from Mr. S. and the family bubble. It had been a long winter.

"So, how do you know my brother?" he asked, glancing at the sky as it suddenly grew dark. I felt a little disappointed that Dock hadn't told him.

"He saved me at a bar one night," I answered, frustrated.

He paused, bringing the bottle to his cheek, scratching it against his face scruff again.

"Oh, yeah, that's right." He pointed the bottle toward me. "You're leather jacket girl." He laughed.

"Good lord." I rolled my eyes but felt happy that he knew.

"My brother gets himself into some shit sometimes, but I was glad to hear this time was for a good cause." He looked to the sky again.

"Where is your brother, anyway?" I asked, trying to be casual, unsure I pulled it off. I suddenly felt like I was prying.

"He'll be here tomorrow. At least, he better be." He looked up again. "I better get going before I can't find my tools to pack up."

"Me too." I pulled at my necklace. Hobo ran barking toward the house. "I have to feed this beast."

"We'll try not to be too loud in the morning tomorrow, and thanks for the water." He turned and strolled toward the truck, then turned back and smiled again.

"Nice meeting you, Will," I said, hating how I sounded.

I headed into the cottage. A few minutes later, a horn beeped as the truck rolled up the gravel drive.

CHAPTER 9

July 11, 1992
Just Dad and I here, no escaping.
Funny—I think we might be okay.

"We are coming into Vineyard Haven," my father said as the freight boat slowly spun, backing up to the dock. The truck jarred forward as we listened to the sounds of cranking metal while they secured the ship to the landing. The captain's voice came over the loudspeaker, reporting the weather and welcoming us to the island. Out in the harbor I saw sailboats, big and small, scattered about.

"We are staying in Oak Bluffs, which is that way." He pointed again, past a small bridge.

"Wherever, whatever," I said, shrugging. I bit my lip and pinched myself on my leg.

I can't stop. Fuck, fuck, fuck.

He ignored me now, mostly, which annoyed me greatly but at the same time made me feel better about my bitchiness.

We pulled off the boat and waited for the policeman directing traffic to wave us on.

"It's nice here," I said, watching two kids eat pizza on a bench when we stopped in the traffic.

"It feels like we're in a different time. Like when I was a kid." He looked at me and changed gears, causing us to jerk. "I have to figure out where to park this thing," he said as we began moving again.

"Yeah, where no one will see it. Or me in it," I murmured, although loud enough for him to hear.

"No one will see it, no one will see it. Calm down."

I hated it when he repeated himself.

So stupid.

"Be on the lookout for the Island Inn, okay?" His eyes darted around. "It should come up on the right once we turn onto the beach ahead. We're staying there."

I nodded. *I hope it's not a dump.*

"There's a big lot to park. I'll drop you off and make the delivery, and then we can park her for good. Maybe take a cab around." He shrugged.

"Sounds like a plan," I said, taking it all in.

I checked us in at the inn, and he took off to make his delivery. I wondered when he would be back, still never trusting him.

He's probably going to buy weed, or maybe he has illegal immigrants in the back he's unloading. I laughed nearly uncontrollably as I opened the door to the room and plopped on the bed.

My father wasn't just a guy who drank too much on occasion, and he wasn't any type of functioning drinker either. He couldn't only drink a few beers or even a sip of a beer without ending up on a week or monthslong bender. Next, he'd attempt to detox himself or have to go to detox. It was always the same.

He was a "gutter type of drunk," I heard my mom say to her friend outside a meeting one night. There was no hiding his drinking, which my mom always said was a good thing and that we were lucky. "If we could hide it," she'd say, "we may not have gone to the meetings to get healthy. We'd probably keep his disease and all of its craziness a secret like a lot of other families do."

I wasn't sure how lucky any of this was, but I knew early on there was no hiding him. We were lucky that where we lived, everyone had a crazy in the family or something to hide, although I felt like our crazy was the biggest and the most on display.

No one cared that our neighbor Lenny's grandmother slept in a tent in the yard with a bunch of stray cats she rescued from the marsh behind us. Nothing was said about Lisa's house missing a few windows and her asking to take showers at our house because there was no hot water. Or how they fed their dog Lucifer whole potatoes or even had a dog named Lucifer. The two brothers who lived next door to us would fistfight in front of their house nightly until the police showed, and nobody treated them any differently. No one judged each other, or at least that's how it felt.

Being Richie from the Beach's daughter was hard. One day in fifth grade, Lynn Melody, one of the popular girls, saw my dad on the beach. She recognized him from the time she came by selling Girl Scout cookies. She told the class all about how my dad was "stinking drunk" and how he slid off a bench, and it scared her. I'll never forget her nasal voice and the lisp I was jealous of saying those words. She put her hand up to cover her mouth like she was telling a secret to someone but said it loudly for all to hear.

"George's dad is a stinking drunk." She giggled.

I sat frozen at my desk in horror, watching her tell Michael Tarantino, the boy everyone had a crush on, including me.

Lynn giggled some more across the room and said again, "Stinking drunk" as she looked at Michael, twirling her hair and tapping her pencil. Ms. Pappas, our teacher, was talking to someone in the hall, although I couldn't see who despite sticking my neck out, trying to look. I listened to the evil giggle again and glared in their direction. Michael said nothing, looking for something in his pencil case.

"Maybe they named her George because they were drunk," she said loudly enough for me and everyone to hear, keeping her eyes on Michael.

The kids at school already made fun of my name. Lynn usually was the ringleader. "Georgie Porgie pudding and pie," she'd say, laughing.

I couldn't control my rage any longer. I knew my father was a drunk.

I knew he had a problem, a disease. I learned all about it every stupid Thursday at our stupid group. I knew it too well. I was sick of knowing it. I was angry about it, and that's what I'd speak of every stupid week there. I drew pictures of my ruined birthday party when he came out in his underwear, locking himself in the bathroom. I told the story of finding the hidden bottles in the house and me emptying them, filling them with a concoction I created. I thought it would impress the others in the group because I impressed myself. I used soy sauce, maple syrup, and Moxie soda, all the brown liquids, so he'd think it was whiskey or rum and, aha! It wouldn't be.

One night as I was just getting into bed, I heard him stumbling around the kitchen. The kitchen cabinet squeaked open where I knew a bottle I'd messed with was, and I sat up, excited to listen. I next heard him spitting and coughing. Figuring he took a swig, I giggled myself to sleep.

Lynn continued to tap her pencil. I watched her occasionally smirk at me, and I noticed she was about to speak again. The rage swelled from my stomach into my throat. I ground my teeth, feeling my face turn red. Lisa was behind me, and I heard her say something, but it was too late. Lynn's lips moved again, but I couldn't hear what came out.

I don't remember anything after that except sobbing at my desk with my head in my hands and Ms. Pappas yelling and questioning what happened, threatening to keep the whole class after if someone didn't come clean. I lifted my head and raised my hand, looking at Michael and Lynn. The words "stinking drunk" replayed in my head on repeat over and over. Lynn was holding her nose as blood poured from it. My pencil case lay open, spilled all over her desk. She screamed something about how I was an animal and was raised by animals, proceeding to tell the teacher how I hurled my pencil case at her nose.

Ms. Pappas put her arm around her and yelled for someone to get tissues and to follow them to the nurse. They walked from the room, leaving a trail of blood droplets out the door.

"I will speak to you later, Georgette!" Ms. Pappas said with her eyes wide and angry. She suddenly had a look of disappointment, turning once more in my direction before they left. I felt Lisa's hand on my back as I cried into my hands.

"Who cares anyway?" I said, lying on the bed, swinging my legs. The weight of my boots pulled my feet toward the floor. I laughed again, thinking of my father unloading illegal immigrants from the back of the truck.

I pretended I didn't care, but I did. I always wanted him to know I had his number. I had to play it cool because there might be nothing to know. Sometimes there wasn't, especially lately. But if there was, I couldn't have him thinking I didn't know. It took a lot of energy, but I could get hurt—more hurt, anyway—if I didn't stay suspicious.

I took a lighter out of my pocket and went over to my backpack, grabbing the cigarette I'd stolen from his pack when he got our ferry tickets. I lit it just after the breeze passed and then settled on a little chair on the patio. Hating the menthol taste, I coughed, then stubbed it out half finished, trying to make it last, not knowing if I'd get the opportunity to snag another one.

I began wondering what time my father would be back or if he would be.

He had been sober for a while now, and I wondered if I'd ever get over this kind of thinking. I was tired of it but didn't see any other safe way to be around him. I'd thought of alienating him and had tried before, but the problem was I didn't want to. I liked him in some ways. He seemed to understand me better than my mother. She and I hardly spoke anymore, at least not about anything real.

Does she ever have any fun anymore? I would see her laugh with my aunt sometimes, and she enjoyed going to thrift stores, but was that all life was for her? It seemed pathetic.

Maybe marrying him and his fucking disease took her fun away.

An hour or so passed, and I peeked out the window as he parked the truck. He came into the room, and I was glad he seemed okay, but something seemed different. Not in a high, drunk way. He didn't smell of weed or booze or the extra cologne cover-up scent to mask the bad smells—that was gross, and I never understood why people did that.

It did nothing but make it worse.

He appeared suddenly stressed and tired. I changed into the one decent thing I had to look like I kind of fit in. White shorts and a black floral sweater with a hole in the armpit I tried to sew with green thread a few weeks ago. I wished I had some sandals, but all I had were my stupid boots. At home, I loved wearing them, but here I wanted to burn them.

"Let's grab some dinner in town," he said, putting on his glasses. "And I wanted to ask if you'd mind something." He sat on the bed across from mine.

I crisscrossed my legs, leaning a mirror on them, and put on mascara. I looked over and thought how creepy it was we were in the same room. It wasn't a big deal to me, but I wondered what the people at the inn could be thinking.

So gross. I giggled, looking at his ridiculous boots, having trouble seeing why any woman liked him.

"What would I mind?" I asked, returning to the mirror and holding it up for a final check.

"Would you mind if I went to a meeting? Not now, but after dinner?"

While he smoked outside a few minutes before, I'd noticed him looking at the little blue book he kept with him that listed his meetings.

"I guess," I answered, watching his expression.

My father had been sober for close to four years. I wasn't sure of the actual date. He did, and he got a chip, as they called it, every year at his AA meeting to mark the milestone. We never asked why then, why that was the day he stopped, and we never questioned how he did it. I think we all assumed it was some sort of miracle, especially my devout Catholic mother.

Ray and I felt it too because it seemed impossible to us, and strangely, for a while, it was uncomfortable. We weren't used to this new person, the not-drunk man in our home. Everyone's role had changed, and it felt weird. We didn't believe he'd quit for good. That took a long while, but we couldn't help but notice something was different. I only remembered the general time he gave it up because of how ugly it got before. They say you have to hit bottom to see the light, maybe. From what I could see, he had many bottoms; I didn't know which was his, but in the end, there were a few, and then by some miracle, it was over.

He stared at the ceiling with his hands behind his head. He didn't say anything, but I could tell he wanted to. I debated on saying anything more, thinking I probably shouldn't, but I couldn't help myself as usual.

"What do you want to drink?" I snarked, hating myself for it.

He let out a long sigh, although I knew he saw it was coming.

"It's part of the process, George. It's just part of the damn process."

"Is it? Is it?" I said twice to remind him how annoying it was to say things twice. I didn't care what he did. I only wanted to get out of the room and, for once, didn't want to get into it.

"It's fine," I said. "Let's roll."

CHAPTER 10

March 31, 2003
Love, whether blossoming, lasting, breaking,
or unseen, is an experience orbiting us all.

The ferry horn sounded as it passed by, and I listened to the rain tap loudly on the roof, wishing I could go back to bed. A feeling of relief came, remembering Lilly had said we wouldn't fly to New York today if it was raining badly. I closed my eyes, thankful I could take my time before heading to the house. I tried not to move so Hobo would think I was still sleeping. Mr. S., for sure, would sleep well past ten today. He always did when it rained, so there was no urgency.

I rolled over, hoping for another ten minutes.

Shit, I fucking moved.

I kept my eyes closed, sensing Hobo's face near mine.

"Let's go!" I yelled, annoyed, jumping up and ripping the covers off, tossing them over him. He scooted out, wagging his tail, and trotted toward the door, turning back to bark at me.

Asshole.

I grabbed the leash from the hook by the door, smoothing my hair back under my beat-up Red Sox hat, and threw on my jacket.

"You're a pain in the ass," I said, watching him spin around as I opened the door.

"So, I'm told," a man's voice came from nowhere.

"Holy shit, oh my God!" I screamed, jumping back.

I hit the side of the door as Hobo pulled through my legs, barking ferociously. It was Dock. He held three coffees in a tray from Mocha Mott's; I could tell by the white-and-black cup label. I wiped my face with my sleeve, hoping I didn't have night cream on it, trying to remember if I put any on.

Oh my God, how do I look? Jesus. What the hell am I wearing?

I looked at my sweatpants, one leg pulled high to my knee, and I saw I had two different socks on.

"Sorry to scare you," he said, handing me the tray. "I thought I'd be a nice guy and drop you a coffee."

"You scared the hell out of me," I said, still in disbelief he was here. "Why are there three?"

"One's mine, and I wasn't sure if you wanted regular or decaf. Sheila said you change it sometimes." He squinted as a few raindrops hit his face from the overhanging gutter.

Did he ask Sheila about my coffee?

"Oh, um, do you want to come in?" I asked reluctantly, hoping it didn't sound that way.

He could be a friggin' serial killer. What's my house look like? Jesus!

He hesitated. "Sure." I turned to step back inside, quickly scanning the room, and he followed. I pulled two stools back from the island and set down the tray. It surprised me again how deep his voice was.

"I'm no murderer, in case that's what you're thinking." He laughed, sitting on the stool closest to the door.

I didn't want him to think I was suspicious. "I wasn't thinking that," I scoffed, wondering if anything was in my teeth.

Where is my pepper spray? I looked around, trying to remember where I'd put it. I didn't feel the need to have it here like I did in the city.

"Yes, you were." He smirked.

I handed him his coffee and perched halfway on the stool next to him. He sipped, and I sipped, choosing the regular; I'd need it today.

"Seriously, I wanted to bring you a coffee." He brushed his hair back with his free hand. "I didn't mean to scare you, and I didn't expect to come in."

He stood and meandered the room, and I followed him with my eyes. I felt my cheeks turning red and wanted to take my coat off, but I had no bra on and just my holey T-shirt, so I left it.

"Well, thank you, but my appearance . . . and my place." I pulled at my hair ends, looking around. "I wasn't expecting guests." I laughed nervously, licking my teeth under my lips, attempting to clean them.

"I know, but it's fine. I like your place. It's a great spot." His eyes seemed to see through me.

"Thank you for the coffee, though," I said again.

"You're welcome." He sat back down. "And you look great."

I rolled my eyes, but he didn't smile or change his face. He looked serious, and I felt my face getting hot again, hoping it wasn't red.

"I figured you wouldn't work today in this weather." I tried to break the awkwardness.

God, this is not how I planned things.

"No work. I just had to pick up a check at the club. Will forgot it yesterday."

"Oh." I blew into the slit in the coffee cover.

He seemed so comfortable, almost *too* comfortable. It was odd, like he had been here before or we knew each other well—as if I could relax and just be myself; not that I had a choice, at least appearance-wise right now. Weirdly, I liked it, but I wasn't used to it.

"I'm sure you're working today, though. Do you ever get a break?"

"I am," I said, glancing at the clock on the stove that didn't work.

His eyes were a little bloodshot, making them seem a darker green than I remembered, almost like emeralds. He had long, jet-black eyelashes, the same color as his hair.

"I'm in and out all day, but another nurse is coming on board next week, so I'll have some free time, I hope, now that the warm weather is coming."

I put the word out in the hospital, and two nurses had already called, interested in a night or two to cover for me and give me a break. Karen, whom I knew from the emergency room, was coming by next week.

"I'm ready for the spring, especially for work," he said, stretching. I looked at his hand again as he reached up.

"What's the tattoo about?" I asked, lightly touching the dots with my finger when he put his hand down.

He turned his hand, looking at it.

"It's the five islands of Portugal. I'm Portuguese—if you couldn't tell."

"I figured." I laughed, remembering thinking this the night I first met him, and the other day I'd noticed the way he talked with his hands.

Does Portugal have five islands?

I didn't know much about Portugal, but they reminded me of Italians, and I knew a lot about them.

He smelled good. I'd noticed it when I leaned in toward him. It was subtle, sweet, and earthy—jasmine and wood. It wasn't a cologne. It was him, and I liked it.

"I better let you get going." He got up and reached in his pocket, pulling out his keys.

Surprised, I'd thought I would have to be the one to end the conversation.

"Okay, well, thank you for the coffee." I got up too.

He towered over me, staring down at me again, then stepped onto the porch. I stood in the doorway. My coat hung off my shoulders, and I wrapped it gently around me, crossing my arms. He pulled his collar up again on each side with one hand, holding his coffee with the other.

"I'd like to see you again." He squinted, watching as the rain poured. A drop fell, then another and another, making him look like he was crying.

"Okay," I said, leaning against the doorframe.

"Tonight?" he asked, then reached toward me, moving my hair from my face, and I pulled away, taken off guard.

"Okay," I said again.

What is wrong with me? Okay? Just okay?

"You're working, right?"

"Until ten," I said, disappointed, forgetting I had a never-ending job.

"I'll pick you up then?" He paused, waiting for an answer.

I nodded in agreement. He turned and jogged toward the truck, climbing in, and I watched him as he drove off the grass. He looked at me once more, driving up to Main Street.

• • •

I ran toward the house, pulling my hood up. Unable to find my umbrella, I suddenly remembered it was in the trunk of my car when I was a few feet from the door. I thought of tonight and what had just happened, feeling nervous and excited. I'd forgotten to ask his age. I figured he was older by at least by five years, and I was okay with that; it was time to stop dating boys anyway.

Delia wasn't in the kitchen, which was unusual. I headed up the back staircase, poking my head in the door, not hearing a sound.

"Mr. S.," I whispered into the dark.

He said nothing but gurgled and coughed.

"Mr. S., it's George," I whispered again, coming in.

"George," he whispered; I could barely make it out.

I could discern his shape in the bed as my eyes adjusted. His body slumped toward the middle, and one of his legs dangled off the side.

"I'm turning on the light."

He said nothing, only coughed and choked and gasped. He was struggling to breathe. I ran, putting my arms through his, lifting him high in the bed, leaning him forward. This wasn't good.

"George," he gasped.

"It's okay, Mr. S., it's okay," I tried to reassure him while I grabbed my stethoscope. "Mr. S., I'm worried. We will have to go to the hospital. I'm so sorry." I held him, turning to speak to him face-to-face.

He nodded, and I held his hand tightly, feeling him try to squeeze mine. He was scared, I could tell, and I felt awful, like I'd failed him.

I called 911 and yelled for Lilly, letting her know what was happening. She rushed in and moved close to him, touching his arm. Lilly was used to this, I figured. He'd been in and out of the hospital for years now, but he hadn't been since I started. I'd wanted to keep it that way but knew it was inevitable.

"Are you coming?" he said, looking at Lilly and me.

I nodded, barely able to make out what he said through the oxygen mask the EMT placed on him.

"Yes, I'll be right behind you." I spoke loudly, assuring him.

Delia appeared at the bedroom door. She still had her coat on, and moisture dripped onto the floor.

"Mr. S., oh no, not again," she said.

I could tell she was upset. I watched her wipe at her cheek, unsure if she was wiping a tear or if the wetness was from the rain. I couldn't picture Delia crying.

"I'll be there soon, darling. I just have to let Kelly in on a few things," Lilly said, retreating past Delia to the hallway. He nodded as they lifted him on the stretcher.

Delia and I hopped in the BMW and followed the ambulance over the bridge toward the hospital.

· · ·

After giving all his information to the nurse, I chatted with Dr. Mac in the emergency room.

"We'll take good care of him, George. Miss you around here."

I stared. I'd forgotten how handsome Dr. Mac was. I remembered the rumor about him and Kate, the night nurse manager, and that they were having an affair, and I could see why. But he was an excellent doctor, and that was what mattered most to me now. I was glad he was working. I suddenly missed the hospital. I'd been in a bubble for a while.

Delia went to the cafeteria to get us a coffee. I sat in the metal folding chair by the stretcher, shut my eyes, feeling exhausted, and then heard his voice.

"George."

Thankful he sounded better, I opened my eyes and saw him staring at me.

"I'm here," I said, coming close to him.

He looked comfortable and said nothing else, closing his eyes again. I leaned back and did the same.

"Will they give me morphine?" he asked.

When I looked at him, his eyes were still closed.

"Why? Are you in pain?"

He didn't appear to be, and I was unsure why he would be.

"No."

I stared at him, puzzled. "Then why would they give you morphine?"

He coughed and took a deep breath, and I got up and adjusted his pillow.

"My mother had morphine." He paused. "When she was dying, she had morphine," he said quietly, then coughed and reached for the tissue box I'd placed on the bed.

I wasn't sure what to make of this. I knew he was young when his mother died, leaving him and his father.

"You're not dying, Mr. S." I touched his hand, watching his eyes open, seeing the fear in them. He looked childlike, and it made me uncomfortable. He closed them again, and I kept my hand on his until he fell asleep.

They admitted him at least overnight, which concerned me, but I was glad they would monitor him closely. Delia and I said our goodbyes, and I reassured him I'd be back tomorrow. He already seemed better, and I was glad. It was nice seeing all the hospital folks again, and part of me wished I hadn't left, hating how I felt right now. I hadn't felt this way about another patient before. They were never solely mine, but he was, and it made me feel inadequate that he was here, like I didn't care for him well. I knew it was bullshit but couldn't help how I felt.

Sometimes there is nothing you can do or could have done differently.

My mind spun as Delia and I walked down the hall to leave.

You learn this repeatedly in medicine, but it doesn't matter. Knowing something doesn't change the feelings. I hated he was in the hospital, and I hated leaving him here. Most of all, I hated that I cared for him.

I shouldn't have become a nurse.

I didn't feel like talking, and it seemed Delia didn't either. Walking quietly through the automatic doors, we stood, listening to the rain banging on the metal awning above us.

"I'll grab the car. Wait here," I said, pulling up my hood.

She nodded, and I darted into the parking lot, making a run for it. Delia didn't know how to drive, which hadn't bothered me but now irritated me to no end. She got rides from the cleaning people to the grocery store or whoever was around the house, including me. I asked one day in the kitchen if she wanted to learn to drive. "No!" she snapped at me angrily, and I made a mental note never to bring it up again.

Her being quiet was unusual, and I worried about her after the annoyance wore off. She always had something to say, and she didn't seem herself, but I didn't feel like getting into it. When she was standing by the bed, looking at Mr. S. in the emergency room, I'd never seen her look sad like that before.

I was almost to the car when Kelly and Lilly pulled into the spot next to me. Seeing me, Lilly got out quickly and opened her umbrella.

"How is he, George?" she asked in a serious tone.

I hoped she would lift the umbrella higher and put it over both of us, but she didn't.

"He's on the floor. They brought him about ten minutes ago." I lifted my hands over my head to block the rain, which did nothing.

"Let's get in the car for a minute," she said, opening the door.

It relieved me she'd noticed I was getting soaked, although it didn't matter, as I was already. I jumped in the back as she closed her umbrella. She got in and turned toward me.

"Hey, George," Kelly said.

"Hey there. Long time no see." I smiled, touching her shoulder.

Over the summer, I had met Kelly when she came a few times but spoke to her regularly about all types of things. Divorced with a young son, she lived in Connecticut, not far from Lilly and Mr. S.'s house. We had a glass of wine on the porch in August when she was on the island to organize Lilly's office.

"Should I call the Harvard group, George?" Lilly asked, referring to the doctors from Boston.

"No, I don't think so. They have it under control here, but I can let them know." I tried not to sound too annoyed. *What the fuck are they going to do for him here?*

"Okay, please do that, George," she said in her formal tone. "The New York group as well," she went on, staring past me.

"Of course." I nodded.

"We must reschedule Carly for dinner." She looked at Kelly.

I watched the windshield wipers move back and forth, not caring about their conversation.

"Got it," Kelly said, reaching for the small notebook on the console and jotting something down.

"I'm flying out tomorrow instead for New York, George. Can you reschedule his therapy appointment?"

"Yes," I began, but she kept going.

"I still have the gala for the Stewarts. Do you think I should cancel?"

I don't give a shit about a gala, Carly, or the fucking Stewarts. Who are the friggin' Stewarts? Why is this my decision?

"I'm not sure, Lilly. I don't want to make that decision for you."
I hate it when she thinks out loud.

"How long do you think he'll be in the hospital for?" she snapped. Her voice was higher, and she let out a long sigh.

I forgot about Delia, who would be wondering where I was now, but I wouldn't interrupt Lilly because Delia was waiting.

"I'll go talk to the nurses and doctors," Lilly said, grabbing the door handle.

"Did you want me to come?" I asked, praying she'd say no. I had already been in there for hours, talking to all of them.

"No, no." She turned toward me. "Just come back tomorrow. Then, if I go out of town, you can update me on anything they say." She paused, looking down at her hands. "George?" she said softly.

"Yes."

"Do you think he'll be okay?" She appeared strange and vulnerable.

"Of course," I said, leaning between the seats, hoping to comfort her.

"Where's Delia?" she asked, returning to herself. She opened her umbrella as she climbed out of the car. The rain poured off the sides. I pulled my hood up and got out behind her.

"She's waiting by the emergency room for me," I said, crossing my eyes to watch a raindrop fall from my nose.

I wanted to end the conversation, but I went on a little, seeing if she had any insight. She was walking away when I spoke.

"She seems upset, Delia. I'd never seen her like this."

She spun, and I quickly moved back to avoid being hit by her umbrella.

"She's in love with him, George. Of course she's upset," Lilly said, loud and nonchalant.

I thought I'd heard her wrong at first or maybe misunderstood. She stared at me, confused, and when I said nothing, she hurried toward the hospital.

I got in the car and put it out of my mind. I was too cold and tired to care.

"They're all crazy," I mumbled as I pulled around to get Delia, unsure I could look at her without feeling awkward.

We drove back in silence. I glanced at her a few times, looking for a sign of something, but I wasn't sure what. I didn't enjoy thinking of Delia as vulnerable or want her to see I was acting different. I felt like she knew when something was off with me, like when she wanted me to elaborate after saying something about my mother. She said she could tell something wasn't right there. I dismissed it but knew then she was intuitive. I looked at her again, watching her stare quietly out the window. Something was different about her now, and I wondered how I didn't see it before.

Of course, she loves him.

CHAPTER 11

July 11, 1992
This island, Dad and me, it's changed us.
It's changed things—me.

I t cooled off some, and the wind blew from the water. We decided to head back to Vineyard Haven to eat, catching a cab at the gazebo after a short walk along the road by the beach. We didn't say much to each other except a random comment here or there about how nice everything was.

"I've always loved the Cape," my father said, his boots clicking away.

"This isn't the Cape," I schooled him, glad I knew something he didn't.

"Well, what is it? Smart-ass." He laughed, pointing to the ferry coming in ahead.

"It's Martha's Vineyard. It's a whole separate thing."

He groaned.

"Why don't you get some new boots?" I said. The clicking made me want to scream, and I envisioned pushing him over the wall.

"Why? These are fine," he said confidently.

I nodded, not feeling like arguing.

He appeared thoughtful as he stared ahead.

We drove the bridge into town and got out at the corner, noticing a small restaurant. *The Black Dog Tavern*, it said in weathered, dark letters. People were in line on the porch, and I caught him looking nervously at his watch. We put our names in, then were told it would be a thirty-minute wait or so. He looked at his watch again, then smiled, giving the lady his name. He had a charismatic smile, and he knew it. I'd watch him sometimes smile and speak differently to people when he wanted something from them. He smoothed his voice and took his glasses off to look them in the eyes. He'd grin and laugh at the littlest thing they said.

"Will you make the meeting?" I asked, noticing him glance at his watch again.

"I think so," he said. Across from me, he leaned against the railing of the stairs. "I may just make it."

He stood with his arms folded as a couple passed between us, dressed beautifully. The woman wore a white linen dress with beaded sandals. He had on tan pants with a whale belt, just like the kid at the ferry. They moved up the steps, and my dad came into view again. I laughed at how obvious it was we didn't belong.

I want to take that sleeveless T-shirt and pull it over your head!

I glared at him, then at my boots. I wanted to get rid of them, along with the tough persona I wore like armor after seeing the people here. My cutoffs and stupid boots felt comfortable and like me back home, but here they didn't. I didn't feel like me as much here. I liked it, and it had been less than a day.

I looked over toward some tall ships, noticing a small beach.

"Let's check out there." I pointed.

We walked to the little beach and sat on an overturned rowboat on the sand. The orange summer sun hung low in the sky. Its reflection spread across the water and created a trail of rippling gold that went on for miles.

We were quiet for a good while, taking in the surroundings. I felt calm and not as angry. I was sure I wasn't angry all the time with him, but being here was the first time I was aware of it.

"I'm glad you came," he said, nervously clearing his throat.

He put his hands behind him and stretched out his legs. He tilted his head to the sun, and I suddenly wanted to take his aviators and throw them.

"I'm kind of glad I came too."

It was hard to leave it at that without a snarky remark at the end or making a joke of it all, but I did. I left it alone, hanging there, feeling awkward. I figured he was feeling the same, and that made it tolerable.

"Where's the meeting?" I asked, changing the subject.

I could tell it relieved him.

"Up the street." He stood and stretched his arms wide, then reached in his pocket. "We should head back. They'll probably call us soon." He coughed. It was a deep one, and I knew what was coming. He conjured a giant loogie, launching it like a rocket toward the water.

"Really, Dad?" I said, brushing sand off me, rolling my eyes. "Really?" I stared at him as a mother would a poorly behaved child. "Gross."

"Let's go." He ignored me, lighting a cigarette and walking up the sand.

I followed behind. Suddenly he stopped and turned to me.

"George," he said, clearing his throat.

"Yeah."

"I'm glad you came. I am," he said again, smiling weirdly.

I stared at him, confused.

He turned and continued walking.

• • •

"Vineyard Sound," he said, looking at the map under the glass tabletop. We tried to figure out where we were.

"What's that?" I asked.

"The water there." He pointed.

Vineyard Sound was written in black cursive, surrounded by blue on the map.

The waitress dropped the check, and he squinted at it, which I knew meant it was too much.

"Maybe we should have ordered sandwiches instead," I giggled.

He looked puzzled, pretending not to know what I meant.

"I'm sorry I'm going to a meeting, George," he said, reaching into the breadbasket for the last roll.

"You got to do what you got to do, I guess. Right?" I shrugged.

"Yeah. But I know it sucks sometimes."

I didn't know who this person was, being so honest with me. I didn't know who I was either; I was suddenly understanding. It felt like some weird shift had happened, and I couldn't figure when or why. Maybe it was being outside our usual environment. I couldn't be sure, but it was nice, even if it didn't last.

"What are you going to do?" he asked.

"What do you mean? While you're at the meeting?"

"You know you can come if you want," he went on, throwing a bunch of money on the table. "Family can come. They recommend it."

I paused, thinking of how awful that sounded.

"I don't know; it's all so depressing." I sighed. "I'm not sure I feel like listening to a bunch of drunken sob stories." I regretted saying the last part, but it was true.

"Well, if you want to, I wouldn't mind, but if not, here." He went into his wallet and handed me some cash. "Go get yourself some sandals." He laughed, rising from his chair.

The buildings on Main Street were mainly white with black shutters. Shops and a few eateries lined the long street, and people slowly walked on the red brick sidewalk, enjoying the hot but beautiful day. We stopped in front of a small art gallery, and he pointed to a little white church up the side street. A sign in front of it read LOBSTER ROLLS FRIDAY NIGHTS in big black letters. I smiled and waved, watching him leave.

We'd agreed to meet at the movie theater a little after nine. It was just before eight o'clock, judging by the time on the large clock in front of a bank, and I was glad he would be on time.

Who am I?

He disappeared up the path on the side of the church. I noticed a small store across from the movie theater that looked like it might sell sandals. I was heading over when something caught my eye in the art gallery's window, and I turned back to look. It was rare that art made an impression on me, but I was entranced.

The painting was large and surrounded by an ornate gold frame that looked Italian. But I thought anything gold and elaborate was from Italy; that was how every house in Revere was inside. I stared into the frame at the small sailboat in the middle of the ocean with a large red sail. That was all it was, but something about it made me want to be there, on that boat wherever it was, envisioning myself feeling the rocking waves.

I continued on to the shop and passed all the tourist stuff on the way to the back where the clothes were. Shirts, sweatshirts, and anything you could put *Martha's Vineyard* on hung all over. A smiling lady came from the back.

"Can I help you, sweetie?" she asked.

A little white dog followed behind her, wagging his tail happily. I let him lick my hands, probably smelling the remnants of the fish I had for dinner, which seemed to make him happy. I noticed the woman's gold sandals. They had a small shell in the center of them that was gold too, so it blended nicely and didn't appear too beachy.

"Do you have anything like those?" I asked, pointing at her feet.

"Why, yes, I do." She walked behind me, grabbing a pair from the shelf, asking if I wanted gold or silver. Silver was in style now, but I pointed to the gold, liking them better.

"Thank you." I smiled as she handed the receipt over the counter.

She waved when I glanced back from the entrance, and then I headed down the street, looking back one more time, at her little dog standing beside her, wagging his tail in the doorway.

Maybe I've wanted to feel this way. Maybe it's okay to be normal—or pretend to be.

There was a bench in front of the ice cream parlor on the corner, and I walked over to sit. I took my notebook and pen from my backpack and wrote my thoughts. Then, reading them back to myself, I became annoyed and shut it, putting it back in my bag. I tried to write my thoughts and feelings when they came most days, at least the big ones. I wanted to write something profound today, but it wasn't coming to me, at least not that I could put into words, and it frustrated me.

Everything felt so different here, or maybe I just did. I felt happier in this small place where everyone seemed happy.

I wish I had a cigarette.

I looked around for someone to bum one off but saw no one. I glanced at the clock outside the bank again, thinking of him at the meeting. I had an hour to be alone. I stared at my boots. They made me feel dirty.

Maybe they sum up my life, these fucking boots. A scuffed leather outside with a hole on top of steel. Then, underneath, a smelly sock and me.

I laughed, reaching for my notebook again, but somehow, I wasn't in the mood now, thinking it was stupid immediately after I thought it was brilliant. I took the sandals from the bag and kicked the boots off one by one. The sandals slid on smoothly, and I gazed at them, moving my feet, suddenly feeling cleaner and shinier. I wiggled my toes, smiling; though they still had chipped pink polish on them, I didn't care. I looked across the street at the clock again.

Maybe I'll go to the meeting.

I scanned the street; a barrel was on the corner near the church. I hurried quickly across and dumped the bag along with the boots and socks.

"Bye, guys." I waved into the barrel.

I walked the small path on the side of the church, seeing a woman smoking a cigarette. All the addicts smoked, especially those in recovery, so I figured this was the right door. Smoke and drink coffee; it seemed to be all they did. It made sense to replace one thing for another, and coffee didn't make you an asshole, at least that I'd ever seen.

"Is the meeting downstairs?" I asked the woman, startling her, which I found strange, unsure how she didn't see me walk up.

Probably drunk or high.

She blew a cloud of smoke out of her nose and stubbed the cigarette on the ground, then walked in the door. I followed her, feeling nervous, not knowing what to expect. I remembered going to an AA meeting once, a long time ago, when my mother took us.

"It's an anniversary meeting," she said to Ray and me after we moaned about going.

It was long and lasted the whole day. Ray and I were miserable, listening to speaker after speaker. There were people from AA and other groups. Artwork and poetry hung from the kids' groups, like the one Ray and I went to, all over the room's walls. I remembered our group leader asked my mother once if my art could be featured in a special meeting. I couldn't remember if I said yes or no, or if it was up to me at all. I only knew I didn't want a picture of my father with *X*s for eyes, in his underwear, holding a bottle, on the wall for everyone to see.

I didn't recall much of that day except one speaker. It was his tenth anniversary or something like that. He reminded me a lot of my father. They both were horrific drinkers married with kids. He described all the horrible things he did, starting with selling their furniture once for alcohol and drugs. Next, he talked about when he set the apartment on fire, almost killing his family when he fell asleep with a cigarette in his mouth. He smiled a little when he talked, which I thought was odd. He spoke of his kids getting older and how he gave his son his first beer.

"I got his best friend, who was like my other son, high the first time," he said in his gruff voice, still weirdly half smiling.

I sat still, sickened by all of it, mostly how easily he talked about it. I couldn't understand how anyone could do any of this and then be on a stage, telling people who wanted to listen.

He should be in jail!

He told a story of that, too: about being in jail for a time.

We listened to how his son and daughter now had addictions.

"They have to hit their bottom on their own," he said, and everyone clapped.

What he said next destroyed me. His son's friend, his "other son," died of a drug overdose. I remembered grabbing the bottom of my chair tightly, wanting to punch him in the face. All I thought about was the other son. I looked at my mother, who was quiet too and didn't appear happy.

"I'm sober today, and that's what matters," he finally finished.

That's what matters? That? Aliens, drunk aliens! I screamed in my head. I was sure they were all alien nutjobs because when he finished, they clapped and whistled. I shrank in my seat, watching in disbelief as they brought him a cake and he blew out the candles. I hated all of them instantly, feeling uncomfortable in my skin.

I pictured the other son's face, although I didn't know him.

He would never blow out candles or have a cake again because of this man!

I hated him. I hated my parents too and thought the world was crazy, especially these people.

I sat up and gulped for air, then ran from my chair to the bathroom. My heart raced and pounded in my chest. My mother came to the door and tapped on it, letting me know she was outside. I'd had a few of these "episodes" recently, but she said they were only in my head.

"They aren't real," she said, then told me they only felt real, which didn't make any sense.

• • •

The church basement smelled of cigarettes and mold. I scanned the room for my father, unable to find him in the sea of people, surprised at how many there were. I spotted a man I thought was him, walked in his direction, and then realized it wasn't. Trying not to disturb anyone, I hurried to an empty chair in the back behind a tall man while a woman spoke from the front. I searched the room again, seeing him nowhere.

"Fucking liar!" I whispered out loud.

I glanced at the woman next to me, hoping she hadn't heard.

Probably slipped out the back and at a bar.

I planned my exit strategy and was waiting for the opportunity when a door opened near the front. It was him. He carried some books to the desk where the woman was. She'd just finished speaking. He didn't see me behind the tall man, who looked like he was knitting, which I thought was strange. My dad put the books on the table in front, standing them upright to display them. He took a few signs from another box, displaying those too. *Live and Let Live*, one said. *One day at a Time* was the other. I'd heard these sayings so often in my house, and they seemed like a lot of crap. It all felt cultish, like they were alcoholic or alcoholic-affected zombies walking around, chanting these "slogans," they called them, since my father got sober. It reminded me of an episode of *Unsolved Mysteries*, and it scared me. But whatever worked, I figured, and it was better than stepping over him, wondering if he was dead on the floor.

When I looked to the front again, I was confused to see him behind the table.

Why is he there?

My hands felt sweaty as I held them together tightly, then pulled them apart to pick at my cuticles. The scent of lousy cologne and cigarettes lingered in the basement's stale air, and I grew nauseous. I looked at the man next to me, wondering if the smell was from him, though I knew it could be any one of them. I tried breathing only through my mouth so I wouldn't smell. Then I heard his voice.

"Hey, everyone. So, I'm Richie from Revere, Massachusetts, and I'm an alcoholic."

CHAPTER 12

March 31, 2003
His eyes I felt, warm and wonderful on my skin.
He tasted like burnt cherries and winter, delicious.

I dug my favorite jeans from the back of my closet. I hadn't been
out in so long that I had trouble finding them and hoped they
still fit.

"Ass look okay?" I asked Hobo while I pulled them on, turning to
look at myself in the mirror. He wagged his tail, which I took as a yes.

These were the only jeans I owned that made me look like I had
an ass. No one in my family had one, at least on my father's side, and
I inherited the no-ass gene. I remembered my Aunt Rita saying we
were the flat-ass family that summer we went to the Cape. Ray and I
belly-laughed on the floor, and my mom joined us while Rita circled
around and smacked my mom's butt.

"You're not part of the club, Jane," she said. My mother gawked at
her. "You got a little for all of us." Rita opened her arms wide, laughing.

Mom and Rita danced, shaking their butts while Ray and I laughed
hysterically.

In the mirror I noticed myself smiling, remembering, then suddenly
felt the sadness. It always came after, and I hated it. I missed Ray and

wondered how he was doing. I'd called him a few weeks ago and left a message but hadn't heard back. Not that I expected to. It took everything I had to reach out, and I prepared myself for the disappointment, but it hurt more than I'd planned for. I wished things were different, and sometimes I felt he did too.

I tried on three different sweaters and settled on the first one, which always seemed to happen. I quickly did my hair and makeup and gave myself a once-over in the mirror.

"This will do, I guess." I reached in my bag, feeling for lipstick.

I was both nervous and excited, and I liked it. I'd never had a problem with guys liking me. Usually, it was the wrong ones I liked back. I dated a guy from Ireland all last summer, if that's what you'd call it. Lots of transients and people from other countries inhabited here, especially in the summer. They'd come for work and fun, with some overstaying their visas. No one bothered them as long as they kept their noses clean.

Johnny Apples, they called him. He had been living here for three years now. I was never clear why they called him that, only knowing it had something to do with a drunken night in an apple orchard. I never heard the whole story as he and his mates would all break into fits of laughter and end up wrestling and knocking each other around whenever it came up. They were an odd, rowdy group, but fun, and we hung out on more than a few late nights. At one point, I thought we could be something more, but I changed my mind after he pissed his pants in a drunken stupor one night. The worst part was that he still stayed out, continuing at Seasons as if nothing happened. I knew then this wouldn't be good long-term, especially after how I grew up. I hoped for something a little better.

Something about Dock was different. I wasn't sure what it was, but he felt comfortable. He was the blue-collar type, and that was familiar, but it was more than that. I wasn't sure if it was a good or bad thing, but I wanted to see where it led. I looked at my phone again, then heard a car coming down the gravel.

Please don't let him beep. If he beeps, he sucks already.

I heard the truck door shut and smiled.

Yes.

I checked myself in the mirror again and grabbed Hobo's leash to take him out before we went.

"Hey." I smiled, opening the door, watching him come up the steps.

"Hey, you," he said in his raspy voice.

He looked good, better than good.

"I saved you the trouble of knocking." I laughed, opening the door wide.

Hobo darted past his legs, seeing something to chase as the leash somehow slipped from my hands.

"Oh God, he doesn't come back." I raised my arms. "I'm fucked."

Shit. Stop swearing.

I didn't care much anymore when Hobo did this, which was often. Abby from Animal Control knew him by now as I'd called so many times when I first moved here. She would always find him and bring him home.

"It's an island," she'd say. "We'll find him eventually."

"He doesn't?" He started taking off his jacket. I looked at it, noticing it was leather, and laughed as I reached to hold it for him. "I got this." He looked at me seriously, then glanced at the jacket and smiled, seeming to realize why I was laughing.

He slowly came off the porch, and Hobo saw him and ran a little toward the club's dogwood tree. He turned, crouching on his front legs, wiggling his ass in the air and staring at me, then Dock, who kept moving slowly toward him. The motion light came on from above the club doors, lighting the whole scene.

"Oh boy," I called. "You're screwed. He wants to play."

Catlike, Dock made his way toward him, moving his upper body back and forth like a boxer as he got closer. He looked ridiculous, and I snickered, watching him crouch down like a tiger ready to pounce.

Hobo let out a bark, then darted toward him, stopping and quickly moving backward away from him as if to say, "Get me, you jackass." At least, that's always what I envisioned him saying.

"I'm sorry," I shouted so Dock could hear me over the wind picking up from the water.

I lifted the jacket near my face, smelling him. It was that same woodsy jasmine scent from earlier. Something about it made me shiver. I looked again at Hobo making his move. He darted past Dock's legs, and in a blur, Dock swept down and snatched him up. Turning to me, he looked victorious as Hobo's head poked out from under his arm, clearly confused at what had happened.

"How the hell?" I started to say as he put him down, holding the leash as they headed toward me.

"I'm big, but I'm quick." He laughed, stopping to let Hobo pee on the truck tire.

"I don't know what to say. Thank you." I smiled flirtatiously.

"You're welcome," he said and touched my arm, and I handed him back his jacket.

I let Hobo in, grabbing my coat and bag, and stepped back on the porch. Dock was smoking on the grass.

"You look amazing," he said, blowing the smoke toward the water.

The motion lights came on again, putting me on display.

"Not sure about amazing, but I'll take it." I smiled.

He walked to the truck and opened my door. I stepped past him and got in, then leaned over and did the reach thing, although I knew his door was open. I made sure he noticed my effort and smiled as he got in.

"If a girl doesn't reach over and unlock your door, she's not the right girl."

"So they say," I agreed.

He pulled a little toward the club, turning around on the sand and spinning the tires, and drove up the drive, turning on Main Street.

"What's the plan?" I asked.

"You'll see," he said, looking ahead. "You up for some fun?"

God, I haven't been out in ages.

"Let's go," I replied and tried not to sound overly excited.

We drove over the bridge into Oak Bluffs, and he pulled up to the liquor store on the corner by the harbor.

"What kind of wine do you like?" he asked, shutting the engine.

"How do you know I like wine?"

"Okay, what kind of beer do you like?" He wasn't playing.

"I'm kidding. A good Pinot Grigio is perfect. Do you want me to come in?"

I realized he might not know what Pinot Grigio was, never mind a good one.

"Nope, got it—a good Pinot Grigio. Can you spell that?" He laughed, nodding.

I squinted at him, wondering if he was serious.

"I'm kidding," he said and shut the door.

Oh, thank God.

He came out and handed me the bag. "I knew you were a wine girl."

"I drink beer too!" I said, snatching the bag playfully, putting it in the back.

I saw another bag and some neatly folded sweatshirts along with a blanket and wondered if it had anything to do with tonight. He drove toward State Beach Road, taking a right as we followed the shoreline toward Edgartown. We were both quiet, looking at the moon over the water.

"I don't know anything about you." I looked at him, then at his hands holding the steering wheel. It was dark, and I couldn't see them clearly, but there was something about his hands I liked.

"What do you want to know?" He glanced at me, then back to the road.

"What town do you live in, I guess, for starters?"

"Edgartown, in a small house." He paused. "Don't laugh."

"You don't strike me as Edgartown." I laughed anyway.

"I'm not. Will and I are fixing it up. It's got a big garage, so it's good for us." He cleared his throat and rubbed the back of his neck.

"And Will lives here part-time? I think that's what he said."

"He's back and forth," he said, stretching his neck.

"So, New Bedford?"

"Yup, New Bedge."

"Is that the nickname?" I asked.

"Kinda." He chuckled.

"Hard growing up there?"

"It was rough but made us tougher, ya know?" He paused, looking serious. I wondered what he was thinking.

He pulled off the road onto the sand by the lagoon and shut off his headlights but kept the lower fog lights on. I became nervous for a second, wondering what he was doing, and gripped the door handle tightly.

"Is this legal?" I asked, concerned.

"Don't worry, we do this all the time."

"I didn't even know there was a path here."

"Lots of hidden places on this island. I know them all." He smiled, then touched my leg.

"Is that where the bodies are buried?" I tried to be cute but also wondered if I was in trouble here. Feeling the warmth from his hand did something for me, though, and strangely, I became more at ease.

He drove slowly around Sengekontacket Pond, then up a path and down another to where there were sand dunes and another small pond that I wasn't sure I knew existed.

"So, why MV?" he asked as we drove up another hill, then closer to the pond, pulling onto a flat patch of sand by the water.

Is that State Beach there? Where am I?

I pointed to the water in front of us, where the moon shimmered on the ripples of the tide and stars filled the night sky above it.

"Isn't it obvious?" I said, and he nodded, leaning back in his seat. "But the backstory is I came here years ago, in high school, and fell in love with it. I knew I wanted to live here one day." I fidgeted with my necklace. The silhouettes of dunes rose on both sides of us.

"It's a beautiful place." He stared ahead.

The truck was idling, and I wondered why he hadn't shut it off.

"Why are you here?" I looked at him. He seemed lost in thought.

"I needed a change." He paused. "New Bedford isn't Martha's Vineyard."

I felt like there was more to the story, as if he were holding back something. He didn't strike me as the type to move for the beauty of a place.

"Do you mind if I smoke?" he asked, feeling in his pocket.

"No, go ahead."

He put the cigarette to his lips, lighting it. He took a long inhale and handed it to me. I took a puff and rolled my window down, blowing out into the night. It felt good, although it burned a little, reminding me again how I hate menthols, and I coughed a little.

"Oh, wait!" he said excitedly, reaching for the bag from the liquor store. He pulled out a pack of Parliaments and proudly displayed it.

"Parliament, oh my God," I squealed and clapped my hands. "How did you know Parliament was the non-menthol of choice?"

"Lucky guess," he said, opening the pack and handing me one.

I felt like nothing he did was a lucky guess. I handed him back his cigarette, putting mine to my lips. He lit it for me, leaning in close. I closed my eyes and inhaled his smell and the cigarette.

"You know, I only smoke when I drink," I said, blowing out the window again.

"I'm getting to that." He smiled. "But first, a little ride."

Another ride—we just rode here to God knows where.

I sometimes wondered if I was losing my edge here. In the city, I'd never go out with some random guy and drive to nowhere without knowing anything about him or where we were going. I used to carry a knife in my purse and stopped that a few months after moving here because nothing terrible seemed to happen. I sometimes wondered if I was foolish.

He stubbed his cigarette in the ashtray. I took another puff and stubbed mine, waving the smoke out the window, hating the smell.

"Ready?" he asked.

I hesitated, unsure what was happening. "Okay."

"Buckle up and hold on." He looked at my seat belt, then hit the gas.

We launched forward across the sand. My head whirled, and I

didn't know what was happening. He drove crazily in and out of the water, turning the wheel in all kinds of different ways. I grabbed on to the door as he pulled up one of the dunes and then down. We seemed airborne for a moment, and I realized we were when we hit the ground. He cut the wheel quickly as I screamed, feeling the truck was on two wheels and we'd flip over.

"Oh my God!" I yelled as he drove another hill that was steeper than the first.

I gripped the door handle, and we were in the air again and then on the ground, and I bounced high on the seat.

He turned to me, smiling. "You good?" he yelled as I made out the shape of another dune ahead.

"I, I don't know," I said, staring at him.

"I think you're good." He winked.

"I'm good." I looked over as he revved the engine, now feeling confident. "But one thing." I paused, looking serious.

"Anything." He smiled, revving the engine again.

"We need some music." I laughed as his eyes widened.

He pressed play on the truck's radio and listened for a moment.

"Will Zeppelin work?"

"Totally."

My laughs turned to screams as we lurched forward, heading up another hill. He turned the volume high, and I screamed louder, feeling weightless as we went airborne again.

· · ·

He shut the truck's lights off and drove slowly down a small trail overgrown with brush that scraped against the sides of the truck. The trail led us a back way opposite from where we came in and into what seemed to be someone's yard and their driveway, putting us on a county road I recognized immediately. He took a left, turning toward Edgartown and peeling from the driveway.

"How about that wine?"

"I think I need it after that." I sighed loudly as the adrenaline left me.

"Was that too much for our first time out?"

"It was awesome." I looked at him, wanting him to know how much fun I had.

"I'm glad." He smiled.

Suddenly, I felt open, and talking to him seemed natural. He asked about my family, and I told him the basics, not elaborating much, although strangely, I felt that I could. I thought I'd share more if he asked but wanted a nice night, and that meant forgetting things.

We passed through Four Corners and into Edgartown. He turned and pulled into the Harbor View Hotel's lot, one of my favorite places on the island. The hotel was massive, with an enormous porch and a gazebo overlooking Edgartown Harbor and Chappaquiddick Island.

"Are we going in?" I asked, knowing they had a bar. I'd been a few times and knew the bartender a little through Bobbie, but I didn't think they were open this late as the season hadn't started yet; it was only April.

"No, we are going there." He pointed toward Edgartown Light, the small black-and-white lighthouse on the sand in front of the harbor's entrance. It still had Christmas lights on it, which surprised me, but it looked beautiful. The lights lit the path to the small beach, green and red, making it easy to see our way down.

"Can you park here?"

He smirked, grabbing the stuff from the back.

"You just do whatever you wanna do, it seems."

"Drink time," he said, ignoring me, holding the bag and tucking the blanket and sweatshirt under his arm. I followed him down the sand and onto the wood planks toward the lighthouse. Thankfully, it was a warmer night than usual. Although it was the beginning of spring, it could still be cold, especially by the water.

He spread the beat-up-looking blanket onto the sand in front of me, gesturing for me to sit as he opened himself a beer. I laughed, watching him struggle as he worked on getting my wine open, which took him a few frustrating minutes.

"Good thing you brought an opener," I said, impressed, thinking of how many times I'd forgotten one.

"I didn't. Bought one at the liquor store only because they were right in front of me at the register." He pulled, and the cork made a popping sound. "I got lucky."

"No, I did." I looked up.

He began to smile, then suddenly looked defeated.

"Nope, you didn't." He tipped his head back and growled, holding the bottle with his arms wide. His face and neck glowed red and green from the Christmas lights.

I laughed with my hand on my chest, realizing he forgot a glass, and reached for the bottle. Beer in hand, he sat on the blanket next to me, and I nudged him, letting him know it was fine. I clinked my bottle against his, and we both took a sip. The familiar warm feeling I'd grown to enjoy filled my head as we quietly looked at the water. I pulled my jacket tight to my chest.

"Here, put one of these on." He reached behind, handing me a sweatshirt.

He helped me pull my sleeve out of my coat, and I pulled the hoodie over my head, inhaling as it passed my nose. It smelled like him except with a mixture of gasoline or some type of fuel.

"Better?" he asked, putting my coat over my shoulders and moving closer.

"Yes." I relaxed, warm and comfortable as I leaned into him.

I glanced up at him, knowing my face would be in front of his as he adjusted my jacket. Our eyes met, and I smelled the sweetness of his breath warming my cheek. He held my gaze and put the backside of his hand on my face, touching me softly. The red-and-green glow of the lights shined over him, and he moved his hand, his fingertips under my chin, pulling me to him. I closed my eyes, feeling his lips touch mine.

We kissed again and again; then he came behind me, holding me in his arms. I felt warm and wonderful from the wine, resting my body against him. The waves lapped gently against the breaker at the harbor entrance, and the glow of the moon and lights energized me. I hardly knew him, but he felt familiar and like something I'd been missing.

"Wanna get out of here?" he asked, pressing his chin on top of my head.

My mind raced. I didn't want the night to end, although I knew it should. It was late, and I hesitated.

"I don't want to take you home yet—doesn't mean what you're thinking," he interrupted himself, and I felt a pinch on my side.

"Hey!" I laughed, twisting around. "I'm not thinking about anything." I turned serious.

"Uh-huh." He smiled. "C'mon, let's go. One more stop." He brushed himself off, grabbing our things, and I followed him up the path.

We drove out of town to Edgartown Vineyard Haven Road, pulling onto Smith Hollow to the end, to a small house. He drove around back, stopping in front of a giant garage.

"Your house?"

"Yup."

The moon shone through the trees, and I spotted shapes of people sitting at a bonfire in the yard.

"We have fires most nights," he said and got out, grabbing the beers and wine.

"Fun." I looked at the clock on the truck's dash: *1:00* glowed in green, but I didn't care what time it was.

He passed me my wine bottle, and we walked toward the fire. A man was sitting; I recognized him.

"Hey, Leather," he said, standing, taking a sip of his beer.

"That is getting old." I laughed. "Hi again, Will."

Dock pulled a chair next to him. "This is Tim and Amy," he said, raising his beer to the younger guy and girl sitting there.

"Nice to meet you," Tim said. Amy smiled, and I smiled back.

"Hey, kid, run in and get a wineglass for me?" Dock said to Tim.

"Tim works for us sometimes," Dock said as Tim jogged toward the house.

"If that's what you want to call it," Will chimed in, and they both laughed. Amy quietly smiled but seemed annoyed.

"How old are you, anyway?" I looked at Dock, then Will, who was laughing.

"Uh-oh, Grandpa." Will raised his beer.

"If I'm a grandpa, so are you, so I wouldn't be laughing."

Amy spoke. "This is true."

"Oh no!" Dock laughed. "She's alive!"

"Fuck you, Dock." Amy glared at him.

"So." I paused. "How old are you?" I grew nervous.

"He's too old for you and too ugly," Will quipped.

"He's thirty-something, right, Dock?" Tim said, hearing the conversation, handing Dock the glass.

"Thanks for answering for me, T, but I can handle it." Dock accepted the glass and took the bottle from me, pouring the rest of my wine in it.

"It's not a wineglass, sorry," he whispered.

I took a large sip. "Thank you."

"Not a bunch of wine drinkers around here, that's for sure." Will got up again, lighting a cigarette.

"I figured," I said, smiling. "You boys look a little rough for wine and fancy glasses."

"I can be fancy." Dock smiled, taking a cigarette from his pocket.

"Well, you are in Edgartown," I said, looking back and forth at the two brothers, enjoying the banter.

He touched my leg and leaned over. "Do you want one of yours?" he asked, holding up his cigarette.

"Sure, I can get them. Where are they?"

"I think they're still in the truck."

"I'll get them. Do you have a bathroom I can use, anyway?"

"We have one right in the garage right there, or you can go in the house, but that's closer," Will said, overhearing us and pointing.

I headed toward the truck, feeling slightly unsteady, trying not to look it. My face was warm from the fire and wine, and my cheeks hurt from laughing and smiling. I grabbed the cigarettes and lighter from the console and lit one, taking a long inhale, leaning against the truck. I looked up, taking in the night sky, remembering why I loved it here. The urge to pee overtook the moment, and I hurried into the garage through the side door. Seeing the bathroom in the corner, I felt around for a light.

When I came out, I noticed a large tarp over something and what looked like a chrome fender sticking out under the side.

"That's my baby," a voice said as I jumped, startled, although I saw it was Dock. The alcohol must have given me a delayed reaction.

"Jesus." I grabbed my heart. "You are fucking catlike." We both laughed.

He pulled the tarp off, and I walked over, seeing the letters written in chrome on the side of the gas tank. It was an old Harley Davidson.

"It's a shovelhead." He smiled proudly, running his hand up the side of it.

"I think I've heard of that," I pretended.

"It's what I've always wanted. Will and I have been restoring it. Got her at an auction last summer."

"That's awesome. Will it be finished soon?"

"That's the plan." He clenched his cigarette in his teeth and put his beer on the floor, then stepped back, giving the bike a once-over, wiping some dust off the seat.

"You guys are close, you and Will?" I asked, touching the handlebar.

"We go back and forth." He pulled the cigarette from his teeth and threw it on the floor, grinding it with his boot. "We're eleven months apart. Kind of have a love-hate thing." He moved close to me. "But no one knows me better," he said, turning to face me and wrapping his arms around me. "Are you having a good time?

"I am."

"How good?" He put his fingertips under my chin and looked into my eyes.

I smiled, saying nothing. He bent down, looking at me, then stepped back.

"You're drunk." He laughed.

"I know." I held my jacket tight, swaying a little.

"I should probably get you home."

"I think I need to lie down, actually." The room spun a little.

"Okay, want me to carry you?" he asked, bending his knees so he could look in my eyes again.

"No?" I said, embarrassed. "God, no. Just let me lay down for a minute, and I'll be fine."

My level of drunkenness surprised me, but I remembered I had eaten hardly anything all day.

He put his arm around me, and we headed toward the house. He led me into a room, and I sat on the bed, watching him disappear. He came back and handed me a large glass of water.

"Just give me a few minutes," I said, lying on my side, gazing at him above me. I smelled him on the blanket. Everything looked clean, which I appreciated.

"I'll be right outside if you need me, and I'll check on you in a few minutes." He ran his hand over my hair.

"Okay," I slurred. My eyes were already shut.

• • •

A truck started, and I felt light on my face and heard the calls of birds outside. I quickly opened my eyes, disoriented, unsure where I was. My head throbbed, and I remembered. I looked around the room for a clock, not seeing one, then saw my coat hanging from the footboard of the bed and reached in, grabbing my phone.

Oh, thank God, 6:30. I laid my head back and wiped the corners of my eyes.

"But, Hobo, shit!" I said, sitting up again.

There was a tap on the door, and Dock came in. I could only imagine how I looked, but my head hurt too much to care.

"Hey, drunky," he said, smiling, looking showered and fresh.

I pouted.

"It happens. Stop." He sat on the bed next to me.

"Interesting first date," I said, rubbing my head.

"It was." He lay back and stretched.

"Sorry I took your bed."

"Stop." He locked eyes with me. "I want to kiss you." He looked at me seriously.

"You may regret it." I ran my fingers through my hair.

"I won't." He leaned over and nudged me back gently on the bed, holding my head as he inched closer. Dizzy, I wasn't sure what was happening. He pressed his upper body on me and kissed me softly and slowly. I kissed him back, tilting my head, offering my neck to him as he kissed behind my ear, then down the front of my throat.

"I have to go," I whispered.

He looked at me and whispered back, "I know."

He took his shirt off, walked to the bureau in the corner, grabbed a T-shirt that said *New Bedford Builders* on it, and put it on. His body was tanned, and his shoulders were broad and muscular.

"What's that tattoo?" I asked, noticing one on his forearm of a crown with leaves.

"Which one?" He turned, pulling the shirt down, looking at his arm and hand.

"The one on your arm. You already told me about the dots," I said, standing, grabbing my coat.

"Oh, it's not finished. I let some kid do it when I was younger. I'll finish it someday. Maybe." He pulled on a sweatshirt. "Just dumb kid stuff," he said, brushing it off.

"Let's go, Dock!" Will's voice called out.

"Yup," he called back.

We drove into Vineyard Haven, the three of us. Tools filled the back seat, so I sat in the console between them. They both bobbed their heads to the song on the radio, and I laughed, causing my head to hurt. I wasn't looking forward to today. Mr. S. was in the hospital, and I wouldn't have to do much, but something always came up.

"There's no time for Mocha's, so we are shit out of luck for coffee today," Will said. "We're late." He smirked.

"I'll make you guys some. I feel bad."

Dock rolled his eyes. "Don't feel bad," he said, turning down the radio. "We had fun. Nothing to feel bad about."

"That's your motto, dude." Will side-eyed him.

"Can't think of a better one." Dock rolled his eyes again, tapping the dashboard.

"I'm kidding." Will looked at me. "I'm glad you had fun."

I sighed as we pulled down the drive. "I'll pay for it today."

Dock got out and took my hand, helping me.

"What's your plans tonight?"

"I, I don't know," I stuttered, surprised. "I'll have to go to the hospital. My patient's there. I forget if I said that last night." I nodded, annoyed with myself.

"So, you're home early?"

"Um, yeah, I guess."

I was not used to someone so forward and felt like I couldn't say no. I wasn't sure I wanted to, but he gave me no option.

"How about—" he began.

"Come over at eight thirty," I interrupted, trying to gain some control.

"See you then," he said and kissed me.

"No, I'll see you in ten because I'm making you both some coffee."

"Let's go, Dock," Will yelled.

He kissed me again gently while Hobo barked loudly in the house. I looked in his eyes, lost in them, and then away, heading into the cottage.

CHAPTER 13

July 11, 1992
He was someone before me, and he's still someone,
a person, not just my dad. Now I see.

He's the fucking speaker! I screamed in my head. I felt like a bus had hit me and wanted to run from the room. Instead, I froze.

"Jesus, Mary, and fucking Joseph," I whispered, sounding like my mother, except she wouldn't say the f-word.

The man next to me sighed, but I didn't look at him. *Fuck you.* I nodded in disbelief, crossing my arms tightly. The man turned to me, and I smiled apologetically.

"Hi, Richie," they chanted in cult-like unison.

"So, I wasn't expecting to speak tonight, let alone chair the meeting." He laughed uncomfortably.

He was never uncomfortable for long.

"Truth be told, I didn't plan on coming to a meeting. I'm here for the weekend with my daughter, but I needed to come."

He shifted in his chair nervously while I sank in my seat.

"I knew I had to be in one of these rooms today." He took a deep breath. "But, by the grace of God, I am here and not at some bar in Oak Bluffs."

I sank lower in my chair.

How the fuck do I get out of here?

"I was outside meeting some of you a few minutes ago, and a few of us were asked if we'd be interested in chairing. I guess the scheduled person was sick." He appeared more comfortable now, leaning back in his seat. "Listen," he continued, "I didn't want to. I wasn't even sure I'd speak tonight, but something told me I should, and if you good people want to listen, I'm happy to talk."

It was odd seeing him speak so freely and easily to a room full of strangers. I held my breath and felt the pang of my heart in my chest. He hadn't seen me, and I wasn't sure he would with the knitting man in front of me. I finally gave up plotting to leave as I couldn't without being noticed. I focused on trying to control my anxiety and calm myself instead. I crossed and uncrossed my legs again and shifted in my chair.

I have to just not let him see me.

Tears filled my eyes for a moment, and I blinked them back. I wasn't sure what I was feeling, but I felt uncomfortable and exposed. I looked down at my feet, wanting my boots back. I wanted to be covered.

"I'm from Boston—well, north of Boston—if you couldn't tell. You all may be from the island or from all over. I'm guessing on vacation and needing to be here, like me. It's nice to see you all." He sat back, appearing to think a moment, then leaned forward, putting his elbows on the table.

"So, my story," he started. "My story is sometimes a tough one to tell for me." He nodded and smiled, letting out another uncomfortable laugh. He fiddled with his sunglasses on the table. "It's a tough one to tell because I've already lived it, ya know?"

Someone said, "Yup."

He smiled toward the voice.

"So, where do I begin?" He crossed his legs and turned to the side, clasping his hands on his lap.

I was stuck. I had to listen. I wanted to hear. But from the other side of a wall where no one knew I was there. I didn't want to be in the room as a willing participant. I wanted no one to know who I was. I didn't want him to see me either.

Maybe he wouldn't want me to hear? Maybe he wouldn't say certain things?

My mind raced, but I couldn't come up with any way to fix it. My only choice was to let it happen or run out of the place, crazy. I had to be okay with one of them. I closed my eyes and breathed slowly.

The room was quiet except for the occasional cough or throat clearing. The smell was back and somehow seemed worse. I tried only mouth breathing again, but it didn't work.

"I grew up on the North Shore, as I said, my sister and me. My parents were alcoholics; that's a whole other story." He smiled again. "My mom left us a lot." He paused. "*A lot!*" he emphasized. "She would have a boyfriend or two and leave, then come back home to my father, who always let her. I never understood that, but as a kid, you just want your mom and dad together, ya know?"

He continued to speak with ease. I looked around the room at everyone but him.

Do I even know his story? What's his fucking story?

I knew his story of how it affected me. I remembered hearing about his mom, my grandmother, leaving a lot, but I didn't know why. God forbid we spoke ill of anyone. There were so many things unsaid and not talked about, so I wasn't sure what I knew. And as much as I'd always thought it was strange, right now I wanted to keep it that way.

I looked at his face, and he looked different now. I glanced down at the man next to me's water bottle on the floor. My mouth felt like I had been sucking on cotton balls, and I wished I could steal a sip. I couldn't figure out how I felt. I wasn't sure I even thought of him as anyone except my father until right now. I became angrier. Angry at myself, at him, Ray, my mom. All of it.

Fuck.

"They drank. My mom got nasty sometimes," he went on. "She never thought I was good enough at anything, sports, school, etc., and would tell me. But I really wasn't, so I guess she was just honest." He spun his cigarette pack on the table. "I just didn't give a shit except about baseball.

I liked baseball." He stared down at the table. He looked like a sad little boy. "My dad, well, my dad was my everything. Although I guess I didn't realize it so much at the time." He popped up, smiling, looking at a lady to the right, who smiled back.

For a while, he went on about his father and the bond they had, which I wasn't aware of except from stories my mother had told, always saying they were best friends, him and his dad. My grandfather died when I was two. I recalled her saying once that was when my father's drinking changed, and he never could stop anymore.

He talked about when he knew drinking was a problem for him. He was fifteen years old and had his first night of real drinking at a party with his friends.

"Right then, at fifteen, I knew I didn't drink like everyone else."

He went on about growing up, getting into trouble, stealing cars and drinking, and trying other drugs.

"But never heroin," he said with pride. "I never stuck a needle in my arm."

Jesus. I rolled my eyes, looking toward the door. I was becoming invested until he said that. I looked at the man next to me, who stared ahead. *He's invested, I guess. Stupid.*

At least I was more relaxed now, but probably more from exhausting myself than feeling comfortable; I didn't feel that. I wanted to listen unseen and know. I wanted to know him.

He was surprisingly a great speaker. He had everyone's attention, judging by the expressions around the room. He talked about Kate, his first wife. I looked at his arm resting on the table. I felt weird when he said her name, unsure I wanted to hear this part, as if it were a betrayal to my mother, whom he hadn't even met yet.

Or had he? Jesus. No.

He said he drank through that whole relationship but thought getting married and having kids would change him. He said he wanted to be a better man but never could figure out what was wrong with him then. He just wanted to be normal and like everyone else. He spoke briefly of Mary, and his eyes changed. His voice did too. It cracked a little, and he cleared his throat a lot, nearly every time he said her name.

"My first daughter, I have a lot of regrets. I was drunk a lot. I was useless, although I didn't want to be. I had every intention, every day, of not being that, but it always ended there." He wrung his hands, then clasped them behind his head. "I was drunk and useless to both of them."

My eyes filled and I tilted my head, trying to stop it.

Why am I crying?

"She left me because of my drinking, but we were young, and I used that as an excuse. At first, I tried to see Mary, but my ex wanted to move out of state after meeting her next husband. He was a military guy. I'd already met my now wife." He nodded. "Didn't even tell her I was married or had a baby." He took a deep breath, exhaling loudly. "I lied." He coughed, clearing his throat again. "I lied because it was easier not to tell the truth. I lied to myself and a lot of people. I was ashamed, and I wanted to be normal, like everyone else, but didn't want to admit it was booze." He sighed.

I thought of Ray's constant cry of "Why can't we just be normal?"

Why can't we be fucking normal? I asked myself, nodding in agreement. *I'm seventeen years old on Martha's Vineyard in a fucking AA meeting. Instead of being out with friends on a Saturday night, I'm with a bunch of drunks trying not to be drunks in a smelly church basement.*

What the fuck is normal?

I looked around the room at all of the misfits and uncomfortable-looking people. I didn't think anyone here had the answer. I sighed, noticing the man next to me staring.

What are you looking at? Weirdo.

I wasn't a drunk, let alone a recovering one, but wasn't I closer to fitting in to this group of misfits than anywhere else? I looked at my sandals, feeling sick.

I guess he tried to see Mary at times. She apparently stayed with us when I was a baby and Ray wasn't born yet. One of his biggest regrets was signing papers so her stepdad could adopt Mary. He said his sister, my aunt Rita, told him it would be for the best, and it would give her a chance at a better life. He said it was then he couldn't deny he was a fucking drunk and none of this was normal.

"But instead of doing anything about it, I drank because that's what I do. Then, poof, like magic, the feelings were gone." He raised his hands to his mouth, gesturing as the Italians did.

He tried to make it all right with my mother and having us kids.

"Almost like a do-over," he said, laughing at the ridiculousness of it.

He swore to himself that he'd get it right and tried to cut back drinking. He thought his love for my mother and the way she loved him might fix him. He said he tried only to drink on the weekends for a while, but he would count the hours, minutes, and seconds until Friday night and would be a "fucking prick" all week to her. He drank all weekend, he said.

"A real life-of-the-party drunk from Friday until Sunday." He laughed, spinning his cigarette pack again.

He went on about how he couldn't even pull that off for long, so he gave up trying.

He talked of how he was drinking every day and ended up hospitalized twice after my grandad died. My mother threw him out, and he lived in a broom closet at the train station for almost a year. I never knew that. I felt like I didn't know half of my life. My cheeks grew hot, and I felt naked in a room full of people who needed a bath or a baptism, or maybe I did; I couldn't tell the difference between any of us anymore.

Maybe we're not so different. We're all messed up.

They were all just so unclean to me, and I felt dirty next to them. At the same time, I was also a little envious of their defects and their admission of them by sitting in this room together.

Maybe they were like my father and couldn't pretend even if they wanted to. Maybe the ones who could act for the outside world struggled the most and weren't here. My mother would say that. I understood it in my world. I tried to pretend. I knew it all and had it figured out, always needing to stay one step ahead. It was exhausting.

Maybe it feels better when you just give up.

I didn't have the answers, and although my father was speaking to this room, I knew that he didn't either. But he knew that he didn't, and at least he was up there admitting it. He said every time he thought he had it all figured out was when the rug came out from under him.

"I'm the most dangerous when I think I have all the answers," he said once when we were talking.

I looked at the lady in the front staring at him. She was smiling like a teenager. Her hair had a giant knot in the back, and she was holding a large wad of tissue in her hand. The oversized patchwork pocketbook slung over her chair had a hole in it, I noticed at the bottom. It was wide open, and her car keys with what looked like a rabbit foot and a big, yellow happy face hung out the side. Clearly, she hadn't left 1970, and looking around the room again, it looked like a lot of them hadn't. No one here had it figured out. That I was sure of, but neither did I, and being here made me realize it even more. I didn't like it either way.

He spoke of my mother as a large part of why he got sober, which I knew, saying she inspired him. It was strange when he talked about her sometimes. He seemed disconnected, but I wasn't entirely sure. He spoke like she was some untouchable saint, and weirdly I understood it. You wanted her approval but were unsure how to get it. You could never be real and let go, or maybe she would see and judge your ways. She said nothing and didn't do anything in particular, but you knew when she disapproved, and to me, that was worse. Say it! Yell it! I had a hard time without words. *Maybe it's her way of protecting herself,* I started to realize.

I didn't know what he had to worry about; she saw all his ways and was still around.

I slowly realized I connected with this man more than I'd apprehended. As weird as our relationship was, I liked that there wasn't a lot of bullshit. I could hate him if I felt like it, he could ignore me, and then we moved on. Then we'd hate and ignore some more with an occasional laugh or tiny amount of understanding popping in from time to time. He was easy to talk to and didn't judge, but I guess he really couldn't.

I saw he was tired of talking. Replaying his life seemed to exhaust him. It exhausted me too. *He's fucking exhausting.*

Certain things pained him, and I could tell. His father, Mary—when he spoke of them, you could see the regret and sadness. He probably wished he could skip those parts.

"And I had a relapse." He shifted in his chair again, his finger in the air, looking at the woman with the tissues.

• • •

I remembered the relapse. He hadn't been sober for long, but it was long enough for us to notice, as our lives had become slightly regular and routine.

My mom's cousin Pam from Charlestown threw a party. She and my mother had started taking some college classes and decided to celebrate. I happily watched as my mother strolled proudly around the party, talking to family and friends, which always excited her. I spotted Pam's famous chicken wings and was even happier, making myself a giant plate.

I looked around for a place to sit and saw nothing. I decided to go outside on the steps, pleased that I could enjoy them in peace. Trying my best not to spill anything on my new outfit, I sat on the top step. Then I heard voices and turned to see who it was. Through the window of my father's Cadillac in the driveway, I spotted him and Pam's husband, Billy. I watched for a while, seeing my father laughing, lifting a can of beer to his lips. I knew it was beer. Growing up in my house, I knew every name and label ever created. Rage boiled inside of me, and my stomach churned and gurgled.

Piece of crap! Oh, God, forgive me, please. Now I've broken another commandment.

I tried to remember which commandment it was but couldn't, only knowing it was the you-can't-be-bad-to-your-parents one.

He laughed loudly, and then Billy laughed too.

I'm not going to hell because of this asshole. Asshole, asshole, asshole!

I looked at the big stupid Cadillac that he loved so much. He got it when he stopped drinking after becoming friendly with more people in the union, helping with campaigns and things. He thought he was a big shot, so he needed the Cadillac like the rest of them.

He sneakily took another sip from the can. It was Schlitz. I could tell, seeing the fancy brown *S* through the window. I looked again at the stupid car he'd spent yesterday washing and buffing, and suddenly I stood so they could see me. A chicken wing slid off my plate and tumbled as if in slow motion down my new skirt, plopping onto my shoe, then rolled off onto the porch. Tears filled my eyes, and I gritted my teeth, staring at my lap. I tried with all my might to fight back the tears and rage when a voice called.

"Hey. Georgie." I looked, seeing Billy smiling. My father smiled too, looking surprised to see me and keeping his hands at his side, hiding the can. I stared at him, still holding the plate of food.

"What's wrong, George?" Billy said with fake concern.

I looked at my skirt and back at them and started to cry angrily. I looked straight at my father through the Cadillac's window again and grunted, screaming as loud as I could.

"You are so full of shit!"

I threw my plate with all my might, now sobbing hysterically, glaring at my father. I watched the potato salad and chicken wings soar through the air, landing on the Cadillac's hood and partly on the ground next to it. JoJo, Billy's three-legged German shepherd, came running, devouring the food on the ground, then jumping on the side of the car to get the rest. My father screamed and hollered for Billy to get his fucking dog off the fucking car.

We left soon after that. My mom came out, saw me crying, and looked at my skirt, assuming that's what it was about. My father said nothing, probably hoping I wouldn't either. It didn't matter anyway because if he had a sip of alcohol, he couldn't stop until he had to be detoxed or detox himself. I was twelve and knew this much. And he told me so one day when I saw him change from drinking vodka to beer and asked why he did that.

"I need to taper down, or I could die" was all he said, sitting at the table with his head hung low.

My mother went in and got Ray. She looked at the car, at my plate of food and him cleaning it off. He said nothing, and neither did she.

• • •

He said how disappointed he was in himself and that he nearly crumbled, seeing me crying that day. He described me as a tough little girl, telling them he didn't worry about me much and I'd be fine.

"She has a good head on her shoulders and takes no bullshit." He looked at the table.

Tears fell down my cheeks, and I was holding my breath, my stomach filling with air. I wanted to leave again, desperately. I didn't want him to talk about Ray or me. Something moved in front of me, startling me. It was the man next to me. He handed me a box of tissues. I smiled at him, taking the box. My father was now looking in my direction. I held my breath, moving slightly, trying to position myself directly behind the knitting guy who had stopped knitting and was only listening now. But soon, he talked again, so I didn't think he noticed me.

"My son," he said a few times, touching the corner of each eye with his finger. The tissue lady walked up, handing him some. He smiled and set them on the table in front of him. He didn't cry, but this was the closest I'd seen him come. I slumped, lifeless in the metal chair, not caring if he saw me now. I felt out of my body. I felt nothing, and everything seemed to go blank. His lips moved, but I didn't hear what came out. The tissue box fell on the floor, and all at once, the sounds of the room came back. I wasn't sure how much time had elapsed.

"I'm sorry. I'm just sorry," he said, rubbing his chin.

The room clapped, and the man next to me leaned in, asking if I was okay. I looked at him, attempting a smile. Everyone stood, and I heard my father's voice say something about a break. The knitting man gathered up his things and got up fast. I stood up behind him, wanting to make my way out with the crowd, hoping my dad stayed in the same spot up front and wouldn't see me. I moved close with the group and peeked over. He stood talking to a man by the table, shaking his hand, then stopped, seeing me as I moved from my chair. Our eyes met, and he watched me head toward the door. He turned back to the man, who was saying something to him again, and I turned away. I followed the people up the stairs, moving through them quickly toward the street.

CHAPTER 14

April 1, 2003
Life is a collection of moments. Some are unremembered,
and others are joyous, life changing, and tragic.
I think I'll embrace them.

I wished so badly that I could rest, but I wouldn't be able to with Dock working right outside and knowing I had to go to the hospital soon. My head ached, and my stomach was sour. I had just enough coffee left to brew a pot and brought out two cups, following the buzzing sound.

Will hunched down, cutting something, but there was no sign of Dock. He looked at me and got up, taking off his glasses and brushing his knees. I handed him a cup and a few packs of sugar. I offered the creamer I thought smelled okay, but he waved it off, which was probably in his best interest.

"Where's your other half?" I asked, seeing the truck wasn't there.

"He had to go to the lumberyard."

He poured a few packs of sugar in his cup and stirred it around with his finger, then pulled it out, shaking it.

"Hot," he yelled.

"Um, yeah, coffee is hot," I said sarcastically, to which he smirked.

"Just leave his. He can heat it in the club." He took a long sip, jumping as his phone rang on his hip, nearly causing it to spill. He unclipped it from his belt and made a face at it. "The ex." He laughed.

I raised my eyebrows.

"No one's home." He laughed again, pressing a button to dismiss the call.

"Ex, as in married?" I immediately regretted asking, feeling nosy.

"If that's what you want to call it." He clipped the phone back on his belt.

"I'm sorry," I said awkwardly.

"I'm not." He smiled. "You ever married?" He took another sip and put the cup on the ground next to the saw.

"Me? God, no. Haven't thought of that yet." I crossed my arms over my chest as the wind blew off the water. "That would be too adult-like," I added.

"Yup, stay young forever."

"That's the plan. But maybe someday."

"Don't do it!" He pointed at me. "You'll be sorry." We both laughed. "At least wait for the right guy, anyway." He picked the cup up again.

"Hard to find nice guys anymore." I smiled, uncomfortable.

"You're looking at one, and let me tell you, what they say is true. Nice guys finish last."

"Well, you and your brother seem nice, but looks can be deceiving," I said coyly.

"What?" He raised his voice, smiling crookedly. "I'm the nicest, but Dock, he . . ." He halted, scratching his chin.

"He what?" I couldn't resist asking.

"Let's just say my brother is a little rough around the edges." He put the cup down again, then put his hands in his pockets. "You seem like a nice girl with a lot going for you; don't ever settle. There's my worthless two cents."

I wasn't sure if he was talking about his brother or just in general, but I didn't dare ask. I thought there might be some sibling rivalry between them. I'd felt it last night, and this morning.

"I'm going to head in and get ready. Then off to work. Although I'd rather go to bed," I said, yawning.

"I hear you. I'll leave the mugs on your porch if that's cool?" He pushed his brown hair back. It was long on top, and a piece fell in his face. He looked like Dock just then. He was shorter and stockier, with smaller eyes. He had a sadness about him. I wondered if it was the ex: the sadness. Our eyes met, and I turned away, feeling he could read my thoughts.

"Perfect." Heading toward the cottage, I looked back and waved. My hair whipped in my face, and I pushed it with my sleeve. "Bye, Will."

He raised his cup.

• • •

I got myself together and went next door to check in with Delia and Lilly about the day's plans. Will was still sawing, and Dock hadn't come back yet when I passed through, for which I was thankful as I had no time to talk; I should have already been there.

"Hello," I called into the empty kitchen, surprised not to see anyone. I noticed a breakfast plate with half a strip of bacon and a notebook next to it. I saw black-Sharpie lettering, which meant Lilly was close or had been.

"Georgie," Delia's voice called from the back stairs, "come here. I'm getting him some things."

I darted up the stairs. Feeling my head rattle on the first few steps, I slowed to one by one. *God, I hadn't been this hungover in a while.*

I headed into the bedroom, and Delia immediately shoved a bag at me.

"Here, take this to the hospital. He may want some of his things," she said, walking to the dresser, closing the drawers.

"Okay," I said, confused by her aggression. "Did you want to come?"

"No, no," she snapped. She spun around to look at me. "I have too much to do, and that man is in and out of the hospital." She turned to the dresser.

I'd never heard her call Mr. S. "that man" before. Lilly was always "that woman." I wasn't sure what was going on. I neatened his bed, which was a mess, figuring Lady must have slept on it.

"It's hard seeing him in the hospital," I said, immediately regretting it while I fluffed the pillow, watching her from the corner of my eye.

Her face scrunched angrily. She looked tired.

"The man wants to die," she exclaimed, then looked to see if anyone was around to hear. "I was there this morning." She tapped the bag I placed on the bed. "He wanted something warm. There's a sweater in there. He likes the brown one." She walked out of the room and down the hall.

"Where's Lilly?" I called out. This didn't feel like the right moment, but I needed to know.

"She's in New York. Where do you think?" Her footsteps stopped, and her tone changed. She got a thrill talking about Lilly, and the gossip always seemed to please her, which I found strange. I wondered about it all now. *Maybe she's jealous?*

I would have never thought anything before Lilly's comment the other day, but now I questioned Delia's motives. I'd felt Delia plain old didn't like her before, and that was it.

My head hurt, and I didn't want to think.

"That's right. I forgot," I called back.

"Get with it, Georgie." She laughed loudly and headed down the steps.

I took the bag off the bed and followed her, grabbing the keys to the BMW.

"I'll be back," I shouted over the running water as Delia filled a large pot in the sink. She ignored me or didn't hear me.

There were too many prominent personalities and too much history in this house. I wasn't in the mood to navigate them at all today.

I drove past the hospital and swung up East Chop Drive, taking in the morning view; I'd circle back around. The sky was clear, and a blue fishing boat passed in the distance beyond the lighthouse on Telegraph Hill at the top of East Chop. The giant houses were nearly all unoccupied, which would change soon when the season began. I was thankful I had it all to myself for now, if only for a short time.

I thought about the night and all that had transpired. I looked down at my arm, feeling little shivers, thinking of him kissing me. He kissed well, and I liked it. He seemed to do whatever he felt like, which I found attractive, though I wondered if it was healthy. He was different, uninhibited, and I wanted more with him; but there could be some danger in this, which worried and interested me at the same time.

• • •

"Hey, Mr. S.," I whispered as I approached the bed, noticing his eyes still closed. He opened them, blinking, taking time to adjust before turning his head to look at me.

"George," he said, clearing his throat and coughing.

I handed him the tissue box on the table.

"How are you feeling?" I asked as I gently touched his arm.

The was uncharted territory for us. A caring gesture of touch wasn't something we did. I wasn't a touchy-feely person, and it was blatantly obvious he wasn't either. I'd felt compelled to but now felt strange and uncomfortable.

"Like hell," he coughed, not seeming to notice.

"Delia packed a few things for you." I held the bag up for him to see.

"Why?"

"She thought maybe you'd like your brown sweater. I don't know."

"Why?"

I ignored his last "why" and walked to the other side of the bed to look at his IV to see what medicine they were giving him.

"Did you sleep okay?"

He ignored me, staring at his hand.

"Hey, George," Pat, the day nurse, said as she walked in with a smile. She went to open the blinds, which I knew wouldn't go over well.

"Hey, Pat. How is he?" I asked, watching for his reaction.

"Jesus," he barked, coughing. "George!"

"He isn't a morning person, Pat. Can we close these a little?" I pleaded.

"Of course." She smiled, shutting them partly but not enough. "I'll be back with your morning medications," she said in his face in a childlike voice.

He said nothing, staring at her like she was a fool.

I laughed as Pat left the room. "They're just trying to help."

"There's no help for me," he mumbled.

"Oh, stop. There is no help for me either, but as long as they physically get you better enough to go home, that's good, right?" I asked, knowing I was pressing my luck.

"Agreed," he whispered and let out a long sigh. "Where's Lilly?"

I felt guilty saying she was in New York, thinking he'd feel abandoned, but it wasn't my guilt, and she'd been going through this for years. I couldn't lie.

"New York, the gala or something," I said matter-of-factly. "I'm giving her an update after I see you, and I think she is coming right back tomorrow if I remember correctly." I sat in the chair near him.

He closed his eyes, and I closed mine, nearly falling asleep until Pat came back in with his medications. I followed her into the hallway to get an update in private, then headed down to the gift shop. I grabbed a *New York Times*, hoping this would keep him content for the afternoon.

"Paper," I said, placing it on the table in front of him. He looked out the window. Someone had opened the blinds.

I opened his glasses case and helped put them on. He pushed them up on his nose, swatting my hand away.

"Just trying to help," I sighed.

He held the paper in front of him, and I watched, noticing again that his eyes were not scanning the pages. I closed my eyes and sat back in the chair.

"You need to work with therapy, Mr. S.," I said, hearing the wrinkle of the paper. I didn't want to argue with him and refused to today. I understood his frustration but was too tired to dance with him. I immediately went in with the big guns. "If you don't, you might not come home, or you'll come home in a wheelchair or confined to the bed." I kept my eyes still closed, hearing the paper rattle again.

He coughed. "Maybe that's where I belong."

Fuck.

I thought hard about what to say next, and then it came.

"If you're confined to bed, there's no more sitting on the porch, looking at the water, no evenings on the sofa with Lilly; do you know that?"

He groaned.

I pulled out the biggest guns. "Lady is getting older, so she won't be able to do the stairs or climb on the bed soon, and a wheelchair is just as bad."

Frustrated, I listened to the silence, nervous I might have said too much. I opened my eyes and looked over at him.

He put the paper down and stared out the window in thought. "Fine."

I closed my eyes again, feeling victorious.

• • •

The sun shone brightly over the lagoon. Two neon finches darted by, and I was excited to see them. I rolled down my windows as I drove over the bridge, taking in the salty smell. I worried his depression had worsened since being in the hospital. It was hard to tell as he was a stoic man, but I saw the subtle changes. I thought about depression and the book he'd written. I'd seen a copy as I was dusting the shelves in his room a few weeks ago and had pulled it from its place, looking at the blue-and-white cover.

Maybe I should get to know his mind better.

I thought about depression and darkness. He seemed to struggle with it his entire life, at least since his mother died, he said once.

All his books are about dark subjects, I realized. The Holocaust, slavery, depression, and suicide were the ones I knew of. I felt guilty I hadn't read them and resolved to do so.

I pulled down the gravel drive and hurried into the house, hoping no one was there so I could grab the book and head out. Luckily, I saw no one. I darted up the back staircase and took it from the shelf, then came quietly down, planning to leave from the porch to avoid Delia if she was around. I made it to the door and stopped in my tracks, noticing Lilly sitting on the stairs outside.

Something about the way she looked stopped me from approaching her—her head tilted back and her eyes closed. The sun hit her face, and it made her bronzed, wrinkled skin glow. She reminded me of my father just then, and I found myself smiling. I'd never seen her still before; something about it eased me. Just then, I felt a hand on my shoulder.

"Oh my God!"

I turned to see Delia giggling. She put her finger to her lips, shushing me, then grabbed my hand and pulled me toward the kitchen.

"Don't bother her now, you fool," she said, walking through the butler's pantry and sitting me at the table. "What's that?" She pointed.

I looked down at my hand.

"His book. I'm going to read it," I said. She peered at me strangely.

"You stealing, Georgie?" She laughed, taking it from me and looking at the cover, then handing it back.

I rolled my eyes. "Yes, I've been planning on taking it for some time."

"Which one is that?" she asked, which confirmed her not being able to read.

Suddenly, I felt terrible for her.

"The one on depression." I tapped the book on the table.

"Oh, that was a dark time, girl, let me tell you. He was dark, so dark," she said, shaking her head. "It was bad, just so bad, Georgie."

I looked through the pantry, thinking I heard a noise.

"I wasn't expecting her home. I've never seen her sit still," I said, looking again, making sure no one was there.

"She never does. Never, never, *never*!" She became louder with each "never," waving her finger back and forth. "Unless that sun is out, and the woman is writing," she finished.

I laughed, watching her dance around the table. "So, you like these times?"

"Yes, yes, I like these times, Georgie. The woman is mad!"

Delia was always saying, "The woman is mad," or "The woman is crazy." I wondered who was crazy or, at least, who was the sanest.

They all are, and so am I. Who cares?

"Well, I'll come by later and give her an update or call. Although I'm sure she has dinner or something, somewhere with someone." I smiled, getting up.

"Of course she does." Delia cackled.

Maybe I'll tell her.

"I'm gonna head home for lunch and pick out clothes for my . . ."—I gave a long pause and headed toward the door, then swung sharply toward her—"date tonight," I blurted, laughing.

"What? Georgie, a date? With who? Tell me. Tell me." She ran to me, grabbing my shoulders.

I wasn't going to say anything but was enjoying my banter with her. I told her all about Dock and last night except that I'd slept at his house, feeling somehow she would disapprove, although nothing had happened.

"I want to see this guy," she said, peeping out the window after I told her he was working on the club, which I now regretted.

"No, stop." I laughed and walked to the table to leave a note for Lilly, figuring it would be easier, at least for me.

"He's the bigger, darker one." I laughed again before heading out the door.

She followed behind me on her tiptoes, pretending to look as I shooed her back in, watching her grab her stomach, giggling.

"Darker is better, Georgie," she called.

I walked through the archway, hearing nothing on the other side. The truck was gone, and the coffee cups sat neatly placed on the bottom step where Will said he'd put them. I was desperately in need of a nap and thankful they weren't here. I took Hobo out, lay back, placed the book on the table beside me, and fell asleep.

I awoke to near darkness in a panic, unsure what time it was, and jumped up, scaring Hobo, who was sleeping next to me. I grabbed my phone from my pocket, but it was dead.

"Damn it!" I yelled, flipping on the light.

I quickly plugged it into the charger on the table, watching what seemed like forever for it to power on. Suddenly, the numbers glowed *6:31*.

I dialed the hospital and asked to speak to the nurse, who took another forever to get on the phone.

"This is Karen."

Thank God, it's Karen.

Hobo stretched on the floor next to me, then wagged his tail and hopped to the door. I put my finger up, telling him he had to wait. He wagged harder, staring at me, jutting out his underbite.

"Hey, Karen. How's the patient?"

"He's the same, sleeping."

"He does that," I chuckled.

"He was in X-ray for a while this afternoon. There was a holdup, so he was there longer than expected."

"Oh? I'm sure he wasn't happy about that."

She laughed. "No, he wasn't."

"Can you transfer me to his room?"

"Sure thing. His wife is there now, so she may answer."

The phone rang a few times before the familiar "Hello" answered on the other end.

Lilly's voice could be intimidating. It wasn't purposeful, just who she was. It always made me think of well-dressed folks with cigarette holders and brandy snifters. I had become used to her voice now, although it made me intensely aware of my blue-collar Boston accent, so I often found myself trying to enunciate more when speaking around her.

"Hello," the voice said again.

"Lilly, hi. It's George."

"Oh, hi, George," she said kindly.

"How is he doing?" I asked quickly, not letting her get a word in.

"He's resting."

I heard someone in the background.

"It's George," Lilly said, holding the receiver away from her. "Well, now he's up." She laughed. "Therapy came in, and he's upset."

"Oh, okay. He needs to work hard with them, Lilly," I said, trying not to drop my *R*s.

"I know; I told him."

"Do you need anything?" I asked, secretly hoping she didn't.

"I think we are fine, George. Enjoy your night."

"Okay, I'll be there in the morning. Call me if you need me."

"Bye now," she chimed. I heard him yell in the background, probably at the therapist.

I brought Hobo out, then took the half sandwich Delia had made for me the other day from the fridge, smelling it, seeing if it was still edible. I sat on the bed and ate, then noticed the book on the table beside me. I had time before Dock got here and opened the book, figuring I'd read a little before getting ready. Putting a few pillows behind me, I cozied up to where the bed met the wall.

I felt strange peering into the past of the ailing man, my patient, whom I looked at every day, watching him at a different point in his life—now trying to come to terms with its end. I quickly became lost in his struggles. I was in a time warp of sorts, reading his past but living his present. It seemed odd and intrusive being in his mind. I read a few more pages and glanced at my phone, realizing I had only thirty minutes before Dock would be here, and I hadn't showered yet.

I was hurriedly pulling on my jeans and cardigan when I heard the truck driving on the gravel. My hair was wet, and I didn't have makeup on yet. I quickly put on some mascara and lipstick as he knocked.

"Come in!" I yelled over Hobo's barking.

He filled the small entryway, and I smiled at him as I plugged in my hairdryer.

"Hey there," he said, looking around. He was holding one yellow rose, which was my favorite. *How does he know?*

He put it on the counter and kissed me.

"Hi." I pulled back, widening my eyes. "I'm so sorry. I'm running so late. I went to the hospital and came home and fell asleep."

"Take your time. There's no rush."

He sat on the stool after taking his jacket off and throwing it over the other one. I hurried, feeling him watching.

"Okay, all done," I said. I pushed my hair back with my bandanna and tied it underneath. "What are we doing?" I hoped for a mellower night than the last.

"I had no plans, really. I sort of dropped the ball getting caught up with some things." He leaned toward me, balancing on the stool with one foot, keeping the other on the floor. "I got wine and some junk food, and I have these." He waved a set of keys at me.

"Where are those to?" I was almost afraid to ask.

"The club." He smiled. "It's a nice night. Thought we could pull a few chairs up on the deck and sit out. Start a beach fire, maybe?"

This sounded perfect. I was tired and loved the idea of being in the Yacht Club when we didn't belong. I had a feeling they didn't give him the keys for this purpose, but I played dumb and didn't ask.

"Sounds perfect."

We walked over and sat on the large deck overlooking the sound, wrapping ourselves in blankets I brought from the cottage. I was nervous we'd be in trouble when the motion lights came on, but he assured me he had permission. I didn't believe him, watching as he climbed up and unscrewed the light bulb.

"Permission, huh?" I laughed, and he smiled.

He pulled chips and powdered donuts from the bag he had with the "good" Pinot Grigio from last night.

"I haven't had a donut in forever," I said eagerly, trying to be cute as he touched it to my nose, getting powder all over me.

We laughed, then kissed, and he brushed off my cheek, licking his finger.

We talked about different things. He had a past. I could tell by how he said things, noticing he left out blocks of time and glossed over some of my questions. I wondered if it was family stuff or something more but didn't want to pry.

"I fished for a while out in Alaska," he said.

Alaska? Was he running from something?

"I was alone on the deck, smoking one night, with icebergs all around us." He settled into his chair, telling the story.

Some people work on boats, and it's not a big mystery. Jesus, stop, I told my paranoid imagination.

"There was a full moon, and the water was like glass. Suddenly, this giant eyeball popped up in front of me, scaring the shit out of me."

I smiled at the way his hands moved as he talked.

"An eyeball?" I raised my eyebrow, not knowing where this was going.

"It was a huge orca. You know, a killer whale?"

"I know what an orca is."

"Can I finish?"

"Sorry, carry on."

Lost in thought, staring toward the water, he murmured that it was the most beautiful moment.

He held me close while we sat under the stars, the ferries passing us one by one, following the path of moonlight on the water back and forth from Woods Hole.

We did this the next few nights. I'd see him and Will during the day, passing between the house and cottage. He'd bring me coffee in the morning, and I'd get them coffee or water after lunch, and we'd chat. He, Will, and I would sit on the porch steps and talk about the summer and how excited we were for the warmer weather coming. I couldn't stop him and didn't want to. He kept coming, and I kept letting him. I tried to put a night apart between us, but he wanted to see me, he said, if only to kiss me goodnight, which he did. I wasn't sure what was happening, thinking I should slow things. I didn't feel I could if I wanted to, and I didn't want to.

Then, just like that, he was gone.

CHAPTER 15

April 5, 2003
There's a place in the world for melancholy people.

*H*appily, Mr. S. was coming home. Although it was Friday and I wouldn't have minded a free weekend, I missed his grumpy, challenging ways. I missed his madness and the melancholy and structure of our daily routine. I sat in the hospital room with him, waiting what seemed like forever for Pat to come and go over everything.

"Glad to be leaving?" I asked as he sat slumped in the wheelchair.

"This place is horrendous." He adjusted himself and turned toward the window.

"Well, they got you better, so they aren't so bad."

He said nothing, gazing at his hands.

Pat came in, cheerful and bubbly as usual. She was always happy and spoke as if she were singing. *She reminds me of someone.*

I watched him stare at her in disbelief, holding myself back from laughing. Overly happy people like Pat bothered him.

My mother.

I liked happiness, like everyone else, but in small doses. I suspected overly happy people, like they were hiding something, portraying overt happiness to cover something sinister.

. . .

I got him into the car with ease; he was stronger than I'd expected.

"You're stronger than when you came." I smiled at him as we headed toward the bridge.

"Not really." He scowled. "Is Lilly home?" he asked, looking at the water.

"She was this morning."

I left it at that. I didn't want to tell him I'd heard there were dinner plans and guests at the house for the weekend. I didn't want to listen to him yell.

"I hear Annie, the kids, and Molly are coming tomorrow."

Molly was one of his other daughters. She was a singer and my favorite. She had a quiet presence about her that was calming. Mr. S. and Lilly had four children in all, three girls and a son. They were all at the house over the holidays, but none of them had come in a while. With summer close, they'd be here more often.

"Oh."

A man of many words.

I'd come to the house early this morning, missing Dock and Will. I thought about the past few nights with Dock and how he kissed me. I had seen him nearly every night this week since Mr. S. stayed in the hospital longer than we anticipated.

He told me he wanted to take me out this weekend, and I was happy to go out amongst the living. Some restaurants had opened, and the island was springing to life again. I thought about the summer and what it would be like with Dock and Will around. Bobbie had called last night, telling me she was coming back early after the hospital called.

"I'll be here at the end of next week," she said as I screamed with excitement. "Ouch, my ears, George!"

"I have news too," I said, concerned it might disappoint her as it could change things. "It's been a long winter, but . . ."

"But what?"

"I have a boy."

"Oh, wow."

"Well, not a boy. I guess he's a man. He's a little older and hasn't peed his pants yet." I laughed.

"That's promising," she said, sounding serious. "And who's this man who doesn't pee his pants?"

"He's—"

"Shit. Fill me in next week. I have to run, duty calls," she cut me off.

I heard someone in the background; I'd forgotten she was at work.

"Will do."

We pulled down the drive and spotted Delia waiting for us on the grass. She ran to the car and opened his door.

"Good to see you, Mr. S." She smiled brightly.

He leaned on her arm, trying to stand.

"He's in good shape, Delia." I tried to sound encouraging. I grabbed his bags, and we walked into the house.

"Take me to the living room." He hurried, stumbling forward.

Delia laughed. "Slow down, Mr. S."

"Be careful!" I shouted.

"Lilly!" he yelled as Lady ran up, sniffing him, wagging her tail. "Lady." He smiled and flopped onto the couch.

Papers were thrown about and crinkled underneath him. He reached, tapping her head while she squinted with each blow.

"Hang on, Mr. S., let's move that stuff under you." I set the bags down and helped him up while Delia grabbed all the papers.

"You're home, darling," Lilly's prep-school voice chimed as she floated in from her office. She walked toward him, smiling. "Kurt is coming for dinner, darling. I thought that might cheer you up."

Do these two even know each other?

I cringed, feeling Delia burning a hole in my back with her gaze. I quickly interrupted before the explosion. "I'm going to go put your things away and then head to the pharmacy, Mr. S."

"Goddamn it, Lilly!" he yelled, interrupting me, then broke out coughing.

"But you love Kurt," she said as I exited the room.

I ran up the stairs, hearing Delia's footsteps behind me.

"That goddamn woman." Delia nodded, smiling.

I headed into the closet and put the bags down.

"Not my business." I pulled a folder from the shelf, putting the hospital papers in. I walked past her toward his room, and she followed.

"What the hell does she have that writer man coming from Connecticut for? The man just got home from the hospital, for the love of Jesus!"

"I don't know, and I don't pretend to. He loves Kurt, I guess." I shrugged, straightening his bed.

"He loves no one but fucking Lady." She slapped her hand on the bed.

I didn't care who was coming. There was always someone coming, and I wasn't sure how this still seemed to surprise her after thirty years, although I figured she just wanted to gossip about Lilly.

"She is a piece of work." She slapped harder on the bed, throwing her head back, laughing.

"You're crazy." Her turban had become crooked. Her hair was falling out, and I laughed with her nervously, feeling she was coming unhinged.

"No, they're crazy, Georgie," she cackled loudly.

"What the heck are all of the papers for?" I asked, putting clothes away in the drawer.

"Who the hell knows, girl." She sat, fixing her turban.

Why am I getting into this?

"It's writing, phone numbers, appointments. It's all of the crazy." She nodded back and forth. Her voice was loud, and I was worried Lilly would hear her. I knew she must have at times, but she never said anything, except for that day with Karla.

"Everything is important! Everything, Georgie!" she snapped, putting her fingers toward her mouth. "Shhh," she whispered, tiptoeing toward the door. "She's coming." She looked at me. The white in her eyes glowed against her dark skin.

"Delia," Lilly's voice rang up the stairs. "Delia!"

"Yes, Mrs. S., coming," she called back, heading into the hall, mumbling, "Crazy."

I went into the bathroom and put the rest of his things away, then noticed the red truck out the window. Feeling a flutter in my stomach, I figured I'd pop over and say hi before going into town to the pharmacy.

What's happening to me?

I rolled my eyes at myself in the mirror. I wondered what it would be like to sleep with Dock. I hadn't yet, and he hadn't tried, which I thought was odd, but I liked the anticipation.

"I'll be back, Lilly," I said, coming down and poking my head into the living room, unsure she'd heard me.

I crossed the lawn and passed through the arch. Someone was in the truck, and I walked up and saw it was him.

"Hey, you," I said into the window, surprising him.

"Hey." He quickly folded a piece of paper and tucked it under his phone. I stepped back as he got out and took my hand, pulling me to him.

"Are you calling your wife or your dealer?" I joked, putting my chin on his chest and peering up at him, wondering about the paper.

"What?" He pushed me away to look at me. "No." He laughed. "It's payday. The job here's done until we get the second permit. I'm buying a part for the bike. The last one I need, and it will be running."

"Oh, nice. That's great." *Why am I always so suspicious?*

"I have to go off-island and pick it up. Leaving on the next boat, I hope, so I won't be back until later." He reached in the truck and pulled the ferry schedule from the console.

"Okay, so maybe I'll see you later? Or let me know?" I finished, annoyed that I sounded desperate.

"I'll call you when I'm back and see where you're at." He leaned down, taking my shoulders. "Jesus, you're beautiful."

"Stop," I said, embarrassed.

"What? You are." He kissed my forehead and walked back to the truck. "Okay, I'll check in later?" he asked, sounding like he was appeasing me.

I smiled but still felt annoyed. Something was different, but I wasn't sure what.

"Gotta run. Two fifteen boat." He kissed me again, then got in the truck.

"Where's Will?" I asked.

"He's off-island too. I'll call you tonight." He hurried off, spinning the tires on the grass.

I stepped out of the way, watching him leave up the drive.

• • •

Days and nights went by, and I heard nothing from him. I couldn't imagine what had changed or happened, and I slowly became too angry to care—at least, that's what I'd told myself. I wracked my brain, trying to figure it out, but I couldn't.

Maybe my suspiciousness drove him off? Why can't I trust anyone?

I called once, and it went right to voicemail. I wouldn't call again, although I wanted to. I just didn't understand. At first, I was concerned something might have happened and hoped he was okay. Then the days wore on, and anger settled in—the familiar anger, where I was the fool.

Fuck him.

I had a burning desire to hunt him down and smack him, but more importantly, I wanted an answer. Was I right that something was off or just paranoid because of my fucked life? I needed to know. I wasn't sure of anything anymore and wondered if I ever was. I knew he cared for me; that was real. I felt it. A few more days passed, and I questioned that too. I questioned everything.

Lilly was away again, and I was at the house most evenings during the week. Mr. S.'s new exercise plan was keeping him and me busy. Mainly the arguing about him not wanting to exercise took up the most time. The exercises themselves took minutes if he'd do them. It wasn't like he was busy doing anything, but it was something to be annoyed about, I guessed.

Control.

He had company in the evenings that Lilly set up before she left. Annie and Molly were there too, so he stayed busy, much to his dismay, although I knew he enjoyed spending time with them. He had a softer look when he talked with his children; I'd noticed the other day in the living room. He could do without the others, the evening company, his friends, and the admirers, and he let me know it every chance he got.

I spent a lot of time sitting alone in his room, reading in the oversized chair I'd pulled close to the door so I could hear if he needed me. I was also trying to avoid Delia as I wasn't much in the mood for talking. Every free moment, my brain was filled with thoughts and wondering about Dock. I tried my best to keep occupied before I did something foolish. In a few days, Bobbie would be here, and she couldn't get here fast enough.

I'd noticed Mr. S.'s book on the table in the cottage earlier after stopping home to walk Hobo. I had forgotten about it but figured it was as good a time as any to read; darkness was the perfect genre for me right now. I wanted to be in anyone's mind besides my own, and Mr. S.'s was as good as any. I opened the cover, rereading the title. The words underneath, *Memoir of a Mad Man,* I stared at, having not noticed the subtitle before. I turned to where I left off, with him in London, and plunged in, leaving Dock and the bullshit behind.

"For those who have never bathed in depression's dark and turbulent seas, and known its torture, the return to life is not unlike the ascent of a mountain, trudging its steep and high rock, upward out of the depths of hell, born into a new and unfamiliar world. Life is now cherished, and a greater capacity for joy and love may be assurance enough for enduring depression's unimaginable despair."

I thought of my struggles with my anxiety over the years and felt I understood. I never thought of myself as depressed but knew they went hand and hand, and I wondered.

"It is the numbness and the hopelessness of it more than the pain that

pulverizes the soul" were the words I ended on and closed the book. My father's face, his eyes, appeared in my mind as the word *hopeless* rang in my head—an accurate description. My stomach sank, picturing those eyes' sadness. I didn't want to think of him, at least not now.

I thought of what he'd said on the island that weekend when he found me after the meeting. I was sitting on the overturned boat by the Black Dog Tavern in the same spot we were before.

"I'd rather be dead than ever drink again, George." He looked at me confidentially as if trying to reassure me. Oddly, he wasn't wearing his sunglasses, and I stared into his blue eyes, the same eyes as mine. Something seemed different, but I couldn't think of what. He paused, squinting back at me, then reached in his pocket, pulling out a small box.

"When I couldn't find you on Main Street, I stopped in a few of the shops looking for you, and I saw this," he said, handing it to me. "I thought you might like it."

I took the box and opened it, seeing a chain with a small gold charm in the island's shape. I took it out and held it, staring past it, watching my feet moving the sand, not knowing what to say when I realized what it was. His eyes, they didn't have the hopelessness in them anymore, and I hadn't seen it for a while. He was working hard to be better; he was better and had been for some time, and I'd fought him every step of the way.

I realized then I needed to let it go. I needed to let my guard down and let my father be my father, and after that weekend, that's what I did.

• • •

Friday finally came. The week felt like it lasted forever. Barbara, the nurse who'd helped last summer, was back on the island. I saw her at the grocery store and asked if she was interested in working again. Between her and Karen at the hospital, I was hopeful for a few days off.

He'll just have to deal with it.

Bobbie said she was on too many shifts at the hospital and didn't think she could. I wanted my days off to go out with her anyway, especially with Dock gone. Barbara agreed to work tonight as I was picking Bobbie up at the boat at seven. I was excited to see her and go out and get everything off my mind.

"George!" Mr. S. yelled.

I sat cozily tucked in the chair overlooking the sound out the window. I had it half opened to air the room, and the warm, salty air swirled around me. I was lost in London, deep into his descension some twenty-odd years ago:

"Loss and all that comes with it is the root of depression. I believed that a devastating childhood loss triggered my disease, and while in it, I felt loss at every turn. There is a palpable fear of losing, again and again, being more alone than you were before."

I enjoyed reading again as I hadn't in a while. Reading and writing were always an interest of mine. I journaled most of my life and wondered why I hadn't lately, feeling the urge to empty my mind. I pulled at my necklace and twirled the charm, trying to remember.

"George!" he called again.

"Yes, I'm here," I called back. I headed down the stairs.

"What's that?" he asked, pointing.

I looked down and realized I was still holding the book.

Oh, boy.

"It's your book," I said nervously, wondering if I should have sought permission from him to read it, although I could get it anywhere.

"Oh," he only said, although he seemed to want to say more.

"Barbara is on her way," I said as he gestured to the porch. "I'm just preparing you." I watched his face for a reaction.

"Who?" he asked, stumbling toward the slider.

I opened the door, and we headed to the chairs. The sun hung low in the sky, and the ferry had just passed, causing the waves to lap against the shore. He pointed up, and I looked as an osprey flew by, heading close to the ferry.

"Barbara. The nurse from last summer." I waited for this to sink in, bracing myself.

"Oh, God!" he choked.

"It will be fine. It's one night," I said, darting into the house for his tissue box. "And I will be back in the morning," I finished. Coming back out, I put the box next to him. "I promise." I lightly put my hand on his arm.

The ferry horn blew as it pulled close to Vineyard Haven, and we sat quietly as the afternoon passed by.

CHAPTER 16

April 13, 2003
The rising light at the start of the Vineyard season awakens
the soul no matter how dark it's become.

"Over here!" I squealed, waving my arms at Bobbie as she rolled her bag off the boat.

"You're a sight for sore eyes," she laughed while we walked toward my car to head up-island to Chilmark.

"I'm so glad you're here!" I tapped the steering wheel excitedly on the drive.

She smirked, sticking her hand out the window. "Don't get all sentimental on me now."

"Why the hell are you in Chilmark, for the love of God?" I asked as we passed Alley's General Store and the fairgrounds.

"They have me here until Monday; then it's back to the log cabin." She tried hard not to smile, knowing how excited I'd be. Bobbie and a few other nurses had stayed in the log cabin last summer. The hospital rented the huge five-bedroom house with a jacuzzi and pool table right in town.

"No way!" I yelled. "How did you manage that?"

"I asked." She shrugged, giggling.

"I'm very excited about this."

"I figured you would be, considering you spent almost every night there last year."

"Yeah, yeah." I waved my hand. "How was the boat? I detect the smell of an Offshore." I leaned over, sniffing.

"Of course I had one. Two, actually, but don't tell."

I noticed the redness in her cheeks, confirming the second beer.

"Best part of the boat ride back." She stared out the window.

"I love coming back. The metal doors close, and the horn blows. I take a sip of my beer, and all's right with the world," I said, thinking of how I hadn't been off the island in a while and had been avoiding it.

I should go and see my mother—shitty daughter.

"You don't have to sell it to me. That's why we keep coming back, and you're here forever, you say." She danced happily in her seat, then changed the subject. "So, tell me about your guy?"

I was hoping she would forget.

We pulled into the driveway to a little cottage nestled in the woods and went in to check it out. It reminded me of the cottage where I stayed, except she was in the middle of nowhere. I told Bobbie all about Dock, bringing her up to speed. Once I started talking, I couldn't seem to stop, and the feelings of it all flooded me.

"Maybe he's in a ditch dead somewhere," she said, pulling on her shirt, looking in the mirror.

"I doubt it." I lay back on the bed and swung my legs back and forth, staring at the ceiling. "Maybe he's just not that into me?"

"You're crazy," she said, sitting next to me. "They are all into you. You got that city-edge thing that keeps them wanting more." She hit me in the leg.

"So, doesn't he? Maybe it repels against itself." I laughed. "Whatever. I don't even want to talk about it. Let's go have fun."

"Perfect." She smiled but regarded me seriously, making sure I was all right.

"I'm fine! Let's go."

We headed to Oak Bluffs and made our way around, meeting up

with everyone who was out and about. Although the season wasn't in full swing yet, it was the weekend, and the weather was warm, so the island was busy. Bobbie was back, and everything felt different. She had been coming to the island for a few years now, and it was like a celebrity had landed. Every bar we went to, she knew the bartender and at least half of the people in it, and they all lit up when they saw her. We walked by the pier and had to stop and talk to three boats full of people she knew from previous summers.

Bobbie enjoyed life, and she didn't have an agenda. Being a non-trusting type suspect of everyone, I enjoyed being with her. She took me out of myself, and everything felt carefree and comfortable. I could breathe, like I was coming to life again.

We ended the night at Seasons, as we usually did. It thrilled Vince to see Bobbie, and he gave her a big hug, letting us in for free without us even asking about his grandmother. I saw a few of the Irish boys from last summer and followed them outside to smoke. We laughed and caught up. I noticed a motorcycle pull in across the street and watched as the man got off and took off his helmet. I recognized him immediately and yelled out.

"Will!" I waved and jumped up and down.

"Hey." He pointed, finally noticing me.

I crossed the street, tipsy enough not to overthink it.

"Hey yourself," I said, coming close, unsure what to say next.

"How goes it, George?" he asked. He strapped his helmet to the seat and doffed his jacket.

"Are you coming in here?" I smiled, putting my hand on the bike and taking a long drag of my cigarette in an awkward attempt to be cool.

"I guess I am now."

"Yay." I pretended to clap, almost burning my hand.

"Who are you with?" he asked as we crossed the street together.

"Not your brother," I said, quickly regretting it. I watched for his reaction from the corner of my eye but didn't see one.

We made our way through the Irish boys, who tried pulling me back in their circle of drunken mayhem, but I ignored them and walked in.

The music seemed louder to me now, and it annoyed me; I wanted to talk and hear him when we did.

"You know those guys?" he asked, peering back, hearing them call my name.

"They're harmless," I said and grabbed his hand, which seemed to surprise him.

I pulled him forward to two open seats in the back of the bar, far away from the stage. Bobbie saw us and waved across the room. I waved back, noticing her puzzled expression.

"*Dock?*" she mouthed when Will turned to sit. I shook my head, shooing her with my hand.

"I guess I dragged you in here." I laughed, realizing how forceful I'd been.

The false confidence from alcohol fueled me.

"I do nothing I don't want to do, George." He smiled, throwing his wallet and keys on the bar.

Betsy put two beers in front of me, and Bobbie waved again across the room. I waved back, and Will held up his beer in thanks.

"That was nice of her. That your friend?"

"Yes, that's Bobbie. We worked at the hospital together."

There was an awkward silence for a moment that seemed to last forever. I swung my stool, turning to him, and crossed my legs, trying to come up with something intelligent to say about Dock. I couldn't think of anything. I looked down, watching my ankle move back and forth, and stopped; it reminded me of my father. I stared at my beer, suddenly wanting to push it away. Instead, I picked it up and rebelliously took a long sip.

I don't care. I'm not him.

"I haven't seen you guys." I tossed my hair and rested my elbow on the bar, looking at him.

He took a sip of his beer and glanced around the room, then at me.

"I've been in New Bedford for a job but back now. A job's about to start here." He looked around again as if trying to avoid eye contact.

"Staying on my friend's boat." He smiled awkwardly, turning toward me. "Boat sitting."

I could tell he was uncomfortable. He drank his beer fast, then waved to Betsy for another.

"Your brother's a ghost."

"I haven't seen him in a while."

"Isn't he working with you?" I perked up, unable to resist.

"Supposed to be. I talked to him the other day but haven't gone to the house. I like it on the boat."

He was clearly trying to avoid the conversation, so I let it go for now.

"What about the rest of the club job?"

"Just waiting on another permit."

Betsy dropped two more beers in front of us. He quickly picked his up and took a long sip.

"Unfortunately for you, we'll be back." He playfully kicked my leg.

Betsy came back and put three shot glasses down, and Bobbie approached from behind, clapping. I introduced her, thankful for the distraction.

"Oh no," Will and I said at the same time, laughing. We all grabbed our glasses.

"Cheers to a great Vineyard summer," Bobbie said, standing between us.

The night went on in a blur. Bobbie and I danced and pulled Will on the floor. They gave the last call, and as usual, Bobbie didn't want to go home, and neither did I. Will and I made our way outside.

"You coming to the house, Georgie?" Mark, one of the Irish boys, called to me. He leaned against the streetlight coolly, talking to two girls smoking. He liked me last summer, but I started seeing his friend, although it never stopped him from flirting when no one was looking.

Will looked at me and rolled his eyes.

"Not tonight, Mark."

"What about tonight?" Bobbie asked as she joined us on the sidewalk.

She was with two girls and a guy I wasn't sure I recognized.

"Our house. Come with us, Bobs," Mark said to her.

"We going?" she asked, as I shook my head no.

"Not me."

She turned her lip in disappointment.

"We're going, Mark," she said, looking at the girl and guy next to her.

"You know where it is," Mark said and walked past. He had a group of people following.

"George and her new friend are too good for us," he yelled back, trying to incite something.

"Watch yourself," Will said, blowing smoke in their direction.

Thankfully, Mark kept walking. He and the other Irish guys liked altercations, although they were usually smart enough to only have them with each other. They didn't want to get deported.

"Are you sure you don't want to go, guys?" Bobbie put her hands on my shoulders. "It's my first night back, George!" She shook me back and forth.

I laughingly pushed her away. I would have gone, but with the way Will wasn't interested, going to Mark's somehow seemed childish, and for some reason, I cared what he thought.

And I'd like to find out more about Dock.

"All right, guys." She nodded, hugging Will first, then squeezing me tight. "Make sure this one gets home okay." She turned again, pointing at me.

Will gave her a thumbs-up.

The street began to clear, and I realized I'd driven and would need a cab. I wasn't driving anywhere, especially now that I was living in Vineyard Haven. The cops always waited on the other side of the bridge for people at this time of night, and I didn't know Vineyard Haven cops like Oak Bluffs ones. I wasn't sure they were in on the stethoscope agreement, and I wouldn't risk going to jail to find out. I looked across the street, noticing Will's motorcycle.

"You drove your bike."

"I did." He laughed at me as I stated the obvious. "I'm not riding it now." He shook his head. "Plus, I don't take passengers."

"Thanks," I said, insulted.

"No, no. It's not you. I just haven't yet, and 'yet' kept, well, getting longer and longer. Now I'm superstitious about it." He looked at my reaction. "I know it's weird." He smiled.

"Cab?" I asked, squinting at the streetlight shining on us.

"The boat's right in the harbor. Can walk. Let me go put you in a cab, though." He paused, scratching his chin. "Or did you want to come back to the boat? I got some beers?" he asked, seeming nervous.

"Sure."

Why did I answer so quickly?

We walked toward the harbor. He was quiet, his hands in his pockets. It was getting colder, and I hugged myself, wishing I'd brought a jacket.

"Here," he said, noticing. He stopped and shook off his jacket, offering it to me.

"Aw, thanks." I reached for it, but instead, he put it on my shoulders and tapped my back like I was his buddy. "Oh my God, it's right here?" We passed Nancy's Bar on the way to the harbor, weaving through the people exiting.

"Yup. Great, huh?"

"Why did you even ride your bike?"

"She needed a ride, and I was coming back from Menemsha."

I followed him up the boat ramp and took my shoes off. He kicked off his boots and took my hand, helping me aboard.

"Taking in sunsets by yourself?" I smiled.

"It's a lonely life, but I do all right." He laughed and grabbed a beer from a cooler. "Hope this is okay," he said, handing me one, wiping the top of his with his shirt before opening it.

"Anything is fine this time of night." I took a long sip, looking around. "Is Dock's bike running?" I figured I'd segue Dock in again. I sat on the bow, leaning back against the windshield.

"It should be. He only had one part left to get, and I thought he said he got it."

Forgetting what I'd asked, I turned, looking at him strangely, then quickly remembered.

I listened to the sounds of the night winding down. The harbor wasn't full yet, but it was all starting. He sat next to me. I took another long sip and felt it. A breeze picked up, and I should have been cold, but the alcohol made me warm and fuzzy.

"What's the big mystery here? Is he, like, married or something?" I was irritated, not holding back anymore.

Will chuckled. "No, he's not married." He seemed uncomfortable again. "He just, he does his own thing," he stuttered. "You probably deserve more, ya know?"

"À la James Dean," I scoffed, tapping my beer can on the deck.

"He's had his issues, George," he said, looking away. "We all have them, right?" He sighed.

It irritated me, the vagueness shrouded in mystery, but I wanted to enjoy the night, so I let it go again. I didn't want to keep pressing him.

"So, what's your story?" he asked, thankfully changing the subject.

"Story? I don't know. Guess it's the same as everyone else's." I wasn't sure what he meant and didn't feel like elaborating. I was tired and becoming fiery.

"What brought you here, I mean?" He nudged me, crossing his legs.

"I came when I was a teenager with my father and liked it," I answered, pointing to two girls dancing funny on the pier.

That day with my father—I wish I could go back to it, feel it all again. My eyes filled unexpectedly, and I put my beer down.

"I think I've had enough." I laughed, touching my face, making sure there wasn't moisture.

"What's wrong?" he asked, his voice solemn and soft.

"Nothing, I'm stupid." I tilted my head back, blinking.

"This is a happy place." He nudged me again. "Vacationland."

"I know. I love vacationland." I cleared my throat. "The weekend was sort of special. I don't know. Whatever. I'm a little drunk."

He leaned toward me, whispering, "Tell me where you were when you realized it. Then I'll tell you where I was." He tapped my knee, trying to change the mood. "C'mon." He stood up. "Then we'll never talk about it again." He laughed. "It'll be our secret," he said, pretending to lock his mouth with his fingers.

"You're an idiot." I giggled. I took a deep breath before I spoke, unsure why this was so difficult. "I was sitting with my father on one of the rowboats on the little beach near the Black Dog, looking at Vineyard Sound." I stared ahead. "I felt different. It felt good here." I realized this didn't sound very interesting and shrugged again, feeling silly.

"I know exactly the spot." He smiled, taking another sip of his beer, tossing the empty can.

"Okay, your turn. Maybe yours is more eventful."

"All right." He looked serious. "Dock and I skipped school one day. We were stupid, ya know? Dock had money; I'm not sure where he got it, and I didn't ask." We both laughed.

He leaned against the railing, looking up.

"We hitchhiked to the boat and came over for the day, had the best time, swimming and walking around."

I could tell he was enjoying the memory, and it made me smile, eager to listen.

"We somehow got beers," he went on, "and Dock, he had a joint." He brushed his hair back. "We smoked, then fell asleep on some beach near the lagoon and almost missed the last ferry back." He crossed his arms, nodding back and forth. "It was a good day." He moved close, gesturing again like he was locking his mouth.

"I better get going," I said, yawning.

He was gazing at the sky again. He seemed so peaceful. He turned to me, and just then, I saw it. It was quick, but I noticed. He looked at me how Dock did, and I knew he felt something. I wasn't sure if it was the alcohol, but it was there. Our eyes met, and I quickly looked down to stop it. He reached out his hand, helping me up, and I kept my head down, walking toward the edge of the boat.

"Thanks for the beer, Will. I'll just jump in a cab." I stepped onto the ramp and hurriedly put on my shoes.

"Let me walk you," he said, following me as I headed down.

I noticed a cab right in front of Nancy's.

"One right there," I pointed out, smiling, and kept walking.

He stopped at the top of the ramp.

"Okay, well, be careful." He waved, appearing confused.

"Good night."

I waved again and made a locking gesture with my hand at my mouth, pretending to toss the key in the water.

CHAPTER 17

April 14, 2003
There was no insecurity, forethought, or decision.
It was raw, miraculous, and angelic—impossible to resist.
It came from deep within us, a place I never knew existed.

I woke to rain tapping loudly on the gutter, feeling like I had just fallen asleep. Sitting up in the darkness, I heard what sounded like a car door and wondered if I was dreaming. Hobo barked, and I swung my legs over to the edge of the bed as he leaped and ran to the door.

I became enraged, figuring it must be Delia, then looked at my phone and, seeing the time, became more agitated. In the middle of the night, all bets were off, whether it was her or Lilly. I needed a life too. I groggily opened the door and was ready to let her have it when Hobo pushed through, attempting an escape. I pinned him with my leg against the doorframe and reached down for him, then spotted the large work boots in front of me. I jumped back dizzily, still feeling the effects of the sleep, and blinked to focus through the rain.

His face came into view; I wondered if I was dreaming again. I put Hobo behind me, blocking him with my legs, and faced him in silence. Ocean waves broke at the pillars under the club's dock, and thunder shuddered off in the distance. He was soaked and looked thin and tired. The club lights came on, and he squinted, tucking his chin into his jacket.

"George," he said in a low voice, clearing his throat.

I awakened from my trance. "No," I growled.

I went to close the door, giving him a serious look. I wasn't interested in what he had to say, but he grabbed the door, preventing me from shutting it.

"What do you want, Dock? What?" I threw my hands up in anger.

"Let me talk to you. Let me come in for a minute."

"There's nothing to say. It's the middle of the night. Why now?"

My face grew hot. He looked at me, saying nothing, moving closer under the awning as the rain came down harder. My head hurt, and I wanted to sleep. As much as I wanted answers, I didn't want them now.

He touched my arm, coming closer to tower over me. He smelled like cigarettes, which made me ill but, mixed with the smell of him, was tolerable. Grabbing my shoulders, he moved me back into the cottage. I looked at his hands on me, then at his face. His eyes were wild now, and his bottom lip trembled. He stepped over the threshold, moving me with him.

"What are you doing?" I demanded.

I felt his hand shaking on my shoulder.

"I need you," he whispered and leaned down, putting his lips to mine.

It was dark, and I stepped away from him, but he stepped closer. I tried to speak, and he stopped me, grabbed me, and kissed me hard and forcefully. I pushed my hands against him, but he didn't move. I tried turning my head from him, and he touched my face, turning it back to him. He shut the door behind him, not breaking his gaze. I stood like a statue, unsure of what was happening, wondering how to stop it; but I was unsure I wanted it to stop. I'd never seen anyone like this. I'd never felt anything like this, and I tried hard to make sense of it all. He didn't seem drunk. He seemed crazed, desperate, and exhausted. He moved me again, and I felt the bed against the back of my legs. He let his coat fall to the floor, brushing the wetness from his hair back. I said nothing as he grabbed my face with both hands.

"Look at me," he whispered.

A strong wind blew, and the motion light came in dimly through the blinds. I could see his face and watched him closely. He stared at me as if seeking approval for what was about to happen. I dropped my gaze to his boots, suddenly feeling vulnerable and childlike. He touched under my chin and pushed his body against me, and I smelled him again. The familiars of him came rushing back.

He whispered something I couldn't make out, then nuzzled his head against my cheek, moving down, kissing behind my neck and ear. I tilted my head back, letting him, suddenly becoming lost in it all.

He moved to my lips again, and I felt the warmth of his hands under my shirt.

"It's you; I need you," he whispered again. "I can't stop needing you, George. I'm sorry. I'm so sorry."

He stopped, hanging his head low for a moment, then moved in again, kissing me hard, putting his hand on my back, and looked into my eyes once more. I stared at him sternly but couldn't help surrendering.

He smiled and gently laid me back on the bed. He kissed me fiercely now, feeling me succumb to him, and I kissed him back. He stopped, bracing himself over me with his hand, and looked as if he was about to cry. Leaning down, he pressed his lips to my forehead. I pulled him toward me, and the lights outside went off, and I was his.

• • •

The wind howled, banging the screen door against the doorframe. I lay trembling, naked, wrapped in his giant arms that engulfed me in the small bed that barely fit us. He kissed the back of my head and stroked my hair while I cried. I cried so hard I could scarcely breathe, and he pulled me closer to him, sweeping me up on his lap, holding me like a baby. I tucked my face into his chest, feeling foolish as the tears poured, and I softly wailed along with the wind, unable to stop what was happening.

I tried to explain but was unsure if I made any sense; none of it made sense. It was the first time I had ever really cried about my father. I was so confused, wondering why now; it seemed strange and inappropriate. I was exposed and vulnerable, allowing him in, and it felt like a dam had broken, and everything inside of me came rushing out uncontrollably. Dock's lips, his smell, and how he made me think and feel was nothing I'd ever experienced, and I let go for the first time I could remember.

"It's okay, baby," he said, still holding me.

He rocked me like an infant, watching as I sniffled, trying to breathe. I caught his eyes, then turned back into his chest, feeling dizzy.

"What about your dad? It's okay; tell me." He wiped the side of my face.

Feeling me shiver, he pulled the blanket up over our naked bodies, then tucked it under my side.

"He's gone," I yelled, throwing my arms back as if expecting him to know. I pressed my hands over my face. "I'm sorry, I'm sorry." I grabbed the blanket, wiping my eyes.

Why is this happening? Why now?

I rested my neck on his arm, gazing up while tears continued to fall. I felt my nose run but didn't care. He gently moved me off his lap and placed me on the bed, fixing the pillow behind my head. I watched the silhouette of his naked body move across the room, then come into full view as the light came through the blinds when he opened the door. I stared at the ceiling, wiping away the tears, trying to make sense of the madness. I heard him light a cigarette and I looked over, watching the wind take the smoke as he blew out into the night.

"You're so beautiful." He turned to me, inhaling. "I hate seeing you cry."

I felt foolish, but I was too exhausted to care. I wrapped the blanket around me and went over to him at the door. He put the cigarette to my lips, and I inhaled. My head pounded, and I needed sleep, but I was overrun with emotion and felt as if I were on another planet.

"Tell me what happened to your dad." He looked at me, then took a long drag.

"He's dead." I stared at the ceiling again. "He's just fucking dead," I said, walking back to the bed.

I curled into a ball, putting my face in the pillow, trying to silence my cry. I couldn't stop crying, and I didn't want to relive it. He was gone, dead, and not coming back. It was nearly ten years ago, and it felt like I had just found out.

His arms were back around me, and he kissed my head.

"Just cry. Let it out. I'm here," he whispered.

"I'm dying," I said.

"Out drinking will do that." He got up again and went to the fridge, grabbing some water.

How does he know? This island is too small. Does he know I was with Will?

My stomach twisted nervously.

"Hair of the dog, maybe? Do you have any beer?" He laughed, opening the fridge again.

"No. God no."

I attempted to sit up, pulling the blanket to my chest. My eyes felt swollen, my mouth like a desert.

Hair of the dog was something I would never do. Being Catholic and living in alcoholism my whole life, I felt I deserved the suffering. It was a sort of penance for partaking in something I should know better not to.

I grew annoyed with how easily he assumed things were fine between us; I was angry with myself.

Why wouldn't he?

But they were fine. I didn't want to discuss anything. I hadn't demanded to know where he was and what happened. I asked but didn't push it, and asking now seemed odd, and I was too tired. I liked being with him and wanted it to continue, so I pushed the thoughts from my head.

"You okay?"

He pulled the blanket around my shoulders, and I nodded, feeling exposed and powerless.

I don't want to cry.

"Wanna talk about it?" he asked as he sat next to me.

"I don't know where to start." I sighed.

"How did he die?"

I hesitated, lip quivering, unsure I wanted to do this.

"Why am I telling you this?" I stared into his eyes, blinking back the tears.

"Because you can." He touched my hand.

I rested my head on his shoulder and permitted myself to trust him. I wanted to trust him; although I shouldn't, I was already there. I felt feminine and alive. In succumbing to him, there was a beautiful vulnerability I'd never known. I knew I shouldn't trust him. I shouldn't trust anyone, but I needed to. He felt safe and like everything I'd ever known and unsafe for the same reasons. I didn't understand it, but I couldn't escape. I didn't want to.

I gave him the backstory of growing up and when he got sober. I told him of the weekend on the island and going to the meeting and how things changed. I still hadn't processed why now. Why, after sex, making love, did this come out? I felt dirty and strange, hoping he didn't think the same. No one had ever made me feel the way he did.

No one has ever made me feel much at all. I want to feel.

I wanted to feel everything, even if it was only today. I started and didn't stop, telling him all of it.

Fuck it.

CHAPTER 18

December 11, 1995
If I say goodbye, it's real. I won't say it. I'll say—fuck you.

*A*fter the Vineyard trip with my dad, things were different. Listening to him at the meeting and suddenly seeing him as a man, a person other than just my father, changed things. He had been sober and stayed sober long enough for all of us to feel like it was our new normal. The insanity we lived in started to feel like some other lifetime. He and I had changed.

It was weird at first, living how "normal" people lived. That's all we'd ever wanted to be, and now we were, mostly. Mom and Dad went to work and came home at the same time every day. Grocery shopping was Friday. Tuesday and Thursday, Dad went to his meetings, and Sundays, we had a family dinner. A life of predictability was foreign, but we settled right in, finally free from the troubled world and on our way to becoming like the families Ray and I envied from TV: the Keatons or the Cosbys—those normal, happy ones, except we'd be the gritty Revere version. There was nothing to be unhappy about, except regular stuff. I used to tell myself and Ray that it was all phony, the people on those shows, and no one lived like that, but I knew now they kind of did. Maybe not as perfect, and perhaps they didn't go to AA or Al-Anon, but we were still pretty close.

In the meetings, they tell you that you are never really free of the disease, whether you're the alcoholic or the one affected, but I didn't believe it. We were content, and I let my guard down. I was safe, and we were normal.

Everything felt right until the day everything didn't.

It was five o'clock, and he wasn't home from work yet. It wasn't that big of a deal at first until the hours crept by. I saw my mom trying to read at the table but could tell she was unsettled. I went to my room in disbelief, thinking of other reasons he could be so late without calling, but couldn't shake what I knew.

All the familiar feelings came rushing back as if they'd never left, and my stomach was in knots. My body immediately recalled how to feel this way; it remembered, and I hated it. I sat in my room waiting, finally hearing the door open downstairs, and leaped from the bed. I crept to the hall softly, trying not to make a sound, listening to the voices. Adrenaline filled me, and I was like a tiger ready to pounce. I hoped I was wrong.

Please, God, let me be wrong.

Ray's head popped out of his room, and I waved him back with my hands.

"Dad?" he whispered.

"Shhh," I said, nodding.

Ray had been doing the same thing, waiting.

Minutes felt like hours, then my mother's voice, clear as day.

"Richie, have you been drinking?"

Her voice trembled, and a burning rage rose in my throat. I felt like I could breathe fire. I knew but struggled to believe it was all over. I had hoped, something I knew better about if you wanted to survive. I regretted letting him in. I regretted it all. My entire world was crashing, and a crushing pain entered my chest.

"It was only a few beers," he said, slurring.

I felt Ray's eyes on me, but I wouldn't turn my head. I couldn't look at his face, somehow feeling I'd failed him by showing him it was okay to let it go and let him in, knowing now I should have never. I should have been the smarter one who showed them both you couldn't ever let them get close.

My father started to say something else I couldn't make out. I wasn't listening anymore, anyway. I looked at Ray, his eyes fearful and sad. I became unhinged. I sprang off the steps, barreling down, hearing Ray crying and calling my name.

"You're going to fucking die! Do you hear me? Do you fucking hear me?" I screamed, spitting and crying. "You're fucking dead! Dead!" I sobbed uncontrollably, not remembering how I got there. I had him by the shirt, throwing him as hard as I could against the fridge. "It's done, it's done, Dad. You're, you're . . ."

I collapsed, crying into his chest, feeling someone pull me off him. His eyes were wide and terrified. I stared at him, his face blurry through the tears, wanting to remember what he was or could have been. I felt my knees buckle.

"Stop it, George! Leave him alone!" Ray screamed from the kitchen doorway.

"Don't any of you fucking get it? What is wrong with all of you?" I yelled, wiping my eyes.

I turned back and forth from him to my mother at the table, feeling like I was dreaming. She looked dead inside, numb. Anger raged within me again.

"Fuck you, Dad! Fuck you." I pushed Ray's hand away and glared at my mother.

I went to the closet and grabbed my coat, and left, slamming the door behind me. I heard one of the stained-glass ornament things my mother hung on the window squares fall and crash to the floor. I hoped it was the JFK one. That was her favorite.

I walked and walked until I couldn't anymore. I crossed the street and sat on the beach wall, staring at the ocean. It was dark and cold, and I shivered but stayed where I was. Things would be different now or the same as they once were. Whatever happened, it would be bad. I shouldn't have trusted him and any of it. He was gone, and it was over.

Things will never be the same.

I came home after midnight, and my mother was still at the table. She had a small candle lit and her Al-Anon meditation book opened in front of her. Her face was stiff with worry, and she looked older than her fifty-one years. I walked past, ignoring her. I blamed her, too; I blamed her more.

"George?" she whispered.

I stopped, not saying a word. She said nothing either, and I went upstairs and went to bed. There was nothing to say.

• • •

I avoided being home as much as I could now that he was drinking again. I picked up extra shifts at the Chowder Pot and stayed at my boyfriend's and friends' houses a lot. I took college classes, too, so I kept busy and avoided it all as much as I could.

Just like before, when he started, he didn't stop; he couldn't. Things were different this time. He spiraled fast, faster than I remembered he used to.

He lost his license after getting pulled over for drinking and driving. He sold his beloved Cadillac and anything he had for drinking money, which was new for him. I remembered him once having me sign my mother's names on a few checks when I was small, but he never sold things. His drinking seemed worse; it all did.

"Georgie." I woke up, hearing my name.

I adjusted my eyes and saw my mother leaning over me.

"I'm sorry, George, can you drive me? He took my car."

The sun hit the side of her face, and I noticed dark circles under her eyes I'd never seen before. I stretched, looking at the clock.

He stole my mother's car at night sometimes to go to the bar, and she'd wake up with no way to work. I had a car with my boyfriend, a Camaro. I kept it at our house most nights because we had a driveway. We also raced it down Route 107, the straight stretch of road behind us, for money on late nights, unbeknownst to my mother. She'd anxiously wake me up at six in the morning if I was home, asking me to drive her to find her car. I'd gripe and groan sometimes, but I couldn't help but feel bad for her.

"Did you hide the keys?"

"Yes, of course I did, but for the love of God, I don't know how he found them. Thank God he never finds the spare keys, too," she said, dangling them. "C'mon, I'm going to be late. I'm sorry." She tapped my leg.

She walked downstairs softly. I sensed her embarrassment, and I didn't know how to handle it. She looked worn down.

I'll kill him.

"How the fuck can a blackout drunk find hidden keys?" I mumbled.

I threw my sweatshirt on and grabbed my keys from the bottom of my underwear drawer. He knew better than to take my car, but I hid them, just in case.

Can't trust them.

My anger for her had turned to pity in the past few months. She was only trying to get to work. I calmly drove, but anger built, consuming me this time. I gritted my teeth, envisioning running him over, then backing up and running him over again. I took a sharp turn angrily onto the open stretch of the boulevard, scanning the street for her car. My rage wasn't evenly displaced between them anymore. She seemed weak, and I suddenly felt this incredible need to protect her somehow, thinking she must not be capable of defending herself. I wasn't exactly sure when the change happened, but it caused me to feel murderous toward him. The disease had got her, by all appearances. She was a shell of herself, and though she still went to her meetings, to me, she was a goner.

"There." She pointed.

I spotted the car and pulled over.

"Thanks." She mustered a smile.

I waited, idling, watching her drive off.

I pulled into the street and looked at the Shipwreck Lounge across from me. I looked again, adjusting my eyes, spotting a figure sitting at the bar through the large window. It was a little after seven. It was him.

Who the fuck is still serving him at seven in the morning? I'll fucking kill them too.

I stared at him, revving the engine a little. I made a mental note to call the city to report the shithole bar when I got home. The beach was quiet and still, and the sun was almost up over the water. I felt strangely calm and started to leave, then looked at him once more and thought about my mother's face.

Fucking drunk garbage!

I swung hard left so I was directly in front of the window. I stared at him, enraged, revving the engine. I hated the anger and the power it had, and I had no control when it came. I idled in the street, waiting, wanting him to see me—if he could see anymore. I revved the engine loud, the car shaking underneath me. He moved his head, lifting it. He looked right at me. He stared a moment, then put his head back down. I saw the shame, and it made me happy.

I pressed my foot on the brake as hard as I could and pushed on the gas pedal, slowly advancing pressure. The tires started to screech and spin, turning and turning, and I pressed harder. The smell of rubber burning poured in through the window, filling the car. Smoke was everywhere and about to block my view of him in the window. I stuck my arm out into the smoke, holding up my middle finger, pressing the gas all the way. I let off the brake and launched forward, peeling away like a rocket down the boulevard, leaving a stretch of rubber on the road.

"Motherfucker!" I yelled, feeling out of my mind.

I gripped the steering wheel tightly, trying not to lose control of the car. I felt powerful and released from the anger as I drove, looking in the rearview, seeing the smoke roll toward the water, hoping a police car wasn't anywhere in sight. My heart raced, and I slowed, turning easily onto the back roads in case there were any cops ahead. The good feeling and the anger disappeared into sadness like it always did, and tears filled my eyes. I brushed them away, continuing home.

I left for a few days, needing a break from all of it. I'd stay away when I could and pop by sometimes for clothes or a shower between classes. I hated that things were like this, but nothing was changing. He wasn't going to detox, and my mother and Ray seemed to have accepted it all. She wasn't leaving him, that was clear, but then there was Ray. Ray dealing with it destroyed me. I wanted him to have somewhere to go and not be around it. I hated them both for Ray.

I came home early one afternoon after they canceled my morning class. No one should have been home, but I heard a noise in my parents' bedroom. I nervously poked my head in, scared of what I might find—sometimes you just never knew—but it was only Ray. He was sitting on the edge of the bed. I was surprised to see him.

"Why aren't you in school?" I asked, startling him. "You didn't hear me come in?"

"George! Jeesh, you scared me!"

I looked past him, seeing my father lying there like a corpse. The room smelled of stale booze and cigarettes.

He looked at me and then at Dad.

"What are you doing?" I asked, frustrated.

"Nothing, it's just I was worried. I didn't want to leave him alone. I don't know." He shrugged.

I felt my face turning red, and I envisioned dragging my father's body to the curb for the trash, then going to my mother's work and driving my car through it.

"Go to school, Ray. You can't stop your life, okay?"

He said nothing, shrugging again. His face turned pink in anger, and his eyes moist with tears.

"Do you want me to drive you?" I asked softly, trying not to upset him more than he was.

He stared at the wall, motionless.

"No. I can't leave him," he said, gritting his teeth, turning sharply toward me.

"Okay."

I shut the door and left.

I'm talking to my fucking mother.

I decided she needed to hear about Ray staying home and how this couldn't go on any longer. I was sick of always being the one to say it. I was the loud one, rocking the boat and making waves. The only one who brought up the drunk elephant in the room no one wanted to acknowledge. I was sick of it but told myself maybe that was just my role.

Maybe if I try once more, they'll listen.

I couldn't get Ray's face out of my mind. Skipping school to care for the man, his father, the only father he had, who was sick and dying as far as I could tell.

Him and his fucking disease taking everyone down with him. I'm not going down with them.

I wasn't going to sink, not without a fight, and I wasn't letting Ray go either.

We still had family dinners sometimes, minus one. My mother asked me to be home at least one night a week for them. I came sometimes, and I decided I'd bring it up then, which wouldn't go over well, but it wouldn't anywhere. I came in that Sunday, smelling her sauce, excited. I'd been eating like shit and was starving. My mother was straining the pasta and turned, happy to see me, as I came in the door.

"Hi, George." She touched my arm, half hugging me.

Hugs? Weird.

"Smells good." I opened the fridge to get water and sat down at the table.

"Did you tell her, Mom?"

Ray came from behind and sat next to me.

"Tell me what?"

My mother put plates in front of Ray and me. He took the parmesan cheese and dumped half of the container on his spaghetti. I made a face, and he made one back.

"Dad hasn't been home in two nights," he said with his mouth full, chewing loudly.

"What do you mean?" I asked. I twirled the spaghetti on my fork, looking at my mom for clarification.

He always finds his way home.

I couldn't remember him ever not coming home. The song from camp popped into my head, and, amazingly, I still remembered the words:

> *But the cat came back, the very next day,*
> *The cat came back. They thought he was a goner,*
> *But the cat came back. He just wouldn't stay away.*

"Well, has anyone called around? The bars, police station, or maybe Marty's? I don't know."

My mother just shook her head. I worried, but only for a moment. *He always comes back.*

I wasn't even sure how he found his way home most of the time, but he did. The song wouldn't leave my head.

"He'll be back," I said confidently, punching the side of Ray's leg.

"Stop." He laughed and tried to hit me back, but I was too quick and jumped up, causing him to miss. I grabbed my dish and put it in the sink.

"Thanks, Mom."

"You're welcome, George." She smiled.

I saw the worry in her eyes, and I hated it, so I avoided looking into them. I decided not to bring up Ray staying home. They were worried, and I didn't want to add to it. I went upstairs and opened my nursing book, but I didn't read it. It was odd he hadn't been home, and I started to worry too.

I hope he's okay.

I flipped the pages, remembering the last time I'd seen him a few weeks ago. But I didn't talk to him, and he didn't know I was there. I came in and almost fell over him passed out in the doorway. He looked crumpled and broken, his keys in his outstretched hand over his head. He didn't moan; I didn't check if he was breathing. I did nothing, not caring if he was alive or dead. I stepped over him, then showered and got something to eat. I left, stepping over him again, and tried not to think about it.

• • •

"George! Ray!" my mother called up the stairs. I'd heard the phone ring and wondered if it was him, feeling my dinner move up my throat. Her voice didn't sound weird, so I figured it must not be bad.

"What?" I yelled. I heard Ray's door open.

"Come down."

I swallowed hard, hoping I wasn't wrong.

She stood holding the phone by her side. Her hand covered the receiver so whoever it was couldn't hear.

"It's Dad. He wants to know if he can come home," she said, looking at Ray, then at me.

I'm confused. "What do you mean? Did you throw him out?"

"No, I didn't. He just didn't come home and is asking if he can." She looked confused too.

"Yes," Ray interrupted, "he can come home."

This didn't make any sense, but why should he come home? Why?

I felt like this was an opportunity.

"You know what, Ma, he can come home when he's sober! He can come home when he gets his shit together, Ma!" I yelled, suddenly feeling empowered. "This is ridiculous! Living like this is nuts!"

I watched my mother's face. She knew I was right. She knew things couldn't go on like this. I knew she knew, but I wasn't sure she'd act on it, so I went on.

"How much longer can this go on? Why should we keep living like this?" I looked at Ray, who was shaking his head. "Ray's been staying home from school to take care of him. Did you know that?" I said, pointing.

Ray glared at me.

"Let him come home, Mom," Ray pleaded.

She looked at Ray and put the phone to her ear, taking a long breath.

"Richie, go get sober and then come home," she said and hung up, gripping the phone tightly.

I put my hand on her back as she stood staring at the phone, not letting it go. Ray stomped up the stairs and slammed his door. I kept my hand on her back a moment, then headed upstairs to bed, hearing her hum quietly as I lay there, unable to sleep.

The following day I was working my usual Saturday shift at the Chowder Pot. It was busier than usual, and I ran ragged, trying to get the orders to the front. I was doing the back, in charge of wrapping the takeout and answering the phone. It rang, and I quickly grabbed it, watching the food get cold as the new girl wasn't getting it out fast enough.

"Hello, Chowder Pot," I said in my phony customer-service voice.

"George?" said a voice I didn't immediately recognize.

"Yup."

"It's Maria."

"Oh, it didn't sound like you. What's up?"

"Well." She paused.

"What is it?" I urged. "I'm in the weeds over here."

"I don't want to freak you out or anything, George, but Billy thought he heard your dad's name on the police scanner," she finished in a nervous voice.

Billy? Your loser boyfriend, who nobody likes?

I nearly said it out loud but stopped myself, remembering she was one of my best friends.

"Maria? I mean, Billy isn't the brightest, and I'm working. Like, everyone better be sure before calling me with this shit."

"George, let's go," Stan, my boss, said.

He stood at the grill, waving his hand for me to get off the phone. I put my finger up, telling him one minute, holding the receiver with my shoulder while I bagged the orders.

"I was just letting you know, George," Maria said, sounding annoyed.

"Okay, well, now I know, thanks." I hung up the phone, instantly regretting how I'd talked to her.

I bagged a few more orders and stared at the next ticket that came in, unable to focus.

"George, what's the order?"

Stan banged on the table.

What if Billy was right and something is wrong? Maybe he got arrested or in an accident?

"Stan, I have to take a break for a minute," I said, dropping the ticket in a panic.

"George!" Stan called behind me as I rushed into the dining room.

I headed to the back office. He always left it open when he was there. I picked up the phone and dialed, knowing the number by heart; I'd called looking for my boyfriend more than a few times.

"Hello, Revere Police, this call is being recorded," a robotic-sounding woman answered.

My heart thumped in my chest and my stomach soured. Smelling the fried seafood odor that clung to me made it worse. Calling the police was nerve wracking. I always felt I'd be in trouble just for asking a question. Like if I said something wrong, they'd come for me, or I'd blurt out something insane and end up in jail.

I thought of my father saying, "You have to be careful trusting cops."

"H-hi," I stuttered, sitting down in the chair. "This is a strange call, but my friend thought he heard my dad's name on the police scanner?" I cleared my throat. "I just wanted to make sure he was wrong, which he probably is." I laughed nervously.

"What's the name?" she said coldly.

I answered her, and she put me on hold for what felt like forever. I nervously tapped Stan's picture of his son with my fingernail.

"Why is this taking so long?" I said aloud and swiveled the chair around. I nearly jumped from the seat, startled, when I saw Stan in the doorway. "Sorry, Stan, just one minute."

But I immediately saw something was wrong. His face looked weird; he scratched the stubble on his chin and slowly approached me. Two police officers appeared behind him, and I stared at Stan, confused, still holding the phone.

"I'm sorry, George," he said, kneeling in front of me, taking the phone from my hand.

My eyes darted from Stan to the police and the phone.

"What? My dad? Is it my dad?" I said, alarmed.

Stan looked away, nodding.

"Stan, is it my dad?" I screamed, watching him and the officer.

CHAPTER 19

December 16, 1995
Goodbye. You died, and so did we.

I stood at the podium, trying not to cry or panic. Adjusting the microphone, I looked at the pews filled with people, suddenly feeling my heart race and my eyes fill. I'd bargained with God not to let me have an anxiety attack, but I was too broken and tired to muster the energy for one anyway. I was numb. It was vital for me to give my father something—a send-off, a tribute; I wasn't sure, but I needed to. Maybe it was the closure thing or having the final word.

I always had it. Why stop now?

I laughed thinking this and thought he might be laughing too, somewhere, wherever he was. I felt myself holding my breath as I smoothed the paper in front of me, staring at the words I had spent hours struggling to write the night before. Suddenly they all looked illegible. I tried hard to focus and began to speak, my voice cracking. I stuttered the first sentence, reaching to my neck, pulling at the small pendant, twisting it around and around. A tear slid down my nose, then another onto the paper, blurring the black ink. I wanted so badly to run, but I wouldn't.

"My father was complicated," I began.

I saw my aunt Rita in the first pew crying uncontrollably. I took a tissue from my pocket and wiped the moisture from my nose. Unexpectedly, a strange feeling of calm came, and I went on, shoving the tissue back into my pocket.

"I'm not here to talk about what complicated him, though. I'd rather talk about what made him *him*, and so much more."

I looked up again and saw my mother lift her head and smile. She didn't know what I'd written or what I would say. The priest asked yesterday if anyone would like to speak, and I said yes, quickly, without thinking. I didn't know what I would say either and had spent most of the previous night regretting I'd agreed. Then the words came, and I realized now, more than ever, his disease didn't make him a bad man. It never had, and he wasn't. He was more than his problem. He was so much more than that; it made it more tragic. He was a good man, which made the disease that much worse, but I wouldn't speak of his illness today. I wouldn't give it one more breath when I spoke of him. It took him from me and us. It took him from everything, and I wouldn't let it take him anymore.

I recognized a lot of the people I'd met at the wake the night before. So many of them told stories of how Richie from the Beach helped them get clean or sober, gave them a ride, lent them money, drove them to detox. The stories were endless and nothing I'd ever known about.

I held on to the paper, noticing my hands shaking. I turned my head carefully so I couldn't see Ray, who was next to my mother. I coughed, a tightness in my chest, feeling it was all a dream.

I steadied my hand and continued to read.

"And I am so very proud to be his daughter, I am," I sobbed, clutching the wood. "I wish I told him."

I wish I knew.

We never knew what happened. Someone found him in a room above the bar where he was staying, and he was alone. Nothing was definitive except the autopsy showed no alcohol in his system. This made me happy for him. I wasn't sure why, but to me, it was necessary. He didn't die drunk.

We buried him in the cemetery near his mother. Mary came, and it was awkward. She rode in the limo with us, and we sat in silence for most of the ride until my mother started making small talk. I felt terrible for Mary, realizing how weird it all was. I wanted to fix it but couldn't, and it wasn't my mistake to fix.

Maybe someday we can talk and be friends.

I stared at her, noticing she had the same color skin and eyes as him, our father.

• • •

Soon people stopped coming by, and life slowly returned to some familiarity, at least by outside appearances, although everything was different. Not only was he gone, and we grieved, but so was the disease, at least the active part, the part that held us together. It had unified the three of us in the battle against it for most of our lives, keeping us close.

Everything was different.

Ray soon became withdrawn and slowly stopped speaking to me. My mother: I sensed resentment. I didn't understand at first but figured it out one evening when the three of us were together, which happened sparingly now. Ray said something about wishing we'd let him come home that night, the night he called. I watched her nod in agreement and suddenly understood; they blamed me. I was the one who wouldn't let him come home.

If he were home, one of us would have found him. How could they think any differently?

I struggled not to say anything. I wanted to scream, but I didn't. Sometimes it was easier to blame, and I let them.

I couldn't deal with it for long. The resentment was subtle, but it was there. Ray became increasingly angry at everyone. He was hurting, but I couldn't help him—my mother, either. Anger consumed me too; I'd drive by the Shipwreck Lounge at night, planning some type of revenge against it and those inside. I wanted to blame, just like they did.

I drove the beach home, going by the bar, telling myself it was the last time. I thought of going in but wasn't sure I could. I was tired of anger. I was tired of it all. Instead, I kept going and pulled in across from Kelly's and sat on the wall. A homeless man dug through the barrel next to me and pulled out two cans, putting them in his shopping cart. Some trash spilled out as he moved on to the next barrel. I watched as the wrappers rolled down the boulevard toward my house in the wind. I spun my necklace around and pulled on the chain, suddenly feeling the urge to rip it off and throw it in the water below. It was high tide, and the waves lapped against the wall. The smell of salt and trash whirled around me.

I looked at the moon over Nahant, the town across the water. The small square windows glowed yellow from the apartment buildings on the point. I remembered how they always looked odd from here, almost like subway cars. The red lights blinked on the hill's water tower, and an airplane flew low overhead toward Boston. I'd been here my whole life and seen these things so many times, but they all seemed different. I never wanted to see any of it again.

CHAPTER 20

April 14, 2003
I'd never planned for tears. I fought them for so long
they stopped trying to come, until now.
How will I ever get them back in?

I didn't cry anymore, telling him. I had never cried so much in my life, and I had no tears left. My mouth was dry, and I took a sip of water from the table. Dock continued to listen, pulling me into him and holding me.

"Gotta get that stuff out." He kissed my forehead.

I sighed, exhausted. "I guess."

I headed into the bathroom, looking at the mess in the mirror. My head throbbed, and my eyes ached.

"Shit, I gotta run," he called out.

I peeked out the door.

"I hate to leave you, though. Are you good?"

I hopped over, careful not to trip on the blanket. He put his finger under my chin and tilted my head up.

"I'll see you when?"

I suddenly narrowed my eyes at him, irritated, thinking of him disappearing again, so I kept it cool.

"I guess whenever. I'll see you around." I smirked, baiting him.

He looked at me strangely, and I could tell he saw through it.

"Okay," he drawled, turning his mouth at one side. "I will see you." He stared at me intensely, squinting. He turned and headed out the door, looking back to see my reaction.

I shrugged like I didn't care. He knew I did.

My heart ached, and I felt empty, as though I was missing something now—the anger and resentment, the grief, the power it held; I suddenly felt like I didn't know who I was.

• • •

"You up late, girl?" Delia laughed as I came through the door, studying my face. "You okay?"

Crap. I could never get away with crying—not that I did much—or being sick, hungover, or tired. It was apparent, and my eyes were still swollen, so I lied. It was easier.

"Allergies, I think." *I hate lying.* "I was up all night with them."

I opened the fridge, grabbing water and chugging nearly all of it, then felt Delia staring and stopped mid-chug.

"If you are getting sick, girl, stay away from me." She laughed, rolling her eyes.

I was too tired to care if she believed me or not.

"You ever see that man again?"

"Who?"

"That man you were liking."

She kept her back turned to me, peeling a potato or something I couldn't see.

Can she smell him on me? I looked at my pants, feeling naked.

"Um, yes and no," I said, hoping it would end there.

She smiled, tossing her head back, laughing again.

"You's a bad girl, Georgie." She grabbed the dishrag on the counter and tossed it at me. I caught it and threw it back at her.

"Get your mind out of the gutter."

I tried not to look in her eyes, as though she could read my thoughts. As I headed up the back stairs, her laugh echoed behind me.

God, I need some fucking privacy.

I tossed my bag in the closet and poked my head in the door.

"Mr. S.?" I paused, listening. "Mr. S.?" I said again, raising my voice, hearing a cough and spit.

"Yes," he whispered, wheezing.

"Do you want to—"

"No."

"Okay."

I figured I'd head to Mocha Mott's for coffee, hoping it would help me get through the day. I hollered, telling Delia I'd be back, and took the BMW to Main Street.

"Can I help you?"

"Sure, I'll have a medium coffee light, no sugar, please."

I wondered where Sheila was. I didn't recognize this new guy at the counter. I hated when there was someone new; they never seemed to make it right. Summer was nearly here, though, and everything was busier. New faces were everywhere, and I'd have to get used to it again.

"Do you want sugar?" he asked, looking at the buttons on the register, confused.

"No sugar," I said again kindly, trying my best not to get aggravated. Everything was slower on the island, and people were mainly patient, especially the year-rounders. Summer, everything was so much busier, and things were slower than usual; sometimes, my patience wore thin.

A tall older man appeared at the register. I'd never seen him either but was glad someone knew what they were doing.

"You punch it in like this," he explained, and I watched his fingers hit the keys. Then I noticed it. He had the same tattoo as Dock, the five dots. It was in the same place, too, on his hand.

What is it again? Oh yeah, the five islands.

My mind was mush.

I handed the struggling man my money and waited at the end of the counter.

"Coffee light!" the tall man yelled.

"Right here." I took the cup from him. "The five islands?" I said, pointing at his tattoo.

"Excuse me?" he mumbled with a frown.

He had black hair with flecks of gray at the sides and pale skin and didn't look Portuguese, I thought, with those freckles on his nose and pale-blue eyes.

"Your tattoo on your hand. The islands of Portugal," I said, smiling again.

He stared at me, seeming to not know what I was talking about. He glanced at his hand and quickly put it by his side as if to hide it.

The man at the register called for help again. The tall man smirked and walked away.

I pulled in the driveway back at the house and sat a moment, dreading the day. All I wanted to do was sleep, but that wouldn't happen until maybe a nap later if I was lucky. I was dying to call Bobbie to tell her about the night, the Dock part, but was too exhausted. I took a long sip of coffee and closed my eyes, thinking about the tattoo.

Why did he seem not to know what I was talking about?

Dock and last night interrupted my thought as shivers ran up my arm. I noticed the time on the dash, envisioning Mr. S. calling for me. I headed into the house.

"George! George!" he bellowed from upstairs.

Great, a double George. I'm in for it now.

"Hey, George," Lilly said, coming through the kitchen carrying her notebook and tennis racket.

"Hi, Lilly. Great day for tennis."

"It sure is." She smiled. She appeared lost in thought, opening her notebook as she sat at the table, scribbling something.

Bracing myself for the usual, I went up.

"Where were you, George?" he said sternly. I pushed the door open and mouthed it at the same time he said it. I said nothing and went to the window, opening the blinds halfway.

"Jesus!" he yelled, blocking his eyes.

It was medication time, and I went into the closet to gather them. I noticed the calendar I kept posted on the wall had the word *therapy* written in the small block with today's date.

"Shit!"

I panicked; he should have already been downstairs. I hurried back into his room and pulled his clothes from the drawers, flinging them on the bed.

"What are you doing?"

"What? Huh?" I turned to him, then back to the drawer, holding up a pair of pants, making sure they were the right ones. "Sorry, Mr. S., you have therapy early today, and we are late. Very late! They'll probably be here any minute." I cringed, knowing this wouldn't go over well, but nothing usually did, so it didn't matter.

"Oh God," he coughed, shaking his head.

"It's physical therapy, your evaluation, and we need to hurry."

"George?" Lilly called from downstairs.

Fuck.

"Yes, Lilly," I called back, simultaneously helping him put his shirt on.

"The physical therapist is here."

Fuck, fuck, fuck.

"We will be right down," I called back as I put his shoes on.

"This is ridiculous!" He spat into a tissue and tossed it toward the bucket, missing like he always did.

"I'm sorry, Mr. S., but all they had was an early appointment."

"Tell him to leave," he barked as I brushed his hair.

He reached up to snatch the comb from me but couldn't lift his arm high enough.

"You need this. It's for one day." I stopped brushing and stepped back, giving him a severe look.

He said nothing, and I handed him a cup of mouthwash, watching as he took his time swishing and spat in the basin.

The therapist was waiting patiently on the sofa in the living room.

He noticed us on the stairs and ran toward us, grabbing two bags blocking the bottom of the staircase, allowing us to pass.

Ugh, Lilly.

"Thank you, Tom," Mr. S. said kindly and headed into the living room. I held on to him with one arm and moved the pile of papers and books off the couch, shaking my head in annoyance.

"Do you guys know each other?" I asked, just as he plopped down, nearly missing the couch.

The therapist, who I gathered was Tom, looked concerned.

"Yes, what was it—two years ago?" Tom smiled, sitting next to him.

Mr. S. always remembered people. People he had just met or hadn't seen in forever, and it mattered little what impact they'd had on his life. It impressed me.

"My father instilled it in me. It's important to remember names in the South," he answered me after I asked him about it once.

He grew up an only child in Virginia, raised mainly by his father after his mother died of cancer she'd suffered through for years. He spoke of her suffering sometimes, asking me medical questions, wanting to know more. Medicine seemed to intrigue him. He wrote about studying depression in the book I'd nearly finished, trying to figure out his mind and possibly his father's, who I had heard also suffered from the disease. His interest in the darkness and the pain of others was evident in his writings and his questions. I wondered if through his immersion in it all, he had taken it on himself, causing him to become withdrawn and dark, or if that was just him.

"Do you think I'll have pain, like hers?" he asked me after telling me about her cancer. He rarely spoke of it. He rarely spoke of anything, so I was intrigued.

"You don't have cancer," I answered.

He said it like he wanted me to say he would, wistfully, as if this would make him understand what she went through. It reminded me of the times I drank when I wanted to know my father.

I went back upstairs, tidied up a bit, and then sat in the chair by his bed, resting my eyes. They still felt swollen and heavy.

The wind blew in, and the blinds tapped against the window, startling me; I had nearly fallen asleep. I got up and stretched, noticing the books again in the bookcase, remembering I wanted to dust them, but it wouldn't be today. I kneeled and looked at the titles: *As I Lay Dying, A Rose for Emily, The Hamlet*. There were tons by William Faulkner; I took one and brushed off the cover, then put it back, looking at the next shelf. I pulled a few others from different authors and opened the covers, some signed or with an inscription. Then I noticed it: another of his books, arguably the most famous.

I struggled to remember any of it except for the ending. Everyone knew the end. I pulled it from the shelf and ran my hand over it, noticing the cracked binding, trying to be careful. I opened it and found folded page corners and pieces of paper stuck in different places. I turned to one, seeing a pencil scribble in the margins. I could tell it was his writing. I'd seen it many times in various things he had written, old forms he filled out in his records. I thumbed through a few of the pages, stopping wherever there was a pencil.

Wrong! it said in big letters next to the German word *wahlen*. I read the passage.

"'Being a Polack, not a rat, gives you more. You can choose.'

"She felt her legs buckle and began to scream. The unbridled screams of those slaughtered in the chambers simultaneously rang out from her as she collapsed to the dirt. 'I won't choose! I won't choose!'"

My heart pounded, reading the words, remembering, and I wondered now if the story was true. In the horrors of the Holocaust, I was sure it could be.

But did he know her? Was she real?

The story took place on Long Island, New York, and Germany during the Second World War. The main character, I knew now, was at least mostly Mr. S. when he was a young writer trying to make it. Lilly confirmed it to me one day, driving back from Boston. We drove instead of flying, and although it was longer, I was happy not to be on the plane.

"Oh, look at this quote. How wonderful," she said, passing me the folded *New Yorker* magazine. It was a quote from some movie director mentioning Mr. S. and his talent and genius.

"The movie, or book, I should say, is quoted a lot, Lilly," I said, wishing I had only said book. I didn't want her to know I had only seen the movie.

"Is it?" she asked, seeming not to know, wanting to hear more. "Do you remember any?"

As she had put me on the spot, I couldn't remember anything specifically, except Alan Alda mentioning it in a movie I'd watched on Lifetime a few weeks ago.

"Really? Alan Alda? I've never seen it. I don't believe it."

"Any time there is a difficult choice, I think mentioning the book is the go-to."

"Makes sense." She adjusted her glasses as I handed her back the magazine.

She began reading again, then stopped, turning to me.

"Did you know he was going to make the end the beginning?"

"What? In the book?" I said, feeling foolish as the words came out.

"Yes, isn't that wild?" She looked at me over her glasses.

"How would that even work?"

"I don't know, but it didn't matter. I told him not a chance when he said it, and that was that."

"Good thing he ran it by you. Maybe you should have won the Pulitzer," I said, and we both laughed.

"I should have won the Pulitzer for a lot of things, the Oscar too!" She laughed again, opening the magazine.

I closed the book, putting it back on the shelf, letting it stick out as a reminder that I wanted to read it. I heard Tom still talking downstairs and figured I had a few more minutes. I grabbed my phone from my bag and went into the guest bedroom, and closed the door.

"Hello," the voice on the other end said.

She was getting older, and she sounded tired. I hated it when she sounded tired.

"Hey, Mom." Tears filled my eyes, and I leaned my head back, blinking hard, not expecting them again.

"Hi, George." Her voice perked up, which made me happy.

"Just thought I'd call and say hi."

We made small talk for a little while, although I wanted to say more. I wanted to repeat everything that had come up the night before, although I hadn't planned that when I called. I hadn't even expected to call, especially here and now, but I did.

"I sort of feel like we don't talk about stuff," I said, clearing my throat. I instantly regretted it, cringing as she spoke.

"What did you want to talk about?"

Here we go. Let's pretend.

My face was hot. Suddenly, I felt vulnerable, which made me angry. I wanted to lash out but heard voices downstairs again and remembered where I was.

"Just all that's happened, Mom," I said, annoyed, knowing she knew.

"I don't live in the past, George," she said calmly.

"Well, the past has a lot to do with the present," I sputtered, gritting my teeth.

She was quiet on the other end.

"Let's forget it. Gotta run. Mr. S. is calling."

"Okay, I'm here if you need me."

"Uh-huh. Love you. Bye."

I wished I could hang up hard, slamming the receiver down. I hated that about cell phones.

She was there in a lot of ways but not about this, not about Ray and me. Not about my dad or about how it was all so fucked up.

Maybe she's right.

In her world, everything wasn't that bad. Things were okay, even if they weren't.

Maybe that's just easier for her, or perhaps I know nothing, and it's me.

I wasn't sure of anything anymore.

"What's it all matter?" I said out loud, staring at my phone. But it mattered. It mattered to me.

I looked out the window, watching the ferry about to pass, and a sailboat turned hard to avoid its wake. I thought of Dock again, thinking I could still smell him on me. I tried to get everything else out of my mind. I lay back on the bed, dangling my feet, feeling my heels touch the floor, and tapped. I'd met no one like him, and it made me feel young and inexperienced. He was confident and gentle. He was rough and everything else in between, and I wanted more. My heart opened, unlocking somehow, and I liked it. It felt like a drug, and I was high and free. I had kissed him before, but it was different now. I wanted it again. I wanted to feel, and I hated it and reveled in it. I couldn't lie to myself. I was mad about him. I was hopeless and helpless. I didn't have control, and I was going wherever he wanted to take me. I had felt lost for so long, not realizing it until last night; in it all, I felt found.

CHAPTER 21

June 28, 2003
Everything is perfect.

S ummer was in full swing on the island, and so were Dock and me. He and Will seemed to be okay again—not that I was sure they hadn't been, but it seemed strange for a while. Will lived on the boat for the summer until his friend returned, he said. Island work picked up for them, so now he and Dock were together most days. I never asked Dock where he'd gone or what happened, and I wasn't sure why. I think, for the most part, I didn't want to know. I was doing the very thing I loathed: pretending. It was easier, at least for the short term, but it gnawed at me.

Barbara and Karen, the nurses from the hospital, worked a few shifts with Mr. S., giving me a day off, much to his dismay. I still found myself apologizing to him after every day off, which weren't many. He said he understood but wasn't happy about it.

"I don't believe you." I laughed, brushing his hair one morning.

"Fine," he grumbled back.

I knew he was still afraid I wasn't coming back, and I tried to be empathetic.

All the girls from last summer were in the log cabin again, and the fun had begun, although things were a little different as I had Dock now.

"We're headed up to Gay Head if you guys are interested?" Bobbie said, handing me a beer.

I took a sip, enjoying the coldness on my lips. It was hot, and I had just finished my bike ride to West Chop Lighthouse, then over to Telegraph Hill, following the coast. I loved bicycling anywhere on the island. Feeling the wind on my face and smelling the hydrangeas' clean scent mixed with the salty air always exhilarated me. I stopped at the cabin after, sitting with the girls. I did this often last summer; now it was a ritual.

"Are we going naked?" I laughed, taking another sip, untying my bandanna and shaking my hair free.

The beach below the cliffs in Gay Head was a nude one. Not legally, but no one bothered you.

Gay Head—or Aquinnah, going back to its native roots a few years ago—was the town at the western tip of the island. They named it Gay Head because of its beautiful red clay cliffs that swept down to the water. I guessed *gay* implying "happiness" was the meaning. I'd read a book about all of the island's history after visiting with my father.

"The day could lead to nakedness; it has before," Bobbie said, taking my beer off the deck and having a sip. "If it's a good day," she finished.

"Dock has his motorcycle running and is picking me up for a ride. Maybe we can head up there. I think Will is coming too."

"How're things in lover land?" She nudged me.

"Watch it!" I laughed. "And it's terrific." I tried hard not to smile.

"Seriously, though, I'm glad things worked out." She tapped my shoulder, standing. "And I need to meet him!"

"I know, I know. We've been—"

"In lover land," she cut me off.

I headed toward the door, ignoring her. "Okay, we'll be there in like an hour—just waiting for them."

"All right, I'll see you there."

I jumped on my bike and headed back toward Vineyard Haven. Bobbie never asked too many questions, and I liked that about our friendship. She just wanted everyone to be happy. I rode down the driveway carefully, trying to keep my balance as I shook and swayed on the broken seashells and hurried in to change. I slipped on my bathing suit and threw a few things in a backpack, hoping to interest Dock and Will in going up-island for the day.

The blast of the motorcycle engines reached me from Main Street. Hobo barked loudly as they came down the drive.

Oh God, Delia's gonna have a field day.

I threw his leash on and met them outside. Hobo shook at the noise, and Dock smiled, shutting off the engine. He unstrapped his helmet, hopped off, and came over to kiss me. I half closed my eyes and breathed in, smelling him.

"Hey, Hobs," he said, patting him.

Hobo nervously came from behind my legs, looking all around.

"Hey, Will," I called over. He put the kickstand down and lit a cigarette.

"What's shaking, George?"

"Bike looks great," I said to Dock, running my hand over the fender.

"Buffed and polished." He turned and admired it. I could tell he felt proud.

"Watch where you touch, George. He's gentler with her than I've ever seen him with anyone; you might be jealous," Will said, getting off the bike and stubbing his cigarette in the shells.

"Ha-ha." Dock turned and put his arms on my shoulders. "You've got nothing to worry about, babe."

Babe. Do I like it? He's never called me that. Like, does this mean something?

"He's done good, though," Will went on.

I noticed Dock perk up, seeming happy with the praise.

"Any chance it interests you guys in heading to Gay Head?" I asked flirtatiously, looking at Dock, hoping for a yes.

"That's a nice ride. I'm down." He glanced at Will and reached into his T-shirt pocket for a cigarette.

"What's going on there?" Will asked, getting back on his bike.

"My friends are at the beach for the day. Who knows, maybe getting naked." I hoped this would entice him, and only him.

"Naked nurses!" Dock raised his voice excitedly.

"Hey." I nudged him.

Will strapped on his helmet. He looked out toward the water, seeming to think.

"Okay, let's go." He stood up and kick-started the engine.

After I put Hobo in the house, Dock handed me my helmet, helping me strap it under my chin and making sure it was tight.

"You ready, beautiful?" He tapped my head.

"Ouch!"

"Oh, stop it." He laughed and climbed on.

He started the bike, revving the engine. I climbed on the back and peered over the bushes, looking for Delia, but didn't notice anyone.

He put on his sunglasses, and I pressed myself against his back. He reached, squeezing my side, and I moved my hand to touch the skin on his arms under his shirt, feeling the outline of his muscle.

"Ready?" He tapped my leg.

"Yup."

I held him tightly, nervous at first but relaxed by the time we reached West Tisbury, the next town over. I loosened my grip on him a bit, enjoying the open air and the island. It was beautiful out, and I felt happy—the in-the-moment kind of happiness, which was rare, at least for me. I never seemed to realize something was good until after it happened, but holding on to him, feeling the wind and all the smells and sights of the island, felt beautiful.

I gazed at the stone walls lining the roads in Chilmark, remembering they'd been there for hundreds of years. We passed the vast green lawns and rolling hills of the giant estates along the water. The roads seemed empty, which surprised me, as it was summer, but up-island usually wasn't that busy except during the week of the fair. I felt Dock getting antsy, speeding up and then slowing down behind Will, who drove cautiously in front of us. We neared the fishing village of Menemsha, about to head up the cliffs, when he tapped my leg.

"Hold on," he yelled.

I grabbed him tightly again, and he hit the gas. We sped up where the road became a straight right before the twisty part to the top. I hadn't been on a bike in years and leaned into him, both excited and nervous. He turned into the other lane, passing Will, who looked like a blur as we rocketed past. I held my breath and slowly exhaled as he slowed, heading up the cliffs. I looked back and smiled at Will. I stuck out my middle finger and tongue, laughing. He did the same back at me as we sped far ahead of him.

We passed the small coves with moored fishing boats, continuing up to what always felt like the clouds. The lighthouse's red brick came into view, and the sun shined on the cliffs before it. I never got used to the beauty here. It still took my breath away.

Dock slowed the bike, letting Will catch up, and we all turned in to the small parking lot.

"Assholes," he said, pulling next to us and shutting off the motor.

I hopped off and unstrapped my helmet.

"The gas is on the right," Dock said, stretching. He already had his helmet on his lap and was lighting a cigarette.

"Can you guys ever not smoke?" I grabbed my backpack and pulled out my bandanna, tying it in my hair. They both ignored me.

"What do you got on under there?" Dock said as he got off the bike, pulling at the buttons of my white shirt.

"Get out of here." I slapped his hand away with a laugh.

"Get a room." Will brushed his legs off and headed toward the path to the beach. "Are we going?" he asked, looking back at us.

Dock took the backpack from me, and we walked. He put his hand under my shirt, feeling the small of my back, and pulled me close to him. We took our shoes off at the end of the walkway and lined them along with the others whose owners had done the same. Will and Dock's giant boots sat on either side of my little sandals, making me

feel small, and I liked it. I pulled my phone out of my pocket to call
Bobbie but suddenly remembered there was never any service here.

"Shit. No service." I pouted at them.

"We'll find them." Dock started walking.

Will laughed. "We're kind of hard not to notice."

I laughed too, realizing they were the only ones on the beach in
jeans and T-shirts.

Dock took his shirt off and stuck it in his back pocket.

"Do I fit in a little better?" He grabbed my hand and pulled me
to him.

"I don't think you fit in anywhere."

"That's what he strives for." Will rolled his eyes.

I spotted a girl in a red bikini jumping up and down and waving
her arms at us.

"There's Bobbie."

"Hey, Bobbie," Will and Dock said, noticing her at the same time.

I shoved Dock, knowing they were both excited over the tiny red
bikini.

"I only have eyes for you and your bikini," Dock whispered, kissing
the top of my head.

All the girls and a few others I didn't know were there. They had
some coolers and towels scattered with food and drinks.

"What up, Georgie," Jennie said, shading her eyes from the sun.

Bobbie ran over after she brushed the sand off her legs. "How was
the ride?"

"Was good," Dock said and stuck his hand out. "Dock. You must
be Bobbie."

"I figured," Bobbie laughed and hugged him. "And I've already met
this one." She hugged Will, taking him off guard.

"Hey, Bobbie."

Shit, I forgot she met Will.

I looked at Dock, trying to gauge his reaction, not noticing any.

Maybe he already knew we were out that night.

I wasn't sure and left it alone.

"Beers?" Jennie said, sitting up, tossing me one from the cooler.

"Yes, please," Will said. He kneeled in the sand and opened the one she tossed him.

I handed Dock mine and took another one from Jennie.

Will stared at us. "Not too many, guys. We're riding."

Dock ignored him, looking at the water.

I took my shirt off and threw it over Jennie, who had her eyes closed as she lay back in the sun.

"What the?" She sat up laughing and threw it back at me.

I plopped next to her and took a sip of my beer, thankful it was cold.

"He's a hunk of a man, George," she said, trying to be quiet.

Bobbie heard her and agreed with a nod as she sat down next to me.

Dock was still standing, peering around the beach. He always seemed to assess the situation before getting comfortable, I'd noticed.

Bobbie introduced everyone to Dock, Will, and me. I knew everyone except a few girls who were lab techs here for the summer at the hospital. They were younger than us and already seemed drunk. I noticed Will watching them as they giggled, running in and out of the water in their tiny bikinis.

"Enjoying yourself, Will?" I said.

"What?" he looked at me and then back at the girls.

I winked at him.

"Shut up." He laughed.

Dock was looking at the cliffs, not noticing the girls at all, which made me happy.

"Take a load off, Dock," Bobbie said.

He turned, coming out of his trance.

I wonder what he's thinking.

"Yeah, Dock, enjoy the view." Will pointed up the beach as two women came toward us by the edge of the water with no tops on. "Life is good," Will said, running his fingers through his hair.

"And here we go." Bobbie looked down at her chest, then at me.

"I can't compete either." I glanced down, giggling.

Dock sat next to me and rested his hand on my thigh.

The women were in front of us now. They spoke French, which made them that much more appealing—at least, I thought so. Now Dock was staring.

"Hey." I nudged him.

"Sorry." He shook his head. "But, I mean, they are right there." He laughed.

I took my shorts off, exposing my blue-and-white bikini as if foolishly trying to compete with the topless French women. I felt okay until I looked at my pale legs, realizing I needed a tan desperately.

"Oh baby." Dock leaned into me, noticing my bikini.

I pulled the towel from my backpack and flattened it on the sand.

"Stop it." I hit him in the arm, which didn't move. Bobbie rolled her eyes.

He took a sip of beer and rubbed my leg as I lay back on the towel.

"I'm going swimming," Will said, jumping to his feet.

Bobbie laughed. "You have jeans on."

"Shit." He looked down. "Well, I'm gonna look at the water and wish I were swimming."

We all laughed as he headed down near the girls still fooling around in the waves.

The beer was already making me feel fuzzy in the hot sun. I looked at Dock, glancing down at his hand, thinking of the guy in the coffee shop again.

Just then, he stood and reached his hand to me. "Wanna take a walk?" he asked.

I put my hand in his, saying nothing.

"We'll be back." I smiled at the girls, who made kissing sounds.

We walked a while in silence. He stared toward the water like something was on his mind again.

"Hey." I nudged him.

"Hey yourself." He turned to me.

"Everything okay?" I asked, unsure I wanted the answer.

"Yeah, why?"

"I don't know. You seem a little lost today."

"I'm fine." He paused and stopped, pulling me to him. "I'm happy to be here with you."

"Good." I smiled and moved close, putting my head on his chest as he stroked my hair.

We walked on a little farther, following the cliff's bend to a long stretch of open beach that was vacant. It surprised me no one was there.

"I guess we have this all to ourselves."

"Perfect." He widened his eyes and unbuttoned the top of his jeans. "Let's go for a swim."

"You have no suit." I soon realized what he meant. "Oh my God, are you serious?" I covered my mouth as he pulled off his pants, throwing them on the sand.

"C'mon," he yelled, brushing his hair back, then confidently strode into the water and dove in.

I walked in until the water hit mid-calf, and he motioned me further.

"You can do it," he yelled again, moving toward me, the water barely covering him.

"Oh my God, I can't believe I'm doing this," I mumbled, untying my top, throwing it up to where his pants were.

"Live a little. You're beautiful."

I pulled off my bottoms and quickly headed into the water for coverage.

"I'm not French," I said, coming close to him. The sun was hot and bright, and the water felt good, cooling me off. He moved my hands away from my chest, looking at me, then swam out a little deeper, urging me to come toward him.

"Come here, you good Irish Catholic."

The water was clear, and it was quiet. It felt like we were the only two people in the world. I swam to him, wrapping my legs around him, and he put my arms around his neck. I gazed past him at the stretch of the ocean against the red-and-gold clay shimmering on the cliffs. I turned my chin up, looking into his eyes. Beads of water glistened in his eyelashes. His eyes were greener than I'd ever seen.

"Listen to me," he said, grasping my legs and moving me closer to him, looking serious.

"I'm listening," I breathed. I felt his heartbeat as I pressed against his chest.

"I'm falling in love with you, George."

I felt breathless, not expecting this. Without thinking, I spoke.

"Me too," I whispered.

He kissed me for what seemed like forever, and it still wasn't long enough.

CHAPTER 22

August 30, 2003
The worry, fear, and uneasiness transfer to the page.
All contained in the lines, dots, and swirls instead of banging
around in my head. It's marvelous. Hello, friend.

I t was a typical summer on the island, by all accounts, but this
one was different. I was falling in love, hopelessly in love, and
so was Dock, telling me every chance he could.

Even Mr. S. seemed in better spirits. We sat on the porch most
afternoons, watching the ferry pass back and forth. It was calming, and
I liked the slowness of it all. He was more amenable to whatever I asked
of him, which was a nice change. He also appeared to enjoy his children
and grandchildren visiting. They rotated through the guesthouse now that
the weather was warmer. The shift in him was subtle, but it was there. A
tiny upturn in the corner of his mouth as he watched the kids play or the
hint of a smile while talking with his daughter. It made me happy for him.

Dock, Will, and I had become inseparable, and Dock even started
occasionally working at the house for Lilly. I recommended him after
she asked if I knew anyone for a small job. Initially, it was just to fix
the porch stairs, but it turned into more. He did odd jobs here and
there and drove her if she needed it.

The three of us spent most nights in Oak Bluffs harbor, meeting up with the girls and other people we befriended along the way.

"Get a room." Bobbie rolled her eyes.

This had become her usual catchphrase with us, and Will nodded in agreement. We were outside Nancy's bar, figuring if we wanted to stay or go somewhere else. Dock had just told me the story of how he got the large scar on his hand after a guy came at him with a knife. I held his hand and looked at it. We kissed, and Bobbie made a gagging noise.

"Shut up." I turned to her.

"Hey, Dock," a voice from behind me said.

I spun around to look and saw Dock's face change.

"Hey, Misty," he said, looking past her.

He sounded irritated or uncomfortable. I couldn't tell which.

She had stringy blond hair and leathery skin with acne scars on her cheeks. You could tell she was pretty once. She was with a younger guy, and they continued past us. She glanced back at us again, then kept going.

"Who was that?" I asked, trying to sound casual.

"Just a girl. She's no one." He reached for my hand.

I looked at him strangely. I didn't believe him but wanted to. He brushed my hair away from my face, and his eyes met mine.

"I'm gonna pop over to the Sand Bar next door and see if Tom is working," Bobbie announced. "If he is, I say we go over. Anyone want to take a walk?"

"I'll go," Dock said, to my surprise. "A guy over there owes me money."

"What?"

He stubbed out his cigarette and leaned down to give me a quick kiss.

"What? A kid who works there, I let him borrow a few bucks. I'll be right back." He took some cash from his wallet and tossed it at Will. "Will, settle us up inside," he said, watching Will count the money.

"Looks like you're short some," Will joked, sticking it in his pocket.

"Be back in a flash, guys." Bobbie grabbed Dock's hand, and we watched them walk toward the bar.

Will and I headed back upstairs to Nancy's. I noticed a spot had freed up overlooking the harbor.

"Should we pay or have another? Who knows how long they'll be," he asked, pulling my stool out.

"Okay." I laughed, sticking my arm out and turning it, making a twisting motion.

He headed over to the bar and brought back beers, and we watched the people walking on the boardwalk.

"Hey, look, you can see those guys." I pointed as Bobbie and Dock headed into the bar.

Will sighed.

"What?" I asked, noticing he looked concerned.

He turned to me quickly, changing his expression to a smile, pushing my leg.

"Nothing, I'm just tired." He picked up his beer and took a long sip.

"Any luck on the girl front?" I asked, knowing it would annoy him.

"A night here and there." He rolled his eyes. "It is summer, but no one worth keeping yet."

"Picky, picky," I teased.

"Have to be a little picky; otherwise, you get burned. I've already been down that road."

"What about any of my girls? Bobbie?"

Shit, I should have said something to Bobbie first.

"Bobbie is great, but I don't know."

"What's not to know?"

"Sometimes, you *just* don't know."

"What the hell does that mean?" I laughed, looking at the Sand Bar again.

"I don't know what it means!"

We both laughed.

I noticed Bobbie walking back up the boardwalk but didn't see Dock. "Here comes Bobbie."

"Hey," Bobbie said, coming over. "Tom's working—wanna go?"

"You know, you could've called us instead," Will said, watching her catch her breath.

"She never has her phone." I smiled and rolled my eyes. "Where's Dock?"

She looked toward the bar, then back at me. "I don't know; he went to the bathroom, and then I didn't see him again. He's probably there still."

"Okay, let's go," Will said, throwing some cash down.

The bar floor was sand with palm trees planted all around, emulating a tropical island. It was crowded but not enough where you couldn't see everyone. I scanned the room for him, but I saw him nowhere. We sat down, and Will went to the bar for drinks. I began to feel foolish, wondering where he was, but didn't want Bobbie to notice, although I knew that she did.

"He probably ran into someone outside," she said. "You know how it is here."

"I'll call him to let him know we're all here now."

I put my phone to my ear and my finger in my other so that I could hear over the version of "Margaritaville" the two-piece band in the corner was playing badly. It went right to voicemail.

"Hey, we're all at the Sand Bar, all of us now. Wondering where you are."

Will came back with our drinks and a few guys behind him, and he introduced us.

"This is Tim and Mike," he said.

"Hey," Bobbie and I said simultaneously.

"They work with us sometimes."

"Nice to meet you guys," I said, remembering I'd met Tim before. I looked around again, feeling Will watching me.

"You call Dock?" he asked quietly.

"I let him know we're here. He didn't answer," I whispered.

Will sighed again.

What the fuck is going on with all the fucking sighs?

I was about to ask Will what he knew or if he knew anything because it felt like he did, and I was sick of it. But a waitress came with a tray of shots, and all the guys started laughing and talking loudly.

"I don't want this," I said to Bobbie, uninterested in the party.

"It's medicinal." She laughed, taking hers.

"Take mine then." I pushed it over.

"Don't mind if I do." Will reached over, picked it up, and tossed it down his throat. "Jesus." He shook his head.

"You'll be fucked up soon." Bobbie chuckled, and I nodded, agreeing.

I looked at my phone and tapped my nails on the table. "I'm gonna go smoke," I announced, picking up the shoes I'd kicked off and heading outside. I suddenly realized I didn't have a cigarette. I was unsure I even wanted one but felt awkward standing there doing nothing.

"Hey, you okay?"

I hadn't noticed Bobbie walk up. "Yeah, I'm okay."

"He probably ran into someone. You know how the island is."

"Whatever." I avoided her gaze.

"Will is on his way to drunk town, just so you know." She laughed, trying to change the subject.

"Oh? More shots?"

"Yup. Let's go back in and have a good rest of the night. Whattaya say?"

It annoyed me that she was in cheer-up mode. I put my finger up and moved away from her a little, pulling my phone from my pocket. "I'll call once more."

I decided to forget him after one last attempt. He was supposed to drive Lilly to the airport tomorrow, so I hoped he'd be around by then. I went back and forth, thinking something terrible had happened, but then anger came; he'd ditched me.

The call went right to voicemail again, and I left another message and suddenly wanted to throw my phone in the water.

I nodded to Bobbie, who raised her eyebrows. We headed back, and then I saw her—the rough-looking girl from earlier, walking toward us. She seemed to be in a trance with her eyes half shut.

"She's fucked up," Bobbie said.

I wonder if . . . A feeling came over me, and I needed to follow it.

"Go back in so Will doesn't think we left. I'll meet you there in one second. Just gonna run to the bathroom."

"Okay. Hurry up."

I headed over to the wooden walkway and up the alley. There was a public bathroom there and some apartments, usually rented by boaters. I was unsure what I was doing or what I thought I'd find, but I kept going. Some people passed, and I listened, hearing loud music from a half-opened door in the unit closest to the street.

"Hey, gorgeous," an Irish voice said, and I felt hands on my hips. I jumped, spinning in surprise. It was Mark, standing there with a few of the other Irish boys.

"Hey, Mark; hey, guys." I relaxed.

"Where are you headed?" Mark slurred.

Oh, God, he's drunk. I was unsure I wanted him to know. I wanted no more drama tonight. "Probably home soon." I smiled.

He grabbed me by the shoulders and pretended to shake me. "C'mon, Georgie girl. Party with your old friends here." He swayed side to side. "God, you're beautiful, Georgie." He moved his hands to my hips, coming closer. I took a step back, strategizing how to get away from him, when I heard his voice.

"Yeah, she is. And get the fuck away from her."

I started to turn, but Dock pulled my body back and moved in front of me. He towered over Mark, and I took a side step, quickly considering how to defuse the situation.

"Relax, mate," Mark said in his cocky Irish way.

"You got two seconds to step away." Sweat trickled down the side of Dock's face, and his voice sounded funny, raspier than usual.

"All right, all right, mate." Mark looked around.

"Listen, guys, let's not do this. Mark, I'll see you around, okay?" I smiled as sweetly as my face would allow.

Mark paused, looking at Dock, smiling devilishly. "Okay, George.

Anything for you," he said, picking up my hand.

His blue eyes sparkled, and he had a grin on his face. He looked at Dock and slowly brought my hand to his lips. Realizing what he was doing, I pulled it away. A breeze blew past my shoulders. Everything moved in slow motion as Dock hit the side of his mouth, and Mark spun, falling to the ground.

I gaped at Dock, then at Mark on the ground, not moving.

"Anyone else, boys? Now's your time." Dock held his hands up, waving them forward.

I kneeled next to Mark, heart racing, hoping he was okay. He was breathing, and he started to open his eyes.

"Hey, George," he said. He blinked a few times and reached for his lip, laughing.

I glared up at Dock. He was sweating heavily now, his eyes wide and scary.

"You didn't need to do that," I said softly.

"Don't worry about what I need to do, George," he said.

His voice was very strange. He looked strange.

"Let's go." He grabbed my hand and turned, pulling me up the boardwalk. I looked back at Mark, who was standing now, which made me feel better.

"Will and Bobbie are back there," I said as he pulled me along. We passed by the open apartment door, and I looked in, wondering if that was where he came from. "Where were you?"

He stopped to look at me and then all around him. He took my hand and resumed walking with a sense of urgency. We came to a bench on the other side of the building behind the bar, and he sat me down. I stared up at him.

"Are you okay?" I demanded.

"I'm fine. I'm fine," he breathed. "Listen, babe." *Babe again.* "I'm sorry I left you. I'll explain later, but I have to go meet this guy about a job." He peered around again.

"Now? What's going on, Dock?" I asked seriously.

"It's no big deal. This kid I know owed me some money, and he has a job coming up and . . ." He paused, looking toward the alleyway.

"And what?"

"And I have to talk to him about it," he said, now staring ahead.

"Okay. So why now? Why not answer your phone?" I stood and put my face in front of his.

He paced in front of me, then stopped.

"I love you." He half smiled. "You're my entire world. Do you know that?"

He'd never said that before. His words always fell short of it.

"I love you too."

His eyes smiled, and he leaned over and kissed me.

"Let me walk you back to those guys, and I'll go meet him and then meet up with you guys after."

"I'm fine walking back. I'll cut through the bar," I said, still uneasy. "How long will you be?"

"I don't know. I'll call you." He turned away and then back. "What's with the third degree, George?" He kissed my forehead softly as if to console me.

"Are you drunk?"

"No. I smoked a little weed with the guys. Maybe I shouldn't have." He smiled, then once again glanced over his shoulder. I'd never seen him so distracted.

"All right. I'll talk to you soon." I put my hand on the side of his face and looked into his eyes. He wasn't coming back.

I was troubled about it all. Something wasn't right, but I wasn't sure what. The music seemed louder, and Will danced with Bobbie as Tim swayed in front of the band. I sat by myself, tossing my shoes on the ground and wiping the sand from my feet.

Maybe I'm paranoid. I had grown up questioning everything and everyone, and I didn't want any of that to ruin this.

Will stumbled over, bumping into my chair and nearly knocking me over.

"Hey there, girly." He had a smile plastered on his face, which looked funny as he rarely smiled.

"Whoa there." I tousled his hair, and he pushed it back away from his face.

"No signs of my asshole brother?"

I thought about telling him the truth; I wanted to say that Dock had acted strangely and see what he said, but I didn't.

"Nope. Maybe he found someone more interesting." I rested my chin on my hand.

"Doubtful, George. Maybe he's drunk; probably just went home," he slurred, staring at me.

I could tell he was trying to make me feel better, and it bothered me.

"Forget it, Will. Have a good time." I tapped his shoulder.

"I think my time is up. I'm pretty buzzed." He sat next to me, almost missing the stool. Tim and Bobbie were still dancing.

"Why don't you let me walk you back to the boat so you don't kill yourself," I said, getting my shoes.

"Whatever you think is best, boss." He laughed at himself, and I couldn't help laughing too. I'd never seen him like this. He was always so reserved and serious.

I told Bobbie I was leaving but was unsure she heard me over the music. Tim grabbed her and spun her away from me. I gave him a look, making sure she was okay, and he smiled.

I took Will's arm, and we walked to the boardwalk. He stumbled, holding on to a lamppost to correct himself.

"Jesus, Will." I laughed. "I've never seen you like this."

"Don't do shots, George!" he yelled.

"I try not to!" I yelled back.

"I'm freaking starving," he said as we passed the takeout window below Nancy's, which was closed.

"Do you have food back on the boat?" I asked.

He didn't answer. We turned the corner to the ramp and went up. He took his shoes off and tossed them. One fell into the water.

"Will!" I laughed, nearly hysterical.

"What?" He stood up, climbing onto the boat, reaching for my hand.

"Your shoe!"

He looked at the water, waving his hand dismissively, and I took his hand and climbed on. I was nervous about leaving him like this.

"Let me make you some food, and you can eat and go to bed. Deal?"

"Deal," he said, sitting hard on the bow and lighting a cigarette.

I went into the galley and opened the fridge. He didn't have much except a few staples and two boxes of mac and cheese.

"Slim pickings in there."

I came out with a bowl of mac and cheese and toast. I put it in front of him.

"Oh man, this is perfect! Thank you." He picked up the bowl and took a few bites, oohing and aahing. I sat next to him, and he put a forkful to my mouth, so I took a bite.

I wonder what he's doing.

I suddenly became irritated.

"What do you wanna be when you grow up, George?"

I barely made out what he said through the food.

"What?" I looked at him strangely.

"What do you wanna do with the rest of your life?"

"Where the hell is this coming from?"

"I don't know?" He shook his head back and forth, then up and down. "I don't know?" he said again. He put the bowl down in front of him, becoming serious. "Sometimes, I think I want to do something different. No more breaking my back. Ya know?"

"I do." I smiled.

"Yeah, but you're a nurse. That's a great job, and it seems like you're good at it. At least, from what you say."

He took another bite of toast, then tossed the crust, missing the plate.

"I didn't grow up wanting to be a nurse," I said.

"No?"

He turned to me, and I stared, thinking how drunk he looked.

"What?"

I stopped staring. "Nothing."

"What did you want to be?"

"I used to journal and write all the time. I guess I wanted to be a writer."

"Really? That's cool. Dear diary, today was a good day." He laughed, pretending to write on his hand.

"Shut up." I pushed him, and he fell on his side.

He righted himself and looked at me again, his eyes gray and dark. The scruff on his chin seemed to have grown in the minutes we'd sat here. He looked like Dock. It was apparent they were brothers.

"Do you still journal?"

"Some, but it's been a bit. I don't know." I shrugged, wanting to change the subject.

"Well, you should. Dear diary, Dock sucks." He laughed, then turned serious, noticing I was quiet. "Haven't heard from him, huh?"

"No, it is what it is."

"Yup." He sighed and looked ahead. He seemed to want to say more but remained silent. He took a few more bites, then leaned back, sighing again.

"You and your sighs."

"George. I think you are the best," he said, glancing away from me.

"Thanks." I nudged him.

"I'm serious, George." He put his head in his hands. "It should have been me. I should have met you first." He looked up, nodding. Sighing yet again, he leaned back on the boat's windshield.

I wasn't expecting this. I didn't know how to respond. My mind whirled.

"Listen, George. I know I'm drunk, and I shouldn't be saying any of this. I know it. Hopefully, I don't remember." He breathed deeply, reaching for the cigarettes next to him and lighting one. "I just—"

"I think you're great too, Will," I said, making it seem like I didn't understand what he meant.

He stopped talking and took a long drag. "Yeah. We're both great," he said softly and closed his eyes.

I got up and walked down the ramp, putting on my shoes. "You okay?" I called back.

He crossed his legs, watching me. "I'm good, George, and thanks."

I headed up the boardwalk to the cab stand and home.

CHAPTER 23

August 31, 2003
It can't catch me. It's not supposed to; otherwise,
I wouldn't keep finding escape hatches.

*M*r. S. was in a foul mood that morning, which was perfect, as so was I. I felt like our moods had synched after spending so much time together. He was never entirely chipper anyway, but today he seemed extra glum. I hadn't heard from Dock, and I went back and forth, thinking I was paranoid and overreacting or that he had a family somewhere with two kids and a dog. I felt upside down.

Maybe he's not into me.

I struggled to believe that, as his actions showed different when we were together. Whatever it was, it drove me mad and made me somehow want him more. I couldn't figure any of it.

I brought Mr. S. downstairs and handed him the *Times*; we were silent in our routine, and I was glad he wasn't complaining. I headed back up, starting to tidy things, and noticed his book I'd left sticking out of the bookcase. I pulled it from the shelf, running my hand across the cover, watching the dust dance in front of me. I'd finished the other one a few weeks earlier, and I was sure I'd be alone tonight, so I put it in my bag.

I'll escape in his stories; they're more tragic than my own.

I glanced out the hallway window at the club and spotted a truck, but it wasn't his.

Am I crazy? Do I even know what a normal relationship is?

I felt defeated, suddenly hating myself, figuring it was probably me. *I'm so fucking damaged.*

I reached in my bag and took out my phone. I stared at it, wondering if I should call.

"George!" Lilly called from across the hall.

"Coming, Lilly," I shouted, heading toward her.

As I walked by the open window in the hall, a large gust of wind blew the curtain across my face. The weather would soon be changing. I could smell it. Fall was coming, and the air would grow crisper and colder. I was ready for it, especially now.

Lilly was half dressed as she pulled things from her top drawer. She mumbled to herself, holding a top in front of her, making faces in the mirror. She frantically tossed clothes at Delia, who folded them and put them in the open suitcase on the bed.

"Which one, George, the red or the white?" She held two blouses, draping the white one across her, then holding up the red. "Which is best for Italy?" Her eyes widened in urgency.

"I'd say red for sure." I looked at Delia, who was trying to hold back from laughing, then headed back toward the doorway.

"You look wonderful lately, George. Have you done something differently?"

I turned, leaning against the doorframe. "No, I got some highlights a month ago. That's the extent of it." I tossed my hair.

"So, George, how do you think he is doing, health-wise?" She put the shirts on the bed and came closer.

"Oh, he is doing well lately. So far, knock on wood," I answered, tapping the wooden door, unsure where this was going.

"Well." She hesitated. "I was hoping to return to our Connecticut house for a while. I think he would enjoy being there and seeing old friends. So, I was wondering what you thought?" She picked up the red shirt and handed it to Delia.

I wondered what she meant.

Delia shook her head.

"So, my question to you is, George, could you go with us?" She smiled, pushing back her silver hair, tucking it behind her ear. "He won't go without you, I'm sure of it." She looked at me seriously as she sat on the bed.

It was odd seeing her sit. It made me uncomfortable. I didn't know what to say. I wasn't expecting this or excited at the prospect of picking up and moving, though it was only for a few months. I pulled at my necklace, looking at Delia, who was fixing things in the suitcase.

"Hmm, this is tough, Lilly."

"I know, George. It's only for a little while, and Dock could come."

"Dock?"

"Aren't you in a relationship?"

Delia giggled. Lilly turned to her, and she bit her lip, falling silent.

"Oh, well, I guess." I became flustered. "I just wasn't sure everyone knew." I stared at Delia.

"We need help at the house, anyway, odd things. It's an old farmhouse."

"Where would I stay?" I hesitantly asked.

"You'd stay in the guesthouse. Where he wrote most of his books," she said excitedly, as if this would sway me. "It's a barn we converted." She went over to the dresser, opening another drawer. "Why don't you think about it and let me know soon."

"Okay, I will." I headed down the side stairs toward the living room, stopping in front of the glass slider to look at the water.

I don't even want to think about this now.

"May as well add it to the plate," I mumbled, wiping a fingerprint with my sleeve.

Mr. S. was sitting with his eyes closed on the sofa where I had left him.

"Any interest in going for a walk?" I asked softly, trying not to startle him, bracing for the no.

He opened his eyes. I noticed Lady sitting by his feet.

"Lady probably would like to go," I said before he could talk, pleased with myself.

He reached down and tapped her head. "Okay," he grumbled, taking a tissue and wiping his mouth. He grabbed the side of the sofa to get up. The tissue box fell onto Lady, causing her to jump and scurry off. "Goddamn it!" he yelled.

I rolled my eyes, helping him and handing him his cane.

We headed to the door off the porch. He stopped suddenly and screamed up the stairs with urgency.

"Delia! Delia!"

Footsteps hurried across the ceiling above us.

"Yes, Mr. S.," she answered sweetly.

She was always sweet to him.

"Can I have a sweater?"

"Which one?" she said, now appearing at the top of the stairs.

Lilly came behind her, still in her bra.

"Is everything okay?"

"Jesus Christ, I just want a sweater," he barked, coughing.

"We're about to go for a walk, Lilly." I sat him in the dining chair. Delia raced down and handed me a sweater.

"I'd love to walk with you, darling," Lilly chimed.

"Okay," he said, attempting to look at her but unable to.

I walked behind them, staying close in case he became tired. Lilly talked mostly, occasionally peering at him. The large willow tree swayed in the breeze off the water, and the sun hung low over the Yacht Club. I wondered what they were like when they were young and falling in love. I knew they'd met after he spoke at her college when his first book was published, and again in London, later. She often told that story. They seemed secure in each other, having been together for so many years. Lilly seemed genuinely interested in everything he had to say, although now that was minimal. You could tell she valued his opinion and held it in the highest regard, often speaking of his intelligence, which he undoubtedly possessed in spades. He needed her to be close, almost like a child relying on its mother. I'd heard he was fiercely independent when he was younger, although I wondered if he'd always needed her there in some capacity.

They walked along the lawn, then back up to the porch to sit just as the ferry passed. I went inside, staying close in case he called, knowing Lilly would leave soon. I looked at the clock, and my stomach suddenly knotted. Dock would need to be here soon if he was taking her to the airport. I didn't want to be here either way, whether he came or left her in the lurch, so I headed into the kitchen to ask Delia if she could help Mr. S. if he called. I told her I had to run up the street for some things.

"Sure thing, Georgie," she said, stirring something on the stove that smelled awful.

I grabbed my bag and headed toward the door.

"So, what do you think about Connecticut?" she called after me.

"I don't know, haven't thought about it."

"Your tall, dark man can come." She laughed, continuing to stir.

"He has a job here, and I don't know what's going on with him." I tried sounding aloof but regretted saying the last part.

"Trouble in paradise?" She stopped stirring. I could tell she wanted the gossip.

"No, I don't know, maybe." I laughed nervously. "What are you cooking?"

"Just some chicken bones for that dog of his." She waved the spoon around, shutting off the burner. "Listen, Georgie," she began, wiping her hands on her apron, "don't let no man"—her voice rose to a yell—"*no man*"—she paused—"steal your smile. You hear me?" She put her hand on my shoulder, coming close enough that I felt her breath.

"I hear you," I whispered.

"Good!" she yelled, leaning away from me. "Okay, go."

She swatted at me with the dishrag she'd pulled off the counter as I jogged out the door.

I hopped in the BMW and headed up the drive, thinking I'd take a ride to clear my head. I drove over the bridge into Oak Bluffs to grab an iced coffee and maybe stop by the log cabin. Pulling in near the carousel, I crossed the street to Dippin' Donuts, and then I saw it—the gold lettering; it was his truck, parked by the Sand Bar, where we were the night before.

Did he meet that guy? Did he ever leave?

My mind raced. I wanted to snoop around but didn't want him to see me.

I ordered, staring out the window, wondering if I should walk over, feeling terrified. I thought of the apartment in the alley.

Is he there?

I took the coffee to the counter and added an extra splash of cream. I had a clear view of the truck. I started to take a sip when I saw her, the stringy blonde, walking from what looked like the alleyway toward the truck. My eyes darted around, and then a red shirt came from behind her. It was Dock. My heart sank as I watched them. He opened the door and grabbed something; then they both walked back, disappearing into the alley again. I stood frozen, unable to move.

"Excuse me," a voice said.

I jumped, spinning around.

The woman looked at me kindly. "Sorry, just want to get some cream."

I grabbed my coffee and walked back to the car, unsure of what to do. I wanted to go over there; I wanted to scream, but what would that prove? I started the car and headed to the cabin.

"He doesn't deserve me," I mumbled, unsure I believed that. I drove past the harbor, looking at Will's boat. The anger subsided to heartbreak, but only for a moment. I quickly became angry again, yelling, "Fuck you" as loud as possible, pulling up the dirt drive.

"Hey, George," Jennie said as I came up the steps.

She was lying in the hammock with some guy I'd never met.

"Bobbie around?" I asked, not interested in introductions.

"Yeah, she's inside. You okay?"

"Awesome," I answered sarcastically and headed into the house.

Bobbie was sitting on the couch next to a pile of unfolded laundry. She turned to me, and the sun caught her face through the window.

She is beautiful.

I stared at her features, resenting she didn't need an ounce of makeup.

"Hey, George, take a load off."

She started to laugh, then stopped, seeing something was wrong.

"Men suck." I plopped next to her, half on her laundry. I took a sip of my coffee, feeling bad as I'd meant to get her one and forgot.

"Dock still MIA?"

"Yup, and I just saw him"—I paused for effect—"with that ratchet-looking blonde."

She looked confused.

"The one who said hi to him last night."

She said nothing, appearing to try to remember.

"Well, whatever. I'm done."

"Maybe it's nothing. Try talking to him, why don't you?" She picked up a shirt and folded it.

I suddenly wanted to change the subject.

"When are you all leaving?" I asked, surveying the packed boxes, sad that summer was over.

"A few weeks. I tried to stay on, but they didn't need anyone." She picked up another shirt.

"This sucks." I got up and headed toward the door. "Gotta go. I'm sure he is yelling for me now." I turned back to her and tried to muster a smile.

"Call me later." She tossed a pair of underwear at me, and I moved to watch them fall to the floor.

I shut the door and headed out.

I thought about how long the winter would be, alone now, on the drive back, wondering where my life was headed.

The thought of his arms around me intruded.

My chest was heavy, and I wanted to run away or sleep. Then it came to me. I pulled down the drive and jogged into the house.

Lilly was sitting at the table, writing in her notebook; she didn't look up.

"Lilly," I said cautiously, praying I wasn't interrupting some poetic genius.

"Oh, hi, George." She glanced over but continued to write.

"My answer is yes."

She stopped writing and shot me a questioning look.

"Connecticut. I'll go with you to Connecticut," I said, sitting across from her.

"Oh my, that's wonderful!" She put down her pen and pressed her hands together.

"When would we leave?" I asked.

"Well, I hadn't thought about it much yet, but you both can leave as early as next week if you'd want to?" She picked up the pen, tapping it. "Delia could go along with you all, and I'd come back here after my trip to make sure the house is shut down. Kelly could come, and someone else could pack things." She was thinking out loud. "Or we could wait, too, until I—"

"Next week would be perfect."

CHAPTER 24

September 10, 2003
The only thing that's real is my feelings.
They are pure and loud.

The weekend came, and I scurried back and forth between the house and the cottage, packing and getting things ready to go. I wasn't sure I'd made the right decision or if I was running away, but I didn't plan the escape. It fell in my lap, so I felt better about it. I never knew if Dock showed to take Lilly to the airport. Delia said someone drove her but didn't see who. I didn't want to get into details and have her ask a bunch of questions I didn't have the answers to.

I made myself scarce at the cottage, staying with Hobo at the main house while Lilly was away. I didn't want to know if anyone came by or not, and I didn't think he'd come here to find me if he was looking. Part of me wanted him to, most parts anyway, but I wouldn't make it easy. I was out of my mind trying to understand what had happened between us and why the disappearing act again. I tried hard to put it all out of my head, and now I could with my escape—or at least I hoped so.

I walked through the archway, planning on finishing packing at the cottage while Mr. S. was visiting with the specialist staying in the guesthouse who Lilly failed to mention was coming. It was eleven in the morning, and I was already exhausted from arguing with him after he refused to get out of bed, knowing he'd have to sit with her.

"George," a voice called from behind, scaring me half to death. It was Delia, rushing down from the porch and through the archway. "A man stopped by for you, Georgie."

She was holding something in her hand.

A man? Oh my God, was it Dock?

My stomach fluttered with nervous excitement but quickly soured; Delia knew Dock. She wouldn't call him "a man."

"The man, he kind of looked like that Dock of yours. He said he came to the cottage a few times, but you weren't there. Said to give you this. What is it, George?"

She handed it to me.

I took it from her, puzzled, and lowered myself to the step. I wanted to be alone, but I could tell she was curious, so I felt obligated to open it in front of her, which annoyed me.

It was small and square, wrapped in brown paper with a yellow string tied around it. I untied it and tore at the corner, pulling off the paper, seeing the leather cover. It was a book, a journal. I opened it and beheld an old-world map imprinted in gold on the blank pages and an inscription in blue pen.

I heard you were leaving, and I wish you told me. I thought you might need a new one. Safe travels, George. Don't be a stranger. Ever—Will

I closed the cover, smiling. Delia pretended to adjust her skirt.

"Will, Dock's brother. It's a journal," I said, holding it in her direction.

"Oh, that's nice. A journal, huh?"

She sounded unsure of what that was but pretended to know.

"It's a book where you write your thoughts and things every day, or whenever."

"Oh, yes. I see," she said.

I was still unsure if she understood, catching her look at me funny. "The brother?"

I saw the mischief in her eyes and knew what was coming.

"Does he like you too, Georgie?" She laughed, slapping at her knee.

"What? No. We're friends."

I can't believe Will remembered.

"They all like ya, Georgie!" she shouted, disappearing through the bushes.

I opened the cover again and reread the words: *Ever—Will*

I went inside and placed it on the bed. Grabbing a water, I saw Dock's face in the picture on the fridge and remembered the day we went to the fair. I pulled it from under the magnet, staring at the way he'd held me as if looking for an answer. Without thinking, I grabbed my phone from my bag and dialed. It went right to voicemail. I hung up, wiping away the moisture beginning to form in my eyes, angry at myself for calling.

Just then, my phone dinged, notifying me I had a voicemail. I picked it up and stared at it. The missed call was from him.

I listened and nearly lost my breath at the sound of his voice.

"Listen, can I see you tonight?" He paused, clearing his throat. He sounded nervous. "Can you come by the house?" He paused again for a long while. "Please?"

I paced around the cottage, listening to him over and over.

"What is going on here? What do I do?" I said out loud.

I looked around for Hobo, forgetting he was next door. Then, staring at the phone, I went to call him back but stopped myself.

What is there to say?

I headed back to the house, determined to not see him. I especially wouldn't come to him.

But maybe he'd come?

I tried to make myself believe I wouldn't go but knew I would no matter how much I wrestled with it.

I went into the living room after Delia gave me the all clear. The doctor had left for the time being, and Mr. S. was sitting on the sofa with his eyes closed.

"Did you want to go for a walk? It's not too chilly."

"No." He coughed slowly, opening his eyes. "I'd like to go lay down."

"Okay. Are you feeling alright?" I was concerned, as this was unusual.

"That woman wore me out," he griped, attempting to stand.

I helped him over to the stairs.

"Quackery!" he yelled as he climbed to the bedroom.

He tripped on the last step, and I caught him under the arm.

He plopped on the bed. I helped him off with his shoes and lifted his legs, putting the throw over him. He looked tired and over it all. I felt the same but in a different way. I stared at him, feeling a connection.

"I'm going to run up the island and get a few boxes at the grocery store. I'll be back soon, okay?"

"Delia is here?"

"Yes, downstairs."

"Okay." He closed his eyes.

I told Delia to listen for him and bring him downstairs if he called, to which she gladly agreed. She liked when Lilly was away and it was just him and her. I wasn't sure why; they didn't seem to talk much, although I caught them once having a conversation. They spoke of living in Greenwich, and some dinner party years earlier, so apparently they had moments. She laughed, and he was engaged and smiling. You could see the history between them. The conversation with Lilly that day outside of the hospital popped into my head.

"She's in love with him, George."

I got in the car and headed toward Edgartown. I felt crazed, unsure if what I was doing was right or wrong, but did it matter?

I'm doing it anyway.

Excitement gave way to anger and doubt. They all swirled together, and I breathed deeply, hoping I'd get an answer, hoping I'd understand. I fixed my hair in the mirror and thought of what to say and why I'd come. I didn't want him to think I'd jumped when he called, although that's what I did.

What is it about him? I asked myself, remembering his smell and kiss, realizing the answer.

I didn't want it to be over, but I couldn't handle another disappearing act. Something wasn't right, and I wanted to know what. I turned onto Smith Hollow and collected my thoughts, stopping in the road in front of the house. I tapped my foot on the floorboard, hearing myself hum. I stopped and cleared my throat. I wanted to throw it in reverse, but it was too late. He had probably seen me, and I'd look like an idiot.

Why didn't I think this through better?

I got out, shutting the door softly, and went up the steps to the door. I hesitated, then tapped lightly. A large shadow moved toward me from behind the curtain.

"Hey," he said softly, opening the door wide. He stared into my eyes, then down at his feet. I couldn't tell if he was nervous or ashamed. I swallowed hard, my throat suddenly a desert.

"Hey" was all I could muster back.

He looked up, and we both were quiet.

"I was headed up-island and got your message. So, what's up?"

I tried sounding casual, needing to break the silence, although I knew he could see through me. I felt an overwhelming desire to kick him.

"Come in," he said, moving to the side.

I walked by him. The house looked nothing like before; it was a mess. A giant pile of laundry sat near the basement door; an ashtray overflowed with cigarette butts. All different cans and take-out wrappers were scattered around. I stared at him.

"Cleaning lady quit?"

"Just been busy and in a weird place, I guess." He looked around and picked up two cans, moving them near the sink. I noticed the cigarette butts were different brands; other people had been here.

"Looks like you've been having houseguests."

I grew hot with anger, thinking of the blonde.

He was fast to answer. "Some workers have crashed once in a while."

"Will been by?" I asked, knowing the answer.

"No, I think he's pissed at me for some reason."

He pulled up a chair and motioned for me to sit, then pulled over one for himself.

I tugged at my necklace, thinking of what to say.

"Pissed?" I paused, suddenly feeling nervous. "I'm a bit pissed too, so maybe it's a theme." I glared at him.

He looked defeated, rubbing his head, then seemed annoyed, which surprised me.

"Look, I know I've fucked up here. I get it." He sat back in the chair, sighing.

"Actually, I don't get it."

I was aggravated. I glanced at the door and thought about leaving, regretting that I'd come. He got up and paced in front of me. I smelled him as he walked by, and it made me realize how much I missed him again.

He stopped and crouched in front of me, taking my hand. "Listen, I'm scared. This all scares me."

He let my hand go and rubbed his face as beads of sweat formed in his hairline. I stared at his shirt. He was wearing a long-sleeved flannel with a T-shirt underneath, which I'd never seen him in before, and it wasn't cold.

"Why don't you take this off? You're sweating," I interrupted him, pulling at the sleeve.

He looked at me, confused. "What? I'm fine, it's fine."

He went over and opened the window in front of the sink; twisting around, he leaned against the counter.

"Listen, George, I'm in love with you and, and I want to be with you."

He came back to me and pulled me up from the chair. I stood in front of him, listening attentively, liking what he was saying, although hating that I did.

"Come here."

He took my hand and walked me back into the bedroom, sitting me on the bed.

"Wait, before you say anything else. I saw you. I, I saw you with her," I stuttered, desperate to get it out. I wanted him to tell me it was in my head and explain it was all innocent.

"Who?" He looked confused.

"The blond girl. The one who said hi to you the night we were out before you *disappeared*," I snarled.

"What? Where?"

He sat next to me, seeming nervous; then suddenly he seemed to know who I was talking about. "She's no one, George." He laughed.

I glared at him, not thinking it was funny, and he stopped.

"I saw you walk to your truck together the day after behind the Sand Bar."

He touched his face again, appearing to think. "She knows the guy I was getting the job bid from. I don't know. Maybe I was getting a cigarette or something? I can't even remember."

I observed him as he spoke. He seemed truthful, and I wanted to believe him.

Maybe I just want to believe.

He turned my face toward him, and I smelled the sweetness of his breath. I wanted his lips on mine, not caring about any of this, but a part of me didn't believe him or knew I shouldn't.

"Listen to me. I love you." He stared into my eyes and kissed my forehead.

I turned my head, not wanting to get lost, trying to stay focused.

He turned my face back to his and closed his eyes. "I'm so sorry. It all scared me."

I hesitated in speaking but had to say something. I shut my eyes, listening to my voice.

"Something is off here, Dock." I opened my eyes again, looking up at him. "It's just . . ." My lips trembled.

"George, I love you," he interrupted. "I've never felt this way before about anyone." He sounded desperate. "I just never expected this. I don't even know if I'm capable of it."

"Capable of what?" I stared at him intensely.

"Being the man that you need, the man you deserve." He hung his head, appearing exhausted.

I looked at my hand now against his head, caressing it, wondering how it got there. He turned his face and kissed my arm, then wrapped his arms around me, leaning me back on the bed, and again I was his.

• • •

We lay there for a while, staring at the ceiling, seeming unsure of where to go from here. Feeling strange and vulnerable, I sat up, looking under the blankets for my shirt, and felt him get up from the bed. I put my arm in the sleeve and glanced over. I quickly looked again, not understanding what was happening. He was on one knee on the floor, staring at me.

"What are you doing?"

"Listen to me, George."

He picked his shirt up from the floor and put it on, not moving from his spot, then took my hand. "You're the one for me. I've known it since we met."

"What are you doing?" I laughed uncomfortably, taking my hand back, pulling my shirt on. He grabbed my hand again and reached to the top of the dresser, picking up a small blue pouch I hadn't noticed before. He let go of my hand and pulled open the strings. My mind raced, watching him take my hand again and open it. He tipped the pouch over and dropped something into my palm. I looked at the sparkling stone in disbelief, feeling him take my other hand in his, unable to move my eyes.

"George, George," he called again, snapping me from my trance.

I looked up, and his eyes met mine.

"I want to marry you. Marry me, George."

He moved closer to me, putting his face near mine.

"George?"

"What? Yes, yes, I-I . . ." I stuttered, looking at my hand again.

"George," he whispered, smiling, then kissed me.

I closed my eyes, and he kissed me long and hard. I pulled away from him and put my head against his.

"So?" he breathed.

My mind raced. I've never felt like this with anyone before. It was real, our feelings. I knew that.

But is getting married right? Is he capable? Like he said. Am I capable, even?

I didn't want to think. I only wanted to feel. I wanted us together.

I looked at my hand, then up at him.

"I would have married you yesterday," I whispered.

CHAPTER 25

September 15, 2003
Remote, rustic, and farther still, this will be our time.

"*A*re you ready, Mr. S.?" I asked, twirling the band on my finger. I'd put the diamond in my jewelry box to keep our secret, wearing only the band on my right hand until we were ready to tell everyone.

"No," he grumbled, staring at the ceiling.

"We have to get on the road. Bob is here to drive you."

He conceded as he usually did—by saying nothing. I got him ready and brought him downstairs. Delia and I helped him into the car, meeting each other's eyes in surprise at the lack of yelling or complaints.

"See you tonight." I waved, watching them drive off.

I walked out on the lawn and gazed at the whitecaps rolling in. The air was colder, and the wind blew, causing a rustling sound as clusters of leaves from the willow tree swirled at my feet. I thought of how much had changed, still unable to believe I was married—married, and leaving the island. Although it was only for a short time, I still felt sad.

It all happened so fast. I had no time to think and preferred it that way, enjoying being caught up in the moment. I loved him and believed we'd make it. We'd live here, and he'd build our house. We'd grow old in it and maybe have a family. I'd never been more excited or happy, and he seemed to feel the same. I didn't think of him disappearing and my suspicions. I wouldn't let that ruin anything and kept telling myself it scared him, feeling this way, and that I was paranoid. The way he made me feel couldn't be wrong. It was too primal, like he was a missing piece of me I'd longed for, although I didn't know it. I wouldn't let myself ruin it.

We'd met that Sunday under the gazebo at the Harbor View. He didn't tell anyone, and neither did I, agreeing to keep it a secret, except I convinced him to let me tell Bobbie because I'd burst if I didn't tell someone. She thought it was all crazy, but romantic too, and gave us her blessing. I felt terrible not telling my mom and Ray; we didn't tell Will either, and I felt guilty, thinking he should be there too, but Dock said no one, and I didn't want to make waves. I also didn't want disapproval from anyone who thought things had gone too fast, so I didn't mind keeping it from them for now. I figured he felt the same.

I thought we'd wait until spring or summer, be engaged for a while, but he convinced me it would be romantic marrying now, just the two of us. He knew the justice of the peace and the clerk at the town hall, so it wouldn't be hard. We talked it through, and I felt swept up in it all.

I'd leave for Connecticut, and he'd meet me there after tying up some loose ends on the island. When I told him about going, he seemed unsurprised but denied it when I asked if he'd heard. The island was a funny place, where everyone seemed to know everything, and he always seemed to as well.

I found a dress at one of the Edgartown shops on sale. It looked vintage with long lace sleeves and a short train. It hugged my body perfectly, making me believe it was all meant to be. We got two white-gold bands from the jeweler on Main Street. He also gave us a deal, placing the diamond in a beautiful antique setting that he had in the shop. It was from the estate of one of the island's older families and fit as if it were made for me.

"You're beautiful." Dock had smiled, rising from the rocking chair as I walked under the gazebo.

"You're looking pretty handsome yourself." I laughed, watching him pull at his suit lapel.

I fixed his tie, and he kept his eyes on mine, then leaned in and kissed me.

"Hey, not yet!" I pushed him away.

A man walked up the stairs, pulling on a black robe. I assumed he was the JP, and he came over, introducing himself. Dock shook his hand.

"Are you both ready?"

I was ready. I wanted this and wanted Dock. But I hesitated a moment, feeling caught in a whirlwind, wondering if my head was about me. *Am I sure?*

The moment didn't last. I envisioned us living here, finally happy. I'd never believed before in happy endings or fairy tales, but I felt sure this was mine.

He took my hand, and we stood close, listening. The JP read verses of scripture, saying something about Dock being a carpenter like Jesus. We tried hard not to laugh, rolling our eyes at each other, knowing the comparison was silly. A large catamaran passed by the lighthouse through the channel; everything felt magical.

"Wait!" Dock yelled, startling me and causing the man to drop his paper. He hopped the railing into the blue hydrangea bushes that lined the front of the hotel, hurriedly picking a few, then rushed back up the stairs and handed them to me.

"You're crazy." I laughed.

My head spun, and my heart felt full. I felt complete and happy. I belonged to someone, and he to me. And I mattered; it was something that had been missing, and now it wasn't. I found a quote about marriage, and I read it to him as a surprise during my vows. I asked what an individual life was worth in the grand scheme of things. And I told him what his was worth to me. All of the mundanities, the tragedies, the joys—I swore to love him through it all as our futures intertwined. We would both matter to each other, even if everything else fell away and there was no one else to care. His life mattered; I would be there to make sure he knew it. "I will be your witness," I swore.

I looked up after reading and saw his lips closed tightly, quivering. He had tears in his eyes, and I could tell he was trying hard to keep from crying. My eyes filled too, and I smiled. He smiled back as a tear rolled down his face, and we both laughed. Holding hands, we turned to the man, and repeated our vows.

"I do."

"Then I do too." I laughed again, kissing him before being told.

• • •

I headed to the cottage and heard the crunching of seashells as the truck came into view.

"Hey there," I said, coming through the archway.

"There's my beautiful wife." He smiled and jumped out of the truck.

He had on his work pants and a knit hat. His green eyes stared through me, and he grabbed me in his arms.

"Ouch!" I giggled as his stubble scratched my face.

"Look at you." He pushed me away from him.

"What?" I pressed my hands to his chest.

"You're glowing."

"Shut up."

I pretended to slap his cheek, knowing he was remembering last night, our wedding night, when we came back here.

"So, I'm leaving. What's the plan again?"

"I'll tie up all of my loose ends here and talk to Will; then, I'll be there hopefully by the end of this week, or next at the latest. I'm gonna talk to Lilly, too, once you leave," he finished.

"I spoke to her this morning, checking if the offer still stood about you coming. She said yes, but I still think it's a good idea for you to go over."

"I'll miss you." He pulled me close again, holding me against him.

"I love you," I said and pulled away.

"I love you too." He kissed my forehead.

I stepped back abruptly, pulling at my shirt as something cold slid down my chest. "What the heck?"

"I said I love you too." He laughed.

"No, I think my necklace broke." I felt down my shirt and pulled out the chain, looking at the small charm dangling at the end of the broken clasp.

"Oh no." I stared at it in my hand.

"Give it to me. I'll get it fixed for you; I got a guy."

I handed it to him, smirking. "I'm sure you got a guy for everything."

• • •

I left the island on a late-afternoon boat, hopeful that this was the start of something beautiful. From the top of the ferry, I watched East Chop become smaller and smaller as we headed toward Woods Hole. I hated leaving, especially now. Just a few days ago, I was eager to go, but only to get over him. I never wanted to leave the island and always hated going off. I sometimes wondered if I'd lived here in a past life because of how strong my attraction to it was. I realized it that first day with my father all those years ago.

My eyes filled suddenly, wishing he were here, wondering how it would be if he were alive. I felt an absence, that feeling of having a protector that all girls need and seem to look for if it's missing. I was unsure I'd ever had it at all. My father spent so much of my life drunk; I never thought of him as someone safe. But now I had Dock and somehow felt whole in that way. I was safe, and I mattered. I never expected the feeling. I reached for my necklace, forgetting it wasn't there, feeling naked without it.

It was early evening when I arrived in Connecticut. Thankfully, Hobo slept most of the drive. I pulled into the small town of Greenwich, immediately noticing its charm—the rolling hills and winding roads. Older farmhouses blended with large estates nestled in the trees by the coast. I passed a covered bridge and understood why writers and artists made their home here. Creative types always seem to gather in the most beautiful places—no doubt finding inspiration in their charm and beauty.

I pulled up to a long cobblestone drive leading to a large yellow home set back off the road. The lawn and surrounding landscape were meticulous, and upon a hill sat a giant barn with a path connected to the house.

"Right here!" a voice called out. Delia stood on the front steps, waving her arms.

Hobo hopped up the steps, and we headed into the house to find all kinds of people I didn't recognize moving about: landscapers, cleaners, etc.; it seemed a small army was here to get the house in order.

"Are these people here all the time?" I asked Delia, following her into the enormous kitchen.

"These are the Connecticut folks." She introduced me to a few of them. "He's in the great room there." She pointed.

"How is he?"

"Eh." She smirked. "You know him, Georgie." She smiled, swatting at a fly.

"George!"

"He's heard you already, girly." Her large white teeth gleamed as she tilted her head back, laughing.

I headed down the corridor, following his voice. He was sitting in an armchair by an enormous stone fireplace that took up the entire wall. He looked small and frail in the large chair. I scanned the room, noticing the dark wood beams and high ceilings, the smell of musty books; every wall had a bookcase filled from top to bottom.

"There are more books than in the library."

I sat in the chair next to him.

"Glad to be back?" I asked while he ignored me.

"When's Lilly coming?"

"She'll be here. I think tomorrow or the day after."

There was an awkward silence that I'd become used to now, but somehow it was more uncomfortable.

"Lilly thought we could answer your fan mail." I stared, trying to engage him.

"No."

"Oh, c'mon, it will be fine."

He said nothing. I walked back down the corridor, past a small door with a desk and chair I'd spotted on the way in. I noticed black-Sharpie writing on notes stuck to a large bulletin board, along with notebooks and scraps of paper with scribbling on them scattered about; it had to be Lilly's office. She'd told me he got tons of mail here and never wanted to answer any, and she hoped maybe I could get him to. A small wicker basket in the corner had a pile of envelopes in it. I figured this was it. I picked it up, seeing a Post-it stuck to a small notebook on top.

If he has anything profound to say, it read in the usual black lettering.

I wondered how she even got it here and figured Kelly must have brought it.

I started to feel annoyed, wishing I hadn't told her about a few of the conversations he and I'd had where he spoke of his drinking, his mother, and other private things.

"He has another book in him, George."

"I'm sure he does."

"It bothers him." She sighed irritably.

We talked for a while that day about things he had said. I could tell he wanted to write more too, and I thought about how hard it must be to lose your purpose and identity. Lilly was quiet, appearing captivated with what I was saying.

"Maybe you could write these things down?"

I shrugged and agreed.

I grabbed the basket and headed into the living room, placing it on the table.

"What's that?"

"The mail."

"Jesus Christ."

"Don't sound so excited." I smiled. "We don't have to do it now. Let me go settle into wherever I'm staying, and I'll be back."

I touched his knee, feeling awkward afterward, and headed to find Delia again.

"Wait, can you help me to the bathroom?" he called behind me.

Why does he always wait until I'm out the door?

I rolled my eyes, turning to him. In his struggle to get up, he knocked his cane to the ground, causing a loud clap that echoed through the room.

"Goddamn it!" he yelled and continued into a coughing fit.

"Don't get all worked up," I ran. I helped him to his feet and handed him the cane. Then I stared at my hand on his arm, noticing the ring, remembering I was married. I felt my cheeks get hot and a flutter in my chest as he led me down the hall.

"The barn is where you're staying. It's a wonderful spot," he said.

"Oh, nice. Isn't that where you wrote?"

"Yes, mostly." He stopped and lifted his arm to wipe his chin. "It's right here," he said, pushing the door with the cane.

I walked in behind him. A few pictures of the Vineyard hung on the wall. I looked closely at a sizable golden plaque over the toilet.

"Mr. S., is that your Pulitzer?"

"Yes," he grumbled, fiddling with his pants.

I helped him with the button. "Why is it above the toilet?"

He paused, looking at me, struggling now with his zipper. He finally got it, and his pants fell to his ankles. "Isn't that the perfect place for it?"

I settled him back in his chair and grabbed a few bags from the car, heading to the barn with Hobo, who lagged behind me. I struggled with the door, finally hearing the click. Pushing it open, I immediately noticed the smell of wood and earth as I stepped into a hallway. The barn was old and rustic, with a fireplace like the one in the main house. It was dark, and something about it was spooky or romantic—I wasn't sure which.

I climbed the steps to the loft with Hobo nervously by my feet. More shelves with books lined the bedroom walls, and I walked to a small desk in the corner, feeling the wood, wondering if this was where he'd sat. Suddenly inspired, I reached in my bag and pulled out the leather journal. I sat, snagging a pen from a small silver cup inscribed with something French I couldn't read. The words began to pour from me. I wrote about everything that had happened: Dock and I, the wedding, the feeling here, all of it, nearly losing track of time.

I looked at the wooden clock over the bed and tucked the journal into a drawer, then got up and plopped on the bed. Lying back, I swung my feet from side to side and thought of calling my mom or Ray. But it felt weird, not being able to tell them things.

I'll talk to Dock about telling her.

I grabbed my bag again, rummaging around for my phone, and took out Mr. S.'s book, which I'd forgotten about. I placed it on the nightstand. I figured I'd read a lot this week, especially while Dock wasn't here yet.

The week went by slowly. Lilly came, and the house was in chaos. She appeared crazed, trying to get it ready for the holidays, although I thought it was too early to think about that. I called Dock, and we talked about inviting my mom here for Christmas. I brought up telling her afterward if everything went well, and he agreed, which both terrified me and made me happy.

Most days, Mr. S. and I sat quietly in the great room, or we'd venture out to an appointment here and there. Nights I spent alone in the loft, struggling to sleep. It was eerily quiet, and I tossed and turned, missing the sound of the waves lapping against the shore.

I read until I fell asleep, remembering parts of the movie and the three familiar characters I could put faces to, including the probable Mr. S., a young Southern writer embarking on his first novel. Knowing the main character was obviously him made things interesting. I enjoyed getting a glimpse into his early life, but I questioned if it was all him or partly, although somehow I knew it was the latter.

I felt the darkness, entwined with a Holocaust survivor's guilt and all of the friends' excessive drinking. I could tell the drinking was more than fun through his writing. It was easy to see the pain there. Although I knew the story, I enjoyed reading his words. There was so much feeling and depth within the characters.

Is it because they were real friends in another time and place years ago?

It was apparent he was falling for her, the beautiful, mysterious Polish girl. He seemed so young and awkward. I remembered him being entranced by her beauty in the film. More than her beauty, it seemed it was her brokenness that enticed him.

All things dark intrigue him. Did it start with her?

I stared past the page at the desk chair, envisioning him sitting there, writing it all. He'd write feverishly through the night, drinking scotch and wine like a madman until the early morning. Then he'd give it to Lilly to type, she said.

The stories I'd heard didn't describe it that way. It wasn't so glamorous to live with him at times. But I didn't have to live it; I'd lived with my father's madness, although he hadn't churned out anything except a pile of bullshit most days.

If he had been drinking and achieving greatness, maybe I'd have been more understanding.

I smiled, thinking how foolish it all was, reaching to my neck, still forgetting the necklace wasn't there.

All of the books he's written . . . You'd have to be selfish to create like him. Maybe the alcohol fueled his mind, unleashed something?

I wanted to ask him if it was all real: the story and the characters. I wanted to know if he loved her, but I couldn't envision how I would introduce the subject.

Is Dock my soul mate? My real love? Is Lilly his, or was it her?

I couldn't imagine feeling for someone more than I felt for Dock. I never had.

I closed my eyes, thinking of his arms around me, about him touching me, his smell and warmth. I looked at the clock and grabbed the book, heading back over to the house.

• • •

After the long week of unpacking and getting things settled, Mr. S. seemed more depressed than usual, and I tried to figure a way to get him out of his slump. I went back to the barn for a break after a rough morning. First, there was a blowup again about his hand when he struggled to pat Lady. Then I spilled something and he screamed. He later apologized, then barked about the therapist who came yesterday, who said she thought she could get his hand functioning again if he worked a little harder.

"They're all quacks," he grumbled again.

"What can it hurt? Miracles happen," I said, watching him move his hand in front of him, wiggling his fingers. We did the exercises for a few minutes until he ripped his hand away from me. It was then I decided I needed a break.

I put Hobo's leash on and stepped outside, hearing a rumble coming from the top of the hill. Suddenly, the sound grew to a roar that came closer and closer, sounding impossibly loud against the countryside's stillness. Hobo excitedly pulled me to the front lawn.

"That's all you have?" I asked loudly, motioning for Dock to shut off the engine.

He jumped off immediately, lighting a cigarette and unstrapping the bag, throwing it over his shoulder.

"What more do I need?" He scooped me up with one arm, pulling me into him. "You said we would use their cars."

"It's fine, but I meant clothes."

"I didn't think we'd need much of those," he said. He grabbed at me playfully before following me in the house, where he tossed the bag, then spun me, kissing me wildly. I pushed his chest away in an automatic response. Then I laughed, realizing this man was my husband now, and I could enjoy it. He tilted his head questioningly toward the loft. I nodded, and he took me in his arms, carrying me up the stairs.

CHAPTER 26

December 6, 2003
Is it when you have nowhere to run that you escape
into the poison? It might be easier.

We settled into Connecticut perfectly. I was back and forth between houses all day, and he worked the grounds and occasionally drove Lilly to different events. We took motorcycle rides through the countryside and along the coast as the leaves changed colors and the cold weather crept in. Most nights, we lay on the giant rug in front of a fire, talking about our future and making plans. He seemed happy, and I finally could breathe. I was more in love than I'd ever thought possible, and life didn't feel so lonely.

Months went by like this, and it started snowing early. We had already had a few storms, and it wasn't even Christmas. I wasn't looking forward to a long winter but was glad we had each other, thinking it could be romantic.

"I'm headed out to shovel," he said, sounding irritated as I walked in.

"Oh, I was hoping we could have lunch together." I made a sad face.

He went out the door, and I followed, standing in the doorway.

"My mom called. She said she's coming," I called to him.

He kept shoveling, either not hearing me or ignoring me.

I could tell something had been bothering him in the past few days. He was antsy and bad tempered. The romance of being isolated in an unknown place had worn off for him a little, and I could feel he was struggling. The seclusion didn't bother me; I liked the quiet and being with him. But the island was similarly isolated in the winter, so I wasn't sure if that was the problem and figured I'd better ask.

I made us both sandwiches and put them on the table. I walked to the door again and waved him over.

"Come have lunch with me," I said as he kicked the snow from his boots.

I took his jacket, hung it near the fireplace, and motioned for him to sit next to me.

"Did you hear me about my mom?" I asked, taking a bite, pushing a bag of chips toward him.

"That's cool."

"I'm excited for you to meet her."

He said nothing. My throat felt dry, and I took a large sip of water. I needed to talk to him and had never been one for playing "let's pretend."

"Dock." I reached out, putting my hand on his arm. He set the sandwich down and looked at me.

"What's wrong?" I asked, nervous about his answer.

He leaned back in the chair and looked around, seeming to collect his thoughts.

"Nothing's wrong."

"C'mon. I know something's wrong. Just tell me."

"George." He sighed, picking up the sandwich again, staring at it. "I'm just not used to this."

My back tensed, and I readied myself, although I wasn't sure for what exactly.

"Used to what?"

"There is just nothing here for me and no way to get out of here for a bit. I'm stir crazy, I guess. I don't know."

He put the sandwich down, meeting my gaze again. "I just need my own thing, like side work or—"

"I get it," I interrupted, annoyed. *If he's already feeling this, it's going to be a long winter.*

My mind started spinning.

Plus, we're together. Isn't that enough?

"The island is just as isolating."

"Yeah, but I have my own life and friends there. My truck and . . ." He paused.

"And what?" I was officially irritated.

"It's just different. I'm sorry." He could tell I was upset.

I thought for a minute about what to do. Then it came to me.

We finished lunch in awkward silence. I returned to the house and went upstairs, getting Mr. S.'s medications ready before the therapist came. I heard Delia humming as she put some clothes away in the linen closet outside of his room, and I thought of my mother.

"Hey, Delia," I said, causing her to jump.

"Jesus, Mary. Georgie, you scared me." She put her hand to her chest and smiled. "You gonna give this old girl a heart attack."

"I'm sorry."

"What's up, girly?"

"Is Johnny coming today?"

"Johnny?" She looked at me strangely.

"Johnny, the landscaper."

"Yes, he's downstairs now." She laughed loudly. I wondered what was so funny but wouldn't ask. "That woman has him wrapping Christmas presents!"

I guess that's what's funny.

I headed down to the dining room, Delia's laughter echoing from above. Johnny and another man stood at the end of the dining room table, which was now covered in presents and wrapping paper.

"You're a jack-of-all-trades, John." I smiled.

He nodded, rolling his eyes at me.

He kind of was, though. Johnny was the property landscaper, but I'd see him here nearly every day, doing some sort of job. Last week, he was trying to get a raccoon out of the fireplace.

"I have a question for you," I said, picking up a small truck from the table.

"Shoot."

I chuckled as he tried to wrap a stuffed animal, then became frustrated and tossed it to the side.

"Do you need any help? Like side work help?"

He scratched his beard. "Um, I guess we could always use some help. It depends on who. I have my share of knuckleheads." He laughed, poking the guy next to him.

"Dock, my . . ." I paused, almost calling him my husband before remembering it was a secret. "My boyfriend. I think you guys met. He's working here too but going kind of stir crazy."

"Oh yeah," he said, sticking a bow on a newly wrapped present. "He's a carpenter, right?"

"Yes."

"Okay. Tell him to call me or come over and help me wrap." He rolled his eyes again, then reached into his wallet, handing me a card. Taking it from him, I immediately noticed his hand. The dots, the five dots: Johnny had the same tattoo as Dock, just like the guy at Mocha's. He saw me staring and pulled his hand back slowly.

"It was a long time ago," he said, looking concerned.

"What?" I was confused.

"Jail, it was a long time ago. Dumb youth. Ya know?"

I stared, still not understanding.

"I saw you notice the tattoo on my hand." He held it up, pointing. "I'm not ashamed of it. It's a reminder."

"Oh, um, okay," I stuttered, my heart racing.

"What's the dots mean?" the guy next to him asked. "I thought it was, like, how many people you killed." He laughed.

"Ah, jeesh." Johnny laughed. "The four dots on the outside are the four walls of the cell, and the dot on the inside is the prisoner. It's stupid."

"Well, thanks, Johnny. Bye, guys."

I hurried through the kitchen, feeling frozen.

Could this be real?

I couldn't make sense of it, but I wasn't holding it in. I headed back to the barn, determined to know.

"Dock! Dock!" I called, letting the door shut heavily behind me, and walked up to the loft, seeing him. "What's the tattoo mean, Dock?"

"What? What tattoo?"

"Your hand," I said, sitting down next to him on the bed. I took his hand in mine and showed him. "What's it mean?"

He looked at me, not saying anything. I knew then it was true. I let go and walked downstairs.

"George, come back!"

I went back next door, fuming, and tried to relax with Mr. S. by the fire. Upstairs, Lilly called out for Delia to bring up a dress. When Delia didn't answer, she appeared at the landing in her slip.

"George, where is Delia?" she said.

"I don't know, Lilly. I haven't seen her."

"She was just here," Mr. S. grumbled.

"I'll get her."

I headed to the kitchen just as Delia brushed past me, nearly knocking me into the bathroom door.

"I'm right here," she yelled.

"Can you get my dress?" Lilly huffed, holding on to the railing.

"I was ironing it! I can't iron it and bring it at the same time!" Delia yelled, nearly incomprehensible. She threw her hands up and walked away.

"I'm going to be late!" Lilly yelled back. "George, can Dock drive me?"

I don't want to go back over there.

I headed back up the path, nervous, not wanting to know anymore. At least, not right now. *Was he really in jail? He lied.* I felt like my world was closing in on me.

"Dock!" I called out, then noticed him sitting on the couch. I walked over and saw his bag next to him. "What's this?"

He looked ahead, wringing his hands.

"George, I'm gonna leave for a while."

"What?" I sat across from him, not taking my eyes off him.

"I need to clear my head." He sighed and looked away.

"Yeah, okay. Go clear your fucking head." I felt tears and blinked hard, trying not to let them fall.

"George," he said, reaching his hand out, the tattooed one. He pulled it back, replacing it with the other, putting it on my leg.

"George nothing! Why don't you tell me the truth!" I raged.

He jumped up, his bag falling to the floor. Suddenly he was enraged, which terrified me. I stood and stepped back, the chair bumping against my leg.

"You want the fucking truth, George? You want it?" he yelled, sounding like a monster. He paced back and forth in front of me, then went to the door and cracked it open, lighting a cigarette. The cold air blew in, sending a shiver up my arm. He stared at me and laughed.

"You couldn't handle the truth," he said, blowing the smoke.

"Try me," I whispered as a tear fell down my cheek. Exhausted and frustrated, I joined him at the door to say the only thing I could think to say. "Lilly asked if you'd drive her."

He threw his coat on and pulled up his collar. We stared at each other, saying nothing; then he headed to the house. I pushed the tears away with my sleeve.

I ran upstairs, grabbing my bag and tossing the book and journal in. I went back to the house through the back door to avoid him if he was there. I listened but heard nothing as I kicked the snow from my boots.

"Did they leave?" I asked, looking at Mr. S.

"Yes, just now," he coughed.

He looked pale and a little gray, but I wasn't sure if it was the room's lighting. I grabbed my stethoscope from my bag. As I pulled it out, his book came with it and fell to the floor in front of him. I went to pick it up.

"What's that?"

I pause and placed it next to me.

"It's your book," I cautiously said, waiting for his response.

"Oh," he grumbled.

"I hope you don't mind me reading it?"

I walked behind him, placing the stethoscope on his back. He took in as deep a breath as he could muster, knowing the routine.

"No." He coughed again.

I sat on the couch and picked up the book, opening it to where I'd left off. I struggled to read, feeling strange reading his book in front of him, but I was desperate to get out of my head, at least for a little while.

I read through the evening, eventually forgetting that the older version of the man I was learning about was sitting across from me. Occasionally I'd look up and remember. The once aspiring writer living on Long Island, lost in love with the Polish girl, was right there. I stared at him, then the pages, wondering about it all.

"How is it?"

I looked up, his steel-colored eyes meeting mine.

"I think you know it's pretty good." I smiled awkwardly.

"Do I?" He turned his head toward a noise from the kitchen, and I put the book down, wondering if Dock was back.

Jail? What else is he hiding?

Nothing seemed real.

"I think I'll go to bed." He sighed, looking sad. He always looked sad, but he did more than usual lately.

"Okay."

I hopped up, helping him up the stairs.

"Are you all right?" I asked, propping him high in the bed and placing a pillow under his knees.

"Define all right?"

"You just seem different."

He picked up his hand and stared at it, then let it plop onto the bed as if it weighed a thousand pounds. I knew he was thinking about writing.

"You know, there's new technology to write. You wouldn't have to do it yourself."

I suddenly wanted to hurry and get back to the barn to see if Dock was there.

"I don't have pain. Why?"

Where is this coming from?

"Not all ailments are painful," I answered.

"Oh."

He reached for a tissue.

"Cancer is." He spat into it, crumpling it in his hand.

"Not always."

"My mother's was."

"I'm sure that was awful."

"Yes." He closed his eyes.

I turned off the light and headed to the door, stopping before I left.

"Mr. S.?"

"Yes."

"Was she real, in the book? Did you care for her?"

I cringed after I said it. He took his time answering.

"She was someone."

He coughed again, and I quietly shut the door.

As I jogged up the path, I noticed it seemed warmer than it was earlier. The snow had melted on the stones leading to the barn. I stopped at the door, nervous about what lay behind it. Taking a deep breath, I opened it and quietly stepped in. I called through the house for him, feeling the tears fill my eyes, hearing the emptiness. I went out front and immediately saw the motorcycle tarp on the ground and fresh tracks on the snow. I stared at them in disbelief. He was gone.

I came in and stared at the fireplace. The barn seemed suddenly colder. Hobo lay on the rug, wagging his tail at me. I felt unworthy of even him. My skin crawled, and my body ached. I desperately wanted to be out of it. I grabbed the throw pillow next to me to scream into, placing it over my face, but nothing happened.

I went to the kitchen for water, noticing on the counter the bottle of wine with the red bow Lilly had given me a few days earlier. I opened the drawer with urgency, rummaging for the opener. I pulled the cork as hard as I could, then watched the wine glug into the glass, filling it to the top. The warmth spilled down my throat as I gulped nearly all of it, then grabbed the bottle and went back to the living room. I started a small fire and watched the flames dance and crackle. The silence was deafening. I needed to do something, so I dialed Ray. I wanted to feel more rejection to justify the mess I was and the bigger mess I planned on becoming. He didn't answer, which made it better. I poured the next glass.

Fuck everyone.

I went to my bag and got the journal, opening in the middle, not caring that the pages weren't in order. I began writing frantically, scribbling jumbles of gibberish, continuing to drink until I finished the bottle.

My head spun, and I threw it back, looking at the ceiling, clenching my jaw and my fists. I looked at the empty glass, and the anger turned to tears. Rage burned inside of me, and I felt hotter than the fire. I felt the heat making its way up my throat, forcing me to open my mouth, and I screamed louder than I thought possible. I furiously grabbed and pulled at my shirt. I was desperate to tear it from my chest as if it somehow would free everything from me. Instead, I stopped, collapsing into the pillow. I turned my head, seeing the empty bottle again. I grabbed it tightly, then let go, hurling it against the fireplace, feeling relief at the crash and seeing it shatter.

Hobo leaped from the rug and hurried up the stairs. He shivered as he stared at me from above, looking at me like I was a monster. I closed my eyes, disgusted, wishing for nothing but more wine.

CHAPTER 27

December 7, 2003
Maybe I'll be the man with the cake. They liked him.
They clapped even though he destroyed people.

The sun came in, and I opened one eye. I quickly moved the pillow over my face, feeling disoriented; then suddenly it all came back. Dock leaving, the wine, the yelling. My head pounded, and I tossed the pillow and reached for my phone to check the time, noticing a missed call from Ray. I threw it at the chair across from me, trying to be forceful but not having the strength.

I went to the bathroom and splashed cold water on my face, then hurriedly brushed my teeth, trying to get rid of the sour taste, but it was no use. I glimpsed myself in the mirror. The tired and blotchy reflection terrified me.

I thought of all the misfits at the AA meeting my father had spoken at.

Is this what they feel every morning?

It wasn't the hangover. I'd had a hangover before. It was shame and self-loathing. Those were new. I didn't recognize myself.

Everyday guilt and self-hatred.

The man who got the cake, whose "other son" died—I wondered if he ever felt like this. Somehow, I didn't think so. Not him, anyway. I suddenly understood why they'd drink again if they didn't stop altogether.

. . .

Christmas came and went. I canceled with my mom, making an excuse: I was too busy with Mr. S., and they needed me at the house to help more. I hated lying but didn't want to see her. If I did, I'd break. She had Ray and Aunt Rita, so she wasn't alone. Dock called a few times, and it took everything in me, but I didn't answer. I wanted to, but I couldn't trust myself. I knew I'd believe anything he said, and I loathed myself for being weak, feeling I'd become like my mother.

Maybe it's genetic.

New Year's Eve, I had some wine for courage and called Ray. To my surprise, he answered, and we chatted before he headed out for the night. It was our usual small talk, and I was tired of it. I wanted to say so much. Fueled by alcohol, I thought I could but didn't.

Coward.

I wondered if I'd turn into my father, except I couldn't handle the hangovers.

I could never drink like that.

But the phone and the feelings were there with the booze, and it made me sick.

"Hello," I answered, grabbing the phone next to me, not looking at the number. I thought it might be Ray again.

"Happy New Year," the voice said.

I pulled the phone away to look and saw it was Will.

It was nice hearing a familiar voice that gave a shit on the other end, and I perked up.

"How goes it? Happy New Year."

Does he know Dock isn't here?

"Not great. Happy New Year yourself."

"I know. I'm sorry, George."

I suddenly wanted to punch him. I stared at the wine bottle, feeling the urge to throw it like before but thinking better of it. I wasn't drunk enough not to care that I'd have to clean it up. In the movies, it always cut to the next scene after the dramatic explosion. It never showed the person hungover and cleaning the mess, crying and cutting themselves on the shards of glass in the morning.

"Your brother sucks," I huffed.

"Yup, he can." He let out a sigh.

Here we go with the fucking sighs.

"When are you back?"

"I don't know. Hopefully never," I snapped.

"Oh, stop, George. This is your place. Don't forget that."

Oh, shut up.

"I gotta run, Will. Duty calls, but have a great New Year."

"Okay, well, don't be a stranger. I'm here if you want to talk or need anything, okay?"

Yes, let's talk about everything except the elephant in the room. No thanks.

I wanted to say it all but knew from previous experience that it got me nothing except people annoyed with me.

"I know, Will; thank you."

That was easier. Let's pretend. Maybe it's not so bad.

The winter felt longer than ever. Alone in the country, I analyzed everything he'd said, trying to understand how he had been feeling, but it didn't matter. He left. He was gone, and I tried not to care, but I did.

I spent every day and nearly every evening with Mr. S. when Lilly wasn't home. He and I had become utterly codependent on one another, and I realized it more and more. I knew what he'd say before he said it, and I knew how he felt most times without him saying a word. I could tell it was the same for him with me. I tried hard not to let my thoughts of Dock consume me, so I read. I read slowly, trying to savor the story and make it last, feeling somehow connected to it all: the broken girl, the out-of-his-mind boyfriend, the young writer wanting love and change. I wanted it to last for as long as I could make it.

"Are you okay?" he gruffed, clearing his throat.

I stared over the book at him. I had just been in New York City with him while he lost his virginity to her and felt I'd just traveled to the future.

"Why do you ask?"

He said nothing, only looking down at his hand. He coughed loudly again. I didn't like the sound of it.

"Let me listen to your lungs again."

I got up and fumbled through my bag.

"Good lord," he said, coughing again.

I handed him the tissue box in front of him.

"Deep breath."

He coughed again, unable to breathe. "I'd like to go to bed."

"Okay." I tapped on his back, which always annoyed him. "I think I'm gonna call the doctor tomorrow, though."

He struggled to stand, and I reached through his arm, helping him.

"Fine," he barked, tripping toward the stairs.

• • •

"Looks like you have something brewing," the doctor said.

This wasn't his usual doctor; he was young and looked barely out of medical school. I knew Mr. S. wouldn't take him seriously.

"Why?" he droned, sitting in the wheelchair.

"I think you should go to the hospital for a few days to make sure we get rid of it."

"No," he grunted, refusing to look at him.

"It's the right thing. Let's be safe."

He reached his hand to Mr. S.'s, leaning in close, which I knew would annoy him greatly.

"Mr. S., you should. Just a few days; then we can go home," I pleaded, trying to convince him. "Lilly is away anyway."

I looked at the doctor, nodding, noticing his dimples.

Mr. S. stared ahead, saying nothing. I nodded again, acting as the interpreter I'd become, and we headed to the hospital.

• • •

I awoke to birds chirping the following day. It was becoming warmer.

Outside, I smelled freshly cut grass and waved to Johnny, who passed by on the lawnmower as Hobo sniffed the bushes before finally choosing one to lift his leg on. Spring was nearly here, and I thought of the business happening now on the island and all the sights and smells that spring brought as the locals prepared for the season ahead. I missed it, wishing I were there.

I headed to the hospital, anxious to see how he was doing.

"When's Lilly back?" he grumbled.

It was almost childish how he seemed to only exist now for her returns, but she deserved her life. At least, that's how I felt.

"Soon," I answered him, watching his eyes close and opening the book.

"What chapter are you on?"

He startled me. I thought he was sleeping.

"I realize the boyfriend is quite disturbed. And you—I mean, the main character—is in love, I think. I'm sure he knows it."

Jesus, should I have said that?

"Where's Dock?"

My face became hot, and I adjusted myself in the chair. I didn't think he'd notice.

"He had to go back to the island for work," I said, trying to sound believable. I told Lilly and Delia the same.

I put the book in my bag, searching for the gum I thought I had, frustrated at not being able to find it. I pulled the book back out again, along with the journal and the notebook Lilly had given me. Then I spotted the gum under some tissues.

"What's that?" he asked, looking at the pile.

"What?"

"*That.*" He pointed to the notebook, appearing to recognize the handwriting.

Shit. "A notebook."

"What does it say?" He was becoming irritated.

I couldn't come up with anything, so I said it.

"Lilly wanted me to write things."

"What things?"

He tried to sit up in the bed but couldn't. I went and adjusted his pillows, watching him lie back in exhaustion.

"If you had anything profound to say."

There, I said it.

He lifted his head again and moved his hand, gesturing toward the table for me to give it to him. I handed him the notebook. He read what she'd written, then opened it, staring at the empty pages. After a moment, he shut it, tossing it to the side.

"Empty," he said, closing his eyes again.

His self-loathing was humorous and clever, but I couldn't understand it, mostly. He had achieved so much, and none of it seemed to matter. I had nothing, only a dog who liked me because I fed him, and I spent all my time with a miserable old man who barely said anything to me. I wasn't even sure if he liked me or me him, but strangely I was closer to him than I'd been to anyone in what seemed like forever. I picked up the journal in front of me and began to write, trying to distract myself.

"What are you doing?"

He accidentally hit the button on the call light and turned the TV on.

"Jesus, shut that off." He gagged, spitting.

With a loud sigh, I reached and pressed the button.

"George?" He pointed at the journal.

What is with twenty questions today?

"It's a journal a friend gave me. I've been writing a little." I felt strange telling him this. I didn't want to feel any smaller than I did.

"What about?"

"Originally just journaling, but I started a little story about horses. I'm not sure why." I felt self-conscious and defensive.

I remembered feeling good writing when I was younger. Inspired after reading some cheesy Southern romance novel my mother had lying around, I wrote about a horse farm. It was a short story. I won a contest in seventh grade and wrote nearly seventy-five pages. I thought I'd continue and turn it into a novel, but I stopped.

"Do you know about horses?"

"No."

"Then why write about them?"

"I don't know. I like them."

"Write about what you know, George."

I felt silly, suddenly remembering why I stopped writing at the seventy-five pages. I knew nothing of the South or horses. I laughed out loud.

"Sound advice," I said, closing the journal. "And speaking of sound advice, why don't we answer some mail? I brought it."

I pulled a large envelope out of the bag.

"God, no."

He closed his eyes.

I spilled the contents on the tray table, looking at all the different sizes and colors of the envelopes. I picked one and opened it, reading it to myself first, figuring I'd summarize, knowing he would never want to listen word for word.

"This is from Zachary in New York. He's a huge fan, and thanks you for your work. He's an aspiring novelist and would love any advice on writing you could offer."

He adjusted himself and cleared his throat, wiping at the corners of his mouth.

"Don't do it." He coughed loudly, closing his eyes again.

I sighed so that he could hear me. Annoyed, I tossed the letter on the stack of envelopes when my phone rang. I fumbled through the bag and grabbed it, seeing Dock's name on the screen.

"Hello," I answered quickly.

Oh my God, why did I answer?

I stepped into the hall and walked down the corridor.

"Sorry, hello," I said, making sure I had an angry tone.

"George." He paused and repeated my name.

"What?"

"I'm sorry."

My heart fell in my stomach. "You left."

"I know. I just was . . . I was going stir crazy and—"

"And what?" I snapped, cutting him off.

"I hated that I lied." He breathed out heavily.

"Jail, Dock," I said, my lips trembling, hating that I missed him.

"I should have told you. I hated the way you looked at me when you found out. It killed me. I didn't want that look. I never want you to look at me like that."

He told me about jail and how it was years ago for something small. I didn't ask how long he was there; I never asked too much of anything. I didn't want to know. If I knew and it was terrible, I'd have to leave him, and I didn't want to. I lied to myself, but the truth was there with all the others in the secret place inside me.

"Please, let's make this work. I promise you I'll be the man you deserve, George."

He had me, and he had me before that, to be honest. I told him I'd talk to Lilly and see if we could come back earlier. We talked about a fresh start. I'd move into the Edgartown house with him, and he'd work on it to have it ready.

I hated the power he had over me, and I hated more how I disregarded things.

Do I just need to be loved so badly? But why him?

I suddenly felt ill. I was sick of analyzing everything.

I headed back to the room. He was sleeping again, and I opened the journal, staring at a blank page. I felt whole again, but like a child on the cusp of no longer believing in fairy tales or Santa Claus. My head hurt, the ache moving from the crown to between my eyes. I thought of my mother and how I hated her denial—and Ray's; he had it too. I never did until now. But I was struggling.

I went back for the night to the barn. I had just walked in when

Lilly called, asking me to the house for an update. I told her he'd likely be home tomorrow, and she interrupted, saying the hospital had called her; they wanted to keep him a few more nights.

"He won't be happy." I sat at the kitchen counter, yawning.

"I know. I thought I'd be with him tomorrow and the next day. Why don't you take two days off, George? You must be going crazy."

Suddenly, I didn't feel so tired, happy she'd noticed I hadn't had a day off since I came.

"Thank you so much, Lilly."

"I'm off to bed." She yawned.

I headed to the back door.

"George, wait," she said, pausing, smiling at me. "Thanks for all of your help. You know he adores you."

"Thank you, Lilly." I gave her a half hug and headed out.

I lay on the sofa with Hobo, thinking of the two days I'd have off, not knowing what to do with myself.

"Wait!" I sat up. *I could go to the island.*

I picked up the phone to call him, then stopped myself.

"No, I'll surprise him!" I said to Hobo, who wagged his tail.

I awoke early the following day. Delia agreed to look after Hobo, and I told Lilly. She agreed it was a great idea, knowing how much I loved and missed it there. I packed quickly and sifted through my jewelry box for earrings, seeing the blue velvet pouch. I opened it and dropped the engagement ring into my palm. I stared at it, wondering if I should bring it.

Maybe we can make it official? No more secrets.

I placed it back in the pouch and put it on top of my clothes, then zipped up my bag and left for the three-and-a-half-hour drive to Woods Hole.

CHAPTER 28

March 24, 2004
Everything went silent in the sound. Everything is silent.
I am silent. There is no me. I only exist in my love for him.
Without it, I'm not here. I never was.

*I*t was warm, and the sun was trying to come out from behind the clouds. I pulled into the Palmer Ave parking lot and hopped on the bus to the ferry. I was glad to make the 12:15 as the next one wasn't until 2. The bus pulled down the embankment, and I gazed at the boats, excited. I ran in and got my ticket, inhaling the salty air. I felt alive again as I listened to all the familiar sounds. I walked the passageway, seeing I was on the *Martha's Vineyard,* one of the better boats.

I headed to the top deck and put my feet on the chair in front of me. I considered getting a beer but closed my eyes instead, taking it all in. My feelings quickly turned as I remembered why I was coming. A warm feeling traveled up my legs. I imagined what the night would be like. I smiled, trying to stop myself, feeling stupid.

We passed by West Chop. I could just make out the Yacht Club and the road to the cottage. The porch of the main house came in view. The trees weren't in full bloom yet, and I thought of how strange it was that only a few months ago, I was there with Mr. S., watching the ferry pass. I thought of time and how little there was in life, validating my decision to come. I wanted my happy ending.

"Edgartown, please," I said to the cab driver.

He was wearing a wetsuit and helped me with my bag.

Only on the Vineyard.

I called Dock repeatedly on the way. I wanted to keep my surprise but suddenly thought the worst.

What if he's not on the island or he's working late? What was I thinking?

My heart skipped, and I nervously picked at my cuticle.

We drove into Edgartown. He still hadn't answered, and I hesitantly left a message. Unsure of what to do, I figured I'd go there. I remembered a spare key above the door, seeing him use it after we went night swimming in the lagoon. I spent the whole winter thinking of nights like those whenever I couldn't distract myself with work or reading.

My heart thumped hard in my chest as the car slowed, turning onto Smith Hollow. Seeing his truck, I told the driver to stop ahead of the driveway.

"He's your husband," I whispered, climbing the steps.

I tried to convince myself I was silly, wiped my palms against my legs, and then fluffed my hair.

I went to tap on the door but saw it was open and slowly pushed my way in.

"Dock," I called quietly.

I looked around at the mess. Beer cans and rolling papers sat on the counter. I swatted at a fly, seeing a garbage bag on its side near the door with the contents half spilled out on the floor.

"Dock!" I called louder.

I put my bag down and cautiously walked down the hallway. I went to call his name again, but instead gasped when a woman emerged from the bathroom. She didn't notice me at first, then looked right at me.

It was her—the stringy blonde from the Sand Bar. My heart sank, and I couldn't catch my breath. She seemed to know who I was. Rage boiled inside me. I thought I might lunge at her, but she smiled, nervously stepping toward me. I nearly screamed as tears filled my eyes. I thought I would be sick.

"Dock!" I screamed, pushing past her.

I looked in the bedroom; then, from the corner of my eye, I saw something through the partially open bathroom door. I went to push the door open fully, then heard her voice.

"George, stop, wait! You don't want to see him like this."

I stopped, glaring at her. "Who are you? How do you know my name?"

She stared at me coldly. She was wearing a long T-shirt, and it looked like his. I watched as her eyes partially closed. She swayed back, nearly falling, but caught herself.

"What the fuck is wrong with you?" I asked and turned back to the bathroom.

I opened the door.

I stood, unable to move, feeling as if my legs were encased in concrete. He was nearly unrecognizable. The steam from the hot water in the tub swirled around him, and he was naked and shivering. The smell of vomit filled the air, making me gag. I watched in horror as he lifted his head. I kneeled by the tub to make sure it was him. He stared, reaching his arm as if to see if I was real; then his eyes met mine.

"Dock," I whispered, confused, barely able to speak.

"George, what are you doing here?"

His voice sounded weak and broken.

"Dock, what's wrong?" I brushed back his hair. Tears spilled down my cheeks.

He shivered, and his face felt hot against my arm.

"Dock! What's wrong!"

He dropped his head onto his arm, and I watched his body slide deeper into the water.

Everything was in slow motion. I turned from him, spotting clues piecemeal, unable to process it all. In the corner, pill bottles scattered on the floor. There were needles on the bathroom sink, three of them hanging off the side—their orange caps on the floor below. The toilet seat had droplets of what looked like blood, and the trash was overflowing. I pulled his arm from under him and flipped it over, seeing the marks and bruises, noticing some he tried to hide in the crown tattoo. I fell back against the wall, scrambling quickly to get up.

How could I have been so stupid? How could I not have known?

"Dock," I cried as he lifted his head again.

"He's sick! Don't you get it?" the girl's voice said from behind me.

I stumbled to the door, my heart pounding. I needed to run. I needed to get out. I pushed past her again, and she fell back against the wall.

"He's kicking it for you! For you!" she yelled as I ran out the door.

I stumbled down the stairs, continuing to gain speed until I was running down the street. I made it almost to the end, then fell to my knees on a patch of grass behind some trees and threw up. Tears fell fiercely onto the ground, and I sobbed, wiping my mouth with my sleeve. I misdialed the cab company over and over, watching my fingers shake, pressing the buttons, finally getting it right. The driver came quickly, and I directed him toward Oak Bluffs, watching him stare at me in the mirror as I wiped my face, trying to stop the tears.

"I'm such a fool," I whispered.

He turned past the carousel and drove along the inner harbor.

"Stop and wait here!" I shouted. "Please," I added.

He scowled at me, annoyed.

I looked like a wreck, I was sure, and I didn't care. I figured he thought I was drunk and hysterical, which wasn't that uncommon here, especially in the summer. I raced up the plank and threw off my shoes, stepping onto the boat.

"Will!" I yelled.

I turned the corner as he was coming around, nearly colliding with him. I grabbed the railing to steady myself and watched the water pour from the hose he was holding, unable to speak.

"Jesus, George! I didn't know you were—"

"Shut up," I whispered, glaring at him, finding my strength. I wanted to hit him or slap him across the face.

"George, what is it?"

He dropped the hose, and the water pooled around his feet.

I folded over and began to cry, then felt his hand on my back, and it enraged me. I stood upright, pushing it away. "Why didn't you tell me?"

He looked at me, confused.

"Why didn't you fucking tell me, Will!" I screamed, not caring if the cops came and dragged me away.

"Tell you?" he breathed, looking panicked.

"Don't play fucking stupid with me, Will." I burned a hole in him with my eyes. "He's a fucking junkie! A fucking junkie!" I yelled again, throwing my hands.

He swallowed hard and pushed back his hair. "I tried George. I fucking tried."

He shut off the hose, grabbed his cigarette pack from the top of the boat, and lit one. "I told you, you deserve better," he whispered.

"That's telling me?"

"What was I supposed to say, George? Tell me! What was I supposed to say? My brother's a junkie?" He kicked the hose and leaned against the railing. He took another drag of the cigarette, then tossed it off the side. "It was clear you loved him. And he fucking loved you. He loved you more than I'd ever seen him love any woman. I never saw him try so hard."

He rubbed his forehead.

"He was clean, George! He was clean for a while, and when he met you, I thought maybe he'd be forever. I hoped, which was the worst thing I could have done."

He hung his head, looking like he might cry, but I knew he wouldn't. I did, again putting my face in my hands. I felt his arms around me, and I buried my head in his chest. He felt like Dock somehow, and I pushed him away, but he held on, not letting me.

"I lost my brother a long time ago, George. We were close our whole lives, then things changed. Fucking drugs."

He looked away and let me go, wiping the corner of his eyes.

"I've thought so many times I had him back, and every one of them,

I lost him all over again. He came here to start fresh. But he can't run away from himself. Why do you think I'm on this fucking boat? The business isn't happening here anymore. It's all gone. I put myself in it again because I had hope. I saw the change in him. I saw how different he was, especially after meeting you."

I watched his lips move, noticing the upturned corners, the same as Dock's, but not as pronounced. I felt closer to him, seeing his pain. He understood more than I did.

"You can leave him now. Just leave him. You deserve so much more, George."

Tears poured, and I wiped them away, panic rising. Nothing felt real.

"I married him, Will."

"What?" he said, looking confused.

"I married him. It was a secret. No one knew. We were supposed to have a party or a wedding this spring or summer. I married him."

He let his hands fall to his sides and stared in disbelief or disappointment. I couldn't tell which. The cab driver beeped the horn. I turned away from Will; stepping over the side, I walked back down the dock. I looked back, and he was in the same spot, watching me. I didn't look back again.

I gave the driver the address to the cottage and stared out the window, unseeing, at the clouds moving in over the bridge. We passed through Five Corners on our way to Main Street. My head hurt; my heart hurt.

"Stop here," I said, handing him some cash. I got out, waving him off.

I walked past the tavern and took my shoes off, stepping onto the sand. The little beach was empty, and I was glad to be alone. Clouds came in over the sound. I sat on the overturned rowboat near the water and watched. A raindrop fell on my forehead. I looked at my arm and saw it was shaking, although I felt nothing.

All the signs flashed in my head: the disappearances, the tattoo, the secrets, and myself, all of which I ignored.

Then how he looked. How sick he looked. It was like two different people. I wanted to help him. I wanted to fix him and make him strong again so he could make me feel how he always made me feel. I rubbed my shoulders and rocked back and forth. I closed my eyes, and there was my father dead on the floor. Suddenly, that woman's voice popped into my head.

"He's kicking it for you."

I squeezed my eyes tightly, trying to get her out of my head. I wanted it all out.

The rain fell harder. I opened my eyes, watching the little circles fan out as the drops collided with the ocean. I remembered the thunderstorm I'd watched with my father on the porch overlooking the ocean. I looked at the empty spot beside me, remembering us sitting here. It seemed like forever ago. Him dying alone in that room above the bar came next. I shut my eyes, trying to erase it.

What was it like in the end? That last breath?

I often thought of this but kept it hidden, tucked away with the other unspeakable things. I reached for my necklace, running my fingers over my empty chest.

I felt filthy on the inside and the out. It was all so dark and dirty. I rubbed my legs, the rain pelting the backs of my hands. I headed to the water's edge. I watched my feet sink into the mud and the water fill in around them. I stepped in deeper, shaking, feeling the coldness. I slowly waded further out. I went to my waist, my jeans weighing me down, every step becoming harder. I had no idea what I was doing. I needed to wash away the unclean—wash away my life. I bent down and splashed the water on my face, shivering uncontrollably.

My eyes burned, and I blinked hard. East Chop appeared blurry on the cliff, and everything was silent in the sound as if time had stopped, and I heard nothing except a ringing in my ears. The stillness—the terrifying silence scared me, and I'd never felt more alone. I wanted it all to end: the sadness, the secrets. I wanted it gone, and I wasn't sure what that meant.

It was pouring now, and the waves felt stronger, coming into the shore. I envisioned Dock's face, and strangely I wasn't angry. I still loved him, and that made it all worse.

I closed my eyes and swayed as if I were drunk, feeling the vibration in my throat as I hummed.

I stopped, thinking I heard a voice.

"George!"

I heard it now. *Dock?*

He walked toward the water. I took a few steps toward him and fell to my knees in the mud, putting my head in my hands.

"George, oh my God. George, get up. Let me help you."

He lifted me, carrying me to the beach, standing me in front of him. He took off his jacket and draped it on my shoulders.

"George, it's okay. It's all going to be okay. Let me get you out of here," he said, taking my hand, but I didn't move.

"I have nothing," I said. I stared at him.

"That's not true, George, and you know it," he yelled, stepping backward.

He moved close again and pulled me into him. I leaned my head on his chest and closed my eyes, feeling the warmth while the rain poured over us. I felt safe against him, and that's all I'd ever wanted. He held me tight, then rested his chin on top of my head. I pulled away and looked up at him. He tilted his face toward me, and I felt him shivering as his eyes met mine. I closed my eyes and turned my lips up, offering them to him. He leaned his head against my forehead and closed his eyes as he spoke.

"It's him you want, George, not me," he whispered.

He lifted the jacket off me and over our heads.

"I . . ." I began.

"Don't say anything. It's okay."

He put his face close to mine, trying to keep us covered.

"Will," I breathed, closing my eyes, "I love him."

He took my hand and pulled me hurriedly toward the bike.

"Let's get out of here, okay?" He handed me the coat, and I nodded.

I climbed on, holding on to him securely. We pulled in front of the cottage, and I ran up the steps, grabbing the key from under the mat. He came behind me and stood in the doorway.

"Are you okay?"

"No."

"I know. But you will be."

"I don't think so, Will." I bit my lip, feeling my eyes fill again, amazed I had any tears left.

He came in and pulled the blanket from the bed, wrapping it around me. When he walked over to the cabinets, his boots clicked rhythmically on the floor, and I thought of my father. He opened the cabinets one by one.

"Tea or this?" He held up a bottle of rum. I couldn't remember where it came from.

He found two glasses and poured, handing me one. I drank, the warmth burning my throat. I put the glass down, and he filled it again along with his. I heard my ring tap against the glass and finished it quickly.

"I don't want to leave you alone."

I stepped backward and leaned against the wall.

I sighed. "I don't want to be alone."

I looked down, watching his boot take a step toward me. He reached his arm to me, touching my side, then moved up gently, pushing my hair from my shoulders.

"How did you know I was there?"

"What?"

"Where you found me. How did you know?"

He held my hand, biting his lip. "You told me that night on the boat. You told me about that spot, remember?" He looked at me intensely.

"But you were drunk."

"Some things you just remember." He smiled. "How much that spot means to you. I wouldn't forget that."

Suddenly I wanted it to be him. I wanted it to be him so badly. I closed my eyes, wishing things could change. Wishing it were all different.

He was safe, and I was desperate for safety. I moved away from the wall.

"I'm so sorry, George," he whispered, smoothing my hair as I buried my head into him.

I glanced up at him again. He looked calm and serious, staring at my face. I moved over toward the bed and sat. He followed, settling next to me. Tears broke way to sobs again, and I curled up on his lap.

"It'll be okay, George. Of course it will," he said, stroking my hair. "He loves you, George, more than I've ever seen him love anyone. But sometimes, love isn't enough."

CHAPTER 29

March 25, 2004
The filth on someone else dirties everyone around them.
We are all unclean.

My eyes adjusted, and I saw the outline of the stools at the counter, remembering I was in the cottage. The time glowed on my phone, *9:00*, and I put it back on the table. I reached for the lamp, wondering when I'd fallen asleep. I turned the light on. Seeing the large boot prints and the puddle of water on the floor, I then wondered when he'd left. I rubbed my swollen eyes and wished it were all a dream.

I took a long hot shower to wash it all away—drugs, booze, feelings. I felt dirtier than before, no matter how hard I scrubbed. I put my face in the water and felt my wedding band cold against my cheek, wanting to die.

I looked for my bag and didn't see it, then remembered I'd left it at Dock's when I ran. I had some sweats and a few pairs of socks and threw them on. Everything smelled musty. I wiped the water from the floor. The scent of wet leather filled the air around me. I flung open a window and heard a car coming down the drive. I didn't want to talk anymore. I wanted only to forget.

After a few moments of silence, I opened the door and saw my bag on the steps in front of me. I spotted the back of Dock's truck turning onto Main Street. Grabbing the glasses off the island, smelling the rum, I threw them simultaneously against the wall. Then I fell on my knees and cried again until I couldn't anymore.

I got on the last ferry, desperately wanting to leave and never come back. As I stepped onto the outside deck, I stared at the lights of Vineyard Haven through the fog. I watched them become dimmer, my light dimming with them as we headed back toward Woods Hole. A woman holding a leash attached to a black Lab pointed to the island as she chatted with a young girl next to her. I stood and grabbed my bag; I headed to the other side, taking a seat looking forward. I didn't want to see the island. I didn't want to look back.

Back in Connecticut, I pulled up to the house and headed into the barn; Hobo jumped excitedly. I walked by him, too tired to care. I called the hospital and spoke to the night nurse, who told me Mr. S.'s discharge was tomorrow. My stomach growled, and I opened the fridge, knowing I should eat but having no desire. A bottle of Pinot Grigio stared at me on the counter. I opened it, pouring a large glass, taking a sip, hoping to feel the nothing I so badly wanted. I looked at the glass and watched a drop slide down the side. I dumped the rest in the sink; it was pointless.

Dragging my bag behind me, I headed upstairs, then tossed it on the floor. As I took out the clothes and placed them on the bed, the blue pouch fell on the pillow. I blinked hard and took a deep breath, trying my hardest not to cry. I picked it up, staring at it in my hands. I squeezed it tightly. It felt empty. I pulled the little strings and shook; it was.

Hobo curled next to me, and I prayed for sleep, but it didn't come. I reached for the book and turned the light on and read. I was in Auschwitz now, the Nazi concentration camp. I read and read, escaping into Germany and its hells during the war. My eyes hurt, and my heart hurt, but I continued until I fell asleep.

• • •

"Are you glad to be coming home?" I asked. We both hated making small talk, but the silence was killing me. We drove the whole way without saying a word. I couldn't take it any longer.

"I am," he replied, staring out the window.

We went in, and I got him settled in his chair, then went to put his things away. I heard a noise behind me and saw Delia watching me from the doorway.

"You scared me." I attempted a laugh, hoping she didn't notice my swollen eyes.

"Come sit, Georgie girl."

She sat, patting the bed, and I followed, sitting next to her.

"What's going on? You can tell me now." She put her hand on my knee. "I won't bite, Georgie."

I wanted to tell her everything, I wanted to tell someone, anyone, but I didn't know where to start. I felt ashamed and torn. I didn't understand it all myself. I wanted to start from the beginning, I wanted it all gone, but I couldn't, and I didn't know why.

"I'm okay. Things just didn't go as I'd expected on the island. That's all," I said, unable to look at her.

"Well, I'm here, Georgie. Some men are no good! Some people are no good, Georgie!" She stood up, waving her arms around. "That woman, that woman away all this time while that man is in the hospital. Georgie, they're all crazy, all of them!"

She stopped abruptly, seeming to realize she was going astray. She sat next to me again, taking my hand in hers. "You'll be okay, Georgie, you will." She smiled, and I thanked her.

• • •

Lilly was home for a while, and I spent evenings alone in the barn.

I had just picked up the book, trying to find my page, when I heard a knock on the side door. Delia always went to the back and usually walked in, which annoyed me greatly, and Lilly only called, so I wondered who it could be. I went to the window and gasped, nearly knocking over the lamp next to me. I caught it quickly. It was him.

I tried to compose myself, yelling at Hobo as he barked.

My heart pounded, and I felt a lump in my throat. I opened the door and looked at him standing in front of me, seeming unreal.

"What are you doing?" I asked, my voice cracking.

I turned my back to him and went inside. He followed, sitting in the chair across from me. I wiped at my eyes. I suddenly saw my father. I blinked hard to fix it and saw Dock again. I wanted to be in the water again, in the sound, before, alone in the pouring rain. Everything was a wreck, and I wanted to crawl out of my skin.

He rubbed his hands. "Let me talk to you."

"What's there to say, Dock? You lied. You lied about everything." I was about to burst. I hated him for all of this.

He started to speak, and I interrupted, unable to control myself.

"All I wanted was you! I loved you, Dock, more than I ever knew I could love! You made me feel safe, and it was all based on lies!" I sobbed. "Fucking lies!"

I screamed wildly, feeling unhinged, wanting to throw something again.

"George, stop," he said through clenched teeth.

"I can't stop! You stop! You should have stopped!" I yelled, standing up, then sitting down, wiping my cheeks.

He moved toward me. I backed away in my chair, letting him know I wasn't weak, although I was. His face was angry. I'd never seen that before. He suddenly stood over me, breathing heavily.

"Look, I didn't lie about everything," he said, trying to sound calm, but I could tell he wasn't. "I loved you," he breathed. "I do love you, I mean."

His piercing green eyes stared through me. I wondered if I knew him at all.

"I was clean for a while, a long while. I met you, and everything was right. I never planned on going back, ever."

"Then why did you?" I moved over from under him and shook my head, realizing how stupid the question was. *Why do they always? Why aren't I enough?*

I felt I'd soon crumble. I wanted his arms around me. The smell of him made me weak. The only thing keeping me from collapsing into him was everything, and I hated him. I hated my father and my mother, Ray too. I hated myself.

"Because." He paused, looking at the floor. "Because I guess that's what I do."

"So that's okay? That's supposed to make it okay, Dock? What about me?" I started calmly but heard my voice become louder despite my best efforts. "Is that all of it? When did it start?"

I had so many questions but wasn't sure I wanted the answers.

He walked over, grabbing my arms. "Calm down."

"How bad is it? How long were you in jail?" I wriggled my arms free from him.

I didn't see him as strong and safe anymore. He was weak and unsafe, and he looked it. He wasn't enough, and it was apparent neither was I. He was everything I didn't want but all I wanted right now.

"Who are you?" I whispered, staring into his eyes.

He stepped back from me, shaking his head, getting ready to say something. Then suddenly he came in close, in my face, his eyes red and fiery.

"Do you really want the truth? Really, George? You think you can fucking handle it?"

I was scared at the wildness in him. He seemed unpredictable. I started to say something but didn't, watching him pace back and forth in front of me.

"I've been in jail most of my fucking life because of this. I've been doing dope and everything else you can think of forever. Living on the street, dealing, sometimes shit that would make your head spin, I've done!"

He was spitting while he spoke and seemed to exhaust himself. He sat on the stairs, putting his head in his hands.

"I've gotten clean a million times, but this time was different. I had a business, my brother, then you. It all was perfect." He stood again. "And then you know what, George? I fucked it up. I royally fucked it up. Is that what you wanna hear?"

I reached out, putting my hand on his, and he pulled away. I stepped back. I didn't know him. I knew nothing about him, but I also knew everything.

He turned his back to me as if to collect himself, then slowly turned, scratching his chin. I stared at his face. He lifted his head.

"There! Right there!" He pointed.

I was confused. "What?"

"That look you just gave me."

"What look?" I wasn't sure what he meant.

"The reason I didn't tell you. The look I never wanted to see from you."

"Dock . . ." I leaned toward him.

"Get away from me, George, far away."

My mouth fell open. I wanted to swing at him.

"Now it's get away from me? You know what, Dock?" I swallowed hard. "Go to hell," I said furiously, trying to hold back from crying, nearly biting a hole in my lip.

I went into the bathroom, slamming the door behind me. I sat on the toilet and cried. I thought I heard a door shut and came out. I looked around, not seeing him. I didn't want him to leave. I didn't know what I wanted, but I wanted him here, at least for now.

He came all this way.

"Dock!" I yelled, running outside.

He turned and looked at me. I didn't know what to say.

He walked back toward me, breathing heavily, and my eyes locked with his. He kissed me, and I kissed him back. He picked me up, and I wrapped my legs around him. I could feel how much thinner he was, but I didn't care. I hated it, but I needed him. I buried my head in his neck and closed my eyes, and he walked us slowly up to the loft.

CHAPTER 30

April 14, 2004
Watching him leave, I felt my breath go with him.
I didn't try to catch it. I couldn't.

I sat up in darkness and reached over next to me, unsure it was real. I felt only the blanket and thought he'd left again, then heard a noise downstairs. Throwing on my clothes and going to the railing, I noticed him standing at the door.

"Dock?"

He turned, blowing smoke from the side of his mouth.

"Just smoking," he said, seeming to know I was worried.

He walked back up the stairs and took my hand. We climbed back in bed, both lying there, not saying a word.

I couldn't take the silence anymore. "What do we do from here?"

He reached for my hand. I felt his finger touch my ring. "Your diamond." He sighed. "I'm gonna get it back."

I reached to my chest, wondering about my necklace.

Unable to come up with anything else, I said, "Okay."

He sighed again. Rolling on his side, he faced me. "I could stay, but I don't think you're going to want me to."

I turned to him, seeing his silhouette as the morning light came in. "What do you mean?"

"I'm sick, George." He rolled on his back. "I'm dope sick. It's going to get worse."

He moved to sit at the edge of the bed, annoyed.

"Well, I'm a nurse, and I don't know? What do you want to do?" I put my hand on his back, feeling the need to take care of him, then thought of the blond girl. *She was helping him through this. Why her?* Jealousy ran through me, and I was angry. *How am I here?*

It was all so fucked up, and I couldn't make sense of any of it now. It was like I'd become like them, addicts, acting on impulse. None of this felt right; there was so much that was wrong.

This isn't how it was supposed to be.

"Stay. We can figure it out."

"I don't want you to see me like this." He reached for my hand.

"I know."

I let him sleep and went next door. I wondered what to expect from it all, nervous at what I was getting myself into. I'd seen my father detox himself from alcohol and had taken care of a few addicts here and there at the hospital. But this was never supposed to be my life, the life I chose. I hated him and loved him at the same time, a feeling I was familiar with, which made me even angrier.

I'm sick of being angry.

I hated myself now, more than any of them—the addicts. I was weak for him. I was weak at life, and I had no respect for his addiction, but I wanted to fix it. If I fixed him, fixed us, it could all be better.

I came back and forth, checking on him. He mostly slept, but later, the next day, things changed. He shook and moaned. He was freezing and hot. I covered him with every blanket I could find and started a fire. He was okay for a while; then, he wouldn't be.

I filled the tub with warm water and Epsom salts, bathing him, checking his blood pressure and pulse, trying to keep him hydrated, which was nearly impossible as he couldn't hold anything down. I couldn't understand why someone would do this to themselves. He was sick all night, vomiting and crying, saying how badly his body ached.

Between the moaning and throwing up, he told me things. I wasn't sure if he was delirious or if his emotions were heightened from detoxing, but I was curious and listened.

He told me about the first time he got high. A neighbor who sold comics from his van in the city told him to skip school and help him sell to the neighborhood kids. Instead of paying him cash, the neighbor said he had something better, handing him what Dock thought was a joint, but it had heroin in it. After he smoked it, he knew it had him. He was twelve. After that, he started stealing and got into more fights. He signed up for the Marines, thinking that might save him, but got arrested, and they wouldn't take him. Instead, he went to jail. He cried, saying all he ever wanted was to be normal like Will. I told him I understood but wasn't sure if I did. I understood wanting to be normal—that's all we'd ever wanted as kids, Ray and me—but the rest I didn't know. The addicts to me were the enemy.

"What the fuck is normal, anyway?" I said, taking a long breath. I wasn't sure I'd ever known—except for those few years my father was sober.

He looked at me, trying to muster a smile. I was sick of hearing about normal, but I knew normal wasn't this.

He seemed so different, so raw. I held him, rubbing his head as it rested on the bathroom floor. I continued listening. I kept listening until, finally, we both fell asleep.

• • •

I felt a nudge and opened my eyes, grabbing at my throbbing neck. "Hey," he said.

I struggled to get up from the floor, and he helped me to my feet. "What time is it?" I asked, noticing it was still dark in the hallway. "It's early." He reached up to stretch.

"Feeling better?"

"The worst part's over."

He seems so used to it all.

"I'm gonna take a shower." He grabbed my hand, pulling me toward him as I started out the door. "Join me?"

We made love in the shower, then again after lunch. I couldn't understand; it felt different. He kissed me hard and uncontrolled, tearing at my clothes. I didn't recognize the feeling. I couldn't explain why, only it seemed I could be anyone, like he was using my body, and I didn't like it.

"What?" He kissed my forehead.

"I don't know," I started uncomfortably.

"You don't know what?" He lay next to me, taking my hand. I felt him touch my ring again. He looked away toward the door. "What's wrong, George?"

"It's just that . . . it's different."

He turned back to me. "Different how?"

"I don't know," I breathed.

He started getting dressed. I struggled to think of something to say.

"I'm gonna run to the store."

I looked at the clock. Nothing much was open unless he drove out of town. I hated myself, feeling pathetic and unsure who I'd become with him. I thought of my mother and closed my eyes.

"Are you coming back?" I squeezed the words out.

"What?"

I got dressed and walked to the dresser, brushing my hair, not answering him.

Let him wait.

My phone rang on the nightstand, and he picked it up, looking at the screen. He half smiled, handing it to me. I put down the brush and looked. It was Will.

"You know we're friends?"

I held my breath, thinking about Will and almost kissing him.

"Save it, George. Yes, I know you're friends."

My heart banged inside my shirt. I tried not to appear nervous.

"What does that mean?" I asked.

"Nothing," he said and headed down the stairs.

I ran to the balcony.

"Really, Dock? Nothing?"

He kept walking, ignoring me.

"Well, it means something!" I called louder. I grasped the railing tightly.

"George." He smirked, looking up at me. "I'll never be my brother, George, and he'll never be me if he's lucky."

I felt the breath leave me. My eyes widened.

"Does anyone expect you to be?" I asked.

"Everyone."

He pulled on his sweatshirt.

"That's crazy," I said, feeling like I would burst into flames. I felt myself becoming sick and closed my eyes.

"It's not so crazy," he continued.

I opened my eyes, finding it hard to look at him. I looked past him toward the fireplace.

"Well, I don't know," I started, tears filling my eyes. I couldn't take it anymore. Everything was such a mess. I hated him and wanted to scream. I started to speak, stumbling on my words. "I only have ever loved you! We had all these dreams, and we were supposed to have this amazing life!"

I leaned my head on the railing.

"I know you love me. I know it. I've never doubted it," he said, climbing back up the stairs. I lifted my head from the railing. "And you were right. About it being different, what you said."

I got to my feet in front of him. He gazed down for a while. I watched him. He looked like he was about to say more; then his face changed, and he stopped talking.

"What's wrong?"

He said nothing, turning away from me, walking down the stairs again. I watched him pause at the door. I ran down, following him, stopping at the landing. He opened the door and left. I heard the truck start. It lingered for a moment, and I stood frozen, not allowing myself to move. He was leaving again. He wasn't coming back, and as hard as it was, I was letting him go.

CHAPTER 31

June 3, 2004
She existed in that moment, forever. I'm more than
this moment. I see there is light, and I'll gather it in her strength.

The ferry horn sounded as it passed by the house. I opened the slider for some air, hoping the salty smell would invigorate me.

"Are you happy to be back, Mr. S.?" I asked.

Sunken into the sofa, he opened his eyes methodically, one at a time. He was sleeping a lot during the day now, and I tried to engage him in conversation more, although mostly without success.

"What?" he grumbled, wiping his mouth.

"On the island. Are you happy to be back?"

"No."

"Are you looking forward to anything?"

"Not really."

We had spent the last few weeks preparing to return, and it came before I was ready, although I wasn't sure I'd ever be. I'd changed; everything had changed. Anxiety bubbled inside me on the long drive back to Woods Hole. I felt numb, stepping onto the ferry deck. The island didn't feel like mine anymore, and it had lost its magic, something I never thought possible. Coming back this time, I felt empty. Mr. S.,

I saw a change in him, too; he strangely seemed more at peace. He stopped talking about pain or anything related to death, which he had sometimes done, asking my thoughts on the process. He stopped getting angry about his hand. I could blame it on his depression or his health failing, but it didn't seem like that was it. It appeared he was accepting now, accepting his fate instead of fighting it. He was maybe trusting in life's process. I wondered if I should do the same in my own way but wasn't sure what I'd be accepting, and I needed to figure that out.

"What happened with Dock?"

Jesus.

"What do you mean?" I wasn't sure what he knew.

"Delia said he was in Connecticut again." He coughed. "A few weeks ago."

He coughed more, becoming frustrated.

She's such a stalker.

"He was. I think nothing is happening, if I'm honest." I looked down the hall.

I don't want to talk about this.

"How are you?"

Sometimes he surprised me.

I paused, thinking of what to say, but was sick of not saying things to make others comfortable.

"Not good."

He reached for the paper in front of him without success. I handed it to him and turned on the lamp.

"It's not your fault." He shook it open.

It was upside down again.

There was an uncomfortable silence. I wanted to say something, to ask what he meant. I stared at the upside-down words.

I tried my best to be strong and not think of Dock. It didn't seem to get easier. Being back on the island now was something I wasn't sure about. My once beautiful place was dark, and I wasn't sure how to feel.

I was vulnerable, and I didn't want to be. It enraged me. The island was my place. He took it from me, and I let him.

I thought of the day he left—how he looked at me and how different it was. I knew the truth now, the person he didn't want to be, who he hid and didn't want me to know. I saw how angry he was. I looked at him differently, and he noticed it that moment before he left. Nothing was the same, and he knew it. It was all based on a lie anyway; it always is with addicts. But even in the lie, neither one of us could deny what we felt, even after the truth.

If I knew, would I have still gone?

I was angry, so angry at him. It was easier than loving him, which I did. I didn't think I'd ever stop.

I went upstairs to finish unpacking.

"I should have known better," I whispered, looking in the bathroom mirror.

I wasn't my mother; I couldn't be my mother. I spent my whole life never wanting to be anything like how she was with my father.

"Idiot!"

I tossed a hairbrush from the suitcase.

I desperately wanted to drown myself in a bottle or anything that would take it away, but then I'd be them. I didn't want that either. I wanted to be me—whoever that was; I didn't know anymore.

I lay in bed in the guest room that evening, drinking the ginger tea Delia had made me, hoping to feel better. I had been exhausted the whole week, and nothing I ate agreed with me. I figured all the stress had caught up. I wasn't sure what to do and didn't trust myself to be here, with Dock being so close.

I hadn't heard from him. I had hardly heard from anyone and didn't want to. Will called a few times, and I avoided him. I only told my mother I'd be going back and still hadn't filled her in on everything. To Bobbie, I'd hinted at some problems last time we talked but still told her little. I was sick of the lies and the pretending.

I need to forget him.

I put down the tea and cuddled up to Hobo. I shut my eyes, hoping to be in a better place, a dream, but sleep wouldn't come. It never did lately. I flopped on my back, picking up the book from the table. I had only two chapters left and felt sad; it was almost over.

"'Did you ever dream a dream that comes back over and over? Then when you feel like you have finally escaped it, just then, you dream it again,' she asked."

They rode together, fleeing Long Island to the South. They spoke of marriage; he did. She didn't seem interested, but a man and woman living unwed in those days, especially in the South, wasn't something that happened. He tried to explain it to her.

Did he propose? In real life?

I pictured her blinking softly at him, her porcelain fingers casually holding a glass of whiskey.

The anticipation of the ending frustrated me. I wished I didn't know the story, but it didn't intrigue me any less. I was trying to understand this character more intensely than I'd tried to understand others. But she was real—at least, it seemed she was. I thought of the day I asked him.

"She was someone."

She wasn't living; it was all too much for her or anyone to bear, this burden, this guilt, and pain. She was existing, and he seemed too young to understand, at least then. But later, in writing about her, he must have. He did.

A moment in time forever defined her life, and in that, he would never be enough. No one would. Maybe that was what made her so appealing. This made sense to me. I wanted to understand Dock. I wanted to care for him and fix him like the writer wanted to fix her or take care of her, or both.

Why do we want to repair what is irreparable?

My stomach soured again. I rubbed it and went on to read his response:

"'I've had such dreams. I have one about my mother. It started after her death. She's lying in her casket, somehow asking me why without speaking.

Why her, why? Her eyelids, flat and round, sunken in at the corners. They suddenly open, and I wake up wishing I could have answered her. I never can."'

The recurring dream I had about my father came to me. It was always the same, him above the barroom in that apartment, alone, where he died. He walks to the counter and pours a glass of water. Someone once told me there was a glass of water on the counter where they found him, but I never remembered who. He picks it up and feels pain. His eyes crinkle, and he grabs at his chest, which looks sunken, and his hand becomes lost in it. It's his last moment; he knows it. He has no time, and he wishes he did, and then he's gone.

I blinked back the moisture in my eyes, hoping I wouldn't dream of this tonight; it had been a while.

Am I looking for my father?

I stared at the ceiling, feeling Hobo lick my hand.

The smell of him, the smoking, the similarities—I tossed the book, hearing the thud. I held my face in my hands. A giant wave of nausea rose in my throat. I ran to the bathroom, but it subsided as fast as it came. I grabbed the book off the floor and found my page, continuing.

"'Please get me a drink. I have a secret. But I need to drink before I can ever speak it. But I must tell you. I have to say to you my shame.'"

I couldn't imagine the horrors of the Holocaust: the camps, the death. I wanted to ask him so much about her, so much about them, but I knew I couldn't. This was something more, something his.

I yawned, closing one eye, then the other, shifting my position to stay awake. I wanted to keep reading until the end. I couldn't stop here, not now.

She told him of them being trapped, left in the train car for hours, turning into days. There were children, elderly and sick, all too weak and hungry for any more crying. Someone whispered that the car before them were all sent to the chambers. They all were dead. She wondered if she had fallen unconscious herself, for the next thing she remembered was her presence outside, coming face-to-face with the man who would change her life forever.

I continued feverishly down the page. Then there, the Nazi, drunk and disgusting. Then his words, his unforgettable words:

"'You can keep one of them alive. Which one will you keep?'

"'You mean I have to choose? Why me? Why do I have to choose?' she screamed."

The words were as powerful now as I remembered. Even more so reading them. With her screams and torment, I held my breath, feeling my chest tighten.

"'I can't choose,' she said, her eyes pleading.

"More Nazis came and gathered the men from the train. The women were wailing and crying, watching helplessly as they pushed them in the direction of the chambers. She looked in his bloodshot eyes, dead and cold, as he waved them over, pointing to her two children huddled together before her.

"'Send them both,' he said to a soldier.

"'No! No! Please! God in heaven, forgive me! Take the baby, my little one!' she called out, closing her eyes, falling to the ground."

CHAPTER 32

June 6, 2004
Love was there in friendship and purpose, and I barely saw it.
He had been my reason. They had been, all of them are,
me and mine—always.

I heard a loud banging, thinking I was dreaming. I opened my eyes and listened to it continue. Hobo barked, and I climbed out of bed, the book falling to the floor with a smack, and hurriedly stumbled to the door.

"Georgie, hurry!" Delia cried.

"What? What is it?" I yelled and threw the door open.

"It's Mr. S.," she yelled again, softening as I rubbed my eyes.

It was early, and the sun was rising above the Yacht Club. Delia wore her night headscarf and robe. She turned hurriedly, waving for me to come. I quickly followed.

"He's not good, Georgie. Not this time. He's not good. I heard him coughing."

I walked into his room.

"George," he mouthed, gasping, looking at me.

I ran, lifting him high and straightening him.

"It's okay, Mr. S. It's okay," I reassured him, putting on his oxygen.

"Delia, give me the phone." I looked at her sternly, remaining calm so as not to scare him.

I called 911, giving them the details though they knew the house well. "No need for lights and sirens. It makes him anxious," I told them, knowing he hated the fuss.

"Take some deep breaths, Mr. S., in through your nose. It's okay." I rubbed his back in between taps.

The ambulance came quickly. I assured him I'd be right behind them. I headed toward the stairs and saw Delia's sullen face. I stopped, putting my hand on her shoulder.

"I'll meet you in the car?"

Lilly was on her way back from New York and would stop right at the hospital. We discussed he had been declining. She knew, but it was serious this time. I was scared. I needed to say it. I needed her to hear it from me and wanted no surprises. He always bounced back, but one time he wouldn't. I struggled to think about it and tried not to. After hearing my words to Lilly, I knew I was trying to prepare myself too.

"I understand," Lilly said, her voice calm, but then I heard it: the sadness when she said goodbye.

We came into the hospital. Delia and I waited outside the curtain while he was with two doctors I didn't recognize. I figured they were seasonal. I moved close, trying to hear what they were saying. The reality of him dying had always been there, but somehow, I didn't believe it would happen.

I'm too close.

My heart sank. Then nausea came back with a vengeance.

"Will he be okay, Georgie?"

I looked at Delia quickly, changing my demeanor. Her brow furrowed, and she bit on her finger. She was worried, and it would worry her more if she saw I was.

"I don't know; I think so," I whispered, holding my stomach.

"You can come in," a voice said.

A nurse pulled back the curtain, allowing us through.

I walked over and touched his hand.

A man came in from the other side of the curtain. "Are you his nurse?"

"She is." Delia pointed.

"He's fairly stable but not good."

"Okay," I said, concerned.

He smiled kindly, tapping his pen on his cheek. I lifted my head high, taking a breath. My stomach gurgled loudly, and I hoped he didn't hear.

The doctor picked up the chart on the bed.

I watched Mr. S.'s chest rise and fall as he lay nearly lifeless. My legs felt weak, and I needed to sit. Just then, he opened his eyes. I looked at him and turned my lips up to smile.

"You're not alone," I said, making sure he saw me.

He shut his eyes again.

Suddenly it came. It felt like a freight train tearing through my insides and up my throat. I covered my mouth and ran, almost knocking Delia over. I turned right, then stumbled left. I bolted through the waiting room filled with people and pushed through the bathroom door, falling to the floor.

"Oh my God," I gasped in relief.

A few minutes later, I leaned over the sink, splashing water on my face, looking at myself in the mirror. *What is wrong with me?*

I came back out to the waiting room, feeling everyone staring.

"Are you okay?" a voice said. I felt a hand on my shoulder and turned to see the doctor.

"Um, no. I mean, I don't know. I'm not feeling well."

"Why don't you go home and rest. He's stable for now—nothing you can do."

I watched his mouth move, barely hearing his words.

"Get some rest. Doctor's orders."

I walked back into Mr. S.'s room.

"You don't look so hot, girl," Delia said, stepping away from me.

"I'm gonna go rest. I don't want to give this to him."

"Okay, okay. You go. I am here. I'll call you if anything." She tapped my back.

I looked at him.

"Go, Georgie, he'll be okay. You know him. He's a tough old one. Go now. Just go."

. . .

I felt outside myself, sitting on the bathroom floor in the cottage. I stared up at the sink while Hobo rubbed back and forth against my legs.

I looked at my phone for what seemed like hours, finally lifting it to my ear.

"Mom," I began.

"George, what is it? Are you okay? George?"

I cried. I cried hard, and I told her everything. I said everything I'd ever wanted to say. I wasn't sure I was even making sense, and I didn't stop until I couldn't breathe, and she listened. My head pounded; I needed rest. I needed something—I wasn't sure what. I needed help; I needed answers. I needed someone to tell me what to do.

"Mom." My voice cracked.

She took in a long breath and breathed out for what seemed like forever.

"George, come home."

I lay down, trying to slow my breathing, and squeezed my eyes tightly. I wanted to make everything stop. My phone buzzed. I grabbed it and saw it was Lilly.

"How is he, Lilly?" I answered, not bothering with hellos.

"He's okay, George. Not great, but he's right here awake."

"Oh, good. I was so worried." I talked fast, feeling better.

"But how are you, George? Are you not well?"

I wasn't sure how to answer. "No, I guess I'm not. I'm so sorry not to be there, but—"

"George, stop. If you're sick, you're sick. You're always here. He knows you would be."

My eyes filled, and I took a long breath.

"Get some rest, George. I'll check in with you later."

"Okay, Lilly, thank you." My voice faded.

The island. How can I leave? How can I not be with him when he's so ill? I promised. I can't leave him, my brain screamed.

"I can't leave him!" I yelled, curling into a ball, watching Hobo pee on the floor in front of me. I didn't care.

I tried to sleep and couldn't. I thought of calling Dock, wondering what he'd say.

I tossed and turned. Finally giving up, I read the story to the end.

The rivers of cracks on the ceiling stared back at me, and suddenly, I felt calm.

The end replayed in my mind.

I sat up on the bed, picking up the book again. I traced the large *S* on the cover with my finger.

"She was someone."

I wasn't sure about anything. I only knew what mattered to me, what had always mattered. Everything was different, and there was more now. I had a choice.

I have to go.

• • •

I headed to the house, thinking they'd be back by then. Delia was putting a bag of groceries away, and Lilly was at the table, writing in her notebook.

"George, you scared me, girl." Delia put her hand to her chest.

"Sorry," I said, crossing the room between them.

"Are you feeling better, George?" Lilly began. She looked up at me. Her eyes became large. "Have you been crying? What is it, George?"

She motioned for me to sit.

I sat across from her and looked at them both. I hesitated at first, then told them everything.

"Oh, George," Lilly said while Delia nodded.

"I don't know how I'll leave him."

Tears ran down my face. Delia handed me the box of tissues.

"You have to take care of yourself, Georgie. You'll be back. I bet you will." Delia smiled.

I knew it upset her, but she'd never say it.

"George. He will be okay. He will," Lilly said, wringing her hands. "We will make sure he's taken care of. He's in the hospital now, and we'll get a private nurse, maybe Barbara. Someone good. He might not like it at first, but he would want what's best for you, George. He would," she tried reassuring me. "And then maybe you can come on weekends for a while or—" She stopped herself.

"I'm so sorry, Lilly. I'm—"

"George, stop." She motioned for me to come to her.

She hugged me, holding me a moment, and I collapsed into her arms.

"You've been wonderful to him. You have to all of us."

. . .

The sun was bright, and I wished it were raining. I looked around the cottage one last time, taking in the stillness. I packed my car early, and Hobo and I headed to the hospital. I called the island nurses who had cared for him before, letting them know he would need help, and spent the rest of the morning going over things with Lilly. Delia avoided me mostly and made sure to leave before I could say goodbye.

I gazed at him through the glass. His color looked better, and I stared for what seemed like forever, watching as he slept. I came into the room, close to the bed, and I was happy he looked comfortable. I closed my eyes, trying to fight any tears from coming. Tilting my head back, I took a deep breath, then noticed his eyes now open. I smiled.

"You look better." I put my hand on his arm.

He coughed, then moved his arm.

"You scared me. I'm getting tired of it." I laughed, feeling the tears come again. One fell, hitting his arm. He looked at me with concern.

We said nothing for a while. I finally tried to speak but struggled to say anything.

"Mr. S. I have to . . ." I wiped my cheek. "I have to tell you something."

His eyes widened, and he mouthed something I couldn't hear. I hated doing this to him now. He was sick.

"Mr. S., some things have changed, and . . ." I paused again, moving away from him.

I can't do this.

"George," he whispered so that I could barely hear.

He tried raising his hand, but it seemed to weigh a million pounds. He gave up, moving his finger, telling me to come.

I moved my face close to his, his gray eyes moist and beautiful. A tear rolled down each of my cheeks.

I nodded, closing my eyes. "Mr. S."

"George," he whispered again, struggling.

I felt his fingertips on my hand.

I opened my eyes and looked into his.

"You can go."

I felt his fingers press harder. I put my hand in his, squeezing it tightly. I looked at him once more. Our eyes met, and he nodded. I walked the long corridor through the glass doors, hearing myself hum. I didn't stop.

CHAPTER 33

July 6, 2007
I'm exhausted from goodbyes.

"The weather today in Vineyard Haven is a sunny eighty-eight degrees with a few scattered clouds," the captain's voice chirped over the loudspeaker. "Please make your way to your car, and passengers will unload on the port side of the vessel. Have a good day, and thank you for riding with the Steamship Authority."

I picked up the black dress from the floor and placed it on the passenger seat, smoothing it out before pulling off the boat. I passed the Black Dog Tavern, taking a left at Five Corners toward Oak Bluffs. The beer seemed to suspend my feelings in time for a moment. I was in an emotional limbo, which I was thankful for but knew wouldn't last. As if on autopilot, I drove the long way, as I always did, passing the hospital and continuing up to East Chop, then circling to State Beach. I never missed an opportunity to go this route and see the spots I found the most beautiful. I wasn't sure I wanted the nostalgia today, though, and felt guilty for it. I didn't know what I wanted or how to feel. I wished to feel whole again and have the island be mine, the way it was before. Or I wished things were different for us, for a lot of things. I didn't want to be back—not for this.

I came to say goodbye, and that scared me the most.

The numbness faded when I reached Edgartown. I turned onto North Water Street and drove to the hotel. Pulling into the parking lot, I grabbed the dry-cleaning bag off the seat, crumpling the plastic ends angrily in my hands. Then I looked at his eyes again, his beautiful green eyes, and I smiled, seeing his smile. I picked up the teddy bear from the floor and blinked back the tears starting to form, hiding my face with my hand.

It was hot, and I was sweaty. The drops slid down my back as I walked up the drive. I looked at Edgartown Light, at the sun reflecting off the metal on the double-railed fence that hugged the dunes leading to the beach.

Tossing my things on the curb, I crossed the street. I stared out to Chappaquiddick, the sun hitting my cheeks, and inhaled the scent of salt and flowers. A boat with a pale-red sail floated slowly through the channel, and I watched until it disappeared into the harbor. I turned to face the hotel, its black-pitched rooftops and shiny glazed shutters glistening in the sunlight, all looking freshly painted. The Nantucket beer churned in my stomach. I suddenly felt a swell inside of me and tried to stop whatever it was that urgently needed to burst from me with everything I had. I gripped the fence rail tightly, the wood digging into my palms. I leaned on it with my whole body, not caring if anyone saw me.

"Oh my God," I whispered. A tear rolled under my glasses, and I swallowed hard as all that had happened flooded me. "It's over."

Did I still have hope it wasn't, him and I?

I'd lived in anger for such a long time. I wasn't sure I knew there would be an ending—a real one, anyway. I thought it over. I believed I'd accepted. But in reality, I was waiting for his next move. I wasn't over any of it: Dock, my father; in that, I sought help because there was now more to live for. Somewhere during it all, I found I was worth living for too.

I looked, seeing his eyes again.

I assumed it would be this: Dock's end. Just like my father, I wasn't prepared, although I thought I might be. I was still shocked and in disbelief, even though I shouldn't have been. I felt heartsick and broken. I stared at the gazebo, thinking of it all. Even in the better place I was, my heart quietly still had it: hope—the something you should never have, with them.

I took a deep breath. Tears broke way to sobs as I pushed my glasses high and shielded my face. My lip quivered, and I bit down, trying to stop it. I turned to the lighthouse again. The anger subsided. It usually did, now. I loosened my hold on the fence and watched the blue hydrangeas sway in a breeze coming off the water. I thought of the cottage and closed my eyes, picturing his hands. I envisioned him near me—the sweetness of his breath, the taste of his skin. In the secret compartment, there it still was: love.

• • •

Will stood in the middle of the room, talking to the pastor. Seeing me, he turned and smiled nervously.

"George."

He grabbed my hands, kissing my cheek.

My hands shook in his. I glanced past his shoulder, at the casket. We were alone, to say our goodbyes in private before anyone came. I wasn't sure I could. We turned at the same time, both looking at him in silence. He squeezed my hand.

I squeezed back and let go, walking toward him, feeling like I was floating. I kneeled in front of him on the red velvet cushion. His lips were still upturned, and I smiled through my tears. He looked strange, except for his hands. I stared at the tattoo, touching it, moving my fingers to connect the dots.

Goodbye, Dock.

I still believed the quote I read to him on our wedding day. I was his witness. As I gave my eulogy, I stuttered the first sentence, reaching for my neck, rubbing my chest. A tear slid onto my nose and another on my lips. I tasted the salt. I wanted to run or scream, but I wouldn't. Will stood next to me, holding my arm. I tried hard not to look at him. I looked at my paper, watching it shake in my hands, my words blended.

I struggled to see them. I folded the paper, staring past the people. I didn't speak of his pain or his addiction, the why and how. I spoke of him and what made him more. Like I did my father years before.

I hugged a few people and tried not to get caught up in conversation. Will worked the room, and I was thankful. I glanced at the casket and walked closer once more, seeing his dark hair amidst the pale flowers surrounding him. Tears filled my eyes again, and I took a deep breath, staring at the door, trying to gather my strength to leave.

I slipped out unnoticed and drove back to Vineyard Haven. Going over the bridge, I put my hand out the window, feeling the warm sea breeze against it. I pulled down Main Street. I thought I should stop at the florist, but he would hate the cliché. I rummaged through my bag and found something more fitting, feeling it was a sign that I had one.

West Chop Light came into view, and I parked by the small cemetery on the hill. Taking off my heels, I stepped onto the warm grass and into the darkness under the oak trees. I walked through a few rows, reading the names, and there it was, in front of me. Kneeling, I touched the cold granite of the gravestone.

"I'm sorry it took me so long, Mr. S.," I said, pulling his book and the pencil out of my bag. I stuck the pencil in the grass and stared at the book's worn cover, feeling the tears.

"I miss you."

Mr. S. never made it out of the hospital that last time. He was doing well for a while, and things seemed promising. I spoke with the nurses most days, so when Lilly called, I was in disbelief.

"He's not going to pull through, George," she said, crying.

"What? No!" I shouted.

"He took a turn last night. We don't know."

"Lilly, I, I can't . . ." I wrung my hands, looking for my shoes.

"I think he wants to go, George."

I heard someone crying in the background.

"He's tired. He is."

"I know. I know he is."

I didn't know what to say. I needed to be there, to be next to him.

"I'm coming, Lilly. I'm leaving now."

"George, you won't make it," she interrupted me.

"But I have to—"

"It's okay, George. You won't make it."

I paced back and forth. I had to be with him.

"I have to be with him!" I sobbed into the phone.

"Do you want to speak to him? He can hear, George. He can. Speak to him."

"I'm so sorry, Lilly. I'm so sorry, yes. Can I?"

"Here, George, I'm putting the phone to his ear."

I was quiet, thinking of what to say. My mind spun, and my heart raced.

"Mr. S.," I shouted, fighting back the tears, making sure I sounded clear.

I felt tongue-tied. I thought hurriedly and hard, hoping Lilly wouldn't pull the phone away; then the words came. I thought of him, his words, releasing me that day.

"George, you can go."

I cleared my throat and breathed.

"Mr. S., you can go. It's okay. You can go."

• • •

I left the cemetery and headed back down Main Street, passing the driveway I'd driven so many times before. I thought about turning, wondering if Lilly and Delia were there, thinking how I'd love to see them. I pictured Delia puttering about in the kitchen, and Lilly hurrying off somewhere. But I kept driving, thinking I'd come back, feeling maybe I could now.

I pulled next to the tavern and walked the sandy pavement, stepping onto the little beach to look at the sound. An overturned rowboat lay facedown in the sand, and I sat. I watched boats pass as music played somewhere in the distance.

I still wondered how he'd known that day in the hospital. For a while, I figured Lilly or Delia must have called or gone early and told him, but I knew they hadn't. He knew. I wasn't sure he knew the details, but he knew because he knew me. He knew I had to go. In him, I'd learned that sometimes spoken words aren't needed and observation might let you in more. I guessed he'd known more all along. My patient and friend: I so often assumed he lived in his mind, and for the written words he could no longer write. I never knew how much he saw.

I heard a motorcycle and turned to watch it pull in. Will got off and walked down the sand.

"I thought I'd find you here."

"Take a seat." I smiled up at him.

"You okay?" he said, nudging me.

"I don't know; are you?" I nudged him back.

"Probably not."

He sat, and we stared out at the sound.

"Oh." He reached in his pocket and pulled something out. "I got something you might want."

He put down his helmet, brushing back his hair—salt-and-pepper flecks now showed at the sides. Then he took my hand and turned it, placing something in my palm.

"What's this?"

"Just open your hand."

I opened it and stared at the small charm and chain, watching the sun reflect off the gold.

"My necklace. How did you . . . ?"

"I knew where to look."

I pulled my hair up, and he clasped it behind my neck.

Sand hit the back of my arm, and I turned, hearing a familiar giggle.

"Mommy," she called and stumbled toward me.

"Hey, guys," Bobbie said as they strolled our direction, Hobo leading the way down the sand.

Will stood, and she gave him a tight hug.

"I'm so sorry, Will," she said softly.

"I know. Thanks."

"Thanks for watching them again, Bobbie."

Her red hair blew behind her as she smiled.

"My pleasure." She winked.

"And you! How are you?" I picked her up, kissing her, watching the white teddy bear fall from her grasp. Will picked it up and brushed it off. I fixed her dress, looking up at Will as he handed it to me.

• • •

Sophie Ray was born that winter after leaving the island. It was then everything changed. My mother, Ray, and I became close again. A different kind of close, but it was better. It was ours, and it came from something good. Sophie gave us a reason. We didn't say much, we never did, but it was there: the love. I even started talking to Mary after reaching out a few times. We had a few good conversations, and things seemed hopeful.

Dock called so many times to make promises to change, wanting to be better for Sophie and us. I listened and, sometimes during a weak moment, believed, but it was because I wanted to, not because it was real. I didn't want that life for her. I didn't want it for me. I never had, and I had a choice now. No matter how much I loved him, I loved us more.

My mother and I were different. I finally saw her as human, not infallible, which I thought she was supposed to be. It was when I found I wasn't and that I was human too—flawed, messy, sloppily and disastrously human—that I understood her. Like all of us, she only wanted love.

I started going to Al-Anon. As much as I hated it and still resented the infection some days, it gave me the ability to understand more and be humble. I stopped fighting it, and I finally felt free. I loved them all—my family, my father; I always had, and I liked me again, the different me and the same me, my mother and father within me.

I had a nice life back in Boston, working in the operating room at a local hospital. I was writing more too, but not about horse farms, remembering his words:

"Write about what you know."

• • •

"Do you want to hold her?" I looked at Will. He already had his arms out.

"Hi, Sophie." Will's voice quivered. His eyes were moist with tears.

"Sophie, this is your uncle Will."

"Boat!"

She pointed excitedly at the ferry coming in and blowing its whistle.

"Boat!"

She squealed again, bouncing up and down. Hobo barked with excitement.

"Soph, do you want to go see the boat?" Bobbie took her hand, and they walked toward the water.

"She looks just like him, George—his eyes." A tear fell down his cheek, and he turned so I wouldn't see.

"I know."

We watched Sophie and Bobbie playing in the sand.

"So, what now, George?"

I looked at him, squinting in the sun.

"Think you'll ever come back?"

A ferry left the dock, blowing the whistle.

I put my head on his shoulder and smiled.

ABOUT THE AUTHOR

*D*ianne C. Braley is a registered nurse with a passion for music, poetry, and literature. Dianne has been featured in various online and printed publications, including *Today's Dietician* and *Scrubs Magazine*. Her nursing blog, *Nursing the Neighborhood*, was named one of the top nursing blogs of 2018 by Nurse Recruiter.

Growing up in Massachusetts's tough and turbulent inner cities, Dianne has always walked a thin line between her creative dreams and her strong blue-collar roots, finding solace from her raw and difficult world growing up alongside alcoholism in writing and music. Dianne became a registered nurse, but the friendship that blossomed while caring for a celebrity novelist on the picturesque island of Martha's Vineyard inspired her to pick up her pencil again and dive into her true calling.

Dianne still escapes to the Vineyard every summer to reinvigorate herself and channel her creative drive. She is currently pursuing a degree in creative writing. Dianne and her family are firmly planted in a small town north of Boston—but not far enough away to lose her city edge.

ACKNOWLEDGMENTS

There are so many people to thank for creating any book, and this one is no different. It isn't easy to acknowledge everyone leading me here, but I will try my best and start with my little dog and shadow, Buddy; fuggedaboutit—I'd die for you. My father, Richard: thank you for creating me and getting me—he always did. While life with him was not perfect and often disastrously messy, I wish he were here with every ounce of me. My mother, Jean, the magic: you are my songbird in every type of sky. Thank you for being my biggest fan. My best friend and husband, Jason—I never realized that anyone could love me as much as you. With a dynamic blend of codependency and love, I'm forever yours. My sister, Michelle, has supported me through this entire process. I can't imagine my life without you. Knowing you completes me. Richard, my brother—the only one who's experienced it all with me; I somehow came to love you more in writing this book. My best friends, Keri Pomeroy and Amy O'Boyle—your unwavering support and cheers have kept me alive on my darkest days; thank you. To all of my friends and family and the strong women in my life, especially my aunts, thank you for carving the path. My friend and forever brother, Wayne Pierce, thank you for saving me many times, sometimes in ways you could never know.

The island of Martha's Vineyard, my heart wouldn't have a home without it. The love for my vineyard girls is infinite, and every person whose soul this magnificent place has captured, we remain forever bound. The city of Revere, Massachusetts, my hometown, is filled with a cast of characters that I cherish; I can't even come close to listing them all. Revere is a character in its own right, and I will always be proud I'm from there. Mike D'Amico, thank you for teaching me to "Trust the Process." I'm not sure I could have done this without doing that. Dr. Charles Diamond, thank you for treating me as human and believing in me, seeing me as more than just a defiant kid; till we meet again. Chell Morrow and every single editor, alpha and beta reader, and critique partner who helped me whip my manuscript into shape to submit, thank you. To all of the agents and publishers who rejected me, the gutting got more manageable, and you only helped make both me and my work that much better. To my publicity team at Mindbuck Media, thank you for all of your hard work. A huge thank you for believing in my book and for your no-bullshit approach, John Koehler, my publisher, Greg Fields, Hannah, Joe, and the whole Koehler team. One conversation with you, and I knew my book had found its home.

William Styron, it was an honor to care for you and know you—thank you for inspiring me not to be afraid of the shadowy, unlit places in the world and my soul. By embracing your melancholy, I learned to embrace mine. I miss you. In your home, Rose Styron and the entire Styron family, I saw a life where art flourished. It lingered in the air, reigniting my soul as I remembered art lived in me as a child. I had been missing something, and I found it through my experiences with your father, husband, and you—thank you.

Like many of the men in my life, my ex-husband Dale Pierce is no longer with us. I would never want to revisit the highs and lows and the terrible turbulent times brought forth by your addiction, but without them, I am not sure I would have found my resilience. You, like my father, returned to the earth. Here I remain, thankful that despite it all, nothing remains but love and our son, Christopher, the end of this story, and the beginning of it all. Everything in this, through this, and after this is for him.

Printed in the USA
CPSIA information can be obtained
at www.ICGtesting.com
LVHW091036290923
759460LV00003B/71